The Benediction

The Benediction

To Dottie —
May the wind
be always at your back.
Joyce

Joyce McDonald

Library of Congress Control Number: 2011962866
ISBN: Hardcover   978-1-4691-3928-9
               Softcover   978-1-4691-3927-2
               Ebook   978-1-4691-3929-6

This book is a work of fiction. Except for references to historical facts, the names, characters, and incidences are products of the author's imagination or are used fictitiously. Any resemblance to persons, except for historical personages, is entirely coincidental. The author took the liberty of moving the date of the raid on the Charlestown convent up two years to accommodate the story.

This book was printed in the United States of America.

To order additional copies of this book, contact:
Xlibris Corporation
1-888-795-4274
www.Xlibris.com
Orders@Xlibris.com
107612

DEDICATION

The Benediction is dedicated to the memory of Mildred Marie McDonald, who first suggested the idea of a novel about the Irish immigrants who made their way from County Cork to the town of Benedicta, Maine. It was her persistence that this story was worth telling that stayed in my mind for several years before prompting me to write it. It is also dedicated to the late Fred W. McDonald who urged me on and supported me through the years of research and writing of this story.

APPRECIATION

My appreciation goes out to those individuals in Kinsale and Cork City in Ireland who assisted me in finding the history of the area in 1826–1830 and for telling me the tales they had heard over the years about that time. I also owe thanks to the librarians at the Boston Public Library for their assistance with maps of the early city and of Boston Harbor. Any mistakes are those of the author.

PRONUNCIATION OF IRISH NAMES

CHARACTERS
Liam – Lee-um
Donal – Doe-nal
Niall – Ni-al
Declan – Dek-lan
Maire – Mär-i-ree
Pegeen – Peg-gine
Padraig – Pad-raidg
Jocelyn – Joss-lin

PLACES
Kinsale – Kin-sale
Cobh – Cove

PART ONE

"There is a common spirit which binds a family
together that neither distance nor death can break."

CHAPTER 1

County Cork, Ireland
1826

IT WAS AS dark as the inside of a cow's bladder when Declan awoke. At first he didn't remember what had wakened him. All he knew was that he shivered as goose bumps crept down his arms, and the hair on the back of his neck stiffened. The sound came again, and a chill went through his too-thin body.

A wailing such as he had never heard before in all his fourteen years echoed through the black of the night. It was a screeching like the wind in the chimney pot during a winter's gale, except that the sound was higher, louder, and more terrifying. Declan trembled beneath the oat sacks he used for covers and held them close around his chin, not daring to move, not daring to breathe.

Even in his fright, Declan knew he had had this feeling before. He recognized the stealing of it up his arms and along his shoulders. First he would feel the numbness, then the hairs on his body rising stiffly, and he would quiver with dread and fear of what was to come.

"Did ye hear it, Declan?" The scratchy roughness of Gran's voice came through the darkness of the room below. "Did ye hear the banshee call?"

He couldn't answer. His throat was paralyzed. Gran's voice held the same whine as the strange wailing from outside in the night.

"I know you're awake, Declan, lad," came Gran's voice again. "I know ye can hear the keening, for tis only us with the sight as can hear it."

"I didn't hear nothin'," Declan whispered into the night, but his voice trembled, and he knew that his words didn't fool Gran a bit.

"Tis the call of the banshee, Declan, come to claim a life before the sun rises. Tis ever the same. I hear the wailing in the night, like now, and one I know is dead by mornin'. Listen well, Declan, me lad, so you'll know next time. Like as not twill be for me when ye do."

Declan lay under his thin covers, dreading the next mournful sound, holding his breath against its intrusion. He waited, projecting the wailing in his mind, waiting for the terror of it.

In the darkness at the foot of the mat where Declan lay, an image began to form, seeming to float in the air just above the level of his eyes. A long body lay stiff and quiet, clothed in a shabby suit, black against the white sheet on which it rested. Its arms were folded across its chest, and a string of rosary beads dangled from still fingers.

As quickly as the image formed, it dissipated. The significance of the motionless form on the white sheet did not register in Declan's fourteen-year-old mind. But for Gran's whispered words in the dark night, he would not have realized that it was Da.

The prickly numbness once more paralyzed his mind, not unlike it had done at the sound of the banshee wail. The sight of his father lying dead had no impact on his conscious mind, drifting instead like the foggy impression of a dream that seemed real, but that he nonetheless knew was not.

The vision became part of his mind's confusion as he lay waiting for the desolate lament. He strained to its coming, but the warning was over and gradually he dared to breathe once more, though he knew he would never in his whole life be able to forget the sound.

Declan allowed his breathing to deepen as he became aware of Gran's ragged snoring. Somehow he recognized she was right, that one they knew would be dead by morning. It was a knowing that he could not deny, nor could he deny the burden would be his to carry on after Gran was gone. He wasn't quite sure what Gran meant when she said he had the "sight," but he knew it was true—the way he knew the sun would rise from the Irish Sea each morning. The familiar rhythm of Gran's heavy breathing gradually soothed his fears, and he fell asleep.

He wasn't sure how long he had slept, but he was dragged from its depths by a whispered voice in the predawn dark. Liam, his eldest brother, was shaking Donal, who lay sleeping on the mat beside him.

"Donal! Donal!" Liam whispered. "Wake up! Wake up! You've got to help us!" The sound carried no further than the ears of the two newly awakened boys.

Declan felt his brother moan and turn over. He wondered why Liam was waking Donal before daylight.

"What is it, Liam?" Donal asked.

"Hush now," Liam said softly. "Just get your britches, and come with me."

"What is it?" Donal asked again, sitting up. "What's the matter?"

"I'll tell you when we get outside. I don't want to wake the others, but for God's sake, hurry!" Liam made his way to the ladder that led from the loft, and Declan heard his heavy boots hit the rungs as he groped for them in the dark. Liam stumbled down the last step as Donal sat up in bed and pulled on his britches.

"What's going on?" Declan asked.

"Go back to sleep," whispered his eighteen-year-old brother. "It's just Liam come in with too much drink." He crawled from the mat, and Declan followed the sound of his shuffling footsteps to the ladder and down to the room below.

Declan waited until he heard the door close behind his brothers. He listened for a moment to see if any of the others had wakened. From the room below, Gran's snorts and puffs and the slighter sounds of Mam's breathing told him they were unaware of what was going on. His sister Kate turned quietly in her sleep. Declan rose from the mat, crawled to the tiny opening at the front of the loft and pushed open the shutters.

Liam's voice carried up in hushed tones from beneath the window. "Da's hurt bad, Donal, maybe dying. You've got to help."

"But what can I do?" Donal asked. "Wherever is he?"

"Just do as I say, Donal. For once in your life, just shut up and do as I say. Here, put on Da's coat and cap. If anyone sees us, they'll think it's himself. We'd better hurry. The sun will be up soon." Liam's voice was coming in gasps now. *He sounds frightened*, Declan thought, *not like Liam at all.*

"I don't understand. Why should I pretend to be Da?" Donal asked as the sounds of his shuffling into the coat came up to Declan's straining ears.

"Hurry, or we'll never get there before daylight," Liam was saying. "I'll explain as we go."

Declan heard their boots on the path leading to the shore. As they moved out of hearing, he began to shake. All he could think of was that Da was hurt. Recalling the banshee wail, he whispered into the night, "Oh dear God, don't let Da die."

"Is that you, Declan?" his mother's voice, thick with sleep, called from below.

"Yes, Mam, it's me. I just have to go outside. Go back to sleep." He heard her cough, turn over, and settle down.

Declan moved into the dark and down the ladder. Quietly he opened the door and slid out into the cold predawn.

From the shore, he could hear the gravelly sounds of the curraugh as his brothers pushed the boat over the rocky shore and into the river. He ran down the path, but they had already gone. The shape of the canvas-covered boat showed darkly on the lighter-colored water.

There was no sound of their voices, only the quiet slap of the oars as they dipped into the river. Declan's heart pounded with dread, and his thoughts tumbled in confusion. *What had happened? Where was Da, and what was wrong with him? Why had Liam and Da gone out in the night in the first place? And why had Liam come for Donal? How could Donal help if Da was hurt? And why did Donal have to pretend he was Da? What did it matter if anyone saw them?*

Declan sat down on the giant boulder near the shore path. He breathed the cold morning air deeply, hoping to clear his mind as it emptied his lungs of the stale air of the sleeping loft that hung close under the thatched roof. Dawn would break soon. He had to think things through, had to figure out what had happened. Already the sky was getting lighter in the east. The lads had better hurry.

Several times in the past weeks, Declan had heard Da and Liam go out after everyone else was sleeping. He thought they had just gone out for a pipe or maybe to share a jar. Usually sleep took over before he thought more about it. Sometimes he heard Liam come up the ladder late at night too but had simply assumed he had to go outside to relieve himself.

Sometimes Liam stayed out a-courting too, and fourteen-year-old brothers weren't supposed to ask questions about that. Declan thought of Maire Foley with the tiny waist and of the soft bulges in her bodice. The thought warmed him in the cool dawn. Then he shivered as he remembered that Da lay hurt, maybe dying, and alone somewhere.

Declan heard a sound behind him and quickly made a sign of the cross, but it was only a hedgerow dove coming out to greet the rising sun. Declan picked himself up from the smoothly worn seat on the boulder and walked slowly to the cottage now outlined against the green hills and the pink sky to the east. His throat felt dry and scratchy. He took the ladle from the peg over the rain barrel and, dipping it into the cool water, took a long gulping drink.

He went back to his mat in the loft and pulled the oat sacks around his shaking shoulders. He closed his eyes, but the image of his father this time was clear and real. Da lay dead, his head in a pool of blood. "Oh God! Oh God," Declan moaned. "Please don't let him be dead!" The words clung to his throat, and he knew that his petition was too late. His prayer turned bitter. "How could you allow this to happen? What good is a god who lets someone as good as Da die?"

The outpouring of his resentment released his tears, sliding down his cheeks and running into his ears. He lay there waiting for the sounds of his brothers' return, knowing that Da would not be with them.

CHAPTER 2

DONAL LEANED HARD on the oars, keeping in perfect time with Liam as the two of them pitted their strength against the tide rushing into the Bandon Estuary. Quickly and quietly, the two pairs of oars dipped and rose as they covered the five hundred yards across from the peninsula where they lived to the dock at Kinsale.

The neat little harbour at Kinsale had been formed millions of years ago as the Irish Sea cut a path into the mainland north of the cliffs of Old Head to meet the rushing waters of the Bandon River. Ringrone Peninsula's rocky hills jutted out into the horseshoe curve of the river, providing a perfect lookout over river and sea alike. Now in 1828, the crumbling remains of King James's Fort still guarded the entrance to the harbour, facing King William's Fort across the river. Abandoned for nearly two centuries, the pair was a constant reminder of the importance of the harbour in the distant past.

Thank God for the ferryboat, Donal thought as he pulled on the heavy oars. Otherwise, they would have had to walk along the seven miles of shoreline to cross the only bridge in the area and then walk another seven miles on the opposite shore to reach the village of Kinsale, which lay in view only a few hundred yards across the river.

Donal's mind swirled with images of his father lying hurt. Would Liam never tell him what had happened? He knew that the sound of their voices would carry too far over the water, so he fought to hold his questions until they reached the opposite shore.

Donal watched the faint outline of his older brother's back and shoulders. He often envied Liam's height and strength. He would like to be built more like his six-foot brother rather than his own slight five-foot-seven frame. He knew that he was more like his father, even to the faintly rounded shoulders. He even had Da's sandy colored hair, but it was Liam who had inherited Da's strong facial features with his long aristocratic nose and square chin. His own face, he knew, was like his mother's people—almost round with small blue eyes and a snub nose, causing him to look less than his eighteen years. Liam, who was two years older than he, somehow always looked like a grown man, at least to him.

Donal didn't know why Liam wanted him to pretend he was Da, but he knew that from a distance, the deception would be perfect. The coat and cap fit him snugly, and he knew well that he held himself and walked in the same way as his father did. Just the fact that people would be expecting to see Liam and himself rowing over to the dock about sunup would be enough for them to accept that he was indeed Da.

Donal glanced over his shoulder. They were almost at the dock. Liam spoke for the first time since they had gotten into the boat. "Keep your shoulders bent a bit when you get up, Donal, like Da," he said.

The current gave a sturdy shove, and the curragh slid onto the ramp. Donal shipped his oars with split-second timing as Liam did the same. Liam leaped over the side and pulled the canvas-covered boat farther up the ramp, and as Donal jumped out, they each grasped a side, hauling it onto dry land as they had done countless times before. Without speaking, they turned the boat over and stored the oars underneath. Donal stood, his shoulders hunched, holding them in toward his chest as though it hurt to breathe.

"We've got to walk slowly, like always," Liam cautioned. "We can't run. We must look as if Da and me were on our way to work of a mornin'."

"For God's sake, Liam, will you tell me what's happened? What in the name of Jesus, Mary, and Joseph is goin' on?" Donal pleaded as he matched his step to Liam's casual pace in the direction of the smithy.

"We burned Lord Huxley's barn at Ballinspittle last night," Liam said quietly. "They gave us chase and fired. Da was hit in the head."

Donal gasped. *Da had been shot—shot in the head—and by the English! Damn them! Damn them all to hell!* He looked at Liam and said but one word. "Whiteboys!"

Liam nodded.

"But why? Why you and Da?"

"Someone has to do it," Liam answered with a shrug of his shoulders.

"But what Lord Huxley does don't concern us none. We have to worry about Squire Atkins."

"Nothin' is that simple, Donal. The Ballinspittle lads will take care of Squire Atkins. Works better that way."

Everything Donal had ever heard about the rebel organization called Whiteboys rushed through his mind. He forced himself to concentrate on this in order to keep from thinking of Da, wounded and dying.

The Whiteboy organization had nearly died out when the union between Britain and Ireland had finally become official in 1802. But when it became apparent that the emancipation of Catholic Irish rights was not going to result from the union, the secretive rebel group of the native Irish began again to plague the English landlords with destruction of English property and sometimes even killings. To keep their identity secret, all members of the secret organization wore long loose white shirts over their clothing, which led to their name.

In the past three years, since 1825, the rebel activity in County Cork had been more frequent. The British gentry became fed up with the constant harassment by these unlawful bands of impertinent peasants and recently had begun to set traps for them. If caught, a Whiteboy was as good as dead. Trials were a mockery, if held at all, and the rebel ended his days dangling from the end of a rope.

"Were they waiting for you then? Was it a trap?" Donal asked.

"No, I don't think so," Liam replied, "twas more likely an unlucky accident. There just happened to be several landlords at the mansion last night—maybe a meeting or something. The timing was bad on our part, them being there with horses and all."

"Do you think they know who you all are? Will they guess that you and Da were there?"

"Hard to say," Liam murmured, "but if they follow carefully enough, they'll see the blood. We circled round through Fernald's Woods to throw them off track, but we had to get back to help Da. He's hurt bad, Donal, real bad."

"What are we going to do, Liam? How can we keep 'em from knowing Da's shot?"

"We're going to set a stage. We can't have them suspect that Da was anywhere near Ballinspittle last night," Liam answered. "We're almost there. Not another word now. Just do as you're told and pretend you're Da 'til we're ready."

The blacksmith shop stood at the junction of the two roads that made up the village of Kinsale. The high road led up the hill to the tiny Catholic Church and parsonage, passing the Church of England and the abbey at the halfway mark. The low road wound along the banks of the Bandon River, making a horseshoe hook and then winding its way to Belgooley and Cork City.

Once upon a time, a hundred or more years ago, Kinsale, with its wide harbour and deep channel, had been a thriving port. The largest of the king's ships made their way in and out, carrying the produce of the Irish farmers to the mouths of the London gentry, and their linens and woolens to the beds and backs of Englishmen.

Now the mills were closed, and the harvests of the farms of the southern part of County Cork were not enough for the big merchant ships to stop at Kinsale. They began to call at Cobh, near Cork City, and the harbour of Kinsale was left to the occasional fishing boat and ships that needed refuge in a storm. The once bustling port had become a sleepy village whose inhabitants existed on potatoes and little else.

Squire Atkins's gleaming white mansion rose abruptly on the hill at the far curve of the river known as Summer Cove. It stood majestically amid the giant elms spaced over the rocky hillside and the soft green lawns that sloped down to the blue water. Real-glass windows reflected the rays of the morning sun.

Donal and Liam opened the heavy doors of the blacksmith shop and loudly greeted Paddy the Smith who stood by the forge dressed in his stained leather apron. "Ho, Paddy," called Liam, his voice sounding falsely loud and cheerful in the quiet of the morning. "'Tis another beautiful day we have here."

"Oh, it tis, it tis," Paddy called out. "Mornin' to you, Tim." He nodded at Donal then lowered his voice. "Leave one of the doors closed, Liam, me lad," he said. "The work we have ahead of us this day is best done in the shadows."

Liam swung one of the heavy doors wide to the sun, propping it open with a keg of nails. He always did this first thing of a morning when the weather was fair. The other door he left closed though twas not a natural thing for him to do.

Donal looked at Paddy. "Da?" he asked. Paddy nodded toward the backroom. He shook his head. "He's dead, lads," he said, making the sign of the cross in front of his face. "Just a few minutes ago. May God rest his soul."

"No!" Donal cried out, starting toward the back. Paddy and Liam grabbed him, each holding him by an arm.

"We've got to act normal like," Paddy said.

"Calm yourself, Donal," Liam said softly. "You've got to help us before anyone comes. We've got to set the stage."

"But Da's dead," Donal protested, struggling against their hold. "You heard him, Liam. Da's dead!"

Liam shook his brother. "Stop, Donal! We'll not bring him back now. Tis the living we've got to be thinking of, and it's you who can help."

Gently they led Donal to a keg of nails and set him down. Paddy patted him awkwardly on the back. "Sure, and we know how you feel, Donal lad," he said quietly, "but yer brother's right. We need yer help, and there'll be plenty of time for grievin' before the day's done."

The sound of horses made them stop and look at each other with fear in their eyes. Paddy jumped to the open door. "Tis only Mick the Groom with the squire's horses. I sent him to fetch 'em," he called back with relief.

"Is he all right?" Donal asked.

Liam nodded. "He was with us last night."

"Oh my god," Donal moaned. "Why didn't someone tell me what was going on? Why didn't I know of these things?"

"There's no time for this now, Donal. Besides, two of us in one family were enough to be involved."

"Quick now, Donal," Paddy interrupted. "Pretend like you're yer own father and go out to greet Mick. Take the horses, and bring 'em in fer shoeing."

Donal moved to the door. He felt numb. His mind refused to function, but his body responded to the orders.

"Ho, Tim!" called Mick as though he wasn't looking right into the face of Donal in full sunlight. "Here I am with the squire's horses, like I said. Now you be sure and do a fine job. You know the squire likes a smooth ride."

Donal took the reins and patted the matched pair on their noses. "Liam, me boy," he shouted. "Come and give yer old Da a hand with these fine beasts we're to work on this day." *Even my voice sounds like Da's*, he thought.

Liam smiled his approval, took the reins, and led one of the sleek horses through the open door. Donal followed with the other.

"Is the squire about this mornin'?" Paddy asked Mick.

"Ah yes. He had his breakfast on the porch overlooking the harbour," answered Mick. "He was watching Liam and Tim a-walkin' up from the quay as I led the horses from the yard."

Donal looked quickly at his brother. *Had they fooled the squire?* His heart pounded as though it would burst through his chest.

Mick grinned. "He yelled at me to hurry with the horses, that Tim O'Dwyer and his boy would be there before me and wastin' their time a-waitin'."

They all laughed nervous little laughs.

"We'll carry it off yet, lads," Paddy said, patting the horse's behind. "Quickly now. This has got to be right the first time. Let's set the stage for the squire and his cronies."

"I don't understand what we're trying to do," Donal protested.

"No time to explain now, Donal. Just follow directions, and act like yer himself," Liam said. "Go to the fire and use the bellows. There's an iron heating there which needs to be good and hot."

Donal stood at the forge, squeezing the bellows, and watched as the others maneuvered the horse into place. The heat from the fire added to his anxiety. He wondered why they were all standing around when Da was dead—murdered?

Liam and Paddy removed the old shoes from one of the animals. Donal heard them clang as they were thrown into the corner on top of a pile of old metal.

He watched Paddy move to the door of the back room. Donal knew his father lay dead amid the piles of rusting anchors, bits of plows, and other useless tools that one day Paddy would have time to remake.

"Okay, Paddy," shouted Liam. "We're ready!"

The door of the back room swung open. Paddy and Fergus McGee carried Da into the shop being careful to stay behind the closed door. Donal gasped as he saw his father's injured head.

"Don't look now, Donal," Liam said, his voice strangely calm. "Take the tongs, and pick up the iron. Be sure to walk like Da. Stay in full view of the open door and come around in back of me. I'll take the tongs from you." He paused and took a deep breath. "When I shout, you drop flat on the floor. Make sure you stay out of the way of the horse's hooves. He's going to kick like crazy."

Donal tore his eyes away from his father's head. He nodded at Liam, picked up the tongs, and grasped the white-hot iron. Carefully he held his shoulders like Da and walked directly across the open doorway. The sun poured in on the floor, reflecting rainbow colors from a sliver of metal on the hardened earth. He moved deliberately out of sight and behind Liam. Not sure what was going on, he followed the directions exactly.

As Donal bent over to extend the tongs to Liam, Paddy snatched Da's cap from Donal's head. Liam grasped the tongs firmly. At the same moment, Donal heard Liam shout, "Now!"

Donal hit the floor and only vaguely knew that Liam had touched the red-hot iron to the horse's flesh and jumped out of view in the same instant.

Donal wasn't sure what happened next for he was too busy rolling out of the range of the horse's hooves. The heavy shop door banged open as something crashed. The next thing he knew he was against the back wall, and he realized they had pitched Da outside, and his body was lying on the ground. The sun shone on the bright pool of blood that poured from his father's skull, and his cap settled in the middle of the red puddle.

Paddy's harsh whisper brought Donal to his senses. "Git in the backroom, Donal, quick! You're not to let anyone know yer here. Hide under something in case someone comes in." Donal felt himself being shoved into the backroom, and the door shut solidly behind him.

He heard Liam shouting. "Da! Da! Are ye all right?" And Paddy yelled, "Fer God's sake, Mick, control the horses!"

Donal buried himself under a pile of musty seed bags. He could hear the sounds of running feet and shouts of voices coming from every direction.

"The squire's horse has kicked in poor Tim O'Dwyer's head!" he heard Paddy shout. At the same time Liam bellowed, "He's dead! My god, he's dead!"

Donal pulled the bags tight about his ears. He could no longer hear the shouts, but in his head, the sound of Liam's words echoed, *He's dead! My god, he's dead!*

CHAPTER 3

TIMOTHY O'DWYER WAS laid out in the main room of the thatched-roof cottage. It was, in fact, the only room except for the loft at the top of the wooden ladder. The large four-poster bed, which had been Gran's wedding present to Tim and his wife, Katherine, had been disassembled and moved into the shed next to the cow's stall. The room was now ready for his many friends and neighbors from around the county to pay their last respects.

Tim lay stretched out on a white-sheathed board, which had been placed atop the backs of four chairs, borrowed from Brigid O'Malley for the occasion. He was decked out in his one and only suit and a threadbare shirt to which had been added a stiff, new collar, also borrowed from Brigid.

Although a bit unusual for a corpse to wear a cap, it had been thought best to save Tim's friends and neighbors the gruesome sight of his crushed head. After being wrapped in one of Gran's best tea towels, his head was tucked up into his cap. While it looked a mite too big for the rest of him, he did look natural—as though he had stopped for a pint at the Ferry Pub on his way home from mass of a Sunday, Gran said.

Tim's bier was the focal point of the room; the rest of the hard-packed dirt floor waited for the near neighbors to bring in their stools and benches for the mourners to sit upon.

A candle stood at each of the four corners of this grand bier, and Tim's widow raised herself up on tiptoes to light them; they were *that* high. Katherine stood back to admire the sight, smiling to think how Tim would have loved to see himself in such a grand setting. She sighed heavily and turned to the hearth to stir the kettle brimming with stew the Widow O'Shaunessey had brought. The pleasant odors of rabbit and vegetables wafted through the room, mingling with the waxy blandness of the lighted candles. But there was no time to absorb the satisfying smells; the table must be laid out for the food all would bring with them to the wake.

No time, no time. Time was gone—gone with her Timothy, leaving her alone. Katherine turned her back to the sheet-covered table, not unlike the one her Timothy was laid out on, and leaned against it, looking at himself.

Ah, Timothy, she thought, *'tis over. And what happened to all the dreams we had? What happened to the laughing and the loving? When did life turn to dullness and drudgery? And when had the desire and the delight turned to nothingness and emptiness?* She sighed aloud. *Maybe 'tis just as well you're out of it. Maybe where you are is a better place with better people.* She pushed her faded red hair back from her forehead. *And maybe you won't be missing me the way I'm missing you. Ah Timothy, I guess the love's not gone at all, and I am sorry that I've not been showing it these past years.*

Timothy O'Dwyer said not a word to his wife of twenty-one years, but Katherine felt warmth tighten around her heart and recognized his presence as she had those long years ago. She wiped her eyes on the corner of her apron and turned back to her work.

Katherine had been seventeen when she first noticed Tim. He had come to their home with a group of lads from the surrounding countryside to discuss the suffocating laws that continued in spite of the passage of the emancipation. It was one of many meetings her father held in their small out-of-the-way cottage nestled in the foothills of the abandoned Ringrone Castle. Her father had been Declan DeCourcey and his ancestors once owned all the land on Ringrone Peninsula all the way to Old Head Light. Of course that was generations ago.

Declan DeCourcey's only daughter, Katherine, served tea to the group attending the meeting that night. There were perhaps fifteen or sixteen young men crowded into the small room, and she stumbled over Timothy O'Dwyer's feet, dropping the teapot. Tim jumped up to help her gather the pieces of the broken pot.

As Katherine reached out blindly, she touched Tim's hand. It was only then that he noticed her. Tears streamed down her cheeks, her long red hair shading them from view of the others. "I'm sorry. I'm sorry," Tim spluttered at seeing the tears. "Twas my fault. I'll be getting you another pot."

"I have another teapot," Katherine replied, brushing tears away with the back of a slim white hand. "But this one belonged to my great-grandmother—the last of the DeCourcey china." She rose from her knees, the broken shards gathered in her apron. She flung the red-gold hair over her shoulders and stood tall and proud. Looking around the room, her eyes rested on each face. "The last of the DeCourcey heritage," she said, then turned and left the room.

The men decided that night they would no longer take the lack of freedom that still held them helpless to obtain education or to vote in their own country. The old rebel organization called Whiteboys was revived before they left, and by morning, the grain fields on Squire Atkins's estate were ablaze.

Timothy O'Dwyer called often at the DeCourcey cottage, not always to discuss politics with the old man. Gradually, Katherine realized that it was herself whom the dark-haired Timothy came to see, and she began to feel the longing for a home and a man of her own and children to bring up. Six months later, Timothy asked her to marry him, although she had made up her mind weeks before.

Katherine found that, beneath his solemn exterior, Tim was a thoughtful, caring man with a wry sense of humor. Although he could neither read nor write, his sharp mind was a fair match for her own. The DeCourcey family had always felt the necessity for their offspring to learn their letters, and Katherine had been taught at her father's knee, a custom she carried on with her own children.

Katherine was also exposed to her father's politics and was one of the few women in all of Ireland who was aware of the implications of current events, since most women had no education, no say in governing affairs, or even the right to speak Gaelic in public. Having no sons and left to bring up his daughter alone, Declan DeCourcey exposed his daughter to discussions and reading of the history of English oppression and the un-fair treatment of the Irish citizens. Only a tiny minority of women were allowed to voice their own opinions even in their own households.

At thirty-eight, Katherine's face carried deep lines around the mouth and eyes. Her hair was more gray than red, and her hands, once long and slender, were rough and swollen around the knuckles. A cough constantly threatened to explode the tightness in her chest, and while her mind was still as sharp as ever, she appeared to be twenty years more than her age.

Somewhere along the way, Katherine had lost her zest for life. Had she been asked, she would have said she still loved her husband, but her body no longer longed for his touch the way it had those first few years, nor did she respond when he touched her. Her father's death had been the starting point, although she hadn't been consciously aware that this was so at the time.

Katherine moved to her husband's bier and laid her hand on the bandaged head, but she wasn't seeing her Tim. The smell of the burning candles had taken her back to a time she had tried to forget.

They had seen the smoke rising over the hill from their doorstep. Katherine immediately knew it came from her father's cottage. She ran, holding her skirt up out of the way, all the two miles along the low road to the place she had called home for nearly eighteen years. She could hear Tim's padding footsteps behind her as she flew along the path.

The flames were shooting through the roof by the time they arrived. She pushed open the top of the double-dutch door. The wind rushed in and cleared the smoke for one instant, revealing Declan DeCourcey tied to the center post, his clothes afire. His white hair burst into flames as the wind fanned the fire. He was already dead. Tim pulled her away as the roof caved in, and the fire consumed the rest of the cottage.

Declan DeCourcey had been active in one revolutionary group or another all his life. He had never outgrown the bitterness he felt at the domination of the English. His ancestors had lost everything at their hands, and all hope of ever regaining it had been destroyed. He fought in any way he could, and at last they had caught up with him. He had been the ringleader of the Whiteboys in the area for many years, and the English had punished him without the benefit of judge or jury.

Katherine never complained about Tim's activities in her father's political organization. She had sat in on too many meetings over the years to doubt the necessity of what they were doing. But when he began to involve Liam, she objected. "It's gone far enough," she shouted at him. "Far enough! I am not willing to pay the price of father, husband and son." Her voice rose more than she intended, but she could not keep quiet while her family was destroyed.

After that Tim did not discuss his activities with her, and Katherine said no more even after she found Liam was still slipping out to join his father. Instead she lay awake and died a little every time they left. When she slept, her dreams were of her father's face as the flames crept up around him.

Now what she had dreaded had happened. Her husband was dead by English hands. The "accident" at the forge might have fooled the English, but she was not as easily misled. She leaned over and kissed Tim's cold and unyielding forehead. Suddenly she missed the warmth of him, and the warmth that had been in herself those long years ago.

The door burst open. "They're coming, Mam! They're coming! Look at them, all coming to wake Da!" Kate threw open the door, her black hair flowing around her shoulders, and her delicate ivory face shining from the scrubbing at the rain barrel. Two bright spots heightened her high cheekbones, and a third provided a gleam to the tilted nose. *A beauty she is*, thought her mother. *I must have a talk with her. At fifteen, she's a full-grown woman, and the world is full of temptations.*

Katherine pulled her mind back to the moment. "Hurry, Kate, bring Gran in, and set her chair before the fire. I don't want her out there watching them come up the hill. Then help me with setting out the cups and the poteen." She followed Kate with a worried glance. The girl had refused to accept that her father was dead. She had neither cried nor looked at her Da since he was brought in and laid out in the center of the room. Only the tenseness of her body revealed the change in her.

In the next moment the room was filled with people, all talking at once, and all trying to put food and drink on the table, or placing stools and benches around the room. No one paid the slightest attention to Timothy O'Dwyer stretched out on Gran's best sheet with his feet looking bigger than his outsized head. The din rose as neighbor greeted neighbor and friend, friend. The sound filled the cottage, rising to the loft, and flowing over into the yard and into the cowshed.

Katherine turned first to one and then another, responding to greetings and gifts and condolences. Suddenly a scream pierced the air. All other sound ceased. The wail increased in intensity as everyone instinctively turned toward the center of the room.

Gran was on her knees in front of her son's bier, and she cried out her bereavement for all to hear. Gran was a grand mourner. She was in great demand at wakes for miles around, and many was the time that Tim had placed her in the donkey cart and hauled her off to do her best keening for friend and foe alike throughout the county. This was her grand finale—the wake of her only son.

The piercing wail spiraled into the air. Katherine dropped and crawled to the side of the bier. In a flash the mourners fell to their knees as the keening rose on high. A multitude of voices filled the room, and it was as if there were no air to breathe at all.

CHAPTER 4

KATE TURNED AND ran from the house, her hands clasped over her ears. She had to get out. The sound of the keening was driving her out of her mind. She had to get away. . . run . . . run . . . run . . . She didn't know where she was going, but she had to keep running, running.

The dew was still wet in the long grass on the hillside leading to the abandoned fort. The hem of Kate's skirt and the shoes that Mam had made from the torn canvas of a sail which had washed ashore, were soaked through and slowed her progress. Still she ran, holding the wet skirt bunched in front of her with one trembling hand. The piercing wails rang in her ears, carried on the brisk wind up the steep slope of the hill. Her breath came in great gulping sobs. Her long black hair swung from side to side as she ran, tangling and knotting in the wind, shining in the dampness and the sun.

Kate flung herself over the outer defense wall of the fort, now nearly buried with earth in its century of neglect. Landing in a heap on the other side, she picked herself up and, still stumbling, made her way to the crumbling keep, whose lookouts were once first to give the alarm of approaching ships.

A fieldstone fireplace still stood along one wall and in the corner was a pile of straw. Kate and Declan often escaped to this haven and had piled dry grass to sit upon. Exhausted from the denied emotions of the past two days, her heart pounding against her chest in painful thumps, Kate threw herself down into the straw and curled into a fetal position. She clamped her hands over her ears to shut out the keening, now existing only in her mind. Her tense body shuddered, but the tears would not be released. *Oh Da, whatever shall I do without you? I can't believe that you have left me. Why did you have to die? Why? Why?*

Gradually the trembling slowed. She must have slept briefly; she was not sure. She heard a small sound nearby and felt—knew—someone was watching her. She lay still a few seconds without opening her eyes, knowing instantly where she was and all that had happened in the past forty-eight hours. But who could have known where to find her? Had someone followed her mad dash up the hill and into the fort?

Not wanting to be surprised from behind, Kate turned and sat up in one motion. She caught her breath. There in the archway was a man—a man unlike any she had ever seen except in her girlish dreams. He was framed in the half arch that had once been the entranceway to this three-hundred-year-old keep, now overgrown with the creeping ivy that covered most of Ireland.

The sun from a half-destroyed window fell full upon him, bathing him in light. His fair hair reached his shoulders, and he stood even with the head of the gray-flecked horse he held by white reins. He was clothed in tight white riding britches and a coat of dark green. She saw that he wore a shirt of a paler green beneath his coat, and an ascot in a paisley print the colors of wine filled the opening. Knee-high boots gleamed like the mahogany table she had seen through the squire's window one Christmas Day.

The stranger's face held high cheekbones and an almost-square chin, and his nose was thin and a trifle long. The full red lips were slightly pursed, but Kate thought they looked like they were used for laughter. His clear blue eyes stared into her dark ones.

For a moment, neither spoke. Kate held her breath, not really sure this was not a part of the unreal dream of the past two days. Realizing the predicament she was in, she raised her hand to her mouth in a frightened gesture, scrambling to her feet at the same time.

The stranger moved toward her, and she darted for the doorway. "Wait! Don't be frightened," he called out. "I won't hurt you." His arm reached out and caught her elbow.

He didn't hold her tightly. Kate could have gotten away. In fact, he wasn't grasping her at all, but at his touch, she stopped. She looked up into the blue eyes and could not tear her own away.

He dropped his hand from her elbow. Strange, but she still felt his touch. "Don't go," he said quietly. He turned, not waiting to see if she fled or stayed, and moved with the horse out into the sun-filled day. Only then did he look back. Kate stood, staring silently.

"Don't you speak?" he asked. His voice was low and richly warm, and Kate felt a shiver trickle down her spine.

"Who . . . who are you?" she stammered.

"You're trembling," he said. "Come out into the sun. You'll be warmer here." He did not touch her or attempt to aid her in any way, rather moved farther out into the sun himself, allowing her room to pass through the archway without touching him.

"You look like you've had a harrowing experience," he said calmly. "Is there some way I can help?"

Suddenly Kate became aware of how she must look. Her black hair was a mass of tangled curls, her eyes ringed with shadows, her best frock wet and soiled and wrinkled from lying in the hay, her shoes and stockings stained from the dew. Flustered, she brushed the hair from her face and straightened her clothes. "I'm fine, just fine," she stammered, "but I must look a fright."

He laughed, throwing his head back and releasing the joyous sound to the sky. Kate felt the echoes move warmly through her body. She seemed not to be hearing with her ears at all but absorbing the sounds through her pores. A vibration went through, sending her blood pulsing into her chest. The force alarmed and frightened her. It also angered her for she felt out of control.

"What's so funny?" she asked indignantly. *Who was this man that he could laugh at her troubles?* He probably never had a care in the world by the look of him even if he did appear to be the answer to a girl's prayers.

"I'm sorry," he replied still grinning broadly. "It's just that here I find a beautiful young woman huddled in the corner of an old fort, looking like she'd just been raped by the devil himself, and the first thing she says is that she must look a fright." He laughed again, and this time Kate laughed with him.

The more they looked at each other, the more they laughed. Kate felt hysteria rising, uncontrolled. They sank to the ground, laughing uproariously. She knew she was not going to be able to stop. The terrifying emotions of the last two days overwhelmed her. Tears began to flow down her cheeks, and sobs mixed with her laughter.

She hadn't been able to cry when she heard Da had been killed. The horror she felt had been too much for tears. She refused to admit to herself it was Da lying there dead for when she saw his body lying stretched out on the white sheet, he appeared to be someone else. Now the laughter had broken her denial, and the tears could not be stopped.

The handsome stranger reached out and cradled her in his arms. He rocked her back and forth as though she were a small child, holding her close. "It's all right. It's all right." He soothed. "Sometimes crying helps. Don't hold back." He stroked her dark hair away from her face and wiped the tears that streaked the delicate ivory cheeks. "My god, but you're beautiful," he said softly. He drew her to him again, and Kate felt his hand on the back of her head pressing her into his shoulder.

Kate knew she should move away, but she felt a strange yearning. She had always wondered how it would be to be held like this. And he had called her a beautiful woman! Did he really think she was a woman? A beautiful woman? She was so tired of being a child. She knew her body had changed, but she could not tell if it was more attractive, and there was no one she could ask. Gram would say she was wicked for thinking such things, and Mam would just smile and say she would always be beautiful to her.

The sobs stopped and her trembling ceased, but she didn't want to stir. She felt warm and protected as though nothing would ever hurt her again. She had never known this feeling before. And he had called her beautiful! Was she being wicked?

Kate moved away. "I'm sorry," she began. "I couldn't stop crying. You'd better let me go now."

His arms moved away hesitantly as though he too didn't want the moment to end. Kate felt his hands slide down her arms, caressing her softly, then they were gone.

"Feel better now?" he asked, his rich English voice low and with his eyes holding hers.

Kate felt a sudden shortness of breath. Even her dreams had not prepared her for what she was feeling. Hurriedly she brushed away the remnants of her tears and pulled her long hair back with a sweeping motion, twisting it into a roll at the nape of her neck. Her pale, oval face turned up to the sun. She felt vulnerable—not fully in control of her emotions. "Yes yes, thank you," she murmured. "You're very kind. I guess I just needed someone to comfort me."

"Did somebody hurt you?" he asked, looking away as though embarrassed.

"Oh no," Kate replied quickly. "It's my father, you see. They're waking him down in the cottage below. The squire's horse kicked him in the head."

"Here, here, slow down," he interrupted. "You mean your father's dead?"

"That's what I just said," Kate replied impatiently.

"Quite. I see. That's what they were talking about last night at the manor house. So your father was the smithy who was killed by the horse." He paused. "The squire thought it strange that his horse, which had never before kicked at anything, would do so much damage as to kill a man."

Kate nodded solemnly. "It was queer, all right, but he was quite dead. Liam, that's my brother, he was there, and he said Da went flying through the air headfirst and landed on the stones in front. His head was bashed in somethin' awful. Gran had to cover it with his cap when she laid him out, it was *that* bad."

Kate scrambled to her feet. "Oh my! The wake! I've got to get back!" She pulled her long skirt into a bunch with one hand and dashed toward the path. Suddenly she stopped and looked back. "Thank you," she called. "Thank you!" and she ran through the field toward the crumbling wall.

"Wait! Wait!" he shouted after her. "I don't even know your name!"

But Kate didn't hear. As she scrambled over the wall, she looked back and saw him standing where she had left him. She waved her arm in farewell and jumped to the other side.

CHAPTER 5

DECLAN NEARLY SHOUTED with relief as he saw Kate leap over the outer wall of the fort. Thank God he had found her. Father McBride would kill them both if they didn't hurry. He would know instantly they were missing for the saying of the rosary for Da. Father McBride had an uncanny ability to recognize immediately when anyone committed the smallest of sins.

Declan saw Kate raise her arm in farewell to someone on the far side of the wall. He stopped in amazement. *Who in the name of Mary, Joseph, and all the saints, could be up at the fort this morning? Everyone they knew on the face of the earth was down in the cottage below.*

Declan's breath came in uneven gasps from his run up the hill. His sun-bleached hair fell in damp wisps over his broad forehead. "Kate! Kate!" he shouted as she landed on the ground and started toward him. "Hurry Kate! Father McBride is comin' down the high road for the sayin' of the rosary. There's the devil to pay if we're not there."

Kate caught up to him and grabbed his hand. Together they rushed down the sloping path toward the cottage, Kate's long slim legs keeping her a step or two ahead of her younger brother. One leg of Declan's knee britches had already slipped, and his too-thin face was red and sweaty from his frantic rush to find his sister. The two of them were a sorry sight.

Declan saw that Father McBride was already starting down the incline from the high road, his rosary beads swinging from the corded sash at his waist. "Holy Mother of Christ!" Declan whispered to Kate. "He's spotted us! He'll dole out enough penance to last us a lifetime!"

As Declan spoke, Father McBride stopped in his tracks as though he had heard every word and was about to condemn them to the fires of hell for their outrageous behavior while their father was laid out in their own cottage.

Kate and Declan froze in their flight, but Father McBride was not looking at them at all. His beady black eyes were focused beyond the two of them, and his bony hands paused in their fingering of the beads at his sash.

Declan and Kate turned to see what had distracted the priest's attention. Through the break in the far side of the crumbling wall rode the blond stranger on the dappled gray horse. He sat tall and regal on his steed, his crop held majestically in his left hand. His right hand rose in salute to the two bedraggled youngsters turned toward him. Kate let out a small sound as they watched him ride down the slope toward the beach.

Declan stared at Kate with his mouth hanging open. Suddenly he remembered Father McBride and turned his attention back to the priest. Kate could explain about the horseman later.

Father McBride had not moved. Only the black eyes had shifted. They stared across the seventy-five yards into Kate's frightened face. You could almost see the indignant hairs rising on his body. He stood stiffly at his full height, his chin thrust out beyond his square frame. His prominent ears appeared to stand alert, and the wide-brimmed hat seemed more than ever to be supported by them. Even at this distance, Declan could see he was making a tremendous effort to control his rising anger.

Poor Kate, Declan thought, *she'll be confessing this for years*. He pulled her out of her suspended state. "Let's run, Kate. We've got to get to the house before him." They tore their eyes from the avenging Father and ran for home. Declan saw that Father McBride also moved into action and hurried as fast as he could down the slope in hopes of cutting them off before they reached the cottage.

It looked as if their paths would cross right at the door. In his indignation, Father McBride would never take into consideration the fact that Da lay dead inside and the entire parish was mourning with Mam and Gran. The whole humiliating scene of Kate's imminent trial and conviction would take place within earshot of the total population of Ringrone Peninsula and half of Kinsale and Ballinspittle too.

"Come on, Kate—the back way, quickly." Declan pulled her off the path and down over the rocky incline. "We can go in through the shed. We can't risk the path."

They leaped over the ruins of the guard's quarters, over their own low stone wall, and into the cowshed. The sudden darkness after the bright sunlight blinded them. They leaned against each other, breathing heavily. "I'm a mess," Kate gasped between breaths, "and you are too. What will Mam say?"

Declan ran to the cow's stall and grabbed the pail of water left there for drinking. He dragged it over to his sister. "Here, Kate, wash your face and hands, then for God's sake, do something with your hair." He brushed briefly at her wrinkled, soiled dress, and then hitched up his own falling stockings and pant legs. When Kate had finished washing, he splashed some water on his own face. His breathing slowed, and he saw that Kate had calmed as well. They looked at each other with apprehension and moved slowly toward the door next to the hearth in the room beyond. Kate grabbed Declan's hand as they opened the door and slipped into the room filled with their father's friends and neighbors. "Thank you, Declan," she said softly. He squeezed her hand briefly before dropping it.

As they closed the door behind them, a silence filled the room. Declan drew in his breath, then realized all the faces in the room were turned toward the front door where Father McBride stood in the sunlit frame. The priest's eyes searched for the escaped culprits. Declan quickly looked to the floor, hoping Kate had done the same. He heard his mother's greeting and Father McBride's unctuous response. Declan let out his breath. They had won a reprieve.

Father McBride strode to the splendid figure of Timothy O'Dwyer laid out so grandly in the center of the room. The crowd moved back, making a path for his approach, bowing their heads respectfully. He stopped to lay a hand on Gran's shoulder and sank to his knees beside her. Mam knelt by his other side, and the whole room fell to its knees in one motion. They fished their beads from their pockets, and the rosary began.

"In the name of the Father, the Son, and the Holy Ghost . . ." As one, they crossed themselves and bowed their heads. Declan threw a relieved glance at Kate. She acknowledged it briefly and bowed her head, murmuring the prayer.

Father McBride's thin, reedy voice rose and hung in the motionless air of the overcrowded room. The chorus of voices responded raggedly, not quite together.

Declan heard Niall's tenor tones, sounding like music even in the monotonous repetitions. He could see his brother's red head between that of Donal and Liam in the next row of kneeling mourners. Niall held his head high, not bowed in prayer like the others. His perfectly shaped nose gave his face a Roman look, and his deep, blue eyes gleamed.

Declan noted that Niall's attention was not on the kneeling figure of Father McBride nor focused on the gravity of the moment. Instead, he studied the tempting, ripe figure of Maire Foley, kneeling in front and a bit to the left. Declan could see Niall's face clearly through the row of bent heads. Niall's eyes swept Maire's body and lingered on the slim waist and the rising breasts as they moved with her recitation of the prayer. He wet his lips without missing a single syllable.

Declan was mildly offended at the sacrilege of the thoughts he knew were in Niall's mind. Then he realized the same thoughts were in his own mind as well. He pulled his attention back to the prayers and reminded himself it was Da they were praying for. He tried to concentrate on the words.

"Hail Mary, full of grace. Blessed art thou amongst women, and blessed is the fruit of thy womb, Jesus. Holy Mary, Mother of God, pray for us sinners now and at the hour of our death." The voices droned their repetitions, but Declan was caught up on the word "death."

Da can't be dead. He can't be. Declan couldn't get beyond that thought. "Pray for us sinners now and at the hour of our death," he murmured again along with the others, but his mind cried out over and over, *Da! Da! You can't be dead!*

As the kneeling figures shifted and moved, Declan caught a glimpse of his father's body stretched out on the white sheet. In that instant he knew he had seen this scene before. He recognized the completeness of it—even to the outsized cap on Da's head.

Declan remembered a time when he was about seven years old. His mother and father had just returned from the fire at Granda's house.

They did not say how the fire started, only that their grandfather had been inside the burning cottage.

"Granda was tied to the center post with ropes," Declan blurted out. They looked at him in amazement.

"What did you say, Declan?" his mother asked.

"He was tied to the center post with ropes," Declan repeated. "I saw the English soldiers tie him, and then they torched the house. They watched it flare up and rode away on their horses."

There was not a sound in the room. All eyes turned on Declan in disbelief. He became defensive. "I did see it!" he shouted.

"Where were you, Declan?" his mother asked. "What were you doing there?"

"I wasn't there," Declan said firmly, "but I saw it all the same." He dashed out of the door.

"Declan!" Da shouted. "Come back here!" But Declan was already racing toward the beach.

"Leave him alone, Tim," Gran said quietly. "Declan has the "sight" though he doesn't realize it yet."

There had been other times too, as when he had "seen" Liam's friend Tomas Haggerty strung up on the hanging tree. Declan had been shocked at the sight and dismissed it from his mind as impossible. He only remembered what he had seen when Liam told the family several months later that Tomas had been hanged.

Declan didn't talk to anyone about his strange ability. It didn't happen to him often, and it didn't have much meaning for him until after the event had taken place and his "vision" had been confirmed. After he blurted out about Granda tied to the center post, he knew that he was different.

He sometimes lay awake at night thinking, wondering if he was the only one who saw such things. *Am I a wee bit peculiar, or are there others like me? If so, what did they do about it?* Gran tried to talk about having the "sight," but she frightened him, and he wished it would go away and leave him alone.

Declan often wondered how he could use this strange ability. He should be able to have some control, he thought. So much of the time he didn't even know he had actually seen something until after the fact.

If he could recognize the signs sooner, maybe he could warn people and stop the frightening things from happening. He tried to talk to Father McBride, but the priest said he was trafficking with the devil, and he had better watch out for his immortal soul.

The mumbled prayers circled and buzzed around Declan's head, now sounding low and afar, now loud and too near, deflecting his own thoughts from his consciousness. The prayers seemed caught by the rooftop, blocked from their intended journey to heaven.

Declan was suddenly annoyed with Father McBride for his intrusion into the privacy of their mourning, though he was, at the same time, aware that the familiar prayers were comforting to Mam and Gran. *They should be doing the same for me*, he thought.

Repeating the words, he once more joined the fluctuating voices around him. "As it was in the beginning, is now, and ever shall be." *I do believe. I do believe,* he repeated to himself. *I have always believed. What is the matter with me today? We must send up our prayers for Da to shorten his stay in purgatory.*

Da in purgatory! My god, I can't believe that! What kind of a god would send someone like Da to purgatory? It was impossible! Declan quickly crossed himself at the heresy of his thoughts. *Who was he to question God? But Da—in purgatory?*

Declan was suddenly uncomfortable. He shuffled with irritation. The floor was hard and uneven, and the cuffs of his britches were making welts just below his knees. He shifted again, only to feel Kate's elbow poking him in the ribs, reproaching him for his restlessness. On his other side, the widow O'Shaughnessy gave him a look that would wilt the heather.

Still the voices droned on. "The fourth sorrowful mystery . . ." Father McBride's holier-than-thou tones floated up to the loft and hung just below the roof. "Our Father who art in heaven . . ." followed the cadence from the gathered friends and neighbors of Timothy Seamus O'Dwyer.

"Father . . . Father . . ." Declan stumbled on the word. His throat filled, and he couldn't go on. Tears rolled down his cheeks, stopping to puddle in the hollows around his mouth as he raised his head to look at the roof. *Crying like a baby*, he thought, *and me, fourteen years old.* He felt a handkerchief tucked into his hand and saw Kate's warm dark eyes on him. He nodded his thanks and wiped his tears as unobtrusively as he could without disturbing the Widow O'Shaughnessy.

At last the rosary was ending . . . three more Hail Marys, one Our Father, and another "As it was in the beginning . . ." Declan crossed himself in unison with the crowd. As they rose from their kneeling position, he slipped through the door and into the cowshed.

The warmth of the animal drew him, and he slipped his arms about the cow's neck, cradling her head. But his tears were done with, and all he could think of was how Da had named the creature "Anne Boleyn" after she had been secretly serviced by Squire Atkins's bull, which Mick the Groom called Henry VIII because of his many secret mates. In addition, Da had said, she too would probably lose her head.

Declan closed his eyes and leaned against the warm neck of Anne Boleyn. The acrid smell of her rough skin reminded him of the peat bogs where he had gone last summer to help his father and brothers cut turf for the winter's fires. The same warm, earthy smell clung to the roof of his mouth, and he felt the same sense of companionship he had when sharing the work with his father. The good feeling seemed to be part of the air surrounding the bog, and it had followed them all the long way home as Da told them stories of an earlier Ireland, and Niall sang the old familiar songs in a clear, ringing voice. They had forgotten how tired and hungry they were as his voice rose and fell in the twilight.

The cow stirred against his face, straining to release herself from the tightened arms about her neck. Declan let her go, patting her between the ears. "You're a good friend, Anne Boleyn," he whispered. "I'll bet you're going to miss Da as much as the rest of us."

Declan picked up the bucket he and Kate had left in the middle of the earthen floor, put it back beside the cow's feed bin, and rubbed the warm animal once more along the nose. He swung himself up into the hayloft and stretched full length beside the small open window in the eaves. From there he could watch the activity in the yard below as all the younger men, women, and children burst from the cottage, glad to be released from the somber part of the day.

CHAPTER 6

UPON RISING FROM their collective knees, the mourners moved toward the food and drink spread out on the table opposite Tim O'Dwyer's body. Conversation erupted as though a signal had been given. The solemn part of the wake had ended, and the partying could now begin.

Colleen O'Malley assumed the position of authority behind the serving table. "A wee glass of poteen, Mr. O'Callahan?" she offered an old gentleman who, in spite of hobbling along with the aid of a hand carved cane, was first in line for refreshments.

O'Callahan spoke up quickly, "I don't mind if I do."

Fr. Brendan McBride helped Gran to her feet and turned to Katherine O'Dwyer. The ruddy spots on her cheeks and the dark circles under her eyes emphasized her emotional and physical exhaustion of the past two days.

Her three eldest sons converged on her, surrounding Father McBride. "I must speak with you, Widow O'Dwyer," the priest said, "on a matter of grave importance." He glanced significantly at the young men around him. "Privately, Widow O'Dwyer."

Mam appeared to physically shrink at the mention of the word "widow." Instinctively the boys moved closer. "Later, Father," Donal said. "I'm sure you understand Mam has other things on her mind at present."

Father McBride glared at the intrusion. "This is an important matter between your mother and me, Donal, concerning your sister."

Donal exchanged glances with his brothers. They seemed bewildered at the reference to Kate. A look of agreement passed between them, and Niall and Donal each took hold of one of Father McBride's arms and turned him toward the door. "Later, Father," Donal repeated. "There'll be plenty of time to discuss such things after this is over." The finality in his voice left no room for argument.

As Father McBride gave one last look at Mam, Liam stepped between his mother and the priest. Father McBride's feet brushed only lightly across the floor as Katherine's two sons hustled him from the cottage.

"So good of you to come, Father," Donal said, placing the parish priest firmly on the path leading to the high road.

"We'll see you early tomorrow morning, Father," broke in Niall, "at the chapel."

"But I must speak to your mother about Kate," Father McBride spluttered.

"After the burial, Father," Donal said with finality. "I'm sure it can wait 'til then. Mam has enough to handle today."

"This is very important. Your sister is a wayward, sinful girl. Her mother must be warned."

The brothers exchanged looks over the priest's head. At an unspoken signal, they each put a hand under Father McBride's elbow, closed the other over his upper arm, and ushered him well down the path toward the road. His skirt dangled a good four inches off the ground.

"Eight o'clock tomorrow mornin'," called Donal after him.

"And of course, there'll be a grand breakfast waiting after for us all," Niall added.

The priest narrowed his eyes and looked sternly from one brother to another. He was not more than eight or ten years older than either of the young men, but he took his duties seriously. The parish was his responsibility, and he did not take interference lightly. The O'Dwyer family had been a problem from the beginning, what with Katherine O'Dwyer insisting on teaching English as well as Gaelic to the children of the parish. She overstepped her bounds. Teaching was the job of the parish priest. Father McBride did not speak to the sons of the offending Widow O'Dwyer but jammed his wide-brimmed hat down to his ears and marched stiffly up the high road, his beads swinging violently. The two brothers watched his departure silently, looked at each other with satisfaction, and wiped their sweaty palms down the sides of their britches.

Liam guided Mam to the refreshment table and placed a cup of the home-brewed poteen in her hands. "Drink it, Mam," he said softly. "Twill help get you through the day." She nodded and put the cup to her lips.

Liam joined his brothers outside the cottage door. "You lads were a wee bit insistent, weren't you?" he asked with a smile.

"We should have thrown him out on his ass," Niall spoke up.

Donal crossed himself quickly. "God forgive us," he said. "One of these days, you'll get us all excommunicated."

Liam looked at the two of them. "What was all that about Kate?" he asked, ignoring their remarks.

"I don't know," the two replied at the same time.

"Whatever he meant, it sounds serious," Liam said.

The three watched the figure of the priest move along the ridge of the high road. "I don't know why," said Donal quietly, "but I can't like that man."

"He's hardly what I'd call a man," Niall replied, his lips pursed into a skeptical look.

"For heaven's sake, Niall, watch your tongue. He's a man of God," Donal scolded. He glanced over his shoulder to see if they had been overheard by the young people now crowding into the yard.

"No man of God ever looked at a woman the way Father McBride looks at Kate," Niall replied, perfectly shaped eyebrows arching in amusement.

"Stop it, Niall. That's not funny," Liam interrupted. "Besides, Kate's still a child."

"Maybe you haven't looked lately, my dear brother." Niall said, "but our little sister has grown up and quite nicely too."

Donal and Liam looked at each other in disbelief. Neither had noticed that fifteen-year-old Kate had become a beautiful woman right before their eyes, but if anyone claimed authority on the subject, it was Niall.

"But surely Father McBride never . . ." Donal stammered.

Niall laughed. "Father McBride can look—even if he can't touch." He paused for effect. "And the good Father looks at Kate as though he can't keep those lily white hands off her."

"I can't believe that," Liam said. "I hope Kate hasn't encouraged him."

"I doubt that," Niall said, placing his arm across Liam's shoulders. "Kate's an innocent."

"But what did Father McBride mean when he said she was an evil girl and Mam ought to know about it?" Donal asked. The three looked at each other with blank expressions. None had an answer.

"Obviously Kate will need some watching," Liam said. "Let's all keep an eye on her. Mam's got an apronful right now."

"Sure, sure," they answered.

"Speak of the devil . . ." Niall spoke up as Kate emerged from the cottage with several of her friends.

"My god, you're right, Niall!" Donal exclaimed. "She's a real beauty with that ivory skin and dark hair."

But Donal's two brothers stared instead at the girl on Kate's right. Maire Foley created a perfect contrast to Kate's dark beauty. Though she was a year older, she came only to Kate's shoulder. A peaches-and-cream complexion emphasized her huge violet eyes and light auburn tresses. The small nose turned up gently on the end, and her mouth was temptation itself. Small, pointed breasts strained against the white bodice.

"Now there's what I call a tempting dish," Niall said, licking his lips. "One of these days I'm going to have me a bite of that." Donal tore his eyes away from Maire and glared at his brother. Niall cleared his throat and pulled at the cuffs of his coat. "No time like the present," he said with a smirk. Giving his brothers a slap on their backs, he moved to intercept the approaching girls.

"Damn!" said Liam, scowling at Niall's back.

"Niall should know better than to talk about Maire like that," Donal said almost to himself, watching Niall saunter up to the group of attractive girls.

"He's a turd!" Liam spat out. "Niall couldn't tell an angel from a donkey's ass." He kicked at the dirt on the path and wandered away toward a group of his friends who stood awkwardly nearby, unaccustomed to being dressed in their Sunday best.

Liam's right, thought Donal, *Niall is a turd*. Donal really didn't like his younger brother much, and he didn't like feeling guilty about it. *Niall was a self-centered clod and was happy being just the way he was, never having a thought about anyone but himself*, Donal thought. He watched as each female turned a smile toward his brother and was aware of a wish that he could be as comfortable as Niall with the lasses.

Mam had been hauling Niall out from behind the hedges and thickets to rescue some neighborhood lass ever since Niall was nine years old. Niall thought it was a grand joke, much to Mam's embarrassment. He thought the whole world had been created for his own benefit—especially the opposite sex.

Watching the girls gathered around Niall, Donal wondered if perhaps it was true. Their bright, eager faces turned up in admiration as Niall held sway, his dark copper head standing a good six inches above the curls tossing around him. As Donal watched, Niall reached out for Maire's arm. He couldn't hear their words, but Maire blushed and glanced coyly around at the other lasses. Niall took her arm and led her up the hill path, looking down into her shy smile with confidence.

Donal turned his back on the handsome couple with a restless feeling of regret and joined his friends gathered by the well where they had hidden their jugs of poteen.

"Here, Donal, have a pint," called Morgan O'Shaughnessy. "'Tis a real fine batch, if I do say so meself." Donal took the offered jug and swallowed deeply. He coughed and spluttered, trying to get his breath as the strong drink burned its way to his stomach and exploded there. Morgan hit him on the back. "Hold it down, mate. Ye won't be sorry."

Donal gasped once more and wiped his mouth with the back of his hand. All thoughts of Maire and Niall were erased from his mind. "Now there's what I call a grand drink," he said, reaching for another.

Paddy the Smith leaned against the doorframe lighting his pipe. He caught Liam's eye and motioned toward the shed with a slight movement of his head. Liam nodded in agreement. Moving through the now-crowded yard, Liam paused to speak first with one friend, then another. His black hair gleamed like polished stone in the sunlight as he made his way slowly toward the shed. He stood a good two or three inches above the tallest of the others and carried his head high. The strong bones of his face were chiseled in sharp angles to his square chin, the strong slant of his nose hardly portraying the popular picture of the typical shanty Irish.

Liam shed his black coat, slinging it over his arm as he talked to Joe

Reagan. His white shirt jumped out among the clothes of somber colours worn by his friends. As Joe turned to speak to some new arrivals, Liam slipped from the group and into the cowshed.

Paddy was there before him, the biting odor of his pipe mingling with the familiar smells of the cow and the hay. He stood half in sunlight and half in shadow. At thirty, Paddy was no taller than five two, and his round head was nearly bald. The skin of his face and arms were the color and texture of leather from the heat of the forge where he spent an average of sixteen hours every day but Sunday.

Paddy's cold blue eyes took in everything that went on around him and immediately assessed it. As the recognized leader of the revolutionary movement in the south of County Cork, his opinions were listened to—and often adhered to—by other leaders throughout Ireland.

To the casual observer, Paddy might have appeared relaxed and at ease as he leaned against a supporting post of the shed, but Liam noted the tense muscles and the alertness of his eyes. He knew there was trouble.

"Ho, Paddy," he greeted him. "You have news?"

Paddy drew on the now-cold pipe before answering, his eyes never leaving Liam's. "They've spotted the blood on the path through Fernald's Woods. They know they wounded someone. Mick tells me they're startin' a search for someone with an injury."

Liam crossed himself automatically. "They'll start with the young men, and that means us." He chewed thoughtfully on his left thumb. "Da will be in the ground before noon tomorrow, and we've no sign of an injury. Surely they'll pass us by." He watched Paddy's face as he spoke. The eyes lost none of their concern. "Do you think they have reason to suspect us?"

"They suspect us all. They don't need reasons. They could round us up with no excuse at all. We could find ourselves dangling at the end of ropes, and no one would question or probably even know outside the county."

"But surely that won't happen!" Liam interjected, feeling the fear rush through his body.

"Probably won't come to that, but we shouldn't forget the possibility for a minute."

"What do you think they'll do, Paddy? If they don't find anyone with an injury, will they begin to think of Da and the 'accident' at the forge?" Liam's stomach lurched.

"Seems likely, Liam," Paddy said. "What we need is time. If they search throughout the whole area and Innishshannon too, we'll have the time we need."

"What can we do, Paddy? Even if Da is already in the ground, what's to prevent them from diggin' him up and examinin' his head?" Liam put his hand to his forehead and wiped away the cold sweat. His stomach churned, and he felt the burning taste of bile in his throat.

Paddy put his hand on Liam's arm. "I doubt that will happen, Liam. If enough time has gone by, they won't want to dig up a badly decomposed body. That's not to say they wouldn't, mind you, but the odds would be more in our favor as time passes."

Liam lurched toward the cow stall, his hand over his mouth. When the manure smell hit his nostrils, he knew he could hold it back no longer. He leaned over the steaming pile behind the cow and emptied his stomach. Paddy still lolled in apparent relaxation against the post. Only a faint twitch around his mouth showed his sympathy for the younger man.

Liam wiped his mouth on a handful of hay as Paddy's voice came over the flimsy divider. "I removed the bullet from your Da's head before we brought his body home," he said, almost as though he were talking to himself, "but there's a hole in his skull bone. They'll find it if they look."

Liam came around the divider, wiping his mouth on his sleeve. He studied Paddy's face. His expression gave no indication of his thoughts. "They'll know I was with Da," Liam said quietly. "And they'll know you were involved and anyone else who was at the forge when we staged the accident."

Paddy merely nodded.

"May God have mercy on us all," Liam said slowly. "What are we going to do, Paddy? How did we ever get involved in this?" He stopped, a shocked look on his face. "Oh god, I've involved Donal too!" His whole body shuddered.

"There, lad, nothin's as bad as it first seems. We just need some plans. We must consider every alternative and make a plan for each one. We'll find an answer."

Liam sank to the floor and sat with his knees drawn up and his long arms folded around them. He had never before felt so panicky. His mind jumped from one problem to another like a jackrabbit. Paddy sat beside him, sucking on his cold pipe.

"Poor Mam, she can't even bury Da in peace," Liam spoke his thought aloud. "If Donal and me are both caught, there will be only Niall, and he's good for nothin' and Declan, who is a lad still."

"Don't be crossing those bridges yet, Liam. Tis now you need to control your thinkin'. "But what would they do? There's Mam . . . and . . . Gran . . . and Kate . . . and . . ." Liam's voice took on a note of helplessness.

"There are those of us who would take care of them. Put it out of yer mind for now, Liam. You must!"

Liam swallowed hard. The acrid taste of vomit still clung to his mouth. "You're right, of course, Paddy. You always are. What do you think we should do next?"

Paddy pulled on his unlit pipe. "Fergus McGee has gone to Ballinspittle to alert the lads there. They'll keep the landlords distracted to stall for time and to turn the suspicion away from us—at least temporarily. In the meantime, Mick's keeping track of how the search is going. There may be enough of a pattern to tell us when they'll get here."

"What can I do?" Liam interrupted. He felt better now, but he needed to do something—take some action.

"Nothin', Liam. You're to stay at your Da's wake. Anything else would look suspicious. Just be ready to run if I give the word."

Liam gave him a questioning look and then nodded briefly. Paddy was right. He might have to leave at a moment's notice. It was necessary to accept that. He and Paddy too were in the most immediate danger. If they could get away, hide somewhere, maybe in Cork City, they'd be able to come up with some way to help the others. Liam sighed heavily. *Yes, Paddy is right. I have to be ready to go.*

Paddy clasped Liam's arm warmly and left the shed without another word. Liam leaned his head against his knees, trying to slow his tumbling thoughts. *How can I leave them,* he cried to himself. *How can I leave them?*

CHAPTER 7

IN THE LOFT above the shed Declan knew his slightest movement would send chaff from the dry hay sifting through the wide spaced floorboards. He sat very still, hardly daring to breathe.

He hadn't really intended to eavesdrop on Liam and Paddy's conversation, but there had been no opportunity to make his presence known. He was lying by the open window at the top of the loft watching as the people came out of the cottage and had to smile as Niall and Donal hustled Father McBride up the high road.

He looked on as Morgan O'Shaunessey, Tomas McNally, and Joe Duffy pulled their jugs of poteen from the well. It would be powerful stuff, Declan knew, remembering the terrible fight after they had indulged too much on St. Stephen's Day. They had better take it easy or there would be trouble before the day was over, and Donal, he knew, would have more than his share to drink.

Declan noticed that his three brothers watched the group of lasses as they came out into the sunlight. Kate somehow appeared all grownup from this distance, and Maire Foley looked as sweet as the Virgin Mary herself.

Declan felt a pang of envy as Niall swaggered over to the girls and smiled down into Maire's violet eyes. He couldn't hear what they were saying, but all the lasses obviously giggled as girls do when there's a lad about. He watched as Niall tucked her small hand under his arm and moved away.

Declan watched them disappear behind the cottage and knew they'd be walking up the path beside the old wall and would sit in the tall, dry grass looking out over the harbour of Kinsale. He felt a strange twinge of disappointment at Maire's willingness to go with Niall and a bit of annoyance at his brother.

It was shortly after that when Declan heard someone enter the shed below him. He listened, but there wasn't another sound. Turned back to the window, he heard Liam's voice greeting Paddy. He should have made himself known at that point but thinking they would only be staying a minute, he decided he didn't want to give up his view of the yard below.

The words carried up through the cracks only slightly muffled by the hay. Declan listened with a growing sense of horror as the conversation continued. At first he couldn't follow what they were saying. It seemed Liam and Paddy had been involved in some kind of trouble, and they knew someone was trying to find out who had done it. He could not understand the talk of blood and someone injured. Who had been injured? Paddy and Liam were both all right, but for some reason they thought someone suspected them.

When Declan heard Paddy mention they could be dangling from the end of a rope, the hair rose on the back of his neck. *My god, they were talking about a raid! Paddy and Liam had been on a Whiteboy raid! What if they had been caught?*

Declan held his breath. Liam would kill him if he knew he was listening to all of this! Liam mentioned Da. *What did Da have to do with it? Had Da been on the raid too?*

The memory of Liam waking Donal in the dark a few nights ago filled Declan's mind. Da was hurt, Liam had said, hurt bad.

In all the confusion of Da's being killed at the smithy's, Declan had forgotten about being awakened just before dawn. *Then Da hadn't been kicked by the horse at all! He had been shot during the raid!* The shock of this realization swept over him. *Da had been shot . . . by the English!*

Liam's voice grew louder. *Did he really say they might dig up Da's body from his grave? God in heaven, he wasn't even buried yet!* Declan crossed himself quickly. He heard Liam retching in the cow's stall directly below him. His own stomach soured and churned, and he swallowed noisily. He tried to concentrate on the voices below, but in his mind's eye he saw Paddy poking into his father's skull for the bullet. He muffled a wail of grief as he thought of his poor father.

Declan's mind calmed as Paddy's sensible voice explored the alternatives. Then Liam started talking of both he and Donal being caught and hung. He sounded as if the hanging had already taken place. *Mam and Gran and Kate would have only Niall and me to take care of them.* Declan closed his eyes and took a deep breath. *I could do it! I know I could. Even if Niall wasn't much help, I could do it.* Declan realized that Niall would never change. He would go singing through life. He would always be . . . well . . . he would always be Niall.

Declan wanted to get up and slide out of the haymow to assure Liam that he could count on him to take over, but Paddy was already talking of other solutions. Liam had to be ready if they got too close. He had to be ready to leave.

Paddy went out the backdoor. Declan couldn't hear Liam at first, then he heard the sobs tear from his brother's throat. He wanted to comfort him, but that would let Liam know he had overheard his private conversation with Paddy.

Declan leaned back on the hay and closed his eyes. Liam's sobbing tore at his own throat. *What was going to happen to their family now? What would happen if Liam were caught? How exactly was Donal involved? Liam had said Donal had to pretend to be Da . . . that must be it. Da had already been dead, but they didn't want anyone to know, so they staged a scene with Donal pretending to be Da. They had thrown poor Da's body out of the smithy's as though the horse had kicked him.*

Declan's head buzzed with his improbable conclusions. *What a bizarre idea! But it had worked! No one had even hinted things were not as they appeared. Everyone did, indeed, think that the horse had kicked him in the head. The sight of Da's head wrapped in the towel and stuffed into his cap reinforced the idea. Instead of trying to disguise the head injury, they had simply made it worse. What a fantastic idea!*

As Declan lay in the hay, a familiar, prickling sensation crept up his arms and across the back of his neck and shoulders, spreading up and over his skull. He saw Liam on a ship that was tossing and pitching in a violent storm. A man whose hair was almost pure white stood beside him, a desperately frightened look on his face. A huge wave hit the ship and the white-haired man was swept into the ocean. Liam screamed, but his words were drowned out by the force of the seawater that poured over him. Lightning flashed and thunder roared, followed by total darkness, as though all the candles in the world had gone out.

Declan forced his eyes open. He was relieved to see that there was still light. He tried to focus on the vision, but it was gone. He couldn't understand its meaning.

No sound came from below, and Declan decided Liam had left and he could escape from his hiding place when he heard someone open the backdoor. Declan checked his movement and held his breath. To his surprise, Maire Foley's voice floated up to him. He heard Liam jump to his feet.

"Oh Liam, you startled me! I didn't expect anyone to be here!"

"Don't go, Maire," Liam said, his voice trembling.

"I didn't mean to interrupt anyone. I'd better leave." She paused and then spoke again. "Are you all right, Liam?"

"Don't go, Maire," Liam said. "I'd like you to stay, but what did you want in here?"

Maire laughed with a nervous little gasp. The sound sent shivers down Declan's spine. "It's silly, I guess," she said, "but I was running away from Niall. He . . ."

"Niall!" Liam nearly shouted. "What has he done to you? I'll kill the bastard if he touched you!" The anger in his tone reached Declan through the floorboards.

"Hush, Liam, I'm all right. He . . . he tried to unbutton my bodice. I pulled away and ran . . . He laughed at me." She made little half sobs between the phrases.

"He's a no-good son of a . . ."

"There's nothing to get upset about, Liam." Maire's voice steadied. "I guess I asked for it, going up the hill with him and all . . ."

Liam cut her off. "He ought to know you're not like that. He thinks every woman will run off into the heather with him. You sure you're all right?" His voice was full of concern.

"I'm fine, Liam, just fine." Neither of them spoke for several minutes. Declan wondered if they had gone, then heard Liam say, "Let's go up to the loft, Maire. I don't feel like seeing anyone else just now." He hesitated. "Please, Maire? We could just talk, and I could hold you. No one will know."

Maire must have agreed for Declan heard them move toward the opening above the cow's crib. He scrambled for the corner and scrunched down into the hay. He was going to get caught! He was sure of it! And Liam would know he had been here all the time and heard every word.

Maire giggled as Liam pulled her up into the loft. Liam kind of giggled too. Declan had never heard his brother giggle before. Lads sure act funny around girls. He followed their progress across the loft by the sound of the shifting hay.

"We could sit in the window, and watch everyone in the yard," Maire suggested. Declan held his breath.

"Or we could sit in the corner where it's dark, and we wouldn't have to see anyone but each other," Liam countered. They both laughed, and Declan heard them scramble toward the far corner. *My god, I can't stay here*, Declan thought. *I've heard enough private conversations today.*

Under cover of the sounds of Liam's and Maire's own movements, Declan tunneled toward the opening. Chaff clung to his sweaty face, and the rustle of hay was loud in his ears. *They'll hear. I know they will*, he thought, *and I'll be dead.*

Declan made a little hole in the hay above his face to breathe and brought his head to the surface for air. Carefully he raised his head to see how far he was from the entrance. *Not far to go now.*

"Just hold me, Maire," he heard Liam say. "Just hold me close."

"Oh Liam, I love you so," Maire whispered, the sound just carrying to Declan's ears. He froze where he was, lying in the hay, not daring to move. *Liam and Maire!* He hadn't suspected. He remembered how Donal had followed Maire's tiny figure with hungry eyes, and Niall's had been openly full of lust when Declan had watched him looking at her during the rosary. *But Liam?*

God help them all, Declan thought . . . *and me too*, he added as the sound of Maire's squeal of pleasure came from the dark corner of the hayloft. *I'm as bad as the others. I want her too.*

Declan heard the sound of shifting hay from the corner and made a scramble for the opening, sliding down into the cow's crib.

"What was that?" Maire whispered. "Is there someone there?"

"Twas just some hay sliding down into the crib," Liam said. "We must have loosened it climbing up."

"I was afraid someone was coming," she whispered.

"There is only you and me here, my sweet Maire," Liam answered.

Declan crept to the door and stood outside. He didn't want to hear any more. His heart was breaking, but he knew it was right that she should belong to Liam.

CHAPTER 8

LIAM ADDED A block of dried peat to the dying fire. The night had turned cold and damp for August, and the fog rolled in from the sea, smothering the peninsula in its cocoon. The fire blazed quickly, lighting the room in a yellow glow. The candles at each corner of the table on which his father lay flickered in the otherwise-darkened room, casting moving shadows along Da's still form.

Only an occasional spark from the fire broke the silence of the room and the faint breathing of the sleepers. Both the sleeping loft and the shed overflowed with guests from the day's wake. Those from afar found space wherever they could to lie down for a few hours of rest before the morning's funeral march to the chapel and adjoining graveyard. The near neighbors had gone back to their homes except for those who had too much to drink. These, Liam knew, were to be found under every bush and behind the surrounding stone walls and even up in the fort. Liam had seen Donal and Morgan slumped in drunken sleep, their jugs still in their hands.

The singing and dancing had gone on long past midnight, and the drinking became heavy before it ended, for Tim's friends all enjoyed their jars of poteen whenever the occasion arose.

Liam drew himself up from his stool in front of the fire and walked to his father's side. In the whiteness of death, his face looked more like Liam's own. *It could be myself lying there*, Liam thought. With the sandy hair tucked up under the cap, the long nose and square chin took on more prominence, and Liam realized that he resembled his father more than he had known.

"But we weren't alike in temperament," Liam murmured softly. *I have never made a decision in my life. Always I listened to your ideas and principles and followed wherever you led. I never really stopped to consider whether I believed in what the Whiteboys were doing or not. If you said go and do this, that was what I did. And these past few hours, I have let Paddy do the thinking. My mind didn't seem to function without you there to guide me.*

Liam reached down and took his father's cold hand. *But I must make some decisions now, Da.* The thoughts in his head were so loud and clear he was conscious of the sound, although he had not spoken aloud. He brought the stiff white hand to his cheek, rubbing it against his face in small stroking motions. *Now I must make some decisions you might not like.*

You and I, Da, have put our whole family in danger with what we have been doing these past few years. I have involved them even further, especially Donal, who hadn't the faintest inkling of what was going on. I thought I was protecting you, but it was too late for that. You were already beyond protecting. I guess, after all, I was trying to protect myself.

Liam used the cold hand to wipe away the sudden tears of guilt that flowed without warning. "Forgive me, Da," he said softly, placing the hand back on Da's chest and rearranging the plain glass rosary beads.

Liam studied his father's face for a long moment before moving back to his stool by the fire. He rested his chin on his drawn-up knees and stared at the yellow flames. The acrid odor of the smoke from the burning peat moss filled his nostrils, and the memories of the years of love and contentment spent in this cottage filled his head. He knew that he had to leave, that he would never see his home again.

Leaving was the only way to draw attention away from Donal and the men who had taken part in the raid. If he ran away, the authorities would assume he was guilty, and if the others were questioned, Paddy would insist they were not to admit knowing who else had been involved. Liam was known to be a loner. Paddy would recognize the need to sacrifice one man to prevent suspicion of the others.

Liam realized what he had to do could cause some problems for his family. They would be watched day and night to see if they contacted anyone else or acted in any way suspicious. But allowing the truth to be discovered would endanger the very lives of Donal and Paddy and the others. This way was better.

Liam wasn't sure what he could do or where he would go. He had no money and no contacts. Perhaps Paddy could help. He had to convince him he was doing the right thing. *There was no other way. He had to go.*

Curling up on the floor beside the fire, Liam remembered snatches of conversations around this same hearth—the soft murmurings of Mam and Gran as they sat here spinning wool or stirring a pot of porridge; the excited young sounds of Kate and Declan discussing some pretended adventure in the fort; Niall and Donal's friendly and sometimes not-so-friendly bickering over the chores; and Da and his wonderful stories of the days long past when Ireland still belonged to the Irish.

Another voice clung to Liam's mind, murmuring soft sounds of love. He smiled as he hung on the verge of sleep, remembering the beauty of the words and the smooth sweetness of Maire's yielding body. *Maire, Maire, oh my love, how can I leave you now?* The words echoed as he fell into a deep sleep.

"Liam, wake up! I need to talk to you," Paddy said quietly, shaking Liam's shoulder.

Not sure where he was, Liam raised himself from the floor. The new dawn showed faintly through the window. He stared at Paddy and at the flickering candles behind him. The events of the past two days rushed back. He scrambled to his feet.

"Let's go outside where we can't be heard," whispered Paddy, taking Liam's arm and leading him to the door.

Liam was wide awake and alert now. The decisions made during the night were firmly entrenched in his mind. "Come on, Paddy, we'll walk down to the beach. There'll be no one there. I need to talk to you too."

The dew was heavy as they followed the grassy path in the half light of the breaking day. The fog lifted from the water as the two rounded the corner to the open beach on the far side of the peninsula. Paddy leaned against a huge boulder at the edge of the strand. He lit his pipe and drew several times before speaking. Liam perched on the wet sand, resting on his heels.

Paddy's voice was barely audible when he spoke. "They've organized a house-to-house search in every village," he began. "In Ballinspittle, about midnight, they found a sixteen-year-old lad with his arm in a sling. They beat him senseless before they tore off his splint, only to find there was no bullet hole. He had broken his arm in a fall the day before." Paddy's quiet voice held no expression; he was simply reporting facts. After a quick look of horror, Liam stared out at the gently lapping surf.

Paddy paused and drew on his pipe once more. "They will be here on Ringrone before the morning is over."

"Paddy," Liam spoke quietly and calmly. "I have decided that I have to go—before they get here." He rose from the sand and stood in front of his friend. "I'll run for it. Let them place all the blame on me. The heat will be less on everyone else—at least for a while." Liam's determination was strong. "We'll make it obvious that I was involved. I could show up at the funeral today with a conspicuous limp and make sure several people notice. I'll disappear just as soon as we get Da in the ground."

Paddy's expression didn't change, but he nodded his head.

"I can be a long way from here before they catch up with me," Liam added.

"You know they could get you in the end, don't you, Liam?" Paddy asked, searching Liam's face for some kind of weakness.

"It'll take them awhile first," Liam replied, "and that will give the rest of you a chance to make sure your own tracks are covered."

Paddy knocked his pipe against the boulder and looked across the river to the low hills on the other side. He glanced at Liam and then again at the farther bank. "If we could get you over to the other side," he said, pointing his pipe at the heavy scrub brush across the river, "it would give you a head start."

Liam paced the beach, his hands in his pockets, his shoulders hunched over. He stopped in front of Paddy. "There's an old raft hidden in the rocks just beyond the beach that we used to play with as lads. It should hold me up to get close enough to shore, and I could swim the rest of the way."

Paddy nodded. "Come on, we'll take a look."

The raft had not been used for some time and was coming apart in several places. Liam remembered lacing the logs together with stripped ivy vines for Declan and his friends a couple of summers ago. The vines had rotted in several places and looked as though a light touch might cause them to disintegrate.

Paddy made a careful study, lighting his pipe again. At last he spoke, "Morgan and I will put new vines on it while you're at the gravesite. You should get to the other side all right." He started up the path. His voice came back over his shoulder as Liam followed him. "Make for Oyster Cove first and then cut through the hills to Belgooley. Go to Seamus O'Reilly's place. He takes his milk to Cork City on Fridays by cart." Paddy gestured with his pipe as he spoke, emphasizing each new idea. "Tell him I said to take you to the warehouse in Cobh. He'll know the place I mean. I'll get word to someone there to keep you hidden til they can get you out of the country."

Liam nodded at Paddy's back. *Out of the country*, he thought. *God in heaven, I'll never get back home!*

As they came in sight of the cottage, Paddy turned to face Liam. "Use the tunnel from Ringrone Castle to the fort when you leave the chapel. You'll find a bundle of food and clothes at the end of the tunnel. The raft will be ready for you." He grasped Liam's hand. "I'm proud of you, Liam. I knew you'd decide the right thing to do."

Liam shook his friend's hand. "There is no other choice," he said quietly. Paddy nodded, gave Liam's hand another shake, and disappeared down the path to the ferry.

The sun was already high as the procession straggled behind the donkey-drawn wagon carrying Timothy O'Dwyer to his final resting place. The long line of mourners slowly climbed the high road, passing between tall hedges of ripening blackberry bushes straggling over the narrow path. The scent of the lush sweetness hung in the air of the late summer warmth.

Liam walked between Mam and Gran, supporting each by an arm under a trembling elbow. Donal held Mam steady on the other side, and Gran leaned heavily on Niall at Liam's left. The five of them set the pace for the following mourners. Behind them walked Kate and Declan, with Da's friends and neighbors stretched out beyond.

Liam missed a step now and then as he walked with an obvious limp of his left leg. He deliberately ignored Donal's questioning glance when the rhythm of their march was broken.

They passed out of the shade of the hedges into the sun as they came to the ruins of Ringrone Castle perched at the crest of the hill. The chapel hugged the ground at its base, hardly visible beneath a cover of ivy.

Father McBride stood in the center of the road in front of the chapel. He held his long beads high and made the sign of the cross. The procession halted. The four sons of Timothy O'Dwyer left their mother's side and moved forward to remove their father's wooden casket from the wagon. Liam and Niall took the front corners, and the box tipped precariously as the shorter Donal and Declan raised the back to their fullest height.

Knowing that every eye was upon them, Liam deliberately limped as he and Niall led the procession into the chapel. He pretended not to see Niall's look of annoyance and limped again. They proceeded into the chapel and down the aisle. The procession filed behind them into the pews on either side as the four brothers placed the coffin on the platform which had been erected for the occasion. They took their seats beside Mam and Gran and Kate as Father McBride's voice filled the small room. "In the Name of the Father, the Son, and the Holy Ghost . . ."

Liam shut out the sound of the mass. He had already said goodbye to his father. The responses came with automatic regularity, but his mind was busily trying to figure out how he could get away without being seen.

The mass ended, and Niall poked Liam in the ribs to nudge him to his feet. The four moved into the aisle and picked up their father's coffin for the last time. They walked slowly from the chapel and onto the adjoining graveyard. Their nostrils filled with the spicy scent of the incense wafting back from the censer that swayed from Father McBride's upraised hands.

As they placed the coffin on the slim logs laid across the open grave, Liam leaned toward Donal and whispered, "Meet me at the tunnel when I give the signal." Donal's eyes met his in surprise, but he nodded in agreement.

Liam studied, in turn, each of the faces of his family as they stood around the open grave. The heavily embedded lines around Gran's mouth and eyes were quivering, but they held acceptance. Mam raised her eyes to Liam's as he examined her face. They shared a brief instant of anguish and love before her glance turned back to her husband's coffin. Her head bowed in grief, but her shoulders were straight and firm. *She'll hold up,* Liam thought. *She's strong, stronger than any of us.*

Liam's eyes moved on around the circle. Tears flowed down Kate's unnaturally white cheeks. Even in sadness her beauty showed through. *She really is lovely*, Liam thought. *I wish I could be around to see her grow up. I wonder if I'll remember her as she is today?*

Declan stood close to Kate, his hand holding hers tightly, his eyes fixed to the wooden casket. *He'll grow up quickly*, Liam thought. *I probably wouldn't recognize him if I could meet him in a few years.* He studied the small thin face and found strength there in spite of the sensitive eyes and mouth. *He'll make it*, Liam thought. *Declan has faith. He'll make it.*

Liam's eyes moved on to Niall, who stood with his hands clasped behind his back, his handsome face turned up to the sky. There was no way to read his thoughts, but Liam knew that there was no need to worry about him. Niall would always look after himself.

Father McBride swung the censer in wide arcs over the casket as the slim logs were pulled aside, and the grayed box was lowered by ropes made of vines into the open grave. His intonations rose with the slight breeze that swept the hilltop.

Gran and Mam bent to the ground, scooped up a handful of red earth, and stepped to the side of the gaping hole. First Gran, then Mam threw the small clumps of soil onto the casket below. They moved back and supporting each other, slowly turned away, making room for Timothy O'Dwyer's sons and his only daughter to signify that their father's body was being returned to the earth from whence it came.

Liam stepped forward and grasped a handful of Irish soil. It was damp and cold to his warm hand, but it burned a brand of both love and hate into his palm. As he released it over his father's grave, he knew that he would never again hold Irish soil in his hand. In that moment, he made his goodbye to his home, his family, and his country.

Liam watched Donal cross himself before releasing the earth. As he moved away from the grave, Liam grasped his hand and gave a brief nod of his head in the direction of the tunnel. Donal's raised eyes indicated acknowledgment.

The line of mourners formed behind the family members to follow the ritual of releasing their friend from the living. Their attention was all on their purpose as Liam and Donal moved away and disappeared into the brush beyond the chapel.

The tunnel had been long in disuse. Few had known of its existence, and most of those had forgotten it. Built centuries ago, the passageway had been used by messengers between Ringrone Castle and King James's Fort on the point of the peninsula. The O'Dwyer boys had discovered the entranceway in their play and had explored the entire length, removing piles of rocks and debris.

Liam stepped behind the mass of brambles that hid the entrance, pulling Donal behind him. They looked at each other in silence for a full minute, listening for any sound of pursuit. There was only the mournful murmuring of prayers. Liam dragged Donal into the cool shadows of the tunnel. He caught only a glimpse of Donal's questioning eyes before they were enveloped in darkness.

"Follow me, Donal. I'll catch you up on everything when we get to the other end." Liam's voice echoed from the damp rock walls that lined the black path. The dampness crowded around them, and the musty smell was overpowering. They ran crouched over, their arms almost touching the ground, the sound of their rapid breathing following them in the close air. Everyone from the funeral would be returning soon, and they knew they had to be out of sight of the high road before the mourners reached the turn for the beach.

The two collapsed onto the ground as they came to the end, blinded by the sudden sunlight. As their breathing slowed, they faced each other. They were still protected from view by the overgrowth that shielded the tunnel's exit inside the inner wall of the fort. Donal spoke first. "What are we doing here, Liam? What has happened?"

"I have to leave, Donal. The searchers will be here in a few hours. If I run, they will focus on me, and the others will have a chance to go free."

"But Liam, they'll catch you . . ."

"Maybe—maybe not. I have to take that chance. Paddy has a contact in Cork City who will help me get out of the country. I just have to keep out of the way until then."

Donal reached out and grasped his brother's shoulder. "What do you want me to do, Liam? I'll do whatever you think is best."

"I knew I could count on you, Donal. I just want you to know what's going on. They'll likely ask questions. You'll need to pretend that you know nothing. Tell them you noticed that I had been limping for a couple of days, but I insisted nothing was wrong. That'll convince them that I was the one who was shot instead of Da."

"You're sure you know what you are doing, Liam?"

"I can't do anything else, Donal. If they find out it was Da that was shot, you and me and Paddy and all the rest are going to get caught. I've got to go."

"What do I tell them, Liam?"

"Just say that I never was close to anyone, that I never talked about my friends, or where I went. You can even say you knew that I went out late at night but that you thought I was courting a girl or something like that."

Donal nodded without speaking.

"Paddy will tell you what to do. He'll make sure everyone has the same story to tell. We've agreed it's the best thing to do. He has a contact who is helping me get away." Liam rose from the grass, pulled Donal to his feet, and picked up the bundle Paddy had left for him. "Come on, Donal. Help me get that old raft launched. I'm going to paddle across the river. It'll give me a head start."

They ran across the field, along the hedgerow, and down to the shore as they had done a thousand times when they were boys.

Together they pulled the raft across the rocky beach, grasping the newly wrapped vines that held the logs together. At the water's edge, Liam turned and pulled Donal into a giant hug. "Donal," he said, "look after Mam and the others. I hate to leave you with all this, but there's no other way."

Donal hugged his brother. "I will, Liam. I will. Don't worry yourself none about me."

"Look after Kate. She'll be attracting all the lads now."

Donal nodded, burying his face in Liam's shoulder.

Liam moved away and picked up the vine. "And Donal," he said slowly, "take care of Maire Foley for me." He met Donal's surprised eyes. "Promise me," he said and grasped his brother's hand once more.

"Yes yes, I promise," Donal said.

Liam pushed the raft into the water and climbed aboard.

CHAPTER 9

THE RAFT TIPPED precariously, threatening to upset in the water. Liam shifted his weight to keep afloat. He felt the current take him away from the shore as his craft leveled. The paddle was a homemade affair, cut from a waterlogged board and roughly shaped. He plunged it into the water, and the raft moved out into the river. For the first time, he allowed himself a smile. By god, he'd make it!

A cloud covered the sun, and almost immediately Liam could feel a familiar dampness in the air. The fog would be rolling in soon and would conceal him from searching eyes. *Thank God for wee favors*, he thought. The makeshift boat rode smoothly, and he risked looking over his shoulder. Donal stood on the shore watching his progress. Liam saluted with his paddle, and Donal raised both arms in the air and waved them above his head. The raft tipped sharply, and Liam turned back to the job of keeping his craft afloat.

As he watched, the fog filled the mouth of the river and made its way toward him. He quickened his pace and paddled deeper. The raft responded sluggishly but made steady progress out into the deep water. He knew he would be in full view of Summer Cove for the next fifty feet or more and was in the most danger of being spotted. Studying the shoreline back toward Kinsale, he could see no movement. King William's Fort looked deserted. With any luck at all he'd get to the opposite shore without being seen.

About fifty feet from the mouth of the river, Liam could see a spot on the shore where the branches hung low over the water. If he landed there, he would be able to pull the raft of rotted logs over them and conceal it in the brush.

The water was cold and more than three feet deep, but he was already soaked to the hips from kneeling on the raft. Liam leaped in and felt the sandy bottom beneath his feet. Grabbing the vines, he hauled the raft behind him and waded the last few feet to shore.

Liam scrambled through the prickly scrub, dragging the raft over their tops. A fallen tree had braced itself against a large rock and was nearly covered with new undergrowth. He parted the hedge and saw there was just room enough to push the raft into the space beneath the tree, making a perfect hiding place. He pushed and shoved until it was tightly wedged in place.

Picking up a large stone, he smoothed the earth where his footsteps had made indentations in the damp soil and shuffled the branches near the shore to camouflage any signs of his landing. His hands bled from the scratches of the thorns, but they weren't bad enough to drip any blood on the ground, should anybody look, he assured himself.

The fog gathered in earnest. Liam felt the dampness in his nostrils. Even though it was not yet raining, the heavy mist penetrated to his skin. Pulling his cap down firmly onto his head, he shifted his bundle onto his shoulder. It was necessary to stay near the shoreline to make his way to Oyster Cove. From there, he could cut over the hills toward Belgooley and Seamus' farm. He'd hide in the fields tonight and talk to Seamus when he went out to do the morning milking. With any luck at all, he'd be there by dark.

The wind had picked up all afternoon and approached gale force by the time Liam sighted Seamus' place. The rain pelted against his face and managed to run in rivulets down his neck and beneath his shirt. The bundle across his shoulders was soaked through as well, and he knew he would be eating soggy bread for supper.

Liam hunched himself beneath some scrubby gorse bushes that grew out over the stone wall surrounding Seamus' pastureland. It provided a semblance of shelter, but Liam couldn't stop his shaking. The combination of nervousness and exhaustion had taken its toll. *Maybe if I eat something I'd feel better*, he thought. He had been avoiding eating all day. He hadn't wanted to stop, for one thing, and didn't want to break into his meager supply of food, not quite sure what he was going to do when it was gone.

The serious predicament Liam found himself in ran through his mind all afternoon as he hid in a hedgerow at Oyster Cove. He nearly walked right into three fishermen who were huddled together at a spot where they could watch their boats as the storm threatened to tear them from their moorings. Liam ducked behind a hedge, listening to them talk in low tones, as they alternated between worry about their boats and stories of their sexual pursuits. Liam didn't dare move for fear of being seen. They would surely remember a stranger in these remote parts and might talk to the wrong people.

He stayed hidden for more than two hours, wet and cramped, and aching with misery. Would the rest of his life be like this, running and hiding from every stranger, he wondered. The prospect was frightening. His empty stomach knotted and churned. The three loaves of soda bread and the cheese in his bundle were tempting. *I'd better not,* he decided. *I may need it later.* The fishermen laughed together, and Liam wondered if he would ever feel free enough to share confidences with another person.

The men finally left to check their boats, and Liam scrambled to his feet and cut through the hills away from the shore. The fog had become so thick it was difficult to tell which direction was which, but he knew the hills would lead him west to Belgooley. He trudged through the wet fields feeling alone and abandoned.

A single candle made a faint glow in Seamus' cottage. Liam had lost all sense of direction in the early darkness. He had crawled beneath the hedge, not quite sure of where he was. He must have dozed off for a while; his feet had gone to sleep, and his left knee was stiff. He stood up and stretched. There was no one about, and even if there should be, they wouldn't be able to see more than a few feet in this foggy weather.

The small light seemed to beckon him. Beyond, he knew, was a warm, dry room and a loving family. *Seamus is a lucky man, and so was I just two days ago. Is it really possible I have lost everything in such a short time? I have nothing but the clothes on my back, an extra pair of stockings, a shirt in my bag, and food for maybe three days if I am careful. I have no money and no prospects of work.*

Liam shook off the discouraging thoughts. *I do have Paddy's influence and friends,* he told himself, *if nothing else, I have that. Seamus will get me to Cork City, and Paddy's connections will take over from there. It'll work out.* He refused to think of the possibility of being caught. Images hovered on the edge of his mind, but his consciousness would not accept them as reality.

The shape of the cowshed at the edge of the field came into view, and the thought of the warmth of the animals drew him forward. He couldn't go to Seamus' door after dark. If he knew Seamus, he would be greeted with a loaded shotgun pointed at his chest. No, he couldn't ask for shelter this late at night, but he could creep into the shed to get out of the rain.

Liam crossed the field and slipped into the shed, dropping onto a pile of hay near the cows. The steaming warmth enveloped him as he buried himself. The smell of the cows and the hay were comfortingly familiar. He was too tired to eat. Allowing himself to relax, he fell asleep.

A sharp pain in his chest brought Liam instantly awake. He tried to get up, but the pain increased. A tall, shadowy form stood over him with a pitchfork.

"One move and you're dead, me lad," Seamus said.

"Seamus—Seamus—it's me, Liam O'Dwyer."

"So it tis," Seamus said, not moving the pitchfork. "And what be you doin' in me cowshed?"

Liam gulped. He didn't know Seamus too well. He had met him only a couple of times at Whiteboy meetings. "Paddy the Smith said you'd help me get to Cobh," Liam began with hesitation.

"Did he now?" Seamus said slowly. "And why would I be doing that? What kind of trouble you in, boy?" Seamus's eyes bore into his. Liam knew he was being sized up. The pitchfork didn't move.

"Seamus, if you'd be kind enough to move that pitchfork away from my chest, I'll tell you. I swear I didn't kill anyone, and no one saw me come here."

Seamus studied Liam for a full minute more. The pitchfork moved away and came to rest on the ground beside Seamus's feet. "You hungry?" he asked.

"I am, Seamus, thank you," Liam replied, the relief leaving him limp.

"I won't ask you into me house, Liam, for the safety of me family. But I will bring ye some bread and tea. Looks like ye could use some warmin' up."

"I'd be thanking ye for that, Seamus. I don't want to cause no trouble." Seamus placed the pitchfork by the door and went out without looking back. Liam knew he had been accepted. He dropped his face into his hands and let the air escape from his lungs.

A few minutes later, Seamus was back. He set a cracked teapot, two tin mugs, and a half loaf of bread on the chopping block. "Here," he said, tossing a pair of cotton pants to Liam. "My Mary says to put these on, and I'm to bring yer wet clothes inside to dry. She's a good one, my Mary."

"You're a lucky man, Seamus O'Reilly."

"More than most, I reckon," Seamus said solemnly. He poured tea into the mugs while Liam peeled off his damp clothing. Liam stepped into the too-big brown cotton trews. He held out his wet things in one hand while he clutched the top of the britches with the other to keep them from falling to his feet.

Seamus was a big man, dwarfing Liam's own six-foot height. He handed a mug to Liam. "Have some of Mary's bread too, Liam. It'll fill ye up. I'll be right back to join ye, and we'll talk."

The hot tea burned its way down to Liam's empty stomach, leaving a quick cramp and then warmth. He took another gulp and tore off a big chunk of bread. Never had anything tasted so good. He had taken bread for granted for twenty years and never really thought of its goodness. How good these O'Reillys were! Surely with people like them in the world he would survive in spite of all odds. He chewed contentedly, his faith restored.

Seamus returned to the shed, picked up a milk bucket with one hand and a block of wood with the other. Placing the block next to the cow, he shoved the pail beneath its full udder. "I'll just get me chores done while we talk," he said, settling on the block and reaching his big hands for the pink teats. The first stream of milk hit the pail with a zinging sound. "Now then, Liam O'Dwyer, what is it that Paddy says I'll do?" he asked.

Liam swallowed a mouthful of tea. He watched Seamus's hands

pulling in perfect timing. "I have to get to Cobh today. Paddy says you could get me to the warehouse, that you'd know what he meant."

The ping of the milk hitting the pail stopped. "Are they after you then, lad?"

"Not yet, far's I know," Liam replied. "Probably will be soon though." He cupped his hands around the warm mug and watched Seamus's face, trying to read his reaction.

The steady zinging resumed. "Don't tell me no more. I don't want to know," he said thoughtfully. "A body can know too much, times like this."

"Aye, that's true enough, Seamus. I guess it don't matter much anyhow. It's over and done with. Now I just need to get to Cobh."

Seamus nodded. "Storm's letting up. I'll be taking the milk wagon to the city in about an hour. Ye can hide amongst the milk barrels. Won't be like ridin' in style, but it should get ye there."

"I ain't used to ridin' in style, and I do be thankin' you, Seamus," Liam replied.

"You know how to do milkin'?" Seamus asked.

"I do."

"Then get yourself a block to sit on, grab a bucket there by the door and lend me a hand." He paused. "Or rather two hands," he said, a wide grin spreading over his homely face.

Seamus had never said a truer thing than when he said the ride to Cork would not be a comfortable one, Liam thought as he lay curled around and between the wooden barrels in the milk cart. His back was braced against the plank which supported Seamus's seat, and his long legs were wedged between carefully placed containers, which slopped milk at every jolt of the wagon.

Seamus had covered Liam with burlap sacks that smelled of musty potatoes, leaving only a small opening at Liam's face for him to breathe. As the morning wore on, Seamus discarded his coat and casually slung it over the sacks, just as he would have done on any other trip. One sleeve hung down over Liam's face, cutting off his light and limiting his air. The scratchy material rubbed against his nose, alternately tickling and irritating. He was afraid he would sneeze.

The way was long and rough. Liam thought the trip would never end. He listened with wry amusement and then annoyance at Seamus' off-tune humming, which was just audible under the potato sacks. He heard Seamus hail approaching carts, but no one stopped them, in spite of Liam's pounding heart. Adjusting his body to the jolts and swaying of the cart, he half-dozed.

CHAPTER 10

LIAM AWOKE WITH a start when the jolting of the wagon stopped. He had no idea where they were. It was nearly dark under the covers, and he felt—rather than saw—they had pulled into some kind of shelter. The pressure of the barrels on his legs increased as Seamus shifted his weight to climb down from his seat.

Seamus spoke to the donkey in a soothing voice, and Liam sensed he was tying the reins. "Ye just rest here a wee bit, my faithful friend," Seamus said to the animal. "I'll be bringing ye a cool drink, and we'll be on our way." Liam heard him slap the donkey's rump and felt the slight twitch of the cart as the animal responded.

Dust showered down through the sacks as Seamus picked up his coat from the wagon, and Liam sneezed. "Hush, lad." Seamus responded in the same tone he had used for the donkey. "It won't be long now that we'll have ye out of there."

Thank the good Lord for that, Liam thought as he heard Seamus move away. His back ached, and he felt as though he were paralyzed from the waist down. He wondered if he would be able to stand when the time came.

Liam knew they had pulled out of the sunshine for the light had diminished, and while he still sweated from the heat of the sun-baked sacks covering him, he could feel the slight relief of the shade.

The enormity of his plight swept over him. He was completely in the hands of others. He felt as though he had been dropped into a limbo of nothingness, cut off from his past with absolutely no vision of the future. He didn't have the slightest idea of where he was or where he was being taken. Except for Seamus, no person on earth knew his whereabouts. He dreaded the moment when Seamus would leave. Seamus represented his only link with the past, and Liam knew how fragile that link was.

Hearing someone approaching the wagon, he held his breath as he realized there were two sets of footfalls. Fear leaped into his chest, and the force was as though someone had kicked him. His breath rushed out as he heard Seamus' voice and recognized the calm tone before the words registered in his mind. It was all right. Seamus was not alarmed.

"He's right here," Seamus said, "and none the worse for the ride, I trust." Liam felt his coverings snatched away, and light flooded over him. He was thankful they were not out in the bright sunlight, as it was, he could see only the shadows of the two men who stood by the cart.

The white collar of the stranger's dark clothes jumped out at him. *My god, he's a priest*, Liam thought. His body tensed. All his experience with priests rushed into his mind . . . the heavy hand that Father McBride held over the entire parish . . . the endless prohibitions issued each Sunday from the pulpit . . . the baring of his innermost thoughts at confession . . . the feeling of submission to the Church that seemed to overshadow everybody's actions . . . and above all, his personal dislike of Father McBride.

Liam struggled to keep his thoughts from showing and knew he had failed when Seamus spoke. "Tis all right, Liam, me lad," Seamus said, reaching out to help Liam move. "The good Father is one we can trust."

"I'm not sure I can get up," Liam said. "My legs don't want to work."

"Let's shift a couple of these things, Seamus," the priest spoke up, lifting one of the heavy barrels by himself. "That'll give us more room to get at him. The poor lad has stiffened from the long ride."

Seamus grabbed another barrel, and Liam tentatively stretched his legs. Sharp pains shot through them and up his spine. "Here, lad, don't try to move," the priest said. "We'll lift you out."

Large, well-muscled arms extended from the black sleeves and scooped Liam from the wagon as though he weighed no more than a wee bairn. The shock of being picked up bodily was as great to Liam as was the pain that coursed through his cramped limbs.

Needles prickled his feet as he was set on the ground. His legs refused to support him, and he felt himself falling. The two men grabbed his arms, holding him upright. "Let's try to get him to the door. The walking will help get the blood to flowing again." The priest half pushed and half-supported Liam with his tremendous strength, and Seamus did the same on the other side while Liam made the proper motions for walking. He could not feel his feet touch the ground. He felt only the pain traveling with the newly awakened circulation through his body.

As the two half-carried him to the door and into a small bare room, Liam smiled, remembering how Donal and Niall had escorted Father McBride from their home the day of his father's wake. *Was it only two days ago?*

Seamus talked as he and the priest walked Liam back and forth across the floor. Liam tried to concentrate on the words while he placed one foot after the other on the unevenly spaced slates. It was the slate floor that made him realize they had brought him into a church. Every building he knew had hard-packed earthen floors except for the churches. He was not surprised when they turned him around, and he saw the fieldstone wall and the hanging crucifix. They were in a tiny vestibule which served as the priest's office.

"I'll be leavin' ye with the good Father here," Seamus said. "You can trust him altogether. He's done this before and will see that ye get to Cobh."

"That I will. That I will," the priest responded. "With God's help, you'll get there safely."

"Ye can't ask for more help than that, Liam," Seamus said.

They led him to an old wooden bench by the one window and helped him to sit down. The feeling was returning to his body, and Liam knew that, at last, he was getting back to normal. He looked up at Seamus. In one day's time, this man had become as close to him as his own brothers. *What a good man Seamus is. I wish I had the chance to know him better.*

"I have to be goin' now, Liam. I'm already behind my usual schedule, and we wouldn't want to be raising questions in the minds of others, now would we?" He extended his hand.

Liam pressed it warmly. "Thank you for helping me, Seamus. You'll be forever in my prayers." He studied the round homely face and found it beautiful. "God bless you and yours, Seamus."

"And you too, Liam." Seamus dropped Liam's hand, nodded briefly to the priest and left.

Both Liam and the priest watched the closed door as they listened to the sounds of Seamus replacing the barrels in the cart and giving water to the donkey. The priest broke the silence. "A good man, Seamus," he said. Crossing the room, he sat in the chair behind the desk that was the only other piece of furniture in the room. "His Mary is my sister's lass."

Liam studied the priest. He knew the words were meant to reassure him that he could trust this unknown man of God. The rich, resonant tone of his voice invited confidence as well. Liam felt an urge to blurt out all that had happened in the past few days, but even as the urge struck him, he resisted. He recalled Seamus' words, "Tis better if I don't know what happened and who was involved. It's safer that way." Liam knew he could not place this man, whoever he was, in more danger.

The priest sat behind his desk with his large bony hands folded in front of him. His deep-set brown eyes held a compassion and a sadness that Liam instinctively felt went much further than the present situation. Heavy, dark brows nearly met the bridge of his perfectly shaped nose, which seemed somehow too delicate for the high cheeks and ruddy, lined face. Liam wondered how different the lives of his own parish would have been if this man had been their priest.

Liam cleared his throat. "I'm sorry to have involved you in this, Father."

The priest raised his hand to silence him. "Say no more, lad. I choose to serve God in my own way. I see my mission as one that directs me to relieve suffering wherever I find it. I do what I can, in whatever way I can." He shoved back the wooden chair and coughed. "Enough of preaching," he said. "I'll be bringing you a bit of bread and tea and then I'll have to leave you alone for a wee time. You can rest here while I go out to make arrangements for getting you to Cobh."

Liam munched on the half loaf after the priest had gone. Steam escaped from the cracked pot on the desk, and the strong, tangy odor of tea filled the room. He poured some into the waiting tin cup. The hot liquid burned its way down, and he felt the warmth spread through him. With it a sense of comfort and reassurance flowed, renewing his spirits.

Two good men had been willing to risk their lives to help him. For the first time in his life, he felt that perhaps there was at least as much good as evil in the world.

Liam paced the small room, careful not to let his shadow fall across the one high window. He had heard the key turn in the lock when the priest left and had been cautioned to be silent if anyone approached. It was not unusual, the priest said, for parishioners to come looking for their pastor in the middle of the day. Finding the door locked, they would go on their way.

Had it not been for the priest's parting words, Liam would have felt quite content to wait in the peaceful confinement of this room. Those words echoed in his mind as he alternated between pacing the slate floor and sitting stiffly on the narrow wooden bench.

"You might want to make your confession when I get back, Liam," the priest had said. "Think about it while I'm gone." Liam leaned his head against the ladder-backed bench. *What a relief it would be to tell someone of the guilt I'm feeling*, he thought. *I should have somehow been able to save Da—should have put a stop to the dangerous revolutionary activities a long time ago. I must have known it was only a matter of time before someone was hurt or caught.*

Instead of trying to keep the family from being involved, I've embroiled them even deeper, and I've run away, leaving them to face the authorities alone. He buried his face in his hands, groaning aloud. *How could I have been so stupid?*

Liam's spirits fell lower and lower. *Perhaps it would be better if I were caught*, he thought, *then at least they would leave my family alone. As it was, they would be watching them every minute for some sign they knew more than they were telling.*

The memory of Tomas Haggerty hanging from the tree in the green flooded his mind. The possibility of betraying the others haunted him. He couldn't let himself be caught. He wasn't strong enough to stand up under the torture of questioning.

Liam knew he was rationalizing his actions in spite of the truth of his reasoning. He wanted to live. He had to get away. He could leave no trace of his flight, not even a confession that might be wrung from the unwilling mind of a priest who appeared to be as strong and steadfast as the cliffs of Old Head. Liam instinctively knew Seamus had been right. The less anyone knew about what had happened, the better for them all.

It was nearly dusk before Liam heard the key turn in the iron lock. The faint glow in the sky silhouetted the priest's tonsured head as he opened the door. He smelled faintly of fish, and the bottom of his cassock was stained with mud.

"We'll have time for a wee bite and some tea before it's completely dark, lad," the priest said in a voice tinged with fatigue. "Then we'll be on our way."

"You've done enough, Father," Liam interrupted. "Just tell me where to go and who I'm to meet, and you needn't be involved anymore."

"That's a kind thought, lad, but without me, you'd not get by. I'm the password, so to speak."

Liam felt a sudden exhaustion sweep over him. "I've involved so many people. I'll never forgive myself if I've caused them troubles they never deserved." He turned to the darkening window, his hands deep in his pockets.

"Forgiving one's self is the most difficult part of life," the priest said softly. "God forgives us long before we can come to terms with ourselves. He watches us struggle toward perfection, knowing the end result, and is content with that. We, without that knowledge, see only our own imperfection and the suffering that goes with the struggle to overcome."

"We, Father? Surely, you, as a priest of the Church, could not be classified with the rest of us."

"I wish it were true, lad, but we priests may be even more imperfect than our fellow men. Perhaps that's why we decide to devote our lives to the struggle."

A silence settled on the room with the darkness. The praties and tea had been consumed, and the remains stacked on the desk. Liam finally spoke. "I've decided against making my confession, Father," he said quietly.

"You know that the confessional would seal my lips," the priest answered. It was a statement, not a question.

"I know that, Father, but the knowledge would be dangerous, none-theless, both for you and for me. I cannot expose either of us to the possibility that the methods of British questioning could uncover what neither of us would want known."

The priest nodded. "Since I've just admitted to my own imperfection, I accept your decision." He walked over to his desk and opened a drawer. "However, I shall give you absolution anyway." He took a small stole from the drawer and draped it around his neck. He moved toward Liam, who dropped to his knees. "Do you swear to me, lad, that you did not commit murder nor intentionally do bodily harm to another person?"

"I did not," Liam said steadily.

"Then I absolve you from your sins, both past and present, knowing God has already forgiven you." He made the sign of the cross over Liam's head. "May God bless you and keep you," he said. He turned abruptly and put the stole back in the desk. Liam remained kneeling, reciting the Act of Contrition with a sincerity he had never known before. The priest murmured his own required prayer.

"We're going to have to hurry, son," he said before Liam had completely risen from his knees. He took a black cloak from a peg on the wall. "Put this on and hold it close around you. Should anyone see us you'll look like a fellow priest." He draped the garment over Liam's shoulders. "Get your pack, and we'll be off."

Liam matched his stride to that of the priest as they walked through the darkened streets. The lanes wound toward the quay. Liam smelled the water and the fishing boats before he could see them.

The priest put a hand on Liam's shoulder. "Wait here," he whispered. He moved silently away into the darkness. Liam heard a door close and the faint sound of voices, and the priest was back, urging him to follow. He led him down the length of the quay and handed him into a small rowboat. "God bless you, son," he said quietly and disappeared into the night.

Liam could just make out the figure of the man in the center of the boat as he sat on the narrow seat; he heard, rather than saw, the oars dip into the water. He huddled into the cloak as the dampness of the sea air settled around him. The man at the oars did not speak nor did Liam; both knew how far sounds could carry across the water.

There was no light on the boat nor could Liam any longer see the faint glow that had been visible from the shore they had left. He strained for some indication of life ahead, but there was no sign to be seen, only the blackness of the night.

They rowed steadily northward for more than an hour. Liam had not the slightest knowledge of their whereabouts. Occasionally from the east, there was a faint light; he could hear no sound but the oars dipping in and out of the dark water.

Liam felt the rhythm of the waves change as they pulled into a harbour and made their way into quieter water. Shapes began to appear, and he knew they were approaching a quay. The boat scraped against a piling, and a figure towered above them. His companion stood and flung a rope into the air. It was caught from above and secured. The oarsman turned to Liam and spoke for the first time. "Just here." He turned Liam toward the pier. "There's a rope ladder. You'll be safe above."

Liam grasped his hand and shook it. "Thank you," he said quietly.

"Up you go, quickly now." He placed Liam's foot on the first rung. Liam felt the boat move away before he was halfway up the ladder. Another unknown man had risked his life to help him, and Liam did not even see his face.

As Liam stepped off the ladder, he saw two figures outlined against the sky. One extended a hand to assist him. "This way," he said. Liam followed him along the quay. The other man brought up the rear as they walked close to the buildings lining the dock. There was no sound but their soft footfalls.

The man ahead spoke one word. "Here." He stopped and opened a door. It creaked faintly. Liam followed him in and heard the man behind him close the door and secure it. They led him to an open stairway at the rear of the building.

There was no light, not even shadows here. Liam felt his hand placed on a ladder. "Go up and to the right, lad," the same voice said. "You'll find a pallet to sleep on. There's a packet of bread and cheese alongside— if the rats haven't got it—and some water. Someone will be by about dusk tomorrow. You'll be safe as long as ye don't make a sound or stir about. There'll be people down here by dawn. Don't more than breathe if you don't want to be found out." He gave Liam a small push up the ladder.

Liam scrambled to the top and crawled to the pallet. He let out his breath in one big sigh. He hadn't realized he had been holding it for a long a time. The door creaked below, and Liam knew he was alone.

He felt about and discovered the jug and the packet of food. He took a sip of water and lay back. He would save the bread for tomorrow. Drawing the priest's cloak around him, he huddled beneath it. His eyelids closed involuntarily. He heard a skirmish of rats as he fell asleep.

CHAPTER 11

LIAM AWOKE THE next morning to shouts from the docks below. A man with a Dublin accent called out. "Here she comes, lads, in with the tide! Get a move on now, and give the lady a welcome, old broad that she is!"

"How she do be stayin' afloat is sure a fine mystery," called another. "I'd a wagered my own mother's bedstead we'd never be seein' this' one again!"

"Tis a shame she wouldn't go to the bottom before she's loaded up with Irish passengers, God bless their souls," Liam heard from below.

"Holy Jesus, do you be meanin' to tell me they be goin' to take on passengers in this old tub? Tis a floatin' coffin fer sure." Liam wondered what they were talking about.

"Sure, and ye don't be thinkin' the English would be wasting any other kind on the Irish, do ye?" someone answered.

Liam was wide awake now. He sat up and instinctively wondered if even that slight movement would scatter dust in the lower room. A rat scurried away from the food sack by the side of his pallet.

There was no sound of movement or voices in what Liam assumed to be a warehouse on the lower floor. The shouting came from outside on the quay. *Everyone must be gathered to watch a ship coming in to dock*, he thought as he carefully edged his way over next to the wall where he could see the sun coming in through the wide cracks.

He knelt and placed his eyes against the cracks and peered into the light. The sun was a rosy glow streaming with dark clouds and was just clearing the horizon. The water in the harbour was deep green and muddled by the strong tide that pushed its way inland.

The ship plowing her way in mid-channel was immense and ugly. One patched gray sail flapped loosely, like a wounded goose, catching the slight morning breeze as she turned toward the quay. The other lay in a heap on the forward deck. Liam had never seen so large a ship before nor one so old. There was no semblance of paint on her sides, even the wood seemed rotten and appeared to be peeling away.

Surely they can't be intending to put passengers aboard this rotten hulk, Liam thought. *She could hardly be safe for the crew when carrying light cargo, to say nothing of a full load of passengers and probably cargo too.*

The ship swung round to approach its berth. A stench rose and filled the air, flowing full force through the cracks in the wall against which Liam pressed. "Holy Mother of God, what is it?" Liam muttered to himself, pulling away and covering his nose with his sleeve, his empty stomach protesting. "What could they be carrying to make such a stench?"

The shouts increased as the ship was guided into its berth and made fast. Liam decided to take advantage of the confusion and move his pallet and supplies to the wall where he would have a better view. Quickly and quietly, he shifted his things and settled himself. The day would be long enough; he didn't have to be bored too.

Several more people moved onto the docks. They scurried about, shouting orders and bumping into each other. Liam's few glimpses of faces were brief and distorted by his view from above. Mostly all he could see of them were dirty caps or equally dirty heads of hair. Human sweat and tobacco mingled with the smell of the filthy harbour and the stench of the docked ship.

Liam nibbled on the round, hard loaf from his pack. Although it tasted stale and musty, he had chosen the one from home over the dry loaf the rats had chewed on during the night. He forcefully tore his mind from the memories that rose in him with the first bite and concentrated on the scene on the quay.

It was nearly noon before any cargo was unloaded. There had been much coming and going on the gangplank, but no sign of any other activity. A scurvy looking crew leaned over the rail and shouted back and forth with their counterparts on the docks. As near as Liam could tell, their conversations consisted mostly of obscenities and guffaws. They constantly spit over the rail into the garbage-filled water as he watched. Liam dozed off and on, having become bored with the proceedings.

He was jerked awake by increased noises from the ship and an unidentifiable thundering. He quickly sat up and placed his eyes to the crack. He could not believe the scene that met him. Cattle were scrambling from the ship—bawling, yelling, stinking cattle. A wide gangplank had been built to the dock with high wooden barricades on each side. The cows were being driven from the ship and herded down the quay. Men lined both sides of the wharf; each equipped with a large heavy club. They beat and prodded the animals to keep them from breaking from the herd or from being driven off the sides of the dock into the water. It was pandemonium!

Liam had never seen so many cattle before. They were a strange-looking kind of cow with awkward humps on their backs and strangely shaped horns. *Must be some kind of foreign thoroughbred*, he thought. They ran, pushing the ones in front of them and being pushed by the ones behind. Their horns tossed and their tails swished. They bellowed and bawled, and they stunk. *My god, how they stunk!*

The rotten, acrid, putrid odor rose and spread. Liam pulled away from the scene and covered his face. He gasped for air as the stench leached through the cracks in the walls and penetrated every corner of his hiding place. The odor of animal sweat and urine stung his eyes and dried his throat. His skin tingled with it, his clothing absorbed it.

Still the animals thundered down the quay. There must have been hundreds of them. The floor trembled under him. Bits of the rotted wood fell round him. Dust filled the air, rushing into his lungs, already irritated by the fumes rising from the animals.

The rats scurried from their hiding places in search of safer havens. Some stopped abruptly as though startled to see him there. Others never paused but simply rushed over him, accepting him as part of their environment. One jumped over his face, its tail brushing across his nose. Liam snatched the cloak the priest had given him and huddled beneath it.

At last the thundering stopped, and there was nothing but the shouting below. Gradually the sounds dispersed and the dust settled. There remained only the terrible, penetrating stink clinging to the air.

Liam's water tasted of it and the bread as well. He ate only enough to keep his stomach from gnawing. Several rats watched with hungry eyes as he chewed. He was tempted to throw the tainted loaf to them but resisted. He might need it himself before this ordeal was over.

The day dragged on. There were more signs of cleaning on board the ship and throwing of refuse over the rails, adding to the already stinking harbour. Barrels of supplies were taken on board, and just before dusk, the crew came ashore with much laughing and jostling, ready for a night on the town.

After dusk, the man had said someone would be by after dusk. Liam stowed his few belongings in his sack and settled himself. He would be ready. He couldn't wait to get out of this stinking hole. He stretched out on his pallet as dusk turned to dark. Still no one came.

Liam lay in the black night and fought the panic that threatened to overtake him. He forced himself to think rationally. *What will I do if no one comes? How long can I wait?*

He touched the small bundle of food beside him. A rat scurried away when his hand moved. *How long will the food last? Is it safe to eat after the rats have been chewing on it?* He had heard that rats carried all kinds of diseases.

Where would he go if he were forced to leave here? He knew absolutely no one in Cobh or Cork City. There was no one he could go to for help. He didn't know how to get back in touch with the priest who had helped him. He had never even seen the faces of the men who had brought him here.

Liam sat up and pressed his eyes to the cracks once more. He needed to be reassured there was some other living thing out there. He felt as though he were in a vacuum, as though the past twenty years had been blanked out.

He searched the quay below for some sign of life. Only the lantern on the stern of the ship glowed in the predawn blackness. Nothing moved. There was no sound. He lay back on his pallet and waited, straining into the future.

Liam recognized the sounds from the previous morning even before he was fully awake. Another ship was arriving with the tide. The day before repeated itself in activity. Once more the cattle rushed from the ship and thundered down the quay, the men beating and prodding them. Once more the stench rose to his hiding place, penetrating his very soul.

The dust had hardly settled after the departure of the cattle when Liam heard a new sound. His first thought was that the cattle were returning, but he knew that was impossible. He listened carefully. It was a human sound, lots of human sounds. He pressed his face tightly against the cracks. Far up the quay he could see a darkening mass moving toward him.

The horde swarmed down the quay. They were a ragged bunch, clothed in layers to lighten their loads. They sweat in the August sun. The stench of unwashed bodies rose to the cracks in the wall where he crouched.

Families clung together, afraid of losing each other in the rushing, shoving crowd. They pushed those in front of them and were pushed from behind. Fathers lifted their children to their shoulders to keep them from being crushed and tried to protect their wives and mothers as they were swept along by the mass. Liam thought of the cattle with their heads thrust into the air and their tails swishing. The same frantic rush prevailed.

The forward movement was cut short at the gangplank of yesterday's ship. *My god, these people are going on the cattle ship*, Liam thought. *How could they do this to them? It could not possibly be a fit place for humans after housing cattle for who knew how long.*

A makeshift table had been hastily constructed on each side of the gangplank. Here every would-be passenger stopped, and papers were exchanged. Liam watched as money was handed over by each passenger. He could not believe they were actually paying to board this decrepit ship. It was very doubtful she would ever reach port. It was also doubtful the passengers would survive to disembark. To use the same crowded space that had been occupied by cattle was surely asking for disease and even death.

Liam watched as the passengers streamed on board. They shouted and waved to those left on the dock. "To America!" they called. "We'll see you in America!"

The impossibility of what he was seeing swept over Liam. *This ship might, by some stroke of luck, make Liverpool or some other English port, but America? These people were doomed! Why were they doing it? Why were they leaving all they owned and all their loved ones to risk their lives on a death ship?*

Liam sat back in dismay. He saw in his mind the poorly dressed peasants he had watched board the ship. They carried with them all their worldly possessions—yes, everything. What was there to leave behind? Most of them had never owned anything but the clothes on their backs, and those were probably second- or third-hand.

They paid dearly for the use of the land and their humble cottages. They owned nothing. The rents were high and hard to come by. They lived from one potato crop to the next. The old crop was gone by the time the new crop came in and often long before. One poor season saw many die of hunger before the next crop could be harvested. Even more were evicted before new money came in to pay the rent.

Liam knew that in parts of County Cork and Kerry, there had been potato rot before the last harvest. Last year's few edible potatoes would have been gone long ago. These people could not wait for the new crop to come if, indeed, they had one in the ground. They would be half-starved by now. There was no hope for them here. At least in America there was hope—but they had to get there first.

It was nearly dark by the time the last of the passengers got on board. Liam watched all afternoon, unconsciously absorbing their sense of both dread and anticipation. They were caught in the middle of their fear of the past and their fear of the future as, indeed, he was himself.

Liam lay back on his pallet and nibbled on his last piece of bread. He would have to make some decision about his own future. He couldn't go back, that was for sure; that meant a hanging rope. He had to go forward, but toward what he did not know. If no one came for him tonight, he would slip out before dawn and try to make his way to the city. He didn't know what he would find there. He had never been in a city.

Liam had just taken his last sip of water and lay back on his pallet when he heard a new sound. Someone was making his way up the ladder. Fear leaped into his throat. What if it wasn't the person he was waiting for? What if someone else had found his way here and attacked him in the dark? He reached around for the heavy length of lumber he had seen earlier in the day. It was about as long as his arm, and he could grip it firmly. Quietly he pulled it toward him.

Liam sensed the trap door rising. He poised his club. "Are ye still here, lad?" came a whisper from the dark.

Relief swept over him. "Over here," he said softly, "by the wall." He put down the club.

The disembodied voice whispered quietly. "Sorry we couldn't make it last night, but making the arrangements took longer than we thought. Are ye all right?"

"I'm just grand now you're here," Liam replied.

"Git your stuff, and follow me. We're getting ye out of here."

"I'll be thanking you for that," Liam said, picking up his sack. He could hear his rescuer already scrambling down the ladder. He followed quickly and felt a hand on his shoulder as he reached the bottom.

"I'll guide ye to the door. Me cousin's waiting outside to take ye on board. Ye'll be goin' to America, lad."

Liam gasped. "On the cattle ship?"

"'Tis better than swimmin'," the voice replied, "though not much."

Liam swallowed noisily. He had no more choice than the tired passengers he had watched board the ship that afternoon. There was nothing he could go back to. He had to go on. God grant that the ship was more seaworthy than she looked.

He followed his silent partner through the warehouse and out the door, his eyes adjusting to the lighter atmosphere outside. A shadow moved from a hidden alley at the side of the building. Liam saw a young man in a dark jersey and cap and recognized the attire as that of the crewmen from the ship.

The stranger placed his hand on Liam's shoulder. "Did ye ever work on a ship, lad?" he asked.

"Nothing bigger than a curraugh," Liam replied.

"Ah well, don't really matter. Don't take that much to learn the sort of work ye'll be doin'," he said and motioned for him to follow.

Liam shook his rescuer's hand. "I thank you," he said, looking into his eyes. The man nodded, then turned and disappeared into the night.

Liam followed the crewman up the gangplank and on to the ship. He felt the faint unsteadiness beneath his feet. "Say goodbye to ole Ireland, lad. It ain't likely ye'll ever see her agin'," the crewman said.

Liam didn't look back. He had made his goodbyes back on Ringrone Peninsula three days ago. If it wasn't for his family and friends, Ireland could go to hell for all he cared.

CHAPTER 12

FOLLOWING DA'S FUNERAL, Donal and his friends headed for the home-brewed poteen left from the previous evening's wake. The partially emptied jugs were drawn up from the well, where they had been put to cool overnight. The long funeral mass and the ceremonies at the gravesite were finally over, and the young men's nagging hangovers caused a longing for that first renewing swallow of the powerful drink.

Donal inhaled the heavy fumes as each cup was drawn from the sweating jugs. He would like nothing better than to drown the fear of his new responsibilities in the bitter brown liquid being passed from hand to hand.

I will not, he promised himself, turning away from a proffered cup. *I'll not give in to the craving now. With Da and Liam both gone, I've got to have a clear head. I'm the one who has to face Mam with explanations of why Liam has gone.* Donal forced himself to turn away. He left his friends to their drinking and went inside.

The funeral guests had finished eating the thick crusty soda cakes and potatoes with bits of sausage, and Father McBride held sway. His thin, reedy voice mingled with the noises of plates being removed and pipes lighted. Cups of strong tea were passed down the long table, and friends sat back to relax. Life could return to its normal pace.

Mam and Kate stood on either side of the glowing hearth. Donal met Mam's eyes as he stood just inside the smoke-filled room. He saw the questions there and the hurt. He dreaded the moment when the room would be emptied and he would have to face her with the news that her eldest son was gone forever. At the same time, he wanted the guests to leave so his family could have the privacy they needed after all that had happened.

The room had taken on a strangeness to which Donal could not adjust. He had the weirdest feeling he had never been here before. *Perhaps the events of the past few days have distorted my thinking, and nothing will ever be the same*, he thought. The room still held the old familiar breakfront with Mam's few pieces of blue-and-white delft, along with the cracked bowls and mugs they used every day, but they no longer registered in his mind as family possessions.

Donal let his eyes roam about the room. The guests moved around now that the food had disappeared. Father McBride rose from his seat at the head of the table. He stood behind his chair, his hands clasped over its back, and Donal saw that the priest's eyes were on Kate. His thin face betrayed his desire as he took in her ripened figure outlined by the blazing fire. His fists went white as he tightened his grip on the back of the chair.

Even as he watched, Donal saw the priest's body straighten as every muscle responded to his silent command. The look in the black eyes turned from desire to anger and something else that puzzled Donal. Was it hatred he saw?

Donal could not believe what he was seeing. The priest's mild, bland face reddened and convulsed. His neck bulged above the too-tight white collar. His features, which had seemed so weak a few moments ago, took on a look of strength and determination Donal never would have believed possible. Father McBride raised his fist in the air, and his voice thundered through the room. His eyes never left Kate's face. "Kate O'Dwyer," he shouted.

The silence was instantaneous. Every eye in the room turned first to the priest in amazement at the startling tone of his voice and then to the girl who stood by the hearth. The light from the flames made a flickering aura around her black clad frame, giving it a translucent sheen. Her long dark hair spread out around her head, and the fire shone through it, lending the oval face a cameo whiteness. The beauty was unreal—almost unearthly.

Father McBride's voice broke the silence with an otherworldly quality of its own. "Kate O'Dwyer," he shrieked again, "you are a wicked woman!"

Kate's look of horror, as much as Father McBride's shrill pronouncement, caused all heads to turn toward the priest at the head of the table. "I saw you yesterday up at the fort consorting with the Englishman on the gray horse—and with your own father lying dead here in the cottage. I'll not have the likes of you disrupting my parish!" His voice rose to a screaming pitch. Kate's mouth dropped open in astonishment, her slim body trembling. "You should be sent to a convent so that the men of this parish would be safe from your wickedness. Repent now, Kate O'Dwyer, or you will go straight to hell!"

The silence in the room was profound. Not a soul moved or even breathed. Mam reached out and drew Kate to her. Mam's own hair took on a reddish glow from the flames behind her. Her eyes burned like coals, and her voice seared the air. "Father McBride, you forget yourself. You are a guest in my home. How dare you attack my daughter?"

A unanimous gasp rose from the funeral guests. It was as if her words consumed all the oxygen in the confined room. Their horror now focused on Mam. No one had ever dared speak to the parish priest in such a way.

Mam's voice lost its heat as though the shock of her friends had instantly cooled it. "You will apologize immediately, Father McBride." The ice in her tone brought another gasp from the room. "Or you can leave my house." She drew Kate's body closer.

Father McBride's frame visibly contorted at her words. He shook a clenched fist into the air. "You'll regret this day, Widow O'Dwyer!" he shouted. "God will punish you for speaking to me with such disrespect. You have defied me time and time again by teaching the children of my parish, knowing that it was my duty to perform, but now you have gone too far. From this day you will be ostracized by every member of this parish. No one will speak to you ever again." He turned and made for the door. There he paused and looked at the assembled faces. His defiant eyes met each one. He did not speak but made one beckoning gesture, then turned his back and marched out the door.

Donal went to his mother's side, and Niall joined him. Declan clutched his sister's hand. One by one, the neighbors filed silently out of the room, none even glancing at the group by the fire. Friendship was one thing, but they could not be expected to take sides against the Church. Without it, they had nothing; no hope for the future.

When the last one left the room, Donal closed the door. They were alone.

Donal looked at his family as they huddled by the hearth. Niall stood with his arms about his mother. Kate had dropped her shaking body to the three-legged stool, and Declan knelt with her head pressed into his shoulder.

At the far end of the room, a bench scraped noisily as Gran rose and groped for her cane. She held her body nearly erect in spite of the disease that crippled it. She pounded the cane on the hard-packed earthen floor. "Ye've done it now, Katherine DeCourcey!" she shouted. "Ye always did think ye were better than the rest of us, and now ye've gone and put yerself up higher than the parish priest. Ye'll have us all excommunicated!" She pounded her cane with each word. "I told my son he should never have married one of the almighty DeCourceys." She shuffled her way across the room and stood in front of her daughter-in-law. "My son is gone now. The Church is all I have left. I'll not have ye taking that away from me as well."

She looked Mam straight in the eye. "The priest says we're never to speak to ye. I'm a member of this parish, and I'll go along with the rest of 'em. I shall never speak another word to ye, Katherine DeCourcey." She spat on the floor at Katherine's feet. They all watched in stunned silence as Gran made her way back to the bench at the far side of the room.

Kate jumped up from her stool and rushed to her grandmother, throwing herself at her feet. "Oh Gran, Gran, you can't be meaning that. Mam has always been so good to you, and you love her, you know you do. Please say you don't mean what you said."

Gran patted the sobbing girl. "Don't cry, Kate. This is between yer mother and me. I'm willin' to forgive a lot of things, but defying the Church is not one of 'em."

Kate raised her stricken face. "But it's all my fault, Gran. It's me Father McBride is mad at."

"Whatever ye've done, Kate, love, can be forgiven. But your mother has denied the only thing that can save us all. For that she can't be forgiven." The old woman wiped at the girl's tears. "Now dry yer eyes and make sure ye get yerself down to confession in the morning and clear up all this nonsense about ye being a wicked girl."

Kate walked back to the group by the fire. She knelt before her mother and wrapped her arms about Mam's legs. "Oh Mam, it's all my fault. I don't know what Father McBride is so upset about. I didn't know I was doing anything wrong. I'll go to confession and explain everything. Surely it will be all right again."

"Yes, Kate, you go to confession. I'm sure you'll receive absolution," her mother said, "but leave me out of it. My problem with the Father is a separate thing entirely." She lifted Kate to her feet, pushing stray wisps of black hair from her tear-streaked face. "You're a woman now, Kate, and it's not an easy life as you're already finding out." She gave a small sigh and straightened her shoulders. "And now," she said, shifting her eyes to Donal. "We have some other problems to attend to." She led the way to the table, and one by one, the family gathered around.

Donal sat at the head of the table and faced them. How things had changed in three days. Here he was sitting in Da's place where himself would sit no more. The table looked too long, too empty.

Donal began at the beginning. His voice did not waiver as he explained how Liam and Da had been involved in the outlawed Whiteboy organization and had taken part in the raid on Lord Huxley's barn. He told them Da had been shot as they were being chased following the raid, and of the "accident" that had been staged at the smithy's to cover it up.

"Liam knew the English had discovered the blood on the trail, and they guessed someone had been injured. Unless something was done, they would be led here, to this house, to Da's body with a bullet in his skull." Donal paused and looked at his family. He could see the acceptance of his story already appearing on their faces beneath the shock and the fear.

"Liam and Paddy decided it would be best if Liam disappeared," he continued. "By running, Liam would appear to be guilty. Suspicion would be drawn away from the others."

"Why Liam?" Niall interrupted. "Why not Paddy or one of the other men? Surely there were others involved."

"The others are all married men with families."

"So Liam is the sacrifice!" Niall interjected.

"It was Liam's choice," Donal said firmly, closing the subject. He continued as Niall glared at him. "A house-to-house search is already going on. The constabulary is looking for someone with a bullet wound. They have already beaten up several men who couldn't explain recent injuries."

Donal wondered if they knew how serious this was. Had he already endangered them by telling too much? He wasn't sure. "It won't take them long to remember the unusual accident at the forge; they're not stupid. When they do, we're all involved." Donal paused to let that fact sink in. "Liam will draw their attention away from everyone else, us included."

"But where is Liam? Where has he gone?" Mam's voice was carefully controlled.

"The less we know about that, the better for now. Paddy the Smith has some connections who, with any luck at all, can help Liam get away."

"My Tim and Liam, both gone," Gran said quietly, making the sign of the cross.

"For heaven's sake, Gran, Liam's not dead!" Kate's voice was slightly hysterical.

"To us he is," Gran said, pushing herself away from the table. "He'll never be back, mark my words. He's as good as dead." No one said a word as Gran rose and grabbed her cane. They watched in silence as she hobbled to the stool by the fire.

It was then that they heard the sounds of the English soldiers outside and the banging on their door. Donal glanced hurriedly at each member of his family. "Let me handle this," he said quietly. "We don't know a thing. Liam simply isn't here."

Three soldiers burst into the room as Donal pulled back the door. "All right now," the sergeant said, "over by the fire, all of you." He motioned with his rifle. Donal took his mother's arm and guided her to the hearth, feeling a slight tremor of fear go through her. Niall stood between Kate and Declan. Gran didn't rise from her stool by the fire.

The sergeant gave a motion to his men, and they began to search the room, poking everything with the tips of their bayonets. One of them climbed the ladder to the loft, and straw drifted down as he tore the stuffed mats that were their beds.

Donal recalled the white shirts which had been burned in the fire at the forge. *Thank God they had remembered to destroy that mark of the Whiteboy organization.*

The sergeant looked around the room, taking in the significance of the once laden tables that had fed the funeral guests. "Ah yes, this is the home of the smithy that was kicked to death by the squire's horse. An unfortunate accident and a strange one too." He swung round to Donal. "You the one who worked at the smithy?"

"No, sir," Donal replied. "That'd be my brother Liam."

"And where might he be?" The sergeant looked round at the others.

"He ain't to home," Donal said.

"I didn't ask if he was home. I asked where he is." The rifle swung up at Donal's belly.

"I ain't seen him since mornin'," Donal gasped. "I don't know where he is."

The sergeant turned to Mam. "Where is he?" he shouted into her unresponsive face. "Where has he gone?" Mam said nothing. "Why would a son leave on the day of his father's funeral? He must be guilty of something."

"If you could explain what you're looking for, maybe we could be of some help," Donal spoke up, diverting the attention from his mother.

"You know bloody well what we're looking for. All you Irishers know what we're looking for." He shook a fist in Donal's face. "Now where is your brother? What did he tell you about the night Lord Huxley's barn was burned?"

Donal swallowed noisily. He wasn't sure how he was going to handle this. "Liam isn't one for talkin'. He keeps himself to himself."

"Just the sort we're looking for, a bloody, closed-mouthed, sulking Irisher. Now then, when did you last see him?"

Donal stood a moment as though deep in thought. Perhaps he should play the role of the stupid peasant they thought he was. "Well, as near as I can recollect, twas at the gravesite. I remember he was right in front of me when we threw the blessed Irish soil onto the coffin."

"You better be remembering this is English soil, you sniveling peasant," the sergeant thundered, the bayoneted rifle pressing Donal's belly. "Now think back, did you see him after you got home, after the funeral?"

Donal hesitated. "I don't rightly remember. There were lots of people here. My father had lots of friends."

"All men have lots of friends after they're dead," the sergeant interrupted. "Now did you see him at all after that?"

"No, sir," Donal said. "I don't think I did though I can't be that sure."

The sergeant pursed his lips. He paused, then tried a new approach. "Now, lad," he said, placing his hand on Donal's shoulder, "did you by any chance notice if he had an injury of any kind? A cut maybe? Or a bad bruise?"

"Liam? Oh, I don't think so. He isn't one to get into a fight or such. Liam is a quiet one. A loner." Donal hesitated. *Now was the time to plant the seed Liam wanted in their minds.* "You know, now that you mention it, Liam was limping a bit this mornin'. I noticed it when we were carryin' the casket. He kind of favored his left leg." Donal heard his mother's sharp intake of breath. He deliberately ignored it and turned to Niall. "Did you notice, Niall, when we were carryin' the casket into the chapel?"

Niall cleared his throat. "I didn't notice nothin'."

"Now that I've given it a mite of thought," Donal continued as though Niall hadn't spoken, "Liam has been favorin' that leg for a couple of days. I don't rightly recollect just when it began. I do remember thinkin' that maybe the squire's horse had kicked him too, but in all of the confusion of the past few days, I forgot it altogether." He shook his head as though bewildered.

The family stared at Donal in amazement. The sergeant strode across the room and back again. He glared into Donal's face. "And who else was with him on the raid?"

Donal looked alarmed. "On the raid? Liam?" he spluttered. "I didn't say nothin' about no raid. I'm sure Liam wouldn't do such a thing."

"Don't play the innocent with me. Where else do you think your brother got hurt? He was on the raid, that's where. Now who else was with him?"

"I don't know nothin' 'bout no raid, sir. Liam never talked to me 'bout nothin'. He is a quiet one, like I said. He always keeps himself to himself. I wouldn't think Liam would know anythin' 'bout burnin' a barn."

"Then what has he run away for? Where is he? What has he got to hide?"

"I never said nothin' 'bout his runnin' away," Donal said. *No sense in having them starting a search too soon*, he thought. "He'll like as not be back by supper. I'll bet he snuck off with some lass after the funeral. They're probably up in the hills rolling around in the heather right now." Donal heard his grandmother snort with indignation.

"You better hope he's doing just that," the sergeant replied. With that he marched his soldiers out of the cottage. The family stood without moving, without saying a word. The sergeant's voice could be heard ordering his patrol to surround the property and to wait for Liam's return.

As he heard them move away from the cottage, Donal leaped up to close the door. The day had turned dark; and the rain, which had started to fall, echoed loudly against the walls, driven by a rising wind. He thought of Liam out in the storm as he heard the soldiers milling around the yard, grumbling about the weather.

Once more, the family was left alone in their too-empty cottage. This time, the unwanted guests would always be there—watching, waiting, not to be forgotten for a moment, conspicuous by their presence, as were the others by their absence.

Donal poked at the dying embers in the fireplace and lit the candle on the wooden table before anyone else moved. Quietly, one by one, they set about straightening the room the soldiers had torn apart.

It had been a long day. Their emotions were already stretched almost beyond enduring. The funeral had lent a kind of acceptance to the fact that Da was dead, but in its wake were a painful dullness and the fact that Liam was gone. Donal thought of being in the tunnel from Ringrone Castle. There was the same difficulty with breathing, the same closed-in feeling.

CHAPTER 13

KATE STOOD IN front of Father McBride's cottage door and reluctantly lifted the knocker and let it fall. She half-hoped he would not be in, but she knew she had to face him to clear up this misunderstanding.

Had she really been wicked to talk to the handsome Englishman? She had no sense of shame or of committing a sin, but apparently it was something serious, for now her mother was in deep trouble, and all because of her. Not one of the villagers had come to apologize for leaving the cottage so abruptly without speaking. *I can't let this go on*, Kate thought. *Mam will die of lonesomeness without her neighbors.*

The steady rain had soaked through her shawl and kerchief, and Kate could feel it penetrating all the way to her homespun cotton dress. The long skirt was already clinging to her legs and felt cold and clammy. She shivered as much from the dread of what was to come as from the dampness.

The rain had kept up all night. She had lain awake listening to it blow against the shutters and thinking about Liam out in the night somewhere, running from the authorities.

The parish house before her looked gray and neglected as patches of fog blew across the hilltop. The rain-soaked thatched roof gave off an odor of decay, as though the mice had died in their nests. Kate looked up at the large iron cross that nearly covered the top half of the double-hung door and quickly crossed herself. As she heard the priest's shuffling footsteps approaching from the other side, she took a deep breath. The Blessed Virgin Mary alone knew what was coming next.

The expression on Father McBride's face both surprised and repulsed her. On anyone but a priest, she would have called it an affront. The black eyes gleamed, not with pleasure exactly. They held what Kate could only describe as self-satisfaction, a triumph, and—what she would have called in one of the brash village lads—a leer.

"Well well, if it's not Kate O'Dwyer," Father McBride said, his eyes taking in the rain-soaked girl before him. "How good to see that at least one of the O'Dwyer family has decided to seek forgiveness."

"Good morning, Father. May I come in, please? I need to talk to you," Kate said anxiously.

"Of course, Kate. Come in. Come in." He stepped back and held the door wide.

The atmosphere on the inside was even more dreary than it had been on the stoop. The two high windows in the small room let in little light, and the peat fire belched smoke as the wind drafted down the chimney.

"Put your wet cloak by the fire to dry, Kate," the priest said. "We'll talk in my study." He watched as Kate pulled the shawl from her shoulders and shook out the water. She hung it over the wooden chair that stood before the hearth and spread her kerchief over the seat. Brushing her fingers through her tangled hair, she pulled it into a twist at the nape of her neck, leaving the roped strands to hang down her back.

A shower of droplets flew as she shook out her wet skirt. They caught the light of the fire and sparkled like fireflies before hitting the worn fieldstone floor. Kate lifted her eyes to comment, but Father McBride turned abruptly and led the way into the adjoining room.

The priest motioned her to a small bench placed before a large wooden table. He sat behind it in an oversized chair which Kate recognized as a match to the one at the side of the altar in the adjoining church. On the table, a bound ledger lay precisely in the center. A worn leather-bound Bible and a small pocket missal rested to one side. No fireplace heated the bare room whose only other furnishing was a prayer bench. On the wall hung a large bronze crucifix, supporting a particularly agonizing Christ figure. The one small high window was streaked with dirt, and the rain made muddy rivulets down its length.

Father McBride folded his long white hands over the ledger. "Well now, Kate. What did you wish to see me about?"

Kate looked down at her own tightly clasped hands. "I'm not sure,

Father," she began. "I don't really know why I'm here or what you think I have done, but you seemed so upset with me yesterday . . ."

"You really don't know, do you, Kate?" His voice held puzzlement rather than kindness. Kate looked up and met the intense eyes from the other side of the table. "Don't you realize, Kate O'Dwyer, that you have grown into a beautiful, desirable woman?"

"But, Father," Kate interrupted. "I can't help how I look! I can't change what is!"

"Don't you know that your kind of beauty can drive men mad?" His voice rose as he spoke, and his eyes roamed over her trembling body. "How can you not know that every move you make causes the male members of this parish to lust after you? That soft white skin, those dark inviting eyes, that wild black hair . . ." He gestured erratically. "They're the creation of the devil, meant to tempt all men."

Kate stared at him in disbelief as his eyes lingered on each part of her body. "But . . . but what can I do?" Kate cried out, not sure what was expected of her.

"It's up to you to see that you don't tempt men into sin, Kate O'Dwyer. It's a grave sin to tempt men."

"I don't mean to . . . to be wicked. And now . . . now Mam is in trouble. No one is talking to her . . . and it's all because of me." Her shoulders shook, and her lips trembled.

"Now Kate . . ." Father McBride flustered. "Don't cry." He moved from behind the table and held out his arms. He pulled Kate up from the bench and drew her to him.

"Oh Father," Kate sobbed, "what am I going to do?"

"There, there, Kate. Hush now," he murmured, placing his hand on the back of her head and moving it to his shoulder.

Kate began to quiet, and as she did so, she realized that one of his arms was pressing her against him, and his other hand had moved to her breast. She felt his body tremble. She pulled herself away and straightened her clothing in an unconscious effort to remove all traces of his touch. "I'm sorry. I'm sorry, Father," she said. "I seem to be crying over everything lately."

The priest moved away as though surprised to find himself where he was. He cleared his throat noisily. "It's understandable, Kate," he said in an unclear voice. "You've been under a strain what with your father's death and all." He moved back behind the table as he spoke. He sat down and folded his hands on the ledger.

Kate watched as he turned his hands over and over, studying them as though he could not believe what they had done. He seemed to grow angry under her gaze. His fists clenched, and Kate saw colour spread over his face and neck.

"Do you understand what I've been saying to you, Kate? You cannot go on tempting men."

Kate shook her head. She wasn't sure what was going on. She convinced herself she had imagined his hands roaming over her as he held her and pressed her to his body. She shook her head. "But Father, I . . ."

"Don't interrupt me, Kate," he said. "You have to realize that men are weak. They have little resistance when it comes to women like you. It is up to you to save them from themselves. You will be doubly cursed if you cause even one of God's creatures to commit a deadly sin." His voice rose again as anger possessed him. "It is your sin, Kate O'Dwyer. You sin when you throw your temptations before them. It is the woman who is to blame. Not the man . . . not the man."

He jumped up from his chair and paced the room. He stopped in front of the crucifix and looked up. The expression on his own face was not unlike the one who hung over him.

Kate's voice held its own horror. "What can I do, Father? What can I do?" Even as she said the words she hated the whimpering in her voice. *How could it be my sin? How is it my fault if men were weak?*

Father McBride turned to look at the woman before him. Her hair had come undone and hung in disarray around her face. Her clothing had dried and molded itself against her exquisite small body.

His voice took on the same note he used from the pulpit at Sunday mass. "Keep yourself away from the occasion of sin, Kate. Cover that . . . that wild hair with . . . with . . . a kerchief or something. And you can't go around with your . . ." His voice faltered. "Your chest sticking out like that. Use a shawl. Cover yourself . . . cover yourself." He tore his eyes away from the sin of temptation and turned away.

Kate quickly folded her arms across her offending breasts.

"You will burn in hell, Kate O'Dwyer," the priest pronounced, his eyes lifted to the suffering Christ, "if you don't do as I say."

Kate trembled. *I must be terribly wicked for him to say such things. It must be my fault.* "I will, Father. I will do just what you say. I didn't know. I didn't realize . . ." She crossed herself as she spoke.

The priest turned back to her. He cleared his throat twice and then spoke in a calm tone. "Now, Kate, I want you to think about what happened with the Englishman on the gray horse."

"But nothing happened, Father. I swear it. I never saw him before. He came into the old fort where I had gone. He didn't know I was there." The words tumbled over each other. "When he asked me about my father, I started to cry. He . . . he put his arms around me to comfort me . . . just like you did, Father. It was just like that. He felt sorry for me and wanted to comfort me, just like you." Her eyes rose to meet his. "That's all it was." Kate wasn't sure whether she was explaining the Englishman's actions or justifying those of the priest.

The color drained from his face. "Yes . . . hmm . . . yes . . . well, Kate, you think about it and come to confession on Saturday." He turned away and strode from the room.

Kate followed him and quickly picked up her shawl and kerchief from the chair, wrapping them around her. She did not look at him as she did so. She didn't know if he watched. She walked to the door he held open. "Thank you, Father, for your advice," she said.

Kate stepped out into the rain and paused on the stoop. She turned to face him. "And Father, please forgive Mam for saying what she did yesterday. It's all my fault. She was only trying to protect me."

Father McBride's expression changed instantly to one of iron determination. "That is between your mother and me, Kate. Don't interfere. She has challenged me since the day I arrived with her teaching of the children. I cannot allow a member of my parish to assume my duties or to dispute my judgment, certainly not in front of the whole village. She will take the punishment she deserves." He closed the door in Kate's face.

The weeks that followed were a puzzlement to Declan. It seemed they lived in a different lifetime. Without Da, the household had no spirit.

They seemed to be enveloped in a fog which caused a dread of what lay ahead unseen.

The soldiers had stood at the gate for three days, keeping their silent vigil, their eyes sweeping the hills and the rushing waters. There had been no sign of Liam nor of anyone else, for that matter. No one had approached the cottage from any direction, and after badgering Mam and Donal with instructions to report to them the moment they had any news of Liam's whereabouts, the sergeant withdrew with his troops.

Declan knew there was still a watch on the place. He had seen the lone sentry up on the hill above the high road, where he would be able to see all approaches to the peninsula. Declan had seen the smoke from his fire from the window in the loft, and one day he crept through the thorny gorse and saw the scruffy looking guard as he lay sleeping on the heather.

Liam had been gone for more than two months. Paddy the Smith told Donal his friends in Cork City had gotten Liam on a ship to America, but there had been no more news. *Liam should be in America by now*, Declan thought as he sat in the upper window of King James's Fort.

He watched the small fishing boats in the harbour with new interest and wondered how they differed from the one Liam had sailed in to America. Declan could not imagine one that could sail across an ocean. The ships that passed Old Head Lighthouse in the distance had huge sails shrouded in the mist and masts that tossed in the wind.

It was impossible for Declan to visualize these ships in a storm as there must be at sea. The gales that blew in from the Irish Sea were fierce at times, especially in the autumn as it was now. It must be a thousand times worse out on the open ocean. He crossed himself automatically as he thought of Liam, fear for him rising in his throat.

Since Liam had gone, neither Donal nor Niall had been able to find work. The word was out that the O'Dwyers were under suspicion, and no one was willing to take the chance of offering them a day's work, even when crops must be harvested.

The long winter was settling in, and there would be no more chance for work. The potatoes were in their underground cairns, and thank God for that, Donal said, for there would be little else to eat. But many a family existed for years on nothing but the praties.

What little hard cash they had was used to pay the year's rent. They would have been evicted immediately if Da had not been prudent enough to set aside the cash to pay the rent on time.

The rents were due after the harvest each autumn, and God himself could not help the tenant whose crop had failed. The tenant farmer was completely at the mercy of the landlord or his agent. He could pay his rent in kind if he wished, and the landlord's barns were stuffed with wheat and barley, which would be sold abroad, and with turnips and potatoes and even with pigs and chickens.

Donal decided he preferred to part with the cash rather than with food stuff. There was a long winter ahead and lots of mouths to feed. Better to have potatoes where you knew you could get at them than cash in the teapot when maybe there would be none to buy in the months before the next crop came in.

Brian McNamara, the agent for Squire Atkins, had shown surprise when Donal handed him the rent money. "And what will you be doin' when the next one comes due?" he asked Donal.

"I'll be here," Donal replied. "Will you?" He had taken a chance talking to him like that. It didn't do to make an enemy of the squire's agent.

Agents for the landlords were strange animals. Though Irishmen, they were often more cruel to the tenants than were the landlords themselves. Often the owners never knew what their agents did. Many landlords never even visited their properties. They lived in luxury in London on the proceeds of land they had never seen, leaving the agent to treat the tenants as he pleased.

Declan knew there wasn't enough money in the old cracked teapot for another year's rent. He had counted it one afternoon when Gran was snoozing in the sun and Mam and Kate had gone to pick the last of the blackberries that grew wild on the north side of the fort and up along the high road. There had been only a handful of coppers, not nearly enough to pay another year's rent.

Donal and Niall left early every morning with their slanes over their shoulders to cut the turf for the winter's fires. They didn't return until after dark. Declan went with them twice a week to help pull the loads of bluntly cut black blocks that had been placed on a netting of ivy vines.

The rolling hills and the hard, stony earth ceased to look as beautiful long before the eight-mile trek with the heavy load was finished.

Declan dropped from his perch in the window ledge of the keep and pulled his coat closely around him. The wind had picked up and a heavy mist was beginning to turn to rain. Nearly every day in winter would bring the cold, damp mist and heavy gales off the Irish Sea. While the temperature hardly ever dropped below the freezing point, the cold dampness penetrated everything.

Declan walked slowly toward the cottage. He dreaded going home these days. For one thing, Mam and Gran weren't talking to each other. They hadn't spoken a word since Father McBride had warned the parish that Mam was in the Church's disfavor.

It was really such a stupid thing, Declan thought, *but Father McBride took his authority seriously and was not about to be undermined by one of his own parishioners.* Gran took her religion seriously too. If Father McBride said she should not speak to Mam, she would not.

Declan knew it wasn't just that. Gran was using the ostracizing of Mam as an excuse to get back at her for something. He wasn't sure just what; but he knew, deep down, Gran didn't like Mam very much. Whatever the reason, it sure made things tough, for they all had to live in a small house where two women didn't even acknowledge each other's presence.

Something was wrong with Kate too. Declan couldn't decide exactly what it was. Kate wouldn't talk about it, even to him. They had become almost strangers, when a few short months ago they had shared every thought.

Kate sat huddled by the fire with her cloak drawn around her as though she had the chilblains like Gran. "Leave her be," Gran said whenever Declan tried to get her to go outside or to do something with him. "Lasses her age are moody. You get along and amuse yourself, lad," she said.

Niall talked all the time about getting away. He hated cutting turf. He hated taking care of the cow and the chickens. He hated the harvesting of potatoes and turnips. He hated everything about living the way they did. *Well,* thought Declan, *it wasn't too grand, that was for sure. But they were together, and they had a roof over their heads and food to eat, such as it was. Niall should be grateful for that, like Father McBride said.*

Not everyone was meant to be lords and ladies, he said. We should learn to accept our lot and be content.

Niall stewed about everything and let everyone else know how unhappy he was. Donal told him many a time to stop his sniveling and carry his load like a man. Niall sulked and threatened to just take off. "Liam's lucky to be out of it," he said. Donal was losing his patience, and most of their talk was arguments about the work and Niall's shirking his end.

The fire in the hearth flared up when Declan opened the door. Mam was hanging a kettle of praties over the flame and Kate sat on a stool in front of the hearth, drying her hair. She smiled at Declan. Her long hair swung out around her face, shining in the firelight. She looked like the old Kate. He suddenly realized how much he had missed his sister.

She swung round to face Declan. "Do you think I'm beautiful, Declan?" she asked in a curious, tentative tone. Mam glanced up with a worried look. Kate jumped up and twirled her body around, dancing about the room. "Father McBride says I was created by the devil." Her voice was unnaturally high. "He says I'm a menace to all the men in the parish. He says I'm sinful because I cause all the men to lust after me."

"Kate! Stop that kind of talk!" Gran said from the feather bed at the farther end of the room. "If Father McBride said such things, he no doubt had a reason."

"Oh, he had a reason all right," Kate said, flinging her hair behind her head and piling it on top. "He said I was to cover myself with my shawl so I wouldn't stick out in front." She studied her breasts, unconsciously cupping them with her hands. "I always thought women were supposed to stick out like this."

She turned toward the fire. Her voice held a tremor. "He said I should wear something to cover my wild hair and that I should hide myself from men so they would not be led into sin." Her voice took on a note of hysteria. "I'm a wicked woman, he said, and it was my fault if men were tempted." Her shoulders shook, and her voice rushed on. "It's my fault, he said, not the men's fault if they lusted after me." Tears started to run down her pale cheeks, and her voice lowered. "Cover yourself, he said. Cover yourself," she repeated, almost as if she were talking to herself, "and stay in the corner where they can't see."

Mam rushed to her and gathered her into her arms. "There, there, Kate." She soothed, rocking her back and forth in her arms as if she were a small child. "Go ahead and cry. Let it all out. You can't keep something like this inside."

Gran's voice came once more from the bed. "Have you been flaunting yerself, Kate? Why would Father McBride say something like that if you wasn't flaunting yourself like some hussy?"

Mam turned to her mother-in-law and spoke directly to her for the first time in more than two months. "You're always willing to believe the worst about me and my family, aren't you, old woman? Well, I've had enough. You had best remember that you're in my house. My house, do you hear? And you're here only because I say you can be here. Now keep your filthy thoughts to yourself. Kate wouldn't know how to flaunt if she wanted to."

Kate pulled herself away from her mother. "It's all right, Mam. I'm no longer a child." She wiped her tears away with the back of her hand. "I'm all through crying." She picked up her discarded cloak from the floor, then flung it down. "And I'll tell you this. I can't hide under a cloak for the rest of my life." She looked around at each of them, begging for understanding. "Maybe I am wicked, but I can't help the way I look. If men find me beautiful, so be it. If they are tempted by me, it's their problem, not mine. Let them go to confession, not me. I can't believe that their thoughts are my sin, whatever Father McBride says."

"Stop it, Kate!" came Gran's gravelly voice again. "You listen to what Father says. He knows what's good for us."

"Gran, I'm warning you," Mam threatened. "You keep out of this." Gran snorted and turned her face to the wall.

Kate looked at her mother. "Please don't hate me, Mam, but I can't go on being miserable. If I'm a wicked woman, I'm sorry, but whatever I am, that's what I have to be."

"It's all right, Kate. You just be the way you want to be. Father McBride is wrong about this." She turned to the bubbling pot on the fire and adjusted the cover. "I've had a lot of time to think during this silent treatment I've been getting, and I think Father McBride's been wrong about a lot of things. Maybe it's my pride that's talking, but if that's the worst of my sins, I'm lucky. In my opinion, Father McBride has the same sin of pride. And he'll go to any length to hold his power over this parish." She slammed the cover down onto the pot. "I may rot in hell for the way I feel, but so be it."

"From what I've been hearin' today, this whole family will rot in hell," said Gran without turning from the wall. "God rest your souls."

CHAPTER 14

FATHER MCBRIDE'S WORDS rang in Maire's ears as she stumbled from the confession box in the small ivy-covered chapel. The shocked looks on the faces of the women lined up on the hard benches waiting their turn at the confessional told her that the priest's words had carried only too clearly to their ears.

"You will make a special novena to the Blessed Virgin for your outrageous indiscretion," he had nearly shouted. "May she find it in her heart to hear your pleas and bless both you and your child."

How could he have spoken so loudly? He might just as well have announced from the pulpit on a Sunday that she was pregnant. Could he have done it on purpose? Father McBride took every sin committed in his parish as personal. Maire knew he could be vindictive; look what he had done to Katherine O'Dwyer. Not one person in the whole parish had spoken to her for months. Maire's own sin was much more serious than Katherine's.

Maire held her head high. She would not allow herself to cry in front of the village women—the same women who would leave the chapel and rush out to tell everyone in the parish of her shame. The sin of gossip was one they confessed every week. Maire sunk to her knees before the altar, but she could not pray. How could she ask for forgiveness for loving Liam? How could she be sorry for the few hours they had together? All she had left was the memory of their loving and the feel of his long, lean, hard body pressed to hers.

She looked at her cold hands gripping the rail in front of her. Would it have made so much difference if there had been a ring on her finger?

Would that have made it all right to make love to Liam? Would such a small thing have made God bless them and their child?

Oh Liam, she cried silently, *where are you? Why did you leave me after making it impossible for me to love anyone else? And what of our baby? Will you ever be able to come back and claim it as your own?* She bent her head over her folded hands and forced back the tears that threatened to fall.

She tried to pray, but the words would not come. She could not ask for forgiveness for she did not want to be forgiven. What she wanted was for Liam to be here, for his arms to be holding her, and for their babe to be welcomed, but she knew that none of these things would happen.

Behind her, Maire heard the shuffling of the women as they took turns in the confessional. *What sins did they have to confess,* she wondered, *these long-married women whose husbands were home every night? What occasion did they have to commit a sin even if they wanted? They seldom left their meager, little cottages. They weren't allowed to speak to a man other than their husbands or sons or other male relatives.* Yet she knew they lined up each Saturday with anguished faces, waiting their turns to confess their sins.

One by one, they knelt briefly at the rail to say their doled-out penance, bowed briefly as they rose and quietly moved back from the altar. They would receive communion at the morning mass and start their week absolved of their grievous sins. "Go and sin no more," they were told every Saturday, yet the next week saw the same ones lined up at the confessional.

Are we so weak, we women, Maire wondered, *that we cannot go more than seven days without committing a sin?* The men of the parish were never seen more than once a month and seldom as often as that. Many, like her own father, reluctantly came once a year in order to fulfill the requirements of the Church. *Who,* she wondered, *did all these women commit their sins with if not the men of the parish?*

A sudden thought struck her. *My father! My god, how am I going to tell him? He's been denying for two years that I'm a grown woman. He refuses to admit that I could have a life outside his cottage and the chores I have to do. He's always kept a close eye on everything I do. I never would have met Liam except for the English lessons his mother held.*

Kate had asked Maire to come to their cottage to learn to speak English and to read and write nearly three years ago. She and Kate had both been long-legged, gangly girls then, and the lads paid no attention to them, except of course, Niall.

All the girls in the village knew about Niall and giggled among themselves about his outrageous behavior. *Some of them giggled a little nervously,* Maire thought. So far, she had been able to keep him at a distance. Strange how Niall held a fascination even when you knew he was not the kind of lad you wanted. There was a certain magnetism about him. It was a hard thing to resist.

Her father had warned her about Niall though he had never mentioned the other lads in the village. He had simply said he expected her to act like a lady and to be aware of her immortal soul.

What her father really meant was that she was not to turn out like her mother. He never mentioned her mother's name, not since the day she left when Maire was two years old. They had never heard from her again though someone said they had seen her in Cork City begging on the streets. She hoped it wasn't true.

Maire tried to ask her father about her mother, but he would not discuss it. Katherine had told her, in answer to her pleading questions, that her mother had left with nothing but a bundle of clothing after her husband had beaten her for asking a tinker to come in to warm himself by the fire when she was alone in the house. The tinker had been old and crippled, and she had been a beautiful young woman, but her husband had called her a slut and beaten her almost senseless.

Maire could not face telling her father she was pregnant just yet. She crossed herself quickly, unconsciously; her penance forgotten. She squared her shoulders and prepared to face the waiting women, but the chapel was empty. They had gone while she knelt. She walked up the aisle, not quite sure where she was going or what she was going to do.

As she opened the heavy door and stepped outside, the sound of their voices hit her. The women were gathered into little clusters, their heads together. They turned and watched as she stood on the steps, their faces full of disapproval, and a kind of excitement too. There was a sudden silence; not even the birds were singing. They watched as she descended the steps, then as one, they turned their backs and moved away from her. Not one met her eyes nor uttered a word of kindness or sympathy, not even those whom she had thought were her friends.

Maire was an outcast. She was no longer one of them. They were ashamed to admit that she was of their parish. Maire knew this treatment would continue until she married or, in desperation, moved from the village. There was no forgiveness in this parish for the sin of having a babe out of wedlock.

She gave them one defiant look, swung her long auburn hair, and marched between the groups, looking neither to the right nor left. She moved away from the high road and went up into the hills, walking among the rocks and the heather until dusk fell before she made her way back to her father's cottage.

For three days, no one spoke to Maire in the village streets. Whenever she met any of the women, they abruptly turned their backs. Maire knew they followed an ancient custom, but she was hurt nonetheless. She felt she was being forced into something, but she wasn't sure what. What did they want her to do? She couldn't marry Liam. He was gone.

Maire knew the moment her father came into the cottage he had heard what they were saying about her. He closed the door firmly and stood with his back against it, watching as she ladled the potatoes from the kettle hanging over the open fire.

Maire felt his eyes on her before she turned. Usually he paid her little attention, hardly looking in her direction. The only time they spoke was at the table when he asked for food or muttered about his aches and pains from his work at the slate quarry.

The anger in his eyes burned through her as she faced him. Hate flew out of them, overriding the disappointment she saw at first glance. "I should have known you'd grow up to be like her," he spat out. "I should have seen it in the saucy tilt of your head and that hair." He strode across the room and grabbed her arm. Potatoes flew from the ladle onto the floor. "You're just like your God-forsaken mother—nothin' but a slut!"

The back of his hand hit her in the face, and she would have fallen but for his hand holding her arm. He hit her again, and she felt the blood spring into her mouth. "Whore!" he shouted. "Nothin' but a whore!" He grabbed her by the hair and flung her across the room. She hit the hard-packed, dirt floor, sprawling on her stomach. He kicked her in the ribs, and she heard something crack even as the pain exploded through her. "Dada!" she shouted. "Don't!"

But he wasn't through with her yet. He pulled her up and hit her with his fist, first in the stomach and then a blow that landed on her left eye. She felt blackness swing round her and streaks of light flash in her head. Darkness took over, and she knew she was falling. She still heard his words echoing, "Whore! Whore!" down the endless tunnel.

The cottage was dark when Maire came to. The fire was still smoldering, but she knew by the heavy gray ash that a long time had passed since she stoked it up to cook their supper. The kettle still hung over the hearth, and she could smell the praties gone cold.

She listened for the sound of her father, but nothing but night sounds came to her ears. He had gone—probably gone to the Widow McDougal for comfort. *Funny how it was all right for him to pay visits to her. No one condemned him for that.* She tried to get up, and the pain in her side and back spread like fire. *Was anything broken?* She couldn't be sure, maybe a rib or two. Her head pounded, and her left arm felt like it was wrenched from the shoulder. She rolled over and raised herself to her knees, fighting the sickness that rose in her stomach. She hung her head down until the dizziness passed. The cottage stopped swinging, and she crawled to the stool by the fire and sat upon it. Her lip started to bleed again, and she wiped it with her sleeve.

She picked up the poker and stirred the fire, adding first one brick of turf, then another. There would be light to see by. The flames spurted up, then flared. She walked painfully to the wash basin and splashed water on her face. Her left eye throbbed.

Maire looked into a piece of tin she had polished and hung on the wall. Even in the dim light she could see she was a mess. There were bruises on her cheek, and one eye was almost shut. Blood had dried on her chin and dripped onto her bodice. Her hair was matted with blood too, and her sleeve was torn from her shoulder. But she could move all right though she had to be careful not to move too quickly. Her right side was stiff and sore, and her left arm was bruised, the ache spreading up into the shoulder socket.

How could he have done this to me? My own father who was supposed to love me? But she knew he had beaten her—not for herself alone, but for her mother's sin as well. The hurt was still there—not only the physical ones that showed from the outside, but also the deeper, darker hurt inside that would be there long after the others had healed.

Maire looked around the cottage in the dim light of the fire. She knew she couldn't stay here. Her mother had been right about that. There was no sense in staying around where someone beat you. Having done it once, he would not hesitate to do it again. Anything was better than that.

There wasn't much she could take. She bundled some warm clothing and tied them together in a quilt. The pack was heavy, but she could manage. Looking around the room once more, she found that the potatoes were still in the kettle and was surprised that she was hungry. She ate two of the praties standing in front of the fire, then got a small pot, and put the remaining potatoes in it. It would mean a few more meals. Thoughtfully she looked at the glowing bricks of peat; she would need fire. Finding another pot, she put a couple of bricks inside and placed the first pot on top. The bricks would keep smoldering until a place to make a fire could be found.

Maire took stock of what she had. She didn't know where she was going; but she had warm clothing, fire, some praties, and a pot for cooking. Survival would be possible for a while on her own. With her bundle in one hand and the pots in the other, she left the only home she had known in her sixteen years. She didn't look back.

CHAPTER 15

DONAL'S BRITCHES SHOWED the dark stains of the bog water he had been standing in since early morning. The primeval dampness oozed from the spongy earth as he cut blocks of the solidified peat moss with his slane. The primitive odor clung to his clothing and to the back of his throat.

Niall stacked the uniformly cut blocks in neat rows as fast as Donal could cut them with the sharp curved tool. It was backbreaking work; but the blocks, when dried, would provide fuel for the fires all winter, and possibly they would be able to sell a bit for badly needed cash.

The dried turf would provide a quick hot fire and could be banked to hold the sparks for the beginning of the next day's flame. An earthy odor drifted from its smoke and its yellow ash quickly spread through the air, both of which penetrated every Irish cottage, clinging to the thatched roofs. These roofs of natural fibers, some said, provided the breeding grounds for the plague of consumption that was the curse of all Ireland.

Together the two brothers dragged the netted sling of ivy vines filled with blocks behind them, their tools slung over their shoulders. Tired and dirty, they followed the low road from the strand at Garrettstown, hardly glancing at the breakers rolling in from the troubled sea.

A storm was approaching, that was easy enough to tell from the sound of the surf and the mournful cry of the foghorn from the lighthouse at Old Head. The fog already kept its beacon from warning the ships on the Irish Sea of the treacherous rocks extending out several hundred yards from the point. Neither of the brothers thought consciously of this. Their exhaustion and their plodding steps, which would take them home to a hot meal of potatoes, held all their concentration.

"I'm going up to check on the storehouse," Donal said as they approached the natural bay formed by the turn of the river near their cottage. "You take the load home and leave the slanes for me. I'll bring them along when I come."

"Sure, sure, Donal, let me have the heavy load." Niall complained, but he put his tool down beside Donal's and shifted his shoulder to assume the weight of the loaded sling. They both knew that Niall's complaint came naturally and didn't mean a thing.

Donal knew too the news they had heard that day would give him no rest until he had checked their store of food. The dreaded potato blight had struck a few scattered storage areas in Skibbereen, not thirty miles south. One day the crops were fine, the next they were a stinking, rotting mass.

Donal trudged up the hill, leaning heavily into the climb. Near the entrance to the tunnel, just inside the outer wall of the fort, they had dug a horizontal hole in the ground just below the frost line. Over the earthen roof and the opening they had piled the rounded stones from the collapsed fort wall. It formed an oval, cairnlike structure. A small door of tin, made from a piece of scrap from the smithy, allowed entry. This was the winter storage for food, which had to last until the potato crop was harvested the following autumn. Potatoes and turnips were all it held this year, but there were plenty if they use them sparingly. That is, unless the blight struck.

Donal removed the stones from in front of the small door. A sick feeling rose with his dread. He waited for the stench of the rot, afraid, afraid of what he would find.

The rusty door protested noisily as he swung it open. The stale, alcohol smell of potatoes rushed at him, but there was no odor of decay, no sweet, nauseous fumes of the rotting blight. He stood bent over in the doorway and breathed deeply, relief making him weak. His exhaustion left him. The aches and pains of the day's labor disappeared. A lightheadedness overtook him, and he wanted to run and shout. There would be food for the winter.

Methodically Donal closed the ill-fitting door and replaced the stones. The approaching storm water would drain away down the hill as it always had done. Giving the last stone an extra pat, he turned toward home.

A soft, quiet curl of blue-gray smoke coming from the keep at the south end of the fort caught his eye. *Declan must be playing there again,* Donal thought. *How many times had he been told not to light fires in the fort? It's time the lad was growing up and showing some responsibility.* He quickly smothered the thought. *Declan was a good lad. He carried his load of work, tending the cow and the chickens and cutting and storing the hay. He also kept the ferry running, and that was their only means of getting any hard cash these days. All the same, he shouldn't be building fires in the fort.*

Donal hopped the inner wall and trudged toward the keep. He would warn Declan one more time and then take him home to supper. The wind picked up as he climbed the rocky path. Fog already concealed the mouth of the river and curled over the tops of the hills, and the foghorn from the lighthouse blew on schedule every few minutes. His clothing was soaked through from the thickening gray mist before he reached the dismal remains of the fort.

Declan should know enough to get home before the rain comes, Donal thought as he walked through the scattered rubble in the courtyard. He rounded the keep and crouched to enter the open doorway. Blue smoke filled the circular space, and the damp wind pulled its way down the crumbled staircase from the partially open roof above. "You're the devil's own donkey, Declan, for staying up here with an open fire," Donal began.

He stopped and stared open-mouthed. It wasn't Declan huddled against the wall on the other side of the smoky fire. At first his mind didn't register who it was, not until she rose and cried out.

"Donal! Oh Donal!" Maire dropped the tattered quilt from her shoulders and rushed to him, throwing herself in his arms. "You gave me such a fright!" she said, her small body trembling against him. "I heard someone coming, and I didn't know what to do." She buried her face in his neck. "I didn't know what to do," she said again.

Donal held her close, trying to stop her shaking. His thoughts tripped over each other as he tried to figure out what was happening. He could not believe he was actually holding Maire in his arms, that she had run to him and called his name as though she couldn't have been happier to see anyone else. "Oh God," he groaned, "if I'm dreaming, don't wake me."

The trembling body stilled, and she pulled back away from him. "What are you doing here, Maire?" Donal asked, hating to spoil the dream he was living.

"I didn't think anyone would find me here," she stammered.

"I don't understand, Maire. What's happened? Why are you up here all alone?" He stopped as he looked into her face for the first time. "My god, Maire, what's happened to your face? It's all black and blue!"

Smoke whirled around her as the wind whistled down the broken chimney. He saw that she was dirty and tired, and she was cradling her left arm. "You're hurt! For God's sake, Maire, what happened?" He touched his fingers to her bruised cheek, hurting for her himself. His anger rose. "Who did this to you?"

Maire turned away as he spoke. She went behind the fire in its circle of stones and scrunched down into a ball. She picked up a stick and poked at the fire without looking up.

"Maire." Donal felt the word lodge in his throat. "Please, Maire, tell me what happened. Tell me so I can help."

He felt as though his heart were being torn out of him. His love for her was like a living thing, leaping with joy one minute and writhing in despair the next. He knelt beside her and placed his arm around her shoulders. "Please, love, tell me what's wrong."

Maire pulled away from him. "Don't touch me, Donal. Don't touch me. When you hear what I have to say, you won't want anything to do with me." She pulled the quilt around her awkwardly.

"What are you talking about? I could never feel that way, no matter what you tell me. Nothing could ever stop me from loving you. I've loved you since I first set eyes on you." He hadn't intended to say the words. They bubbled out of him like water overflowing a kettle.

"Please, Donal, don't say that. I can't bear it." Her small white fist clenched against her mouth. He could see she fought to hold back her tears. He looked away to give her time to get control.

Lightning flashed across the sky, casting moving shadows over the stone walls. Donal picked up the blackened stick she had dropped and poked at the fire and added two blocks of the turf that stood against the wall. Flames shot up and gave off a quick light. The thunder rumbled, echoing against the stones.

Beside him, Maire spoke softly. "Has there been any word from Liam? Do you know where he is, when he'll be back?"

Donal stopped poking the fire. He hadn't expected that she would ask about Liam at such a time. He looked at the ugly bruises on the too-pale face. Her auburn hair was damp and matted, and the almost violet eyes looked into his with a pleading he could not understand.

"No," he answered in a quiet voice that matched her own. "There's been no word. Paddy did tell us some of his friends had gotten him on a ship to America. That was two months ago. We haven't heard anything more."

"America." She dragged the word out. "Then he won't be back. He's gone for good."

"Yes yes, it looks that way," Donal replied. *What were they doing discussing Liam's disappearance now?* Donal's mind spun. He could not understand the reason for her questions.

Pain passed over her face and a sadness that was indescribable. He reached out for her hands. They were damp, cold, and almost lifeless. "What is it, Maire? Tell me," he pleaded.

"I'm—I'm going to have Liam's baby," she said quietly.

Lightning struck close by, and Donal felt the shock pass through his body along with the impact of her words. Thunder shook the fort. Surely he couldn't have heard right. "You and Liam?" he blurted out. "You and Liam? A baby?"

Maire nodded her head. "We were so much in love." One tear made its way down her bruised cheek. "And he was so afraid, and . . . and . . ." She brushed the tear away and held her head up high. "And I'm not sorry, Donal. I know it was wrong of us, but I'm not sorry."

The hurt started deep inside him. It was difficult to breathe, and his mouth was suddenly dry. His shoulders slumped as the weight of the pain settled there. A gnawing began in his stomach that was more than hunger.

I should have known, Donal thought. *I should have known Liam had been in love with her.*

There had been plenty of signs, but he had been so wrapped up in his own thoughts of Maire, he hadn't seen it at the time. His throat hurt as he spoke. "You had better begin at the beginning, Maire. I don't understand what all that has to do with your being here."

Maire stretched her hands to the smoking fire. "I discovered I was pregnant about three weeks after Liam left. I didn't know what to do. I didn't know where Liam was or if he'd ever be back." She paused, and the lightning flashed between them, and the thunder pounded the words into Donal's mind. "Last week, I went to Father McBride for advice. He said I was the worst kind of sinner." The violet eyes sought his opinion. "He shouted at me and said I would rot in hell," she rushed on. "The women at confession heard him, and the whispering began. I'm surprised you haven't heard it by now." Shame and exhaustion mingled on her face.

"Not many people come by our cottage these days," he said.

"Yes, I know, then you have some idea of what it's like. And of course my father heard the talk. He was raving mad. He . . . he called me a slut—just like my mother, he said. Then he beat me." Her white hand gestured helplessly at the bruises on her face. "I've been hiding up here in the fort for two days."

"But you can't stay here, love," Donal said, taking her hands in his. He had already guessed what she would say. He knew her father's reputation and his temper. The thought of him beating Maire was unbearable. He had to get her away.

"I can't go home, Donal. I'm never going home again. My mother was right to leave him years ago. No man has a right to beat another person—not the way he beat her—or me. I can't go back there. I won't go back there."

"No, I didn't mean that. I don't want you to go back. I won't let you go back."

"Oh Donal, what am I going to do? Why isn't Liam here when I need him so much? How am I going to take care of his baby?" The dark eyes smoldered black, and the fire reflected there implored him. "Help me, Donal. Help me. Not for me, for Liam and his child."

"Do you love Liam so much, Maire?" he asked, not wanting to hear the answer.

"Oh yes, Donal. I do love him. I will always love him, no matter what happens." The night was black after the lightning. Thunder rumbled in the distance.

"But he's never coming back. You know that, don't you? You will probably never see him again."

"I know that, Donal. I know that." She watched the smoke curling up from the smoldering fire. "But it's not his fault. He never would have left me if there had been any other way. I know that too."

"That's true, Maire. No man in his right mind would leave you if there were any other choice." Donal rose to his feet and reached down to pull Maire up beside him. He pushed the tangled curls back from her face. How he loved her. How he loved and wanted her. He ached with the wanting of her.

As the desire rose in him, an idea formed in his mind, fully bloomed. The words tumbled out. "Marry me, Maire. Marry me, and give Liam's child its rightful name." He held his breath, not daring to hope.

Maire stared at him in disbelief. In the light of the fire, the bruises looked angry and red. She swallowed hard before she spoke. "You would do that for Liam?"

"For me, Maire. For me and for you, and for Liam and the baby." The words rushed out before she could protest. "It's the only answer, Maire. Let me take care of you. No one will have to know it's Liam's child. It'll be our child, yours and mine."

Maire shook her head. "You don't know what you're saying, Donal. I love Liam. I always will. It wouldn't be fair to you. And we'd both know that Liam is the baby's father even if no one else knows."

"Maire, I know all that, and I still want to marry you. I love you, Maire. Nothing else matters. I want you to be my wife, and I don't care about anything else. I'll love your baby the same as if it were my own. Say yes, Maire. Marry me." He watched the emotions fight each other on her face. He began to allow hope to surface. "I love you, Maire," he said again.

The huge dark eyes studied his face. At last she put her hand in his. Her voice was low, but it did not tremble. "All right, Donal, I'll marry you. May God forgive us both."

Donal pulled her into his arms and smothered the white face with kisses. He was not aware of the tears streaming down her face for the storm broke at that moment, and they were immediately drenched.

CHAPTER 16

DECLAN COULDN'T SLEEP. He was as restless as the night creatures that prowled the shore searching for the leavings of the receding tide. He lay listening in the dark, listening even though he knew he could not expect to hear any sound from the nearby cottage that Brigid O'Malley had loaned to Donal and Maire for their wedding night.

Declan's overactive imagination kept him awake. There was something bothering him about the simple wedding ceremony he witnessed earlier in the day. It had been a quiet affair with just Kate and Niall for witnesses. Mam refused to set foot in the chapel, and Gran's rheumatism was acting up, and she could not move. Except for Father McBride, Declan was the only other person present, and he had stood quietly at the back of the church.

Father McBride performed a brief service with an almost disapproving tone, as though he were performing a duty he felt was beneath him. Yet he had done it, and the couple was married—married forever in the eyes of the Church.

How strange that the simple ceremony I witnessed today stripped the sin away, Declan thought, *and made it perfectly all right for Donal and Maire to lie in their bed together and make love with all the world knowing.*

The same parishioners who had cut Maire off—refusing to so much as speak to her or look into her face—now gathered outside the church, smiled, and nodded their heads in approval, commenting on what a grand couple they made. It was as though Donal and Maire had been forced somehow to do the will of the Church, though the idea had been their own. Now they were back in favor. *What a puzzlement,* he thought. There was something else bothering Declan, something in Maire's face, or rather lacking in it. No trace of the happiness one usually could see in a bride shown there; instead, he saw what was almost an expression of tragedy, a lack of hope. Donal's, by contrast, held a look of awe as though he could not believe his undeniable good luck.

Was Maire's stricken face simply the result of her pregnancy as Kate had suggested? Maire had made it quite clear during the three weeks they waited for the banns of marriage to be published that she didn't care what anyone else thought of her—she was not going to be ashamed of her actions. So it was obviously not her conscience causing her apprehensions.

Declan sighed aloud. He hoped Donal could make her happy. If he were the one lying next to Maire tonight, he would . . . but he had better not think of such things. Maire was Donal's wife, and he would wish them nothing but happiness. He sighed again and turned over, much aware of his own body's yearnings.

"Can't sleep, Declan?" Niall asked from the far corner of the loft.

"Just thinking about Donal and Maire," Declan admitted.

"Me too," Niall's whispered voice came back. "I don't know how Donal pulled that off. I tried a couple of times to get her into the heather, but she'd have none of it."

"Niall! She's Donal's wife! Don't talk like that!"

"Aye. Well, she wasn't then, was she now?" Niall responded.

The moon broke through a cloud, flooding their window with light. Declan got up from his mat and sat looking out into the night. After a few minutes, his brother joined him.

Niall spoke in low tones that couldn't be heard by those sleeping in the room below. "You know, I never figured Donal to be one to plow ground that wasn't rightfully his. Makes you wonder, doesn't it?"

"What do you mean, Niall?"

"He looked a mite overanxious today. Not like someone who had already sampled the crop."

"Donal loves her, Niall. You can't doubt that."

"Oh, tis not that I doubt. What I'm questioning is whether his love is returned. Maybe someone else is responsible for the wee bairn in her belly."

"Oh Niall, surely not . . . Maire's better than that. She wouldn't take such things lightly." But suddenly the sound of Maire's giggles in the hayloft the night of Da's wake echoed in Declan's mind. And Liam murmuring soft sounds of love. "My god," he groaned aloud. "Liam . . ."

"My thoughts exactly," Niall said quietly. "Donal's covering for Liam, the poor fool."

"But that doesn't change the fact that Donal loves her," Declan said, gazing out into the moonlit night. He felt a kind of desperation, a yearning, not for Maire's love, but for her happiness. He knew, somehow, that it wasn't to be. "God help them both," he whispered.

A shadow moving across the ridge at the height of the high road caught his eye. "Did you see that, Niall? Something or someone is up on the high road."

"Probably the lookout who's posted up there. They're still expecting Liam to come back or someone to contact us."

"No . . . no. It's not that. Look there, he's striding across the open stretch." There was no mistaking the figure of their brother, his hands in his pockets, his shoulders hunched, stalking along the top of the ridge. "If I didn't know better, I'd think it was Da," Declan said.

"Not exactly my idea of a wedding night," Niall said. "I sure as hell wouldn't settle for that." He turned away from the window and went back to his mat.

Declan watched the spot where his brother's slumped figure had disappeared. *So she's still in love with Liam*, he thought. *Poor Donal.*

Donal's body still ached with the want of her even after what she had said. He could not believe it had turned out this way. Was he not doing the right thing by marrying her? Had his mind been so obsessed with wanting her he hadn't been able to think clearly of anything else?

She was never going to get over Liam; that was clear by what she had said tonight. He had gone outside to give her a chance to get ready for bed without his watching. When he came back, she was standing by the window in what must have been her nightshift. Her wondrous auburn hair hung down her back. His heart had leaped into his throat at the sight, and he felt a yearning in his groin as well. Anticipation made him weak in the knees.

He turned her from the window to face him. The look on her face struck him with the force of a gale. Tears flowed down her cheeks, and the agony he saw there was so real, he pulled her to him and held her tightly to his chest.

"Maire, oh love, what is it?"

"I can't, Donal," she sobbed. "I thought I could go through with it, but I can't."

"Hush, love, don't tremble so." His arms tightened, and he rocked her gently back and forth. "It's all right. There will be lots more nights."

She pulled back away from him. "It wouldn't be fair to you, Donal. I can't make love with you. I'm still in love with Liam. I can't . . . not with anyone but him . . . not with his baby inside me."

"It's all right, Maire. It's all right. We've lots of time. We'll work it out." Donal pulled her back into his arms and buried his face in her hair. The fresh scent brought new waves of desire flooding over him. "Oh Maire," he whispered, "I do love you so."

"I know, I know," she said softly. She pulled away from him and went back to the window. Her voice was low and controlled when she spoke. "Please forgive me, Donal. I never should have married you." She turned and faced him. "I am so sorry. Please believe I didn't want to hurt you."

"You're my wife, Maire, for now that's all I ask. If you don't want me to touch you while you're carrying Liam's child, then that's the way it will be." He couldn't believe he was saying these words, not on his wedding night. His throat felt dry and parched. He ached with a longing he had never known before. "I can wait, Maire. In the meantime, I'll take care of you and the babe." He paced the floor. "I'm not pretending I don't care, Maire. I didn't marry you for the baby, or for Liam, or even to save you from scandal." He paused and looked into his new wife's tragic eyes. "I married you because I wanted you for myself. I still want you." His body was trembling. "I can wait, Maire, but I won't wait forever."

Donal took his coat from the peg near the door and went out into the night. He watched from the high road until he saw she had dimmed the light. *At least she hadn't put it out entirely*, he thought. *She expects me back. Maybe there is some hope after all.*

Donal walked in a daze along the high road all the way to Old Head. He gazed out over the turbulent water, trying to keep his mind from Liam across the sea in another country. He didn't want to think of Liam tonight. But the thought came that by his actions today he had ruined his relationship with his older brother forever. *And for what,* he wondered. *Will I ever be able to erase Liam's image from Maire's mind and heart? Would the child always remind us that Liam stands between us?*

Donal watched as the sky turned pink, spilling its colors into the water. He walked back to the cottage where his new wife lay wakeful, wondering whether he would return.

CHAPTER 17

NIALL LAY WAITING for the first rays of light to show through the small window of the loft. He had been restless all night trying to keep his underlying excitement at a level he could handle. Today was the day he had been planning in his head for weeks. He was impatient for it to arrive. He was done with waiting. The time had come for him to take things into his own hands and make something happen.

Every day for months he had grown more restless. *It must have all started when Da was killed and Liam left*, he thought. The hopelessness of the family's situation was constantly with him. He didn't have Donal's belief in the future nor Mam's acceptance. *If I have to spend one more day in the bogs, I'll lose what little sense I have*, he thought.

Quietly he slipped out of his bed and picked up his boots. Careful not to wake anyone, he crept down the ladder. He went to the shed and shouldered the bundle of clothes and food he had packed and left there the night before. The cow lowed gently as she sensed his presence. "Goodbye, you old fool," Niall said silently. "Thank God I'll never have to shovel up after you again." He closed the door and walked to the shore.

Pushing the curraugh into the water, he jumped aboard. There was no wind at this hour of dawn. He bent to the oars and rowed easily across the river to Kinsale.

Niall didn't look back at the dark cottage. He had not told anyone he was leaving nor did he say goodbye. Nothing they could say would make him change his mind.

He had put in enough time with concerns of feeding a family. From now on, he vowed, he would be concerned with only his own needs. He was going to make something of himself. He was not quite sure what, but he would find a way. If they were smart, his family would be thankful there was one less mouth to feed all winter.

Niall cut through the fields and hills south of the village. No one stirred in the quiet street nor would anyone care where he was going if they were about. He was glad to be finished with the whole village.

He would be able to cross the winding river again at Bandon. From there he would hike to Kenmare, some thirty miles away in the foothills of County Kerry. If he could find no work there, he would continue west and maybe north to Galway. He would find something. He knew he would. He sang as he walked along without a worry for his future. His silvery tenor tones rang in the morning air.

Niall had made up his mind he would not think of his family. From now on, he had no family. Things had become unbearable after Donal brought Maire home to live. Only Kate seemed to be alive again after the disaster of Da's death and Liam's departure. Kate now had someone her own age to talk to, and the two lasses constantly had their heads together.

Meanwhile the tensions in the rest of the household grew. Mam and Gran were still not talking to each other, and the two girls relayed everything they said.

In spite of himself, Niall couldn't keep his eyes off Maire. Her every move tantalized him. He couldn't quite understand his reaction. It wasn't as though there weren't plenty of other lasses in the village, willing ones too. Each toss of her head, each shy smile seemed to suggest that he make an attempt to get her alone.

Did she simply want to reject him again? She had done it before she and Donal were married. Maybe that was what riled him so, the fact that she preferred Donal to himself.

Niall shifted his pack as he walked along. *But did she prefer Donal? Theirs was a strange relationship, and Donal was a fool to put up with it.*

Donal had carefully made a bed for himself and his bride and installed it in the opposite corner from Mam's feather bed. He hung a curtain of Maire's old quilt around it to give them a bit of privacy. Then he slept in the loft with his brothers and left the bed to Maire, inviting Kate to share it with her if she liked.

"Because of her pregnancy," Donal said in explanation. *Rubbish*, thought Niall. *Maire was having none of him, and that was that. I sure wouldn't put up with such nonsense. I'd get into that bed, babe or no babe, and she wouldn't be complaining either.* He felt a sudden swelling bulge in his trousers just thinking of it. *Donal surely is a fool*, he thought for the thousandth time.

There was someone else who wanted Maire. Niall looked on with interest. With lowered lids, Declan followed her every move. He jumped to do things for her. She couldn't start for the door without him leaping to hold it open. He rushed to explain that expectant mothers shouldn't be doing chores as he carried the water buckets or armloads of turf for her. Maire laughed, rumpling his hair to thank him as he passed, and Declan blushed like the innocent he was.

But it wasn't Maire's delicate condition that concerned Declan. He was head over heels in love with her and would do anything to get her attention. His fourteen-year-old sighs were obvious to everyone but himself, and Niall sympathized with Declan's tossings and turnings at night. By marrying Donal, Marie had managed to affect all the O'Dwyer brothers.

Niall pushed the thoughts from his mind. She was a tease, and he wouldn't give her another thought. *Damn her to hell, anyway, for getting herself caught with Liam's babe and involving all the rest of us.*

It took Niall three days to get to Kenmare. He had caught a lift with a farmer on a donkey cart near the bridge in Bandon, and the farmer bought him a meal for helping to unload the cart at the marketplace. Never had thick crusty bread and heavy fish stew tasted so good. Niall went singing along the country road to County Kerry.

It was an unusually warm day for December when Niall approached the village of Kenmare. The waters of a small stream running into the Kenmare River looked cool and inviting. Niall decided to take advantage of it. He could use a bath after his long trip. He removed his travel-stained clothes and dove into a deep pool. The aches and pains from the unaccustomed walking left him as he swam in the cool water. He came up shaking his red hair and reached his arms into the sky. He was glad to be alive. He started to sing. His voice was loud and a strong, pure, clear tenor. As he splashed in the water, he sang at the top of his lungs. "Tra-la, tra-lee, tra-la! It's a day to be glad you're alive."

As Niall paused for breath, the sound of rippling laughter came from the shore. She could have appeared from the fairy bush beside her, so breathtaking was her beauty as she stepped into view. Her slim young body was clothed in a rust-colored riding habit, and a small perky feathered hat perched on her long blonde hair.

Niall stood up in the water in surprise.

"Hold it! Hold it!" she called in a voice like chimes in a church tower. "Don't take another step!"

Niall looked down and saw that the water barely covered his lower body. "Sorry," he said. "I forgot for a moment where I was. Guess it's a good thing the water is deep here."

She laughed again, and Niall noticed that not a trace of a blush showed on the flawless complexion. Only the faintly pouting lips showed red. "Do you realize that you're trespassing on private property?" she asked.

"Now how could I be doing such a thing when I'm not even on land? Is it that you own the waters too, my lady?" Niall responded, taking in the full length of the heavenly apparition before him.

"Now it so happens that my uncle does," she retorted with a toss of blond curls. "But you're welcome to have your swim. Just be sure you don't come onto the land."

Even from the distance of the twenty yards that separated them, Niall could see the twinkle in her eyes. She stooped and picked up his belongings. "I'll just take these things with me to be sure," she said.

"Hold it! Hold it!" Niall shouted, repeating her own words. "You better not do such a thing."

She turned to face him. "And why not, pray tell?"

"Well, you'd leave me but two choices if you did," Niall said slowly, trying to size up her reaction. "First, I'd have to swim around in your uncle's lovely pool for the rest of my life until I drowned in the water. Then every time you'd look at it, you would pine away for the handsome stranger you forced to expire with your own unkindness." He paused for effect. "Or secondly, I'd be forced to come out of the water naked as the day I was born and wrestle my clothes from your arms. And surely

I'd win, being so much bigger and stronger than you." He took a step forward in the water, its reaches hardly covering his privates.

"All right, all right!" she shouted, dropping his clothing on the ground. "You may get dressed, but I'll be waiting on the other side of the fairy bush for you to explain who you are and what you're doing here."

Niall grinned sheepishly. "I kind of thought you'd see it my way," he said. "Now if you'll kindly remove yourself, I'll get out of the water."

She gave him a slow, exploring look from the top of his head down as far as the water allowed. Niall saw the full lips purse into an impudent expression and the blue eyes light up. "Maybe I'll stay and watch," she said, obviously enjoying the prospect.

Niall hesitated only a second. "Suit yourself," he said with a delighted grin and lifted one foot to step forward. The blonde apparition disappeared behind the fairy tree.

Niall shook the water from his head and pulled his trousers over his wet body. He took a clean shirt from his bundle, put it on, and stepped into his boots. How he wished he had some decent-looking clothes. He rolled his pack with haste and slung it over his shoulder. Running his fingers through his hair to clear the snarls, he went in search of the remarkable girl.

She leaned against a gray boulder on a nearby knoll. Her sleek brown horse was tethered to a tree just beyond her reach. She casually examined her fingernails, pretending not to see him approach.

Niall placed his bundle on the ground and paused to look around. He could see the clear water of the river. It ran to rapids as it tumbled over huge rocks and formed a deep frothy pool. The blue sky reflected its deep color into the flowing stream. "What a wonderful place," he said, extending an arm to sweep the entire range of hills, river and sky. "Is it always like this?"

"It's always beautiful, whatever the season," she replied. "It's one of my favorite spots." She paused to study him. "I haven't seen you around here before."

"I just arrived," he said. "Allow me to introduce myself." In a flash he remembered the curse that hung over the O'Dwyer name. News of it could have traveled as far as Kenmare. He made an instant decision.

"I'm Niall DeCourcey from Cork City," he said, "and whom have I the honor of addressing?"

She laughed, the light dancing in her eyes. "Aren't we formal all of a sudden? Well, Niall DeCourcey, I am Jocelyn Winters. My uncle is Lord Kenmare. I'm spending several months at Kenmare Castle while my father is in America."

"I'm very pleased to meet you, Miss Winters. I hope you're a warmer person than your name suggests."

She laughed the tinkling laugh Niall had first noticed. "Oh I am. I am as I'm sure you'll discover." Niall held her eyes for a moment, not quite sure what he was reading there. Was she teasing him or was she really as bold as the words implied? She was the first to tear her eyes away.

She moistened her lips with a dainty wet tongue. "Well now, Niall, what brings you to Kenmare?" she asked, turning away to sit on the ground.

Niall lowered himself beside her, resting on his heels. "I find myself in need of a position," he said. "I had thought to present myself at the castle to see if there was something for a man of my talents to do."

She glanced at him to catch laughter in his eyes. "And what might those talents be, Niall DeCourcey?" she asked innocently.

"As you no doubt have noticed, I am a big, strong, handsome fellow," he said slowly, "and I have a remarkable singing voice as you have heard."

"Well now, let me think. What available position might those talents qualify you?" she responded, placing a slim, pointed finger thoughtfully to her appealing cheek.

"I'm a very handy fellow to have around," Niall offered hastily, "and I do know something about horses. I'd love an opportunity to care for this fine one here," he said, nodding at the gleaming gelding tied nearby.

"What a marvelous idea! I never would have thought of it. We do need someone at the stables. I'll speak to my uncle immediately." She got up from the ground gracefully. "Come by about six o'clock. I'm sure my uncle will agree you're just the man for the job. I'm certain you'll see that neither my uncle nor I is dissatisfied."

She started toward her horse, then stopped and looked at Niall. "There's a nice room over the carriage house I'm sure you could use." Her eyes met his. "I'll be glad to help you get settled."

Before Niall could reply, she leaped on her horse and was gone.

CHAPTER 18

NIALL LAY BACK on the soft bed in the large open room over the carriage house of Kenmare Castle with a satisfied smile on his face. Jocelyn had apologized for the tacky quarters. Little did she know this one room was larger than the cottage that had housed his whole family. He had simply looked around with a noncommittal look and said nothing.

In the days that followed, Niall did not speak of his family to Jocelyn. As far as she knew, he was alone in the world. He didn't speak of the past at all, and if she asked questions, he made up something he thought would please her. Jocelyn was interested only in pleasure, and Niall had both given and received that right here in this grand feather bed.

Jocelyn knew what she wanted and set out to get it with determination. They were a lot alike, Niall thought. He knew what he wanted too, and he was not afraid to use people along the way. He had been using women all his life for his own pleasure, now he saw there was more than pleasure to be gained. He might not have many talents, but he knew how to manage women. For the first time, he realized he could get what he wanted from life by making use of women like Jocelyn.

Jocelyn Winters was from a long line of commercial financiers. They had never been among the aristocratic class, having been second sons of second sons for generations and never in direct line to inherit. But they were socially acceptable because they had money and knew how to earn more with that money. All the members of the upper classes in England, and many from the continent, invested their funds with Wellington Winters Enterprises, Ltd.

The best investment now was lumber from America. The English had stripped most of the woodlands from all of Great Britain and Ireland. Lumber equaled money, and Wellington Winters ventured into both shipping and construction. The more Niall learned, the more determined he became to get his share, and Jocelyn was his entry—if he played his cards right.

Jocelyn seemed more than willing to share whatever she had with her beguiling Irishman, but at the moment she was not thinking beyond her own personal favors. The truth was she had little else. But at seventeen years of age, the only child of Wellington Winters III considered herself an expert on men, her father included. She had been able to wheedle out of him anything she set her heart on since she first smiled at him from her cradle. Niall felt confident that convincing Jocelyn he was necessary to her future was the same as convincing Wellington Winters III.

The sun was already high and Niall had work to do. For the past several weeks now, he had been assigned the duties of overseeing the trainers who were preparing the Kenmare thoroughbred horses for the annual show at Kilarney scheduled in another two months. The six horses that were to be entered would already have had their morning exercise, and it was up to Niall to see that they were rubbed down and cared for properly.

Niall enjoyed his work. It was not something he wanted to do for the rest of his life, but horses were the exception to his conviction that all animals were offensive. He admired the beautiful, sleek, powerful creatures, especially these expensive thoroughbreds in the Kenmare stables. He even found the odors they gave off vaguely pleasant unlike that of other animals; he had never liked dogs or cats, or especially cows. He thought of Anne Boleyn in her stall at home and how he hated the acrid odors emitting from her and her droppings.

The stable boys led the show horses into the stables as Niall approached. The animals' sweating bodies gleamed in the sunlight. They pranced with satisfaction from their early-morning run, their pride shouting in the way they carried themselves. Niall exulted in their condition though he knew he had little to do with it. They would come through with honors at Kilarney, he was sure. Sure enough to bet all his saved wages.

Niall had little to spend money on at Kenmare. He could wait for new clothes and other luxuries until he needed to go somewhere. The tidy sum, more money than he had ever seen in his life, was hidden under a loose floorboard in his room. He could at least triple the sum with winners at Kilarney.

It was the middle of the morning when Niall saw Jocelyn striding toward the stables, her blonde hair streaming out behind her in the bright sunlight. She wore a hunter green riding habit which outlined every familiar curve of her tempting body. Niall knew by the way she swung her crop that she was upset about something. Her green eyes snapped, and the enlarged pupils reflected the light.

"Niall, saddle up Malachi Mor and Disabod and ride out with me." It was an order, not an invitation. Niall bristled at her tone. Jocelyn was getting bolder about their relationship. Niall didn't care that the whole staff knew she met him every night in his carriage house room, but he didn't want anyone from the big house to know. He wasn't ready to jeopardize his position yet.

"I have work to do, Miss Jocelyn," he said, "but I'll be happy to saddle up Malachi Mor for you."

"I said you're to ride out with me." She spoke in her most authoritarian voice. "You know my uncle does not want me to ride out alone. Now get the horses."

"Of course, Miss Jocelyn," Niall replied, turning back to the stable. His face showed nothing, but inside he seethed with resentment. He hated to be ordered about by a mere woman, and Jocelyn knew it. He ignored the snickers of amusement from the stable boys, but he mentally noted which ones he heard. He would keep them late at their duties tonight.

Niall led the two geldings out into the yard and gave Jocelyn a lift to her mount. She took off at a trot. Niall quickly mounted and followed her, leaving a respectable distance between them until they topped the rolling hill toward the river.

They didn't speak until they dismounted and were leaning against the boulders overlooking the pool where they had met. "Did you have to speak to me in that irritating manner in front of the stable crew, Jocelyn?" Niall asked before they had hardly regained their breath.

"Oh Niall, don't be so touchy. Why do you care what a bunch of stable boys think? Besides I've got troubles of my own this morning."

Niall saw the smoldering eyes cloud as though there were flaws in the jewels. *What a beauty she is*, he thought. "What's happened, love?" he asked.

"It's Uncle Ashton," she said with a pout. "He says I can't go to the Kilarney Horse Show without a chaperone, a female chaperone." Jocelyn emphasized her words with her swinging whip. "Aunt Edith is still ailing, and the doctor says she will be confined to her bed for another three months at least. I just know Uncle is going to insist on that hateful Miss Edmonton accompanying me." She plunked her beautiful bottom onto the grassy knoll. "I won't be able to get out of her sight. We wouldn't have any fun at all, Niall, and you know how I've been looking forward to the show."

"There must be some way to keep that old battleaxe at home," Niall sympathized. "Can't you come up with a better suggestion—someone we can trust . . .?"

"I just don't know anybody around here. If there were time I could have someone come over from London, but the show is only weeks away."

"Surely you've met someone here who'd be suitable . . . someone younger . . ."

"Papa has been after me for months to get a companion, someone my own age. He has always felt I'd be more content if I had another girl with whom I could share things. He'd allow me more freedom to come and go if I had someone like that, but I've stalled. The idea of having someone underfoot all the time, knowing my every move, never appealed to me. Now I wish I had found someone."

Jocelyn pursed her full lips in the sulky way that Niall loved. "Don't you know someone we could get, Niall . . . some Irish girl maybe? She could be a combination maid and companion . . . someone my own age maybe. You must know someone, Niall, but not one of your girlfriends. I wouldn't like that."

Niall thought of Kate. *Would it work,* he wondered. *Lord knows Kate needs to get out of there.* "Hmm . . ." he murmured, glancing at Jocelyn with a teasing look. "I just might know of someone who would be suitable. What do I get for bringing her to you?" He flashed his famous smile.

"Oh Niall, love, whatever you want. I knew you'd come up with something." She reached out and hugged him tightly, planting a quick kiss on his waiting lips. "Tell me. Tell me. Who is she, and how soon can we get her here?"

"Now don't get your hopes up. I'm not sure this will be all right with her, and I'd have to go to Kinsale to get her."

"That can be arranged, Niall. Tell me who she is and what she looks like. I want to know all about her."

"Well, she's sixteen, and a real Irish beauty. She's my . . . my cousin. She will have to be trained to do whatever you need done. She has never been around much. God, Jocelyn, you'll probably shock her to death, she's *that* innocent."

"Wonderful! I like her already. I'd rather have someone I can teach to do things my way . . . and she's just young enough that she won't order me around."

"She does have a mind of her own though," Niall interjected. "I'm sure she'll let you know when she doesn't approve of something you're doing . . . like sneaking around at night to make love to me in the carriage house."

"She sounds wonderful! When can you go to get her? I'll write to Papa today and tell him I'm taking his advice and getting a companion. I'll tell him how lonesome I've been. He'll love it."

"I could leave tomorrow," Niall said. "Do you think I could use a carriage? And Jocelyn, she's very poor. You might want to send some kind of outfit for her to wear so she'll make a better first impression on your uncle."

"Of course, Niall. I have lots of them. You do have wonderful ideas. I never would have thought of that. Do you think she could wear one of my outfits? What size is she?"

Niall looked at Jocelyn, trying to compare her to Kate. "She's a bit shorter than you, I think, but that should be no problem, and she may be a bit smaller in the . . . in the . . ." Niall gestured with his hands, then reconsidered and placed them on her breasts. "Yes, a bit smaller, I'd guess."

"You're terrible, Niall," Jocelyn laughed, but she did not push his hands away.

"It'll take me a couple of days, maybe three. She'll need a bit of time to decide."

"I'll speak to my uncle today about the carriage. Oh, Niall, I just know this will work out. We'll be able to enjoy the Kilarney Show after all." She threw her arms around his neck and gave him a long passionate kiss.

Reluctantly Niall removed her arms. "I've got to get back, especially if I'm going to be gone for a few days."

"I'll see you tonight then, Niall, at the usual time?"

"I'll be waiting."

They rode back to the stable, Niall keeping the required respectable distance behind.

CHAPTER 19

NIALL'S RETURN TO his home village was not quite in the grand style he had hoped, but for his childhood friends in his old neighborhood, it was quite grand enough. The carriage that had been provided for him to escort Miss Jocelyn's new companion to Kenmare Castle was not exactly a carriage but a one-horse buggy with a thinly covered leather seat and a black canopy to keep off the sun or the rain.

Niall stopped in the town of Kenmare and spent some of his hoarded savings on a fine wool suit of clothes and a wonderful bowler hat similar to one he had seen Lord Kenmare wearing as he rode off to Dublin one day. He might not be grand, but he would be in style.

Niall held his head high and his eyes straight ahead as he drove the rig through Kinsale, but he kept a careful lookout from the corner of his eye for everyone he had known in the village. *Let them hail me first,* he thought. *Twill do them no harm to have a moment or two to be surprised and to admire my fine fortune before I speak to them.* And indeed they were surprised; in fact, it was in total astonishment that they recognized their fellow parishioner and marveled at his wondrous good luck. Niall O'Dwyer was the last person they expected to see riding in style down the high road.

At the family cottage on the peninsula, there was no less shock and surprise. They all talked at once, hugging and kissing him and admiring the fine rig he was driving. Niall gloried in it all, especially the look of admiration in Maire's eyes.

"Tis surely a fairy tale, Niall," exclaimed Kate. "Wherever did you get such grand clothes and such a fine rig?"

"Tell us the whole story, Niall," Declan begged. "Don't leave out a word. You must have hit on a gold mine, and I'll just bet there's a beautiful woman involved too."

"Well now, Declan lad, I must admit that Miss Jocelyn Winters does have a bit of an eye for me, but let's go inside and have a cup of tea, and I'll tell you why I've come." Niall reached into the buggy and withdrew the purchases he had made in Bandon. *What a fine feeling it is to be able to give gifts*, he thought. It was a completely new idea to him.

When his family was gathered round the table, Niall handed Mam the small box of tea he had bought for her. There was a bag of sweets for Gran to suck on, two colorful scarves, one for Kate and one for Maire, a pocket knife for Declan, and a jug of whiskey for Donal. "Now did I forget anyone?" He looked around the table, then back into his bundle. "Oh yes, a fine new kettle for Mam to boil the tea." He paused, reaching into his bag again. "And a grand bodice of pork for our supper."

"Pork!" exclaimed Kate. "Oh Mam, this is truly a miracle! We haven't had any meat since I can remember! You're a truly thoughtful brother, Niall." They all murmured in agreement.

Niall basked in the attention while Mam put the kettle on to boil and Gran set the pork in a large black pot with some seasonings and hung it over the hearth to slow cook until supper.

Niall sat back and let the satisfied feeling glow inside. How good it was to come home with gifts and with money in his pocket. His resolve to succeed grew stronger. He was never going to live in this miserable village and its poverty again. He would do whatever he had to do to get money. Money was the answer to everything.

He looked around the table at his family. He loved every one of them, but leaving them was a price he had to pay. In a few short months, Declan had grown two inches, and Kate had become even more glorious. What a match she would be for Jocelyn's blonde beauty.

Gran has failed though, Niall thought. *She leans heavily on her stick and can hardly get around. Mam too looks older.* She watched him with a kind of hopelessness in her eyes. *She must miss Da and Liam too, and me as well. The past six months has been terrible for her.*

Donal too appeared to have aged. He wore a perpetual frown, deepening the lines already imbedded in his forehead. It was difficult to tell what Donal was thinking. He kept a pipe clenched in his teeth, preventing one from reading his feelings. You had to judge from the eyes. Niall guessed that Donal didn't wholly approve of him and his gifts. Donal never believed anything came easy.

Niall let his eyes drift to Maire. After that first glance of admiration when he alighted from the rig, she had kept her eyes lowered. She was as beautiful as ever. Her small figure was now obviously filled out. She must be about seven months pregnant, he thought, and it gave her a new kind of beauty. She glowed with health, except for the eyes, that is. The dark eyes verged on violet and held a disturbing disquiet, a brooding even. Niall guessed she was still keeping Donal from her bed. *Why was he putting up with it? No wonder they both looked stricken!*

Niall told his story in his own good time, elaborating where he thought it would make a better tale. He described the castle and the surrounding countryside and the magnificent horses. He talked a lot about the horses and the upcoming show at Kilarney, but he went light on Jocelyn and the role she played, making it sound as though he was just one of the hired hands she had been kind to. Donal raised his eyebrows as Niall described her, and Mam had a bit of a skeptical look. They knew Niall too well to believe it was a totally innocent relationship. He didn't mention he had taken his mother's maiden name of DeCourcey.

They emptied the teapot after adding water twice. Still they sat around asking questions and exclaiming over his good fortune. Niall sat back at last. He looked around at their faces. "Now," he said, pausing briefly for effect, "I've saved the best news for last."

They looked at him in anticipation. "Miss Jocelyn needs a lady companion, and when I learned she would consider an Irish lass, I suggested our Kate." He paused to read their expressions. "I hope to take Kate back with me," he added.

He heard Kate's gasp of pleasure before he saw her face. It held pure light, as though a candle glowed from within. *She does want to get out of here,* Niall thought. *Thank God I've done the right thing.*

Kate ran to Mam's side and dropped to her knees. "Oh please, Mam, can I go?" You could almost hear her hold her breath for the answer.

Mam put her hand under Kate's chin, raising her head so their eyes met. "Is this what you want, Kate? To be a grand lady's maid?"

"It's not just a maid, Mam," Niall interrupted. "It's more like a companion. And she'll teach Kate whatever she has to know. Jocelyn says she prefers someone who doesn't know things so she can train her right."

"I could learn, Mam. I know I could," Kate implored.

"I've no doubt you could learn whatever they want to teach you. You've always been a bright girl. But life would be entirely different, Kate, nothing like you've ever known."

"I know, Mam, but what is there here for me? There is no hope of a future in this village. There, at least, would be a chance for something better."

"I'd take care of her, Mam," Niall interrupted once more. "You know I'd not let anything happen to her."

"Yes yes, I know you'd try, but young girls are exposed to situations you'd not be able to control. It would be very difficult, and it's such a long way from home." She looked back at her daughter. "But you're right, Kate. There's nothing for you here, and I see nothing but worse times ahead. If this is what you want, then go with my blessing."

Kate hugged her mother tightly. "Oh thank you, Mam. Thank you. I won't let you down. I'll be fine, you'll see."

Niall jumped up from the bench. "I almost forgot. I have another package in the buggy." He rushed out the door and returned with a large wrapped bundle, which he handed to Kate. "It's for you Kate, from Jocelyn." He placed the box in Kate's extended arms. "It's an outfit for you to wear on the trip. She said twas for you to keep whether you came or not. It may not fit perfectly, but you can make adjustments however is necessary, she said."

Kate opened the package slowly. In the layers of tissue paper lay a garment like she had never seen before. Her fingers suspended above the deep blue color in awe. A row of black buttons traveled down the front of the bodice, and the small stand-up collar had a pert black bow. Slowly she withdrew the wonderful garment from the wrappings and shook out its length, the look of wonder still on her face. The sleeves held a puff at the shoulders and hung straight to a folded cuff at the wrist. The skirt billowed out in gathers from the waist, and a band of black ribbon circled the hem. The material was of the finest woven wool.

Kate held the dress against her and twirled about the room. "Oh, it's wonderful! It's wonderful! I can't wait to try it on!"

"Look, Kate, here in the box," Maire exclaimed. "There's a bonnet too." She lifted a shaped hat of the same material. A curved brim flared out in front and a fluted feather rose from one side. It sported two long black satin ribbons to tie under the chin. Maire held the unheard of delicacy out and placed it on Kate's head. "How perfect!" she exclaimed, tying the bow neatly. "You look beautiful, Kate."

She turned and shooed the men out of the cottage. "Now you're not to come in until we call," she said, "and then we'll show you our new Kate, a real lady." She closed the door behind them.

"Come on, Mam," Kate called. "Help me get into this. I haven't the foggiest notion of how to put it on."

The three of them, with giggles and exclamations, disappeared behind the curtain. Gran sat by the fire listening to their excitement. When they emerged, she saw a vision of herself at sixteen, her mass of black curls tucked up under a wine-colored bonnet. The tears flowed unchecked down her wrinkled cheeks. *Life has flown too fast. And here in front of me is my granddaughter, looking for all the world like myself at that age, and about to take off on an adventure all her own.* She sat in her own reverie while the men came in and admired young Kate in her new finery.

Early the next morning, Kate and Niall climbed into the black buggy, the fine horse straining at the bit. The tearful goodbyes had been said. Neither looked back as they drove down the low road toward the bridge. Kate was sorry the village was deserted, but she realized that the only people who really mattered in her life were those who had gathered in the small cottage huddled under the hill by King James's Fort. She brushed away a tear.

Niall patted her hand. "Don't look back, Kate. There's only one direction to be looking now. The future's surely to be bright, now we're on our way."

"You're right, Niall, you're right, and I'm after enjoying every minute of it." She gave her brother a wide smile.

Niall let out a war whoop. "That's my girl!" he shouted, giving the horse a slap of the reins.

CHAPTER 20

KATE SAT ON the edge of a fragile chair in the drawing room of Kenmare Castle staring at an ancient portrait of a Kenmare ancestor hanging over the enormous fireplace. She clasped her hands in her lap to keep them from trembling.

Surely the trip Niall had brought her on would be for naught. She would never be able to function in such a setting. Why, this one room was larger than any building she had ever been in. Even the church in Kinsale was smaller than this, and that was the largest building she had seen except for Squire Atkins's mansion.

Huge beyond belief and strangely unattractive, the room was exactly square and had a ceiling at least twelve feet high. The tall narrow windows were covered with heavy drapery, leaving a gloom over the uncomfortable furnishings. *Everything looked too stiff*, Kate thought, *too forbidding*. It held not an inkling of welcome. She swallowed nervously and crossed herself as she heard the footsteps on the polished floor of the entrance hall.

Kate hurriedly rose to her feet as the heavy gleaming door swung open. She felt her hopes rise as she saw the beautiful young woman gliding into the room. *Why, she's not much older than I am*, Kate thought. *And she's beautiful, not in the way of Irish women, but in a delicate, unearthly way.*

Jocelyn came directly to Kate stretching out her arms and taking both of Kate's hands. "You must be Kate O'Dwyer! What a fantastic creature you are! I'm never seen a more glorious Irish woman. Niall was right, you are a real beauty! I'm so glad you're here, Kate. Let's sit over here on the settee where I can look at you."

Jocelyn pulled Kate along and settled the frightened girl beside her. "That outfit looks wonderful on you. The color was not quite right for me, so I never wore it. I'm so glad I thought to send it to you. Such a lovely garment should be worn, don't you think?"

"Oh yes, the dress is lovely. Thank you for sending it." Kate's rich contralto voice contrasted with Jocelyn's lilting soprano.

They sized each other up silently, and then Jocelyn took Kate's hands again. "Do you think we can be friends, Kate? I really need a friend and a companion more than a personal maid. Did Niall make that clear?"

"Are you sure I'll do, Miss Jocelyn? I'm afraid I don't know much about your kind of life." Kate glanced about the room uneasily.

"Of course you'll do fine, Kate. You just be yourself. There's nothing to worry about. And you're to call me Jocelyn, not Miss Jocelyn. We're friends, remember?"

Kate smiled with relief. "Oh, I hope we will be, Miss . . . I mean . . . Jocelyn. I would so like that, and you will please tell me when I do something wrong? I want to learn to be a lady like you."

"Oh, Kate, you're delightful!" Jocelyn jumped up and twirled about the room. "This is going to be such fun! Niall was a darling to think of fetching you."

Kate felt a sudden strange disquiet at the use of the familiar term describing her brother. "It was Niall's idea to have me come here?" she asked.

"Oh yes. He knew my father had suggested I get someone for a companion, and I simply couldn't find anyone I wanted. He told me about you, and it sounded a perfect solution." Jocelyn threw Kate a skeptical look. "Does it upset you that Niall and I have become such friends?"

"No no," Kate said hesitantly. "I know Niall makes friends easily. It's just that . . . well, him working in the stables and all . . . I wouldn't have thought you would even have talked to him."

"Oh, Kate, are you really such an old stuffy? Come on now, we're going to be friends. I'm sure we have a lot to learn about each other, but you must be exhausted after your long journey. Let's go up to your room. Don't bother with your bag. I'll have someone bring it up to you later."

Kate looked around the room she had been assigned. She could not believe it was to be hers alone. Never had she seen anything so heavenly. It was as if she had stepped into a dream. The white canopied bed would have held six people. A ruffled coverlet, decorated in tiny rosebuds and delicate trails of green ivy, gave it the appearance of an arbor. The flowers looked so real she wanted to touch them.

Kate had never slept in a real bed, let alone one so luxurious. She sat on its soft mattress in amazement, then jumped up, thinking that she shouldn't be sitting there. She giggled at herself. *This is my room! My own room! If I want to sit on the bed, I can do so!*

Kate sat down again and looked around. The floor was covered with an intricately designed rug whose flowers exactly matched those in the drapes and the bed covering. The wardrobe and chest of drawers were of a heavy rose-hued wood. Its beauty took Kate's breath away. Her wildest fantasies had never held such luxury. She had not known it existed.

Kate went to the windows and pulled back the drapes. The rolling green lawns flowed to the edge of the wood, and beyond she could see the Kenmare River bubbling over the rapids. The stables were spread out to the left, and she could just make out the carriage house where Niall had his room. She would have to point out her window to him. *Perhaps we can work out a signal for when we want to see each other.*

A soft knock sounded on her door. She turned, startled. "Who is it?" she called.

"It's Cluny, miss. I'm the upstairs maid. I've come to introduce meself."

"Of course," Kate answered, reaching up to smooth her hair. "Please come in."

Cluny was an Irishwoman of about forty, and she carried two buckets of steaming hot water. She wore a gray dress with a tiny white apron with a ridiculous white cap perched on her graying head. She made an awkward curtsy. "I'm Cluny, miss. I'm to see to whatever ye needs. Miss Jocelyn says to show ye where yer things are and to prepare yer bath so's ye can get dressed fer dinner."

"That's very kind, Cluny, but I don't need a maid. I'm to be working here the same as you. No one needs to wait on me."

"I don't know nothin' 'bout that, miss. I just do what I'm told, and Miss Jocelyn said to fix yer bath so I best do it."

Kate dismissed the maid after she had filled the curious brass tub in the dressing room. She was not about to have some strange woman watching her take a bath. She lay in the luxurious hot water. The long trip had tired her more than she realized. She soaped her long slim body with the fragrant, perfumed soap. She would never get enough of the wonderful scent.

The only soap she had ever seen was the heavy bar of strong yellow soap Mam used to scrub the laundry. *How wonderful to know such soap exists, let alone to use it on my body! How good it feels! How soft and smooth!* Kate slid down and let the water cover her dark hair. She rubbed the lovely soap through the heavy strands, making a sudsy lather. She would remember forever the heavenly fragrance that reminded her of an armful of wildflowers on a June day.

Kate dried her hair using the silver-backed brush from the dresser. How easily it went through her tangled curls! The sheer luxury brought tears to her eyes. *How silly of me to cry*, she thought. She laid down the brush and danced around the room. The full-length mirror caught her reflection and she stopped, amazed. She had never seen her whole reflection before. *Why, I'm beautiful*, she thought. *I'm really beautiful!* As her eyes traveled over her naked body, she remembered Father McBride's words. "Cover yourself, Kate. Cover yourself. It is your sin if you tempt men."

Quickly, Kate turned from the mirror and picked up the clothing that had been laid out for her. She put on the soft linen underclothing without feeling the delicate fabric. Slipping into the pale green gown, she buttoned its faintly tinted row of buttons and shook out the full skirt. Only then did she return to the mirror. She saw only the rich color and the design of the gown, not the soft curving body. The person in the mirror had nothing to do with the Kate O'Dwyer she had been for sixteen years. She shook off all memory of Father McBride and his ominous words.

Kate sat at the dining table and stared nervously at the gleaming silver and glassware. The light from the glistening chandelier with its dozens of candles threw flickering rainbows over the sparkling array. How would she ever be able to eat in such a setting? She thought of the rough wooden table in the dark cottage. Jocelyn reached over and touched her hand. Kate smiled timidly, thankful for her reassurance.

Across the table from Kate sat Lord Kenmare's secretary. He wore silver-rimmed spectacles over his piercing blue eyes. Kate had heard of such things, but this was the first time she had seen them. How strange they looked hooked over his ears like that. She had the urge to try them on for herself.

Ian Bentley was perhaps thirty years old and had thin blond hair and a wedge-shaped beard. Kate felt he disapproved of her at first sight. She gave a worried sigh and looked down to the other end of the table.

Lord Kenmare paid careful attention as a uniformed maid held out a silver platter piled high with large slices of meat. His long slim almost feminine fingers held two serving utensils; and he moved an immense slice of roast beef from the platter to his plate. Kate watched how he did it. His gold cufflinks caught the light of the candles as he placed the silver forks back on the serving platter. He nodded his large white head to the server and proceeded to cut the meat on his plate. His shaggy mustache moved back and forth as he anticipated his food. Kate thought of the great wooly sheepdog that worked a herd on the hill near Ringrone.

The maid moved on to serve Jocelyn. Kate carefully observed her mistress's movements as dinner went on and followed her every act. What little conversation there was involved the upcoming horse show at Kilarney. Kate ate nervously, marveling at the amount of food served to four people. This one meal would have fed her own family for more than a week. When at last the meal was over, she returned to the safety of her room.

Kate removed the wonderful dress and hung it in the wardrobe where more than a dozen others had been placed for her use. She suddenly felt overwhelmed. Everything had happened too quickly. She paced the unfamiliar room in disbelief.

At last, she lay down between the silky smooth sheets which had been turned back for her. Despite the softness of the bed and the tiredness of her body, sleep would not come.

The house was completely quiet when she slipped from the covers and went to the window to look out into the cool blackness of the night. The light of the half-moon was hidden by thin racing clouds, but Kate knew the figure she saw gliding silently over the lawn between the castle and the carriage house was that of Jocelyn. Kate didn't have to be told the door her employer slipped through led to the room that held her brother's bed.

CHAPTER 21

AFTER WEEKS OF discomfort on the back of the gentle gray mare, Kate now rode contentedly as she followed Jocelyn across the rolling hills surrounding Kenmare Castle. The terrain was not as stark as the coastline of Ringrone Peninsula in County Cork. Large oak and elm trees spread out their branches to shield the rambling pathways, and small tumbling brooks somersaulted their way to the river. Kate knew the unpredictable Kenmare River rushed on to Bantry Bay, but its rocky bed was out of sight of the peaceful estate through which she rode.

How much difference a few short weeks had made in her life. After some hectic days of being lost in its maze of hallways and side rooms, Kate adopted the routine of the household in the magnificent castle. Her quiet grace earned her the approval of Lord Kenmare and a grudging acceptance by his glowering secretary. Occasionally, she felt the disquieting gaze of Ian Bentley following her as though he expected at any minute to discover she was there under false pretenses.

Jocelyn had accepted Kate as a friend from the first moment, and Kate found that although she disapproved of many of the things Jocelyn said and did, she could not help but like her. Kate began to learn how to laugh and enjoy life. Jocelyn's little escapades, like swimming nude in the quiet pool where she had first met Niall, brought a quick delight to Kate, even while they made her afraid of Lord Kenmare's power to dismiss her.

Jocelyn took Kate everywhere and seemed to enjoy her company. "You're exactly what I wanted in a companion," she told Kate. "It's such fun to have someone to share things with . . . and how much more willing Uncle is to let me go off without one of his elderly acquaintances as a chaperone."

Kate recognized she was being used by Jocelyn to get her own way, but she rationalized that it was part of her job to please her. She shouldn't be making judgments of her employer's action, yet she feared she was opening herself up for criticism, especially in the matter of Jocelyn's relationship with Niall.

Jocelyn would suggest a ride into town and before the afternoon went by, there would be Niall waiting in an out-of-the-way spot; and the remainder of the day would be spent in his company. He might show up at the sheltered pool when they were swimming. He could follow at a discreet distance when they went riding, catching up with them after they were out of sight of the castle.

They did nothing wrong on these occasions, but they were so secretive, so deceitful even, that Kate was made uncomfortable. Despite her reserve, she found it was fun too. She enjoyed their happy banter. They were like children let out after a week of rainy weather. They chased each other over the hills and played silly games.

Kate found herself envying the easy relationship between her brother and her employer. She realized they stole quick kisses sometimes when they were aware she was within sight, and they held hands freely. *There was no harm in that*, Kate thought, but all the time she knew Jocelyn was sneaking into Niall's room at night. From her window, Kate often saw her slip through his doorway. She said nothing to either of them, but she sensed they knew she was aware of it.

Kate wasn't in the least surprised by her brother's actions. Niall had been chasing the village lasses for years, and there had been rumors of his stealing into the beds of one or two young widows who could not resist his charms. *No, it's not Niall that shocks me, but Jocelyn's actions do. I expected more of her.*

Kate could not imagine that a proper English lady could act in such a way. *Why would she prefer someone like Niall, a worker in the stables? Why not a gentleman of her own class?* Kate was not sophisticated enough to figure it out. She simply felt an uneasiness about the whole business and was afraid for the time when someone would be hurt. Jocelyn had confided that she had a terrible fall from her horse when she was nine years old and had needed surgery. As a result, she would never be able to have children. Kate was devastated by this news, but Jocelyn waved it off with a toss of her head and said laughingly, "It's allowed me to have a life without worry, and besides, my father now cannot deny me anything." Kate thought she saw a passing sadness in Jocelyn eyes as she quickly changed the subject.

All talk in the castle was of the Kilarney Horse Show. Kenmare Castle was entering six thoroughbreds. All had won various honors in other shows, and everyone at Kenmare Castle had hopes they would do well in this largest of shows in Ireland. The gentry would be coming from the length of Ireland and many from England as well. It was the social event of the year, and excitement built as preparations went forward.

Lord Kenmare had left three days ago. A round of parties and entertainments was scheduled for a week before the actual show began. A less formal atmosphere prevailed in the castle when the master was gone. Jocelyn and Kate bubbled with exciting plans despite the frowning demeanor of Ian Bentley, who had been left behind to escort the two young ladies to Kilarney.

Ian took his duties seriously and hardly let Jocelyn out of his sight. He had even taken to riding out with them each day, and he curtly dismissed Niall whenever he showed up. From her window late at night, Kate watched as Ian paced back and forth on the lawn between the stables and the back entrance to the castle. The nightly trysts had to be abandoned. Obviously, Kate was not the only one who had been observing Jocelyn's midnight prowling.

Jocelyn was furious with Ian but had stopped short of telling him to mind his own business. Kate watched this new turn of events with interest. "You know, Jocelyn," she told her beautiful employer, "I think you'd be wise to make a friend of Ian. I have an idea he would make a terrible enemy."

"What makes you say that, Kate? He doesn't strike me as one who makes much of an impression one way or the other."

On the way to Kilarney, Jocelyn put herself out to be charming to Ian. Niall had been left with the stable crew to escort the horses to the show, and Jocelyn and Kate rode on ahead in the carriage with Ian as chaperone.

The two young ladies both looked stunning in their new outfits especially selected for the trip. Ian, however, looked exactly as he did every other day. His high white collar was tightly buttoned around his neck, and his black suit held the same creases and prim look that it did every morning when he reported to Lord Kenmare. He obviously felt he was on duty this day as well.

Kate mentally took note as Jocelyn proceeded to ensnare Ian's devotion as skillfully as St. Patrick had charmed the snakes out of Ireland. She was watching an expert at work. Before they reached their destination, Ian was offering to run her errands and carry her messages to friends she planned to see in Kilarney. Kate smiled to herself. She sat back to marvel at how she had accepted this trip, a distance of about twenty miles, as an ordinary occurrence. How far she had come in her thinking in a few weeks' time, she who had never been more than two miles from her home in her entire lifetime.

The streets of Kilarney were a bedlam of people and animals. It was all the village fair days Kate had ever seen rolled into one. Bunting floated across the streets, strung from one building to another. Small musical groups sang and danced at every corner, gathering great groups of admirers. Kate saw that it was not just an event for the English gentry, for the Irish had turned out as well. Not only the well-to-do landowners, but the villagers too thronged the streets decked out in their Sunday best.

The festive atmosphere was contagious, and Kate felt her spirits lift as Jocelyn squeezed her hand. "I just know we're going to have a wonderful time. Ian, why don't you just let Kate and me off right here. I'd like to mix with the crowd. We'll join you later at the hotel." She turned her most charming smile on him.

"I'm sorry Miss Jocelyn, but my orders were to deliver you to the hotel. You'll just have to wait for your fun." Ian carefully avoided her eyes. "I'm sure your uncle will understand you want to enjoy yourself, but that's for him to say. For myself, I don't think the streets are any place for young ladies to be unescorted." He cleared his throat and after glancing covertly at Jocelyn to see how she was taking it, turned to look out the window.

"Oh, Ian, you're such an old stuffy. How do you ever manage here in

Ireland? You belong in London with the rest of the old fogies." But she made no further protest, and Kate was relieved that the holiday was not going to begin with an escapade for which she would be responsible. She noted to herself that even Jocelyn's charms were not always successful in getting what she wanted.

A few minutes later, they stopped in front of the Grand Hotel; and indeed, it was grand. Here, the crowd was more restrained, but nonetheless plentiful. Beautiful women paraded up and down the marble steps, their bright parasols sheltering their elegant coiffures from the sun. *The gentlemen are just as beautiful*, Kate thought. *Never have I seen men in such outfits.* They were as colorful as that of the ladies, with tight-fitting trousers and body-shaping coats. She would never forget the sight, she thought, with excitement rising in her.

Jocelyn was out of the carriage almost before Ian could properly hand her down. She flashed her most glorious smile, knowing all heads turned to admire her blonde loveliness. She moved to gracefully take Kate's arm as Ian handed her companion from the carriage. Kate's dark curls tumbled becomingly from beneath her new flowered bonnet. The dramatic contrast of the two young women caused a stir among those assembled on the steps and in the lobby.

Almost immediately the throng moved toward them. Jocelyn smiled into Kate's faintly frightened eyes. "Come, Kate, love, you must meet all my friends." She tucked her hand in the crook of Kate's arm and ushered her toward the door, pausing to nod at acquaintances and to hug and kiss friends. "And this is Kate O'Dwyer," Jocelyn said over and over, and Kate smiled at the bewildering array of faces until her jaws ached. She soon extended her hand automatically as one gentleman after another bent to bestow a light kiss upon it.

At last, they passed through the lobby and were escorted to their rooms. Jocelyn rushed to pore through the messages that had been handed to her by the clerk. "What fun we're going to have, Kate! Isn't it exciting?"

"It's rather confusing to be truthful, Jocelyn, but it is fun. I can hardly wait for the show to begin tomorrow. I just know there will be some beautiful horses."

"Horses! Oh, Kate, you're so naive! Nobody cares about the horses.

They're just an excuse for some parties." She laughed with delight. "And for the betting. I hope you brought some of the wages you've been saving. I know someone we can get to place some bets for us."

"Gambling? Oh, Jocelyn, you wouldn't!" Kate exclaimed.

"Kate! Kate! When are you going to stop being a nice little Catholic Irish girl and grow up? Of course we're going to gamble. What do you think horse shows are for? And on the last day there will be some races. Everyone will be betting on them—that is, everyone who has anything left after the show."

"Oh, I don't know, Jocelyn. I did bring some money to buy a few things, but gambling . . . I don't know."

"Of course you do, silly. You can double or triple your little hoard of money all at once. I'm certainly going to, and I know that Niall plans to. Malachi Mor is a sure winner in his class, and Niall will have the word on what's good from the stables. He promised to let me know who to put my money on."

"Well," Kate hesitated, "maybe I could risk a wee bit, but only if it's a sure thing."

"Spoken like a true gambler, Kate." Jocelyn grabbed Kate's hands and danced her around the room. "We have only two hours to get ready for the dinner and the ball tonight. Let's get out of these weary clothes and into a hot bath."

As if summoned, Cluny and Avis appeared at the door with their luggage, followed by two hotel clerks wheeling a large container of hot water.

CHAPTER 22

NIALL STROKED THE splendid russet hide of Malachi Mor. He was a perfect specimen of horseflesh, and Niall had placed all his savings on him in the event for three-year-old geldings. No other horse could touch him. Niall had seen them all, and this was a sure thing. It was fortunate that the event came early in the three-day show. His winnings would give him more to invest in the second and third day's proceedings. He had already picked his winners. They were not all from the Kenmare stables, but he felt no sense of loyalty where his earnings were concerned.

He stepped back from the magnificent beast and brushed his own clothing free of hair and dust. The fawn colored trousers and hunter green coat had been selected for the Kenmare Castle crew. Niall had been selected to lead Malachi Mor out on parade, and he wanted to look just right. He brushed his own russet hair, aware that its color was a perfect match to that of Malachi Mor's mane. The effect would not be missed by the admiring ladies of the crowd, and Niall intended to make the most of it.

The parade committee stood near the entrance to the paddock where Niall lined up with the others for the grand entrance. He listened to the heated discussion going on among the committee members. "I tell you he will have to appear anyway," a long-faced matron said emphatically. "I don't care how drunk he is. He must sing in the opening ceremony."

"The man is not capable of singing except in a drunken babble. He can't even stand." Niall recognized the voice of the ringmaster who would be announcing the day's proceedings. "I will not have the entire show ruined by an inebriated singer in the opening number."

"But this has been planned for months. He's the most popular song-ster in Dublin. He must sing!" the woman implored.

"You should have foreseen this," the ringmaster retorted. "He's no-torious for his bouts with the bottle. You should have had someone on guard against just this sort of thing occurring. He cannot go on, and that is final."

"But what are we going to do?" she wailed. "We must have someone sing. There must be someone we can call on."

"My dear Lady Bassington, the show is about to start. There is no time to get a substitute." The ringmaster pounded his crop against his white trousers.

Niall felt his heartbeat quicken. A plan leaped full-blown into his head. Did he dare? Was this his opportunity? He stepped forward. "Begging your pardon, my lady," he said, facing the two ruffled com-mittee members. "If you would permit it, I do a bit of singing." The two stared at him with open mouths. Niall chose to ignore the looks and continued. "I have a pure Irish tenor, and while I've not appeared on the Dublin stage, I have done some public singing." He hoped they would not ask where. They would hardly consider the local pubs as appearances.

The two dignitaries looked at each other and back at Niall. They each grabbed him by an elbow and ushered him into a makeshift office, which had been prepared for the committee. The drunken singer slumped in a chair by the door.

Niall's clear tenor tones soon drifted over the stables. They were cut off after a few bars. "You're wonderful, wonderful!" exclaimed Lady Bassington. "Come along. If you can manage 'God Save the King' and 'The Colleen Bawn,' you're on."

Niall glanced down at his uniform. "But . . . my clothes . . . ," he spluttered.

"They're fine, my boy, just fine. In fact, it's very much in keeping that you're in the colors of one of the stables, very much in keeping. Come along now."

Niall let himself be led out, and he fell into place behind the commit-tee. He nodded to his stablemate to take his place by Malachi Mor. The horns were sounded, and they led the parade of horses into the circle of fences, flanked by thousands of spectators. Niall felt his chest swelling. This was what he had been dreaming of. He was good, and he knew it.

"And now, ladies and gentlemen," the ringmaster called out, "a last-minute change in our program. Our anthem will be sung by that rising young Irish tenor representing the Kenmare Stables, Niall DeCourcey!"

The audience shifted their attention, and a small murmuring started before they scrambled to their feet. Niall stepped forward. He removed his two-colored cap, his russet hair a burnished bronze in the sun. He waited a brief moment before beginning to sing.

The clear tones rang out over the gathered crowd. The shuffling and murmuring ceased. A hushed expectancy fell as they turned to listen. The familiar song became a thing of beauty, full of pride and emotion.

There was not a sound as the last note hung undisturbed on the air, and the applause began, thundering up from the crowd like a covey of partridges startled from their cover. It gathered strength and exploded up into the air. An overwhelming thrill carried Niall aloft. The sound became addictive. He wanted it never to stop, knowing he would never have enough of it. He had found his calling.

Before the applause died away, Niall began to sing "The Colleen Bawn," the ancient Irish song of the long-ago nation. He sang in his own language and with all his newfound emotion. There was not a dry Irish eye within hearing, nor many an English one either.

Niall turned gracefully and left the stage while applause still echoed. He went to his place beside Malachi Mor and stood beside the magnificent animal. He placed his hand on the horse's shoulder and patted him gently, more to calm his own excitement than that of the animal's. Every eye in the audience followed him.

Niall was counting his winnings later that afternoon when he felt a hand on his arm. "Excuse me, Mr. DeCourcey. I wonder if I might have a word with you."

Niall turned to face the speaker. He was startled at the beauty of the striking woman attired in an elegant frock of midnight blue. Plumes of ostrich feathers surrounded the low neckline and fell over one shoulder. She was as tall as he and beautifully shaped. Her frock clung to every graceful line and curve. Her copper-colored hair was only partially covered by a matching blue hat that sported more feathers. They made a flowing frame for her perfectly formed oval face. She was in her late thirties, perhaps even more, but all the more beautiful for the added years.

Niall stuffed his winnings into his pocket. "Of course, my lady," he said slowly, without a trace of excitement showing. He reached for her hand and kissed it lightly.

She withdrew the white hand slowly, holding his eyes. "Well well, a gentleman as well as a songster . . . a fascinating combination." She took Niall's proffered arm, and they moved away from the crowds around the betting area.

"My name is Roxanne O'Flaherty, and I have a proposition for you, Niall DeCourcey," the elegant woman said as they strolled toward the viewing stands.

Niall looked into deep green eyes. "This sounds more interesting by the minute," he said.

She gave a throaty little laugh. "Why do I get the feeling you're a bit of a rogue?" she asked.

Niall laughed in turn. "Perhaps it's wishful thinking," he said with impertinence. "Or perhaps it's just that we're both Irish."

Her laugh came again, and Niall felt it trickle a scale up his spine. She was the most gorgeous creature he had ever seen. She placed a small white card in his hand. "My husband and I own a theatrical company in America," she said quietly, looking into his eyes.

"Now how did I have an idea that you weren't an Irish peasant," Niall interrupted.

"We'd like to talk to you about coming to New York," she continued as though he had not spoken. "If any of this interests you, come to this address tomorrow at two."

He took her offered hand and pressed it to his lips once more. This time he lingered, and she made no move to withdraw. "A great deal of this interests me," he said. "Tomorrow at two. I'll be there." She smiled softly, the green eyes filled with possibilities. She removed her hand and melted into the crowd.

"Niall, Niall! Over here!" Jocelyn's voice called from the crowd in the stands. Kate rushed ahead of her. "Oh, Niall, you were grand this morning. I always knew you could sing, but never have you sung like that."

"It was so thrilling," Jocelyn echoed, "it brought tears to my eyes."

"Well, we can't have such lovely eyes crying now, can we?" he asked, tucking a hand under each of his elbows. "What do you say we have some lunch?" He led them through the spectators now filing out of the area.

Nearly everyone they met nodded and smiled, and it was Niall they were singling out, rather than the young women he escorted. They passed Roxanne O'Flaherty as she stood talking to a pudgy man of about forty, who came just to her shoulders. Niall bowed and tipped his cap, still feeling the excitement she had roused in him. She nodded her head, giving him a small smile.

"Who is that striking woman?" Kate asked.

"Oh, she's just someone who introduced herself to me after she heard me sing," Niall responded casually. *No sense in saying anything further until I find out what it is all about*, he thought.

"I didn't notice," Jocelyn replied tossing her head, "but she must be at least thirty." Niall laughed. An enormous awning had been set up near the show-grounds, and Niall led his companions to a small round table where they ordered lunch. All during the meal, strangers stopped by to compliment him on his moving renditions at the opening ceremonies. Niall took in the adoration as he took in his food, nurturing his pride, his confidence, his very soul, along with his body. He was recognized by everyone, and he gloried in the admiring glances of the women of all ages. He thought of the woman from America and her theatrical company. *Oh, God*, he prayed, *let this be the chance I need*.

"You really should not take all this attention to heart, Niall. It'll be over in a few days, and you'll be back in the stables." Jocelyn's voice interrupted his thoughts. He looked at her beautiful face and read the jealousy there. *You'd like that, wouldn't you, my love*, he thought, *then there would be just you and me*, but *I'm not going back, not even for you*. He smiled their own secret smile at her. "Even Kenmare Castle has its little rewards," he said, watching her face soften with love.

"Excuse me, but . . ." A tall stranger in immaculate English garb approached their table. Jocelyn flew out of her seat. "Edward! What are you doing in Ireland?" She flung herself into his arms.

They hugged each other with warmth, and Jocelyn planted a forceful kiss on his perfectly shaped mouth. Niall turned to Kate with questioning eyes, trying to read the expression on her face. *Why, Kate knows this man*, he thought. *Where did she have an opportunity to meet an English gentleman?*

"Oh, Edward, darling, you must meet my friends," Jocelyn gushed. "This lovely young woman is my friend and companion, Kate O'Dwyer. Kate, this is my cousin, Edward Graham." Edward took Kate's hand and bowed over it.

Niall watched with interest. There had not been a sign of recognition in Edward's face as he looked at Kate, only open admiration as he said, "So you're the companion I've heard about. What a beauty you are." He turned back to Jocelyn. "Sometimes you surprise me, cousin."

Jocelyn ignored the remark. She turned to Niall. "And this is Kate's cousin, Niall DeCourcey."

Niall extended his hand, and Edward took it without enthusiasm. "Well well, the singer from the Kenmare Stables. What an interesting turn of events." Niall could not read the blue eyes that scrutinized him.

"What on earth are you doing in Ireland, Edward?" Jocelyn asked as they all sat down.

"I was sent to fetch you, luv," Edward replied in his clipped English accent. "It seems you have been a naughty girl." He watched her expression with amusement.

"Whatever do you mean?" Jocelyn's voice took on a curt note that Niall knew only too well.

"Your father received a rather intriguing note about your amusing nocturnal escapades from Lord Kenmare's secretary. Your father thought it best to fetch you immediately back to London." Niall saw that Edward did not miss the quick look of alarm that Kate threw to him.

"Ian Berkley wrote to my father?" Jocelyn half-rose from her chair. "How dare he!"

"Hush, hush, my dear cousin. We wouldn't want the whole county to know of your little indiscretions now, would we?"

"Ian Berkley is a jealous prig. He'd say anything!" Jocelyn spluttered.

"I've no doubt he is, my sweet Jocelyn, but he thought it his duty to inform your father nonetheless, rather than disturb Lord Kenmare with such distressing news."

"Then Father is in London? When did he get back? Whatever did he say? Oh god, he'll never let me out of his sight again!" Jocelyn wailed.

Edward laughed. Niall scraped back his chair. "If you'll excuse me, I have to get back to the show-grounds. I'm sure you'd prefer to discuss this alone."

"Of course, Niall," Jocelyn interspersed quickly. "This has nothing to do with you. You may go."

Niall watched the amused look on Edward's face as his eyes darted from Jocelyn to Niall.

"I'd like to get back to the show as well," Kate said, rising from her chair.

Edward jumped instantly to his feet. He took Kate's hand and touched it to his lips. Kate trembled and withdrew it quickly. Edward studied her face. "Have we met before?" he asked with a puzzled expression. "Your eyes are familiar and that lovely oval face. I don't know how I could have forgotten."

Kate turned away quickly. "I don't believe there would have been any occasion where we could have met, Mr. Graham," she said with a slight tremor. "Come, Niall, let's go. I'm sure Jocelyn has much to talk of with her cousin." She took her brother's arm.

Niall overheard Edward's voice as they moved away. "I'm sure I've seen her before. Wherever did you find her, Jocelyn?" he asked. Niall patted Kate's cold hand and led her out of hearing. He recalled Father McBride's displeasure with Kate on the day of Da's wake. He knew now where she had met the Englishman.

"There, there, luv, don't shake so," he said to his sister. "No one would ever connect the lady you are today with the little peasant girl who fled to the old fort." Kate's huge black eyes met his in panic, but she said nothing as they walked toward the show-grounds.

CHAPTER 23

IT WAS EXACTLY two o'clock the next afternoon when Niall knocked at the door of Suite 22 in the Grand Hotel. He straightened his tie nervously and smoothed the tight breeches over his muscled thighs. How thankful he was he had bought this stylish outfit when he went to pick up Kate. He might have lost all his money gambling and had nothing to wear today. He knocked again on the heavy door.

The small stocky man Niall had seen with Roxanne the day before opened the door. His bald head gleamed from the sunlight that streamed through the opened windows. A fat brown cigar hung from the corner of his mouth, which he quickly withdrew with one hand, extending the other to his caller.

"So ye decided to accept our little invitation, did ye, Mr. DeCourcey? That's jest grand. Yer welcome to join us. Come in." He led the way into the suite. "Roxanne, darling, our visitor is here!" he called.

Niall quickly took in the surroundings. A deep cushioned settee and several comfortable armchairs dominated the room. A slight breeze blew the draperies in from the windows. Niall noted several crystal lamps spaced around the room and a Waterford glass decanter and glasses placed on an oak table. His host motioned to a chair, and Niall seated himself.

"Let's have a wee one while Roxanne gets herself ready," the little round-faced man said. His eyes glistened as he poured the clear amber liquid into the glasses. "I'm Sean O'Flaherty, in case you didn't know. Roxanne and I have lived in America for eight years now. Interesting place, America. Plenty of opportunity over there." He handed a glass to Niall and sat down opposite him. "Fer a smart lad, that is," he added.

Niall waited for his host to continue. "Roxanne is a very attractive woman. I'm a very lucky man, wouldn't ye say, lad?"

"I would indeed, sir," Niall said.

"Let's drink to things staying that way, my sweet tenor, if you get my meaning." He held his glass out toward Niall.

"I do indeed get your meaning," Niall said, raising his own glass, "and I'll be happy to drink to that." The two men drank deeply.

Roxanne appeared in the doorway of the adjoining bedroom. She was an undreamed-of fantasy in a gown of white. The skirt was tiered with deep ruffles, and the bodice was cut to show her magnificent cleavage. Tiny sprigs of brilliantly colored rosebuds spread themselves over the soft floating material, and a matching live rose nestled in her red-gold hair. She paused to give them the best view. The light from the window outlined her slim figure beneath the dress.

Niall caught his breath. He tore his eyes away and glanced at his host. Sean O'Flaherty raised his glass once more, his eyes meeting Niall's. The message was as clear as the sound of the starting bugle that came through the window announcing the afternoon's events.

Roxanne took in Niall's entire length with one sweeping glance before moving to her husband's side. "Now then, darling," she said as she sat next to Sean, "this is the young man I was telling you about. He has the voice of an angel . . . a wonderful emotional voice that could make men cry and women want to die of longing."

Sean O'Flaherty looked briefly at his wife, got up from his chair, and paced the room. He stopped in front of Niall. "Sing something," he said.

"What do you want to hear?" Niall asked.

"How the hell do I know? Sing anything you want. If you're as good as she says, I'll know it, even if you sing 'Yankee Doodle.'"

Niall had never heard of 'Yankee Doodle.' He chose a ballad, a haunting sentimental ballad of lost love. He moved to the window where he knew the light would pick up the highlights of color in his hair and give his face a glow. He sang softly at first then increased the volume. The clear, mellow tones filled the room and swept from the window. The words cried out with longing and love. Reaching the high notes with emotion to match, he ended with a cry in his throat to add the richness of unfulfilled desire.

Silence hung in the air when he stopped. Niall bowed low and stood quietly awaiting the verdict. He dared not raise his eyes.

"I'll be good god damned!" Sean O'Flaherty exclaimed. "'Tis the voice of an angel!" Roxanne flew to Niall and flung her arms about his neck. "You were wonderful, sweetie, just wonderful. I knew you would be."

Sean O'Flaherty lit a fresh cigar, meeting Niall's desperate eyes over his wife's head. "Come, come, my dear," he said calmly between puffs on his cigar, "let's not fluster the lad." He sat down in his chair. "Now, Niall DeCourcey, how soon can you be in New York?"

"You mean it?" Niall asked. "You mean you can use me?"

"Oh yes, Niall darling, we can use you." Roxanne put in, and Niall didn't miss her double meaning.

Sean spoke as though his wife had not interrupted. "You will need some training, especially in the new English and American songs, but that's just a matter of time. We can use you with Irish numbers right away."

"And you want me to go to New York? To America?" Niall stammered.

"That's where our theaters are, my boy. Now how would twenty dollars a week sound to start? We have to see how you work out, and we'll have to get the training for you."

"Twenty dollars?" Niall echoed. "How much is that in pounds?"

Roxanne spoke up. "Of course we'll also provide your rooms and your wardrobe. You'll need the latest styles. I'll see to that."

Niall looked to O'Flaherty for approval. He puffed on his cigar. "All right, all right, the rooms and the wardrobe too, but not a penny more than twenty dollars until we see how you go over with the audiences."

"When do you want me there?"

Roxanne broke in. "We're sailing from Galway in two days. Can you join us?"

Niall looked to O'Flaherty. "If that's what you want," he said.

"Grand. Grand." O'Flaherty said. "I'll make the arrangements. Meet us at the Blackstone Wharf in Galway on Friday at half-four. I'll have the tickets."

Niall rose and extended his hand, controlling his excitement with difficulty. He wanted to shout with joy. Instead, he shook O'Flaherty's hand. "Shall we drink on this as well?" Niall asked.

"Excellent idea, DeCourcey," O'Flaherty said. He reached for the bottle, but not before Niall read the relief in his eyes. He handed a glass to Roxanne and another to Niall. He raised his own in salute. "To a long and profitable relationship," he said.

"I'll drink to that," said Roxanne, clinking her glass to Niall's.

The ballroom of the Grand Hotel sparkled with the light of thousands of candles. Their reflections bounced from the gigantic mirrored glass chandelier that hung from the center of the ceiling. As Kate and Jocelyn stood with Lord Kenmare and Edward Graham waiting to be announced, Kate could not believe her grand good fortune in being there. She forgot for a moment the shockingly low-cut bodice of the fabulous gown Jocelyn had ordered for her and looked at the exquisitely dressed people around her.

The colors and fabrics were dazzling. It was as though the entire ballroom had erupted into bloom. Jewels on ears and necks, wrists and fingers glittered in rainbow brilliance as they caught the light. Even the men were elegantly dressed. Their waistcoats were of bright hues of smooth-looking velvet, and the white of their ruffled stocks gleamed.

The orchestra tuned its instruments at the farther end of the ballroom, and the murmur of voices hummed without words. Kate felt her excitement mount as Edward leaned toward her. "You are quite the most enchanting thing in the entire room," he whispered. Kate blushed and lowered her eyes. She could not think of a thing to say to this man she had been dreaming of for months.

"His lordship, Ashton Kenmare and Mistress Jocelyn Winters, his niece," called out the presenter. Ahead of Kate, Jocelyn and her uncle moved into the room and proceeded down the receiving line.

"Mr. Edward Graham of London and Mistress Kate O'Dwyer." The voice echoed throughout the room. Kate felt the eyes turn toward her. She took a deep breath and held her head high. Taking Edward's arm, she moved into the room as though in a dream. Edward gave her hand a squeeze, and she smiled up at him.

The murmuring in the room turned into real words. "Who is she?

She's smashing!" she heard distinctly. She smiled up again at Edward, and he turned to present her to the show chairman at the head of the receiving line.

The orchestra broke into a quadrille just as Kate and Edward passed the end of the line. He bowed formally and led her onto the dance floor. Kate's head felt giddy as the floor spun under her. She was conscious only of the music in her ears and of Edward's arms about her.

Kate gave herself up to the music. The dances were not so different from the ones she had learned at the village fairs. She let the music carry her away. Edward gave her up to other partners reluctantly as they forced him into relinquishing her.

A wineglass was put into her hand whenever the music stopped, but Kate drank sparingly. Still, her head swam, and she could not look away from Edward's clear blue eyes. All else was a blur of unreality. She had to keep reminding herself she was actually here in Edward's arms. Her heart would not stop its racing as she danced on air.

The evening was nearly over when Edward glanced around the room. "Have you seen Jocelyn? I haven't noticed her for some time."

"Oh my, I'd completely forgotten about her," Kate cried. "I'm supposed to make sure she stays out of trouble!"

"And my principal reason for being here is to keep an eye on her," Edward interrupted. "Where do you suppose she's gotten to?"

"Mr. Graham, Mr. Graham!" Ian Berkley elbowed his way through the dancers. "Come quickly. It's Miss Jocelyn." He lowered his voice and spoke into Edward's ear. Kate strained to hear. "She's with that bounder, DeCourcey again. I followed them to his room."

Edward took Kate's arm, and they forced their way to the edge of the ballroom. Ian floundered behind them. "Get your cloak, Kate. We have to get her out of there," Edward said.

Kate dashed to the cloakroom and threw the velvet wrap about her shoulders. Edward and Ian were waiting at the door.

"It's not far," Ian said and led the way down the main street, weaving in and out of the merrymakers who had not been invited to the ball. They had created their own party in the streets and were dancing and singing with abandon. Edward carefully sheltered Kate from the boisterous drinkers as they shouldered their way through the crowd.

Ian led them to a darkened alley and up the porch of a dimly lit rooming house. He stood at the foot of the stairs and pointed. "They're up there," he said, "the second door on the right." His gloating self-satisfaction distorted his face. "Shall I come with you?"

"No. Thank you, Mr. Berkley," Edward replied. "Why don't you stay here out of sight and see that no one comes up the stairs. After all, we do want to keep this as quiet as possible, don't we?"

"Of course. You're right. I'll stand guard." Kate saw the disappointment spread across his face before he controlled it.

She and Edward climbed the stairs. They faced the second door on the right. Edward looked at her for a moment, then raised his fist and knocked. "DeCourcey! Jocelyn! It's Edward Graham. I'm coming in." There was nothing but silence from within.

Edward reached down and turned the knob. The door swung open. Jocelyn stood with her back to the door, her beautiful shoulders bare, her bodice hanging around her waist. Niall's head was just rising from the bared breasts before him. His hands still clung to their grip on her soft rounded buttocks.

"Jesus, Mary, and Joseph, help us!" Niall exclaimed.

Edward threw back his head and laughed. "It'll take more than those three and all the saints combined to help you if we don't get you out of here before Lord Kenmare hears of it."

Kate rushed to Jocelyn and threw her cloak over the bare shoulders. Niall and Edward both watched, their eyes held by the exposed white breasts, as Jocelyn slowly adjusted her gown and buttoned it over them. Deliberately, she fastened the brooch in the center of the alluring cleavage. A becoming blush of pink was the only sign of her embarrassment. She calmly handed Kate the cloak she had dropped on the floor and walked across the room to pick up her own. Niall adjusted his own clothing, put on his coat, and folded his stock. They filed down the stairs behind Edward without another word.

As they left the building and moved into the darkness, Ian Berkley brought up the rear. Edward stopped as they approached the gate. "You will, of course, be dismissed immediately, DeCourcey," he said.

"That won't be necessary," Niall said. "I'm leaving for America in two days." Kate gasped, and Jocelyn began to weep. Niall put his arms around both girls. "I've a chance to sing in the theaters in New York," he explained. "I was going to tell you tomorrow. Kate, please write to my mother and tell her I'll be in touch as soon as I get located."

Kate reached up and kissed her brother. "Of course, Niall. I'm sorry things have turned out like this, but I'm glad you've got your chance to sing." She gave him another hug. "Be happy, Niall. I'll be thinking of you."

Niall turned to Edward. "I'd like a wee minute to say good-bye to Jocelyn."

"All right, DeCourcey, one minute. That's all. She'll be going back to London in a few days herself."

Niall led Jocelyn a few steps into the darkness. She clung to him. "Oh, Niall, I love you. Don't leave me. I'll just die if you do," she pleaded.

"You won't die, love," Niall murmured. "You're a survivor, like me. Give us a smile now and remember the good times." He tilted her head up with a hand under her chin.

She smiled weakly. "I do love you, Niall. I really do." She reached down and unfastened the emerald brooch from between her breasts and pressed it into his hands. Niall leaned down and kissed her lightly. He led her back to Kate and Edward.

"There's one thing more, if you don't mind," he said to Edward.

"What's that?" Edward asked, but Niall had already turned away. His fist shot out of the dark and caught Ian Berkley square on the chin. The pompous secretary fell to the ground with a loud thump. Edward's laugh rang out as Niall disappeared in the darkness. Edward took each of the ladies by the elbow and led them out to the street and through the crowds.

Kate knew her tears were running down her cheeks, but she couldn't stop them.

"What is it, Kate?" Edward whispered. "What's wrong?"

"It's just that Niall is going off to America, and soon you and Jocelyn will be going back to London. I . . . I'll miss you all."

"But, Kate," Jocelyn interrupted, "you'll be coming to London with me. I absolutely refuse to go back without you. Edward, you can just tell my father that I won't return without her."

Edward put his arm about Kate's shoulders. "I'm sure that can be arranged. I'll see that your father understands that you'll need your companion while you recover from this unfortunate affair." He studied Kate's face. "You do want to come to London, don't you, Kate?"

Kate thought of her mother and Declan and Donal and Maire and, of course, her home on the lonely peninsula. London was so far away, and she might never see them again. She looked up into the blue eyes and knew she could not refuse. "Oh yes," she said. "I do want to, very much." She saw the pleasure in his eyes before she looked away.

CHAPTER 24

DECLAN LEANED AGAINST the crumbling outer wall of the old fort and looked at the cottage below. Blue smoke rose from its chimney pot in a steady stream, and he knew that Mam had poked up the fire to set the kettle boiling. The number of praties in the kettle would be pitifully few. They had begun to ration them since he and Donal started planting a month ago. Their supply had dwindled drastically, and it was still a long time till harvest.

There had been a lot of rot in the seed potatoes since fall, and they had to pick them over carefully. It was necessary to add to the seed stock from their eating supply. The shrinking pile haunted Declan. He hadn't been sleeping well for weeks. His lifelike dreams and the seemingly real visions when awake filled his head.

Kate's letter had arrived a few days ago, and there had been something disturbing about it—not in anything she wrote, but rather in what he felt as he read the words. Declan tried to dismiss the feeling from his mind, but it hung on the edges like the fog that hugged the fields. He would miss Kate, but he was happy for her too. She would have a chance at a better life in London.

Declan couldn't figure out what upset him about the letter. His dreams were filled with images of the Englishman on the dappled gray horse whom they had seen at the fort, and of a threatening figure who seemed to be a priest, maybe Father McBride. It didn't make sense to him, but he could not erase the images from his mind.

The blessed Lord knew there were enough real things to worry about. Gran's suffering had become unbearable. Every joint and muscle gave her pain. Donal had sold several of the chickens to buy some laudanum, and even that hadn't helped. Declan heard her moaning in the darkness, and he suffered with her. Mam bathed Gran's joints and applied hot water packs despite her silence, which now seemed a natural part of the day. Any comment either of the two wanted to make was passed through Maire who pacified both with her quiet acceptance.

Declan hadn't been able to keep his eyes off Maire for weeks. He found her enlarging figure a fascination. She had adjusted her walk to compensate for the protruding round belly, her still slim shoulders thrust back for balance and her tempting full breasts jutting forward. Declan thought she was the most beautiful woman he had ever seen. Her auburn hair glowed, and her skin was as creamy as the milk she consumed each day. Only her eyes were clouded and troubled. They no longer sparkled when she smiled. It was not defeat they held, Declan decided, but patience and guarded acceptance. Like Maire, Declan counted the days until she would be delivered.

Declan lay on the sweet May grass beside the wall. His frame stretched out several more inches than it had last year. At fifteen, he was fast approaching six feet. His body was too thin, and Gran said he couldn't keep up with his height.

It was good to relax outside. The planting was finally finished, and the daily backaches disappeared. They could only pray that the crop would be a good one. A lark sang in a tree over his head, trilling a complicated melody. Declan thought of Niall. Niall would do well on the stage. He had always known how to make a good impression, and his voice was clear and strong and true. *I'd like to see him on the stage*, Declan thought. *How grand to think of him as successful and happy. At least one of us is successful*, he thought. He got up from the ground and walked slowly down the hill. He was hungry and hoped it was time for supper.

Maire sat on the edge of the feather bed trying to spoon mashed praties into Gran's mouth. Gran turned her head aside. "I can't," she whispered. "You eat it, luv. It'll be good for the child."

"You must eat, Gran," Maire pleaded. "You haven't kept anything down for three days. Try once more." She offered the spoon again, but Gran closed her eyes and refused to open her mouth. A moan of pain escaped her lips. Maire smoothed her hand across the hot forehead as Gran gave a small sigh.

Maire carried the bowl to the table where Donal and Declan were finishing their supper. "Here, Declan, you have this." She extended the bowl. "You're a growing boy. You need more than the rest of us." She sat down heavily on the bench and looked at the plate in front of her. "I'm not hungry either," she said wearily. She pushed her own plate across the table. "You have mine, Donal. I can't eat."

Donal pushed it back. "No, Maire. You can't go without eating."

"I know, but tonight, I don't have an appetite. I'll drink a glass of milk. You have my share." She moved the plate in front of him again. Food was too precious to be wasted. There was little enough on the plates. The two men ate in silence.

Maire got up from the bench. She held on to the small of her back as she walked across the room to get the milk and gave another sigh.

"Are you not feeling well tonight, then, Maire?" Mam asked as she watched her daughter-in-law.

Maire shuffled to the hearth and sat on a stool beside the fire where Mam was sipping her cup of tea. "Just tired, I guess, Mam," she said. She motioned with her head toward Gran. "Her fever's up again, and she won't eat."

Mam nodded. "I know. I thought this afternoon she was drifting away from us, but she's a stubborn old woman. She'll take the pain until her last breath."

Maire got up from the stool. "I'll do the washing up," she said, taking Mam's cup. An expression of shocked surprise swept over Maire's face.

"What is it, child? Are you all right?" Mam took the cup from her hand. "What is it?" she repeated.

Hot watery liquid rushed from Maire's body as she stood, making long rivulets down her legs. A small puddle spread on the floor. Maire stared in amazement. "Your water! It's broken!" shouted Mam. "Holy Mother of God, child, you're a whole month early, and the midwife gone to Clonakilty!"

Donal and Declan could only stare at each other across the table. The baby coming! Early! They couldn't speak.

Mam led a confused Maire behind the curtained bed. "Get out of the wet clothes, luv, and into your night things. It may be a while before the pains start, but we'll be ready." Marie shuddered, and Mam patted her daughter-in-law's head absentmindedly. "We'll do just fine without the Widow O'Shaunessey." She gritted her teeth. "Wouldn't you know she'd be off visiting just now?"

Maire's pain began about an hour after dark as she sat hunched in her shawl by the fire. With the first pain, Donal turned white and started to shake. Mam banished him from the cottage. "And don't come back till yer called," she shouted after him. "We don't need a fretting father-to-be pestering us," she mumbled to no one in particular.

Declan started for the door. "You stay here, Declan," Mam said, taking his arm to keep him from following Donal. "I may need another pair of hands."

Declan swallowed nervously. What did he know about birthings? He had never seen a baby born, nothing but the lambs and a foal he had stumbled upon at the moment of birth in the hills. He could not imagine that the birth of Maire's baby would be like that. Still, the baby had to get out of her heaving belly somehow. He began to perspire. He remembered the mare's bellowing. He crossed himself. "God help us all this night," he said quietly.

"Don't you panic on me too, Declan," Mam said. "It's mostly Gran I'll need the help with." She leaned over Gran's pain-wracked form and put her hand on the sweating forehead. "Her fever is higher. I'm afraid she's dying." Their eyes met in silent suffering. "May God rest her soul," Mam said.

She returned to Maire's side as another contraction wrenched the girl's body. Declan flinched. "Mary, Mother of God, help us," he prayed over and over. He dipped the rag into the basin of cold water and swabbed Gran's forehead. She sighed with a small whoosh of breath.

As the night wore on, Declan dozed on the stool by Gran's bed. The sound started pounding before he was fully awake. He heard a wailing, an echoing like the wind whistling up over the cliffs of Old Head. He jerked awake. The hairs on his arms prickled and rose, and he felt a tightening of his scalp. The sound came again, and he recognized the shrill cry of the banshee coming to claim a life. He rose and looked over at Mam. She was bent over the bed, pressing on Maire's stomach. "It won't be long now, love," she said.

She hadn't heard the call, Declan thought. Only he had heard. The traces of it still crawled down his spine. He looked at Gran stretched out on the bed before him. Her eyes opened, and he saw the recognition in them. She reached out and took his hand. "Go fer the priest, Declan. Ye know what the call means. Go fer the priest." Her eyes closed, and she said no more.

Declan's eyes flew to Mam's. "Yes, go, Declan," she said. "Get the priest."

Maire's voice rose in a long lingering cry of pain. "Aaaaagh! Aaaaagh!" Declan rushed to the door and grabbed his coat. He turned and looked back at the two beds. "Hurry! Hurry!" said Mam.

He ran to the shore, dragged the boat into the water, jumped in, and picked up the oars. Thank God the tide was slack and the current sluggish. Even so, in his panic the curraugh was difficult to handle. It seemed to take hours to reach the other shore.

The night was dark, and there was hardly a light in the whole village. There was no moon. Declan had no idea of the time, or how long he had slept on the stool by Gran's bed. It had to be long past midnight.

At last, he reached the landing and pulled the boat ashore. He wrapped the anchor line around a post—no sense in turning the boat over—he would be back soon with the priest. He took off at a run. It was a mile and a half to the church at the top of the hill. His footsteps echoed on the hard-packed earth. At the foot of the hill, he stopped to take off his coat, the sweat running down his back. He climbed the steep path as quickly as he could. "God grant that Father McBride be there," he prayed.

The priest's house was dark. The only sign of light was a faint red glow from deep within the church next door, a reflection of the sacramental candle. Declan pounded on the double hung door with the heavy iron knocker. "Father! Father! Gran's dying! You have to come!"

The light of a candle filled a window, and Declan sighed with relief. "Thank you, Lord," he said as he heard the shuffling footsteps approach the door.

"Who is it? What's happened?" Father McBride's voice reached Declan before his eyes adjusted to the sudden light of the open door.

"It's Declan O'Dwyer, Father, sent to fetch you for Gran. She's dying,

Father," Declan said in a quick rush of breath. "You have to come. She's dying."

"Where is she?" the priest stood in the doorway without moving, the candle throwing its light up into his pale face.

"She's in her own bed at the cottage. She's dying, Father. Come quickly!"

"And did the Widow O'Dwyer send for me then?" the priest asked.

"Yes yes. Hurry, Father."

"The Widow O'Dwyer knows that I will not set foot in her house. She should have thought of these eventualities when she crossed me."

Declan stared in horror at the man before him. "Surely, Father, you would not let such a thing prevent you from attending Gran on this night!"

"You have my decision, Declan. Go home and tell Katherine O'Dwyer tis her punishment."

"But you can't take it out on Gran!" Declan protested. "She has always been faithful. She has never spoken one word to Mam since the day you forbid it. Not once. She stuck by you and the Church. You can't take it out on her." Declan stared at the figure of the priest.

Father McBride didn't look much like a man of God at the moment. His nightshirt hung limply below his knees, his bare feet looking white and bony on the dark fieldstone floor. The candle in his hand threw flickering shadows behind him, enlarging his head and extending his oversized ears in wavering images.

The priest hesitated. "What makes you think she is dying?" he asked.

"She's had a raging fever all day, and she's been in and out of the blackness. She said to fetch ye. And . . . and we heard the banshee's call."

"You what?" shouted Father McBride. "How many times have I told you to stop that nonsense? Banshee's call indeed!" His black eyes bore into Declan's. "Go home, Declan. I'll call at no heathen home in the middle of the night." He shut the door.

"What kind of priest are you?" Declan shouted at the closed door. "Gran is dying. You have to come!" But the light of the candle moved back through the cottage, and in a moment the window went dark.

Declan's hope drained out of him as though a hole had opened in the sole of his boot. "Where are you, God, when we need you?" he asked forlornly as he turned toward home.

Declan rowed halfway across the river when a new thought struck him. What if it hadn't been Gran at all that the banshee's cry had meant? What if it had been for Maire? Or dear god, the baby? He had taken it for granted that the banshee had been calling for Gran, that she was the one who was dying. The pain in his chest was unbearable. He tried to row faster, but the boat seemed to make no headway. "Oh, God, let me get there in time! Don't take Maire or her babe!"

The curraugh struck the beach at last, and Declan hurriedly pulled it ashore and ran up the path. He flung open the door.

"Declan, thank God you're back!" Mam called. "Tend to Gran. I can't leave Maire now." Mam was bent deep between Maire's upraised legs, her arms reaching within her. Maire screamed. Declan's panicked eyes met Mam's. "Help Gran, Declan," Mam said calmly.

Declan turned to the bed in the other corner. Gran raised her hand weakly. "Declan, the priest," she said in a feeble voice. "I'm so glad you came." She made a long sighing sound of air sweeping through the hedgerows. Her head fell back, her mouth open.

Declan fell to his knees. "Gran! Gran!" he called. "Wait!" But his cry was in vain. She was gone. Declan buried his head in the blanket. *At least she never knew that the priest hadn't come. Damn his soul! Damn him! Damn him!*

A thin wail broke the silence. Declan turned quickly. Mam held the baby in the air by both feet. It was blue and dripping blood. "My God in heaven!" Declan exclaimed.

"Quickly, Declan, take her. I have to tend Maire," Mam shouted. Declan grabbed the swaddling cloth from Mam's extended hand and held it as she dropped the baby into it and turned back to the blood gushing from Maire's body.

The infant was silent, and the blue color deepened. "Hit her on the back, Declan. Make her cry! She needs to breathe!" Declan could not move. He stared in disbelief from the blood pouring onto the sheets between Maire's legs to the still infant in his arms. "Declan!" shouted Mam again. "Shake her by the feet. Quickly!"

Declan responded at last. He jerked the baby up by her feet and shook. He slapped her on the back. A weak cry sounded. She made a choking sound. "Put your fingers in her mouth and pluck out the mucus, Declan," Mam instructed.

Declan did as he was told, and the baby cried louder. "Thank God," Mam said. "Put her down next to Maire and hand me those cloths. I've got to get this bleeding under control."

As Declan placed the baby in Maire's arms, she stirred and automatically closed them around the bundle. The blueness had faded slightly from the baby's face.

Someone pounded on the door. "Let me in! Let me in!" Father McBride shouted.

Declan met his mother's eyes over the bedclothes. "He refused to come with me before," he said quietly. "What shall I tell him?"

Mam looked at Gran's still form. "Let him in, Declan. Maybe he can still help her."

Father McBride was dripping with sweat. His black robe had been hurriedly put on and hung loosely around him. He had forgotten his sash. "I took a boat," he said, "and I came to give your grandmother the last rites."

Declan held the door partly closed. "You're too late, Father McBride," he said coldly. "She's dead."

The priest threw Declan an agonized look and pushed through the door. "It's not too late. I can still shorten her stay in purgatory." He went to Gran's bedside without glancing at Mam, who still worked between Maire's legs. He put on his black stole and withdrew the Holy Viaticum from a small case he carried. He made the sign of the cross and kissed a small crucifix. Declan knelt at the foot of the bed. "In the name of the Father, the Son, and the Holy Ghost . . ." The words echoed in the silent room. Declan watched as the priest applied the holy oil to Gran's cold forehead from the small round gold pyx that looked like an elegant pocket watch. The prayers continued.

Maire's cry pierced the air. "Declan! The baby's not breathing!" Declan sprang from his knees. He grabbed the baby and shook her briskly. No cry came. He hit her on the back. Still no cry.

Mam sprang to his side, blood still dripping from her hands. "Breathe into her mouth, Declan, and press on her chest. Quickly now." Declan blew into the tiny mouth one, two, three times and pressed on the small chest to expel the air. Again, he breathed into her.

"Father, Father!" Mam shouted, "you need to baptize the baby. She's not responding."

Father McBride looked up at Mam from his bended knees. "Don't interrupt me, Widow O'Dwyer," he said coldly. "The old woman's soul is in danger."

"What of the infant's soul, Father? Baptize her!"

Father McBride turned back to his prayer. Mam thrust her hand into the bloody basin and made a small cross on the baby's forehead. "I baptize thee in the name of the Father, the Son, and the Holy Ghost," she said quietly and firmly. Declan breathed into the baby's mouth once more. She cried feebly, then louder. She kicked her feet and thrashed her arms in protest. She screamed, and the bloody mark on her forehead stood out sharply.

Declan looked from the baby to Maire, to Mam. Tears ran down their cheeks and down his own as well. None of them heard the door open.

Donal crossed the room, his eyes on his wife. "You're all right! Oh thank God you're alive! I saw the priest come across the river, and I was afraid. I was afraid something went wrong."

Declan placed the baby in Donal's arms. "It's a girl," he said quietly.

Father McBride rose from his knees and made the sign of the cross over Gran's body. Without a word, he packed his things. He went to Donal. "Bring your child in for proper baptism, Donal," he said. He glared at Katherine. "Never have I witnessed such a heathenish ceremony. You are in a state of ungrace, Widow O'Dwyer. You have not been to confession for months. You had no right to baptize that infant."

"But you refused, Father, and she was dying," Mam protested.

"As you can see, there was no hurry. The baby is fine, and thanks to me, your mother-in-law's soul is safe." He turned and left the room.

CHAPTER 25

DONAL TRUDGED THROUGH the rain for another look at his potato crop. Not that he expected to find anything new. The field was a sea of slimy mud—gray mud full of clay and water. It had rained every day for a solid month. It had rained in drenches. It had rained in sheets blown by the east wind day and night. It permeated everything in its path. It soaked through the roof. It seeped under the door. It went through one's very pores. And worst of all, it soaked and penetrated and seeped into the potato field, flooding the plants themselves, burying the praties in a sea of mud.

Donal stood up to his ankles in the soaked earth and looked at the gray quagmire that was his field. His crop was covered with a thick viscous, souplike slurry. The rain made small indentations on the surface, like a kettle of porridge beginning to bubble over the fire.

Donal sniffed the air. A stench was rising from the field. Heavy and sickening, the offending odor enveloped his nostrils and throat the way the rain saturated his clothing. It was almost visible as it rose from the mud. He could taste it on the back of his tongue.

"My god, the praties!" he shouted as he rushed to his crop. Before he lifted the limp plants, he knew. He knew with the same sickening certainty that he knew the English now owned all the Irish soil that had belonged to his ancestors.

The plant was rotted at the end of the stem. It hung like yellowed seaweed in his hand, with a stench like he had never smelled before rising from it, clinging to his mouth, his nose, and creeping down into his retching stomach. There were no potatoes on the bottom of the rotted plant.

Donal pawed in the gray slime for his crop. There was nothing but mush there. His hands made a sucking sound as he pulled up a lump of oozing, rotten black potatoes. Fumes rose from them as though from the steaming cauldrons of hell.

Donal closed his eyes, fighting nausea. A fury shook him. "Don't you know that we will starve?" he shouted at the leaden sky. "Don't you know that we have nothing else?" He shook his fists in the air at his unmerciful god. "How can you do this to us? Haven't you tortured us enough? Don't you care?" He buried his face in his stinking, muddied hands and wept, the mud seeping over his knees and up his thighs.

What will I do now? How will I feed my family? Five mouths to go, and the praties not fit for swine!

It had been a nightmare of a year. Nothing in his nineteen years had prepared him for the responsibilities he now endured. Everything had fallen apart, starting with Da's death and Liam's departure.

Donal thought of the dwindling supply of potatoes in the storehouse. There was hardly enough to keep two people alive until the next harvest. *What were they to do?* He was glad Gran was dead, and even as he had the thought he felt the guilt pour over him. He'd had the same sense of relief when Niall left, and again when Niall came for Kate. His guilt was tearing him apart; but every time he looked at their small food supply, he was glad they were no longer here.

Donal thought of the babe, now three months old. Soon, she would want more than the milk Maire could provide. *How much longer would Maire's milk be good?* She looked thin and pale. Her eyes no longer shined but seemed to be covered with a haze, a glaze. The effort of caring for the tiny child sapped all her once vital energy. She needed meat, good red meat. He thought of the cow, still treasured for its butter and milk. He couldn't risk butchering it. They all needed nourishment, but the time might come when tiny Brigid would need the milk.

The last of the chickens had been sold to pay for a coffin for Gran. They missed the eggs, and Donal was sorry to have lost the hidden potential of having a chicken to supplement their diet. But it had been the thing to do for Gran. Somehow, he felt she had traded her life for little Brigid's.

Father McBride refused to come to the cottage for Gran's wake. Donal and Declan hoisted the wooden coffin onto their shoulders and carried it up the high road to the chapel. There, her friends came to pay their last respects. Father McBride grudgingly held the funeral mass, and she was buried in the plot beside her husband.

Mam had not gone to the funeral. She said that she could not leave Maire and the babe, but Donal knew it was because Father McBride would have refused her entrance into the tiny chapel. Donal sighed and was not sure if it was for the loss of Gran or the sacrificed chickens. The guilt weighed heavily on his slouching shoulders.

Now the praties had rotted in the ground. He rose from his knees and looked at his ruined crop. There would not be an edible potato in the entire field, not with this putrid stench. The blight would spread quickly. It would probably carry on the wind and infect the surrounding fields as well.

My god, the other field! He pulled his boots free from the mud and ran up the path and around the wall of the fort. On the other side was a small field where they had planted a new kind of seed last spring. *Maybe, just maybe . . . Let it be all right!* He prayed to the god he had just cursed.

"Donal! Donal! What is it? What's the matter?" Declan had seen his rush down from the field and around the wall. Donal waved frantically for Declan to follow.

The heavy mud clung to Donal's boots and made running difficult. The two brothers reached the top of the hill at the same time. Both stopped in their tracks as the putrid odor struck them. "What is it?" Declan shouted, covering his nose with his hands. "My God in heaven, what is it?"

Donal's arms hung at his sides. His shoulders slumped in defeat. "It's the praties," he said slowly. "They've all rotted." He swung his arm around limply. "The other field too. They're all gone." He stared at the hillside where the mud was already sliding, inch by inch, down the slope, turning the rotting mass over to expose the soft black remains of their only hope.

"What are we going to do, Donal? What will we eat until the next crop comes in?"

"Next crop? Next crop?" Donal shouted, "Where in all of God's creation do you think we'll get seed for the next crop?" The brothers looked at each other in total incomprehension. They could not imagine an existence that did not include a harvest of potatoes.

For generations, the lowly vegetable had been the staple diet of the people of Ireland, always available when there was nothing else. They ate them three times a day, boiled in a heavy black iron kettle over an open fire. Without potatoes, they could not survive.

And now . . . now, they had none.

In the weeks preceding the harvest of a new crop, they could, with careful planning, come down to the last few bushels of the past year's supply. The seed for the next year's crop must come from the ripening harvest in the ground.

Donal looked at the rotted field before him. Not even enough left for seed. He turned to Declan. "I have to see what is left before we eat any more." He walked toward the storehouse buried in the hillside. Declan followed close behind.

Mam stood in the open doorway as they approached the cottage. She sniffed at the air as she wiped her hands on her apron. *She knows*, Donal thought. *She knows*. How he dreaded to place the burden on her. She was not well. He heard her coughing in the night. The wet weather had soaked through the thatched roof, and the fire could not rid the cottage of the constant dampness. Her cough worsened every day.

"Is it the praties, then?" she asked as they walked slowly down the path. "The smell . . . is it the praties?"

Donal nodded. "They're gone, Mam, rotted in the field. All of them gone." He wanted to reach out for her and cradle her in his arms as she had done for him so long ago when he was hurt.

"I thought as much," she said firmly. "I smelled the stench, and I knew. God has not finished with us yet." She turned and went into the darkened cottage.

The bell for the ferry clanged from the farther shore. "Oh dear god, not now. I can't face anyone now," Donal said.

"I'll go, Donal," Declan said. "You go to Maire. She'll need you now." Donal nodded and followed his mother inside.

The bell rang again. Declan hurried to the shore and pulled the curraugh into the water. He could see the stocky form of Paddy the Smith on the opposite landing. Declan climbed into the boat and started to row. He seemed to be rowing into nothingness. He could not throw off the feeling. *Where are you, God, when we need you? Have you deserted us entirely?* His mind would not go beyond that point.

Paddy waved a packet in his hand. "Declan! Declan! It's from Liam! A letter from Liam," he shouted before Declan could beach the boat. "It was addressed to me, but it's for you and the family." Paddy stepped down to the landing. "Here, ye don't need to get out. Take the letter back to yer Mam and Donal. It's good news. He's grand, jest grand."

"Thanks, Paddy. We could use some good news just now." Declan took the packet and turned it over and over in his hands.

"Is something wrong, Declan? Yer Mam, or the babe?"

"No no, it's not that, Paddy." Declan raised his stricken eyes. "It's the black rot. It's taken all our crop."

"Black rot! May the Blessed Virgin help us! The black rot! Holy God in heaven, Declan, how bad is it?"

"Both fields are gone, Paddy. It's a rotting, stinking black mess. There's not a pratie left to be eaten."

Paddy stared in horror, his face drained of color. "I'd better check me own fields, thankee, Declan." He turned away as Declan pushed the curraugh into the water with the oars and rowed back across the river, the letter from Liam tucked under his belt.

As he rowed across the river, Declan could not shake from his mind the vision of Maire lying on a wooden bunk, burning with fever. She thrust her baby into the arms of the strange woman who hovered over her. The woman cradled tiny Brigid to her bosom and turned away. He shook the picture from his mind as the canvas-covered boat slid onto the sandy shore.

The money fell out of the packet onto the table. They all stared. There must be fifteen pounds! It was more cash than any of them had seen at one time. Donal grabbed the letter and read aloud.

> *Dear Family,*
> *I am sending this letter to Paddy in case the authorities*
> *are still watching the house. I know they are looking for me,*

and I'm sorry to have left you all in such a way. I am doing just grand, working in a livery stable, and I also earn extra money helping the smithy.

I recently met Morgan O'Shaunessey, who just arrived safely from home. He tells me Donal has married Maire, and they are to have a baby. I am enclosing some money in hopes they will use it to come to Boston. There is plenty of work here what with the building of canals and such. It's hard work, but I know Donal is a good worker and will want to provide a better future for his new family.

Donal, you come as soon as you can while work is plentiful. Come to the address below in Boston. Ask for Eamon McManus or his daughter, Maureen. They will tell you where to go for work.

I hope everyone is in good health and good spirits. My love to you all. I will send more money when I can.

Liam

Maire went to the cradle and picked up the child, though she hadn't made a sound. Her long hair fell over her face as she hugged the baby close to her trembling shoulder.

They all stared again at the strange looking bills that had fallen from the packet. Donal picked it up in his hands, letting it fall back to the table.

"You must go, Donal," Mam said, watching the bills land lightly. "You and Maire and Brigid, you all deserve more than is here." Her voice was full of the loss of another of her children.

"Yes, Donal, you must go." Declan echoed her words. "Especially now that the praties are destroyed."

Donal met their eyes. "But you and Mam, how can we leave you here?"

"We'll make out all right. There will be only two of us. We'll be all right, won't we, Mam?"

"Yes yes, of course." Mam answered, coughing into her handkerchief. Declan pretended not to notice the blood on it.

"I don't know," Donal said slowly. "But if there's work there, and we have the passage money . . . what else can we do?"

Mam pushed back from the table. "There's nothing to do but go. See the Widow O'Shaunessey and find out how to set about getting the passage tickets. There should be enough money here for the supplies you need too. There's nothing to do but go. Go now." She dragged Donal from the bench and pushed him toward the door. He looked to Maire. Her desperate eyes pleaded silently over the head of the baby. He closed the door carefully behind him. He wanted to escape, but to what? *How can I take my wife to Liam?*

CHAPTER 26

DECLAN WATCHED UNTIL his brother's small family was out of sight. Maire waved as they turned the corner on the low road that led to Cork City. Declan felt sure he would see them again, but his heart was filled with a foreboding, a dread of what was in store for them. He had held the four-month-old Brigid in his arms until the last moment. He had given her life once, breathing his own breath into her; now he was afraid for her without understanding why.

Although they were already beyond sight, Declan waved one last time and walked slowly back to the landing and pushed the curragh into the water. The journey across the river alone was longer than he had ever known it to be.

Mam's eyes were red when Declan got back to the cottage, but she went about her chores as usual. She didn't mention those who had left that morning. *Her cough seems worse*, Declan thought. Perhaps because she was upset, or was it because the house was so quiet and every sound seems amplified?

"I'm going up to the storage, Mam," he said. "We need to know exactly what we have left so we can ration it out. Donal says to sell the cow and buy more praties when they are cheaper during the harvest."

"We'll be fine, Declan. There's enough for the two of us for a couple of months yet. 'Twill be harvest time by then." She paused and looked out the window at their blackened fields. "Strange how only a few scattered fields in the area were affected by the blight. It's almost as though we were being singled out for our sins."

"Now, Mam, you know that's ridiculous! That's not like you at all.

The blight's a disease in the ground. It's either there or it's not. Our fields just happened to be affected."

"Yes, you're right, Declan. It's just that . . ." She didn't finish, but Declan knew she was punishing herself. There had to be some reason for all the terrible things that had happened to them during the past few years, and she could only blame her own sin of rejecting the Church.

Declan went out and climbed the hill to the storage area. He really didn't need to count the number of bushels of potatoes left. He knew exactly how many there were. He just had to look at them each day to reassure himself they were all right. There were exactly twelve bushels of potatoes. Mam was right; by stretching it, they could manage for a couple of months.

A family of five or six would consume about a bushel of potatoes a week when there was nothing else in their diet. He and Mam would have milk and butter too, at least until he had to sell the cow. There were still berries to gather and some hazelnuts, if they were lucky.

The storm began that night, starting with a sudden rush of wind and rain. Declan lay awake listening to its increasing strength. He smelled the rank dampness of the thatch over his head and listened to Mam's almost constant coughing. It was strange how she would be fine one day and the next would find her gasping for breath and plagued with the choking cough. Then the next day she would be better again. The rain sounded unusually loud in the empty house. Morning came before he slept.

The wind increased by the hour until by dusk the next day the cottage shook. Declan pulled the curragh farther up onto the beach and secured it. The wind-driven rain swept the river into sheets of water that seemed to stand straight into the air as it raced toward their cove. Hitting the huge boulders of the seawall, the pounding waves leaped over it, tearing at the low road hugging the shore.

Declan hauled the boat nearly to his front door, securing it with a heavy rope. He dug the anchor into the ground and tested it. The tide would be high before morning. He glanced nervously at the front door. He wished the cottage sat on higher ground. The wind would draw the tide even higher. He wondered if he could get Mam up the ladder into the loft if he had to.

Declan kept the fire going all night. *At least we have plenty of turf,* he thought. Mam slept fitfully, coughing heavily every few minutes, then turning and sleeping again. The wind attained gale force and still it rose. Rain pelted against the front of the house. Declan could not open the door against it when he tried to check the tide. He could hear the waves pounding against the wall and tearing away at the road.

Several times during the night, Declan heard trees crash to the ground. The furious waves descended onto the roof as they hit the wall and rose up in their fury. A tremendous roar shook the cottage as the roof of the cowshed collapsed. Anne Boleyn bellowed with fright. Declan rushed for the shed. Maybe he could bring her into the cottage where she would be safe.

Declan opened the back door just as another wave crashed down on the roofless shed. He saw the cow struggle against the force of the undertow as the rushing water made its way back to the river. She lost her footing, and the receding water carried her across the debris from the collapsed shed, down over the road, and into the raging river. Declan shouted in protest, but his words were lost in the roar of the wind.

Another wave hit the wall and rose above him. Declan slammed the door shut and braced his back against it. The timbers shook as the wind and rain tore at the door. He saw water seep into the room and stared in horror as it swirled under the front door as well.

"Mam, Mam!" he shouted. "The water is coming in under the door!"

Mam sat up and pulled the blanket to her chin. Her face was gray except for two bright red splotches on her cheeks. Even in his panic, Declan knew how sick she was. She coughed again even as she watched the water creep across the floor, swirling around the legs of the table.

Declan went to her and placed his hand against her cheek. "You're burning with fever, Mam," he said calmly. "Is there anything I can get for you?"

Her huge empty eyes looked up at him. A strangling sound erupted from her throat. Declan's own chest hurt to listen. "It's only the dampness of the night," she said when the spasm had passed. "I have the fever when it rains." She wiped at her mouth, and blood stained her handkerchief.

Declan pushed her gently back onto the bed and tucked the blanket around her. "We'll be all right, Mam. You lay back and rest. If the water gets too high, we'll have to get into the loft, but we'll not go up until we have to." She nodded weakly and lay back. "You're a good lad, Declan. This is all too much for a lad your age. I wish there were some other way."

"I'm fine, Mam. You try to get some sleep." Declan added more turf to the fire. The water swirled about his feet. *I'll wait until it reaches the hearth before we climb to the loft. I don't want to be caught up there if the roof blows off.* He sat on the stool before the fire, lifting his feet from the wet floor. He rested them on the hearth and leaned back and listened to the howling wind.

He would not think of the cow washed away into the river. He would not think of the small store of praties in the storage area. He would not think of the long winter ahead. At last, he dozed.

Declan jerked awake. It was the silence that had wakened him. The wind had stopped. The water on the floor ran in trickles toward the door. The tide had turned. He jumped up and ran to the window. Rain still pelted against the shutters, but it was no longer wind driven.

He opened the door. The tide had receded to the shore path. In the dim morning light, he could see the debris from the shed strewn across the road and down to the beach. There was no sign of Anne Boleyn. The curragh rode at anchor on the water-covered yard, stretching out toward the river as the tide receded.

Declan closed the door and went to Mam to feel her forehead. It felt cooler, though the two red splotches were still on her cheeks. He built up the dying fire.

The rain lasted four days. Mam's fever broke, but the cough persisted. Declan ventured out several times to assess the damage. Many large trees had been blown down, and the low road was washed out where it met the high road. The shed was a shambles. Twas a miracle the cottage had not gone down as well.

Declan climbed the hill to check their store of potatoes. Thank the good Lord and all the saints, they were soft but all right. He brought two baskets to the cottage to last until the rains stopped.

On the fifth day, the sun came out. Declan opened the door to let in the drying warmth. He was bailing the rainwater from the curragh when he heard someone hailing him from the high road. Declan walked over the boulders of the seawall to her. "What is it, Mrs. O'Malley? Did ye weather the storm in good shape?"

"We're all fine, bless the good Lord. Tis the praties that have suffered."

"The praties?" Declan lifted his head. The dreaded smell of the blight drifted on the air. "Oh god, not again!" he said.

Mrs. O'Malley nodded her head. "All the fields from here to Old Head and maybe beyond." Tears streamed down her wrinkled cheeks. "There's nothing left. Nothing."

Declan leaped the broken gap in the roadway. He put his arms around Mrs. O'Malley. "Maybe we can save something if we hurry. We can try." They walked up the hill toward her crop.

At the top of the high road, Declan could see his neighbors coming from all directions. They plodded hopelessly over their ruined fields. As they met, they huddled together to share their disastrous news. The blight had struck every field on the peninsula. There wasn't a whole potato left. They stared blankly at one another. The stench hung over them, smothering every hope. "Even my storage bin is infected," Eamon O'Ryan said. "We'll be hungry by tomorrow."

"Storage?" shouted Declan. "Storage too?" He turned and ran, tripping over his boots in his haste. "Oh dear god, not the storage too."

He tore the rocks away from the enclosure. The dreaded odor hit him before the door swung open. He pushed through and fell to his knees groping into the baskets. The damp, stinking mass clung to his hands. Soft black lumps gave way to nothingness in his fingers. The rotting smell clogged his throat. He staggered to his feet and out the door. Falling to the grass, he retched.

Word of the damage spread from tenant-farmer to tenant-farmer. Sixty-five families had been wiped out. Like Declan, most reported they had only the small amount of potatoes in the cottage between them and starvation.

Squire Atkins sent word that there would be a meeting that evening at the crossroads. Rumors spread like the blight. *Was he calling in the rents? Would he put them off his land? Did he know there was no seed for next spring's planting?*

The sixty-five families gathered on the square, silent and apprehensive. The villagers from Kinsale hung on the fringes to hear what would befall their friends and neighbors. At last, Squire Atkins strode across the reserved space before them. His portly body sank into the one chair that had been provided. Brian McNamara, his agent, stood behind the table that had been placed to one side. The eyes of the stricken tenants followed every move. Father McBride waited with folded hands at the edge of the cleared space in front of the speakers.

The agent began to speak. "Today, the squire rode over his lands to assess the damage done by the blight. Every potato field from the tip of Ringrone Peninsula to the strand at Garrettstown has been wiped out." His voice carried out over their bent heads. It held no hint of sympathy. "All sixty-five tenant farms are without means of support, and rents are due in thirty days. The squire is fully aware of the situation and has called this meeting to offer a solution."

A murmur of hope rumbled through the farmers, but it was a muffled, skeptical murmur. They would hear him out before cheering.

The squire rose from his chair. His coat swung open, and the gold chain suspended across his huge belly caught the light from the setting sun, reminding them of his affluence and of his power. "My dear tenants," he began, "my heart goes out to you. I know what you have lost. I realize the hopeless feelings you must have not knowing how you are to pay your rents, or even what you are to eat this winter." He paused briefly and looked out at his tenants. "I am aware there is no seed for next spring's planting. This situation is most serious." He shuffled his feet and cleared his throat before beginning again. "I have given this some thought, knowing I must relieve your suffering in some way." He paused again, thrusting his fingers into the tiny vest pockets where the gold chain disappeared.

"I have for some time felt this land was better suited for grazing cattle, and indeed, in some sections where families have moved on, you have no doubt seen the handsome cattle on the hillsides."

Declan grasped Mam's trembling hand, afraid of what was coming. Squire Atkins continued, "I am prepared to purchase your leases from you for the price of tickets and provisions for you and your families for emigration to America." The shocked intake of breath echoed through the crowd.

"You mean yer forcing us off our land?" The voice came from the center of the crowd. Declan stretched his neck to see who had spoken. The crowd shuffled. The murmur of voices gathered strength and turned to anger.

Squire Atkins raised his hands. "Now wait a minute before you draw any conclusions." He shouted above the voices. The crowd quieted. "Look at your situation!" The squire lowered his tone. "I am offering you a solution. You have no food. Most of you are lucky to have more than a few days' supply. Your rents are due in thirty days. Even if you can scrape it together, most of you can't survive the winter. Those of you who get through until spring will have no seed to plant, which means another year of nothing."

Paddy the Smith shouldered his way to the front. Quiet descended as he turned to face them. "Our troubles have come at a convenient time for our English landlord." Paddy's voice was calm and reasonable. "For years, we have been pushed closer and closer to the sea by the desire to replace us with cattle." He paused as his listeners leaned forward to catch his next words. "And now," he continued, "now we are being pushed into the Atlantic."

An angry shout went up from the farmers as though they had one voice. Paddy let it roar for a few seconds then raised his hands. "Now if our dear landlord really wanted to help us in our hour of need, there are several things he could do." He raised his voice, and the sound sent a prickle of pride through Declan. "He could grant us an extension of rents!"

A cheer went up from the crowd in agreement. Paddy's voice rose even louder. "He could distribute food from his warehouse!" Another cheer came from the throats of his listeners. "He could provide seed for next spring's planting!" Paddy moved back into the group as they shouted and clapped.

The squire stepped forward and waited. The applause drifted into silence. Everyone leaned toward him in anticipation. "There will be no extension of rents," he said loudly and firmly. "You are dreaming foolish dreams if you think you can recoup what you have lost. The land could be unsuitable for planting for several years. It is foolhardy to think short-term measures would solve your problems."

He paced in front of the chairs. His audience held its breath. "Those of you who wish to take advantage of my offer of provisions and passage to America can sign up here with my agent." He gestured toward the ledger on the table.

"And what of those of us who don't want to go to America?" shouted Michael Readon.

"Aye, what of us?" echoed several others.

The squire looked straight at the speaker. "Your rent is due in thirty days. No extensions will be granted. Pay on time or get off the land."

"And where are we to go?" someone shouted.

"I have made my offer. If you do not choose to take it, then where you go is no concern of mine," the squire responded.

"And what of us who can pay the rent? How do we raise crops with cattle roaming over the land?"

"Any who choose to stay may do so, but you will be expected to fence in your land to keep the cattle out. I will take no responsibility for any damage done to property or crops. That is your responsibility." A groan escaped from the crowd.

Father McBride moved to Squire Atkins's side from his place near the offending table. He raised his hands for quiet. They gave him their respectful attention. "My friends," he called out. "My dear parishioners, I think you must give consideration to Squire Atkins's offer. It is a most generous and sincere one. You should be thankful he has offered you a solution to your problems."

Mam dropped Declan's hand. "Are you telling us, Father, that we should be thankful the homes we have lived in all our lives will be torn down and plowed under? Are you telling us we should be thankful that all the lands that were once owned by our ancestors will be used to graze cattle?"

"What of the chapel, Father?" a woman's voice called out. "What of the graveyard where our dear ones are buried, God rest their souls?"

Father McBride raised his arms to quiet the rising murmurs. "The squire has already agreed to place a fence around the chapel and grave-yard. The cattle will not be allowed to disturb your loved ones."

Paddy's voice rose above the noise. "So the Church has already agreed to this whole thing?"

Father McBride had the grace to blush. His ears turned a bright red, but he said loudly, "Aye, I have discussed this offer with Squire Atkins. We have agreed about the church grounds."

"And you sold us out!" shouted Paddy.

"There is no other solution!" Father McBride shouted back to the now-angry crowd. "Go while you still can! Don't stay here and starve!"

Mam straightened her tired shoulders and left Declan's side, seeming to gain strength from her resolve. She forced her way to the front of the crowd. The only signs of her illness were the two overly red spots on her cheeks. She faced her friends and neighbors. They quieted. "Father McBride and I have had our differences in the past, but this time he is right," she said firmly. "There is no other choice. It's time we realized this is no longer Irish soil. It hasn't been for a long time."

"How can you say that?" shouted a woman. "You, a DeCourcey, whose family once owned this entire peninsula?"

"This has not been DeCourcey land for generations." Mam answered, standing tall. "It is time we stopped living in the past. We must look to the future. The future for us is not here. Irish though we are, our future is in America!" She moved across to the table with the ledger. "Where do I sign my name? I wish to go to America."

There was no sound from the crowd as she drew the book to her and picked up the pen. The sound of the scratching was loud in their ears as she scrawled "Katherine DeCourcey O'Dwyer and son, Declan."

There was a moment's hesitation from the crowd, and then they rushed forward to sign their names. Declan went to his mother's side and led her away. Tears made their way down her face, but she held her head high, and she did not tremble until they reached the landing.

CHAPTER 27

MORE THAN HALF the families signed for their passage to America the first day; and for the next three days, nearly a half-dozen more committed themselves to leaving their homeland. Declan watched on the green every day as, one by one, more tenant-farmers approached the table with the open book. The squire's agent entered the names of peasants whose ancestors had lived on this land since before memory. Declan ached for each one and could not understand his uneasy feeling that they were headed for disaster. Surely, to stay behind would be the tragedy; but the sense that they were signing a death roll persisted.

When the book was closed on the fourth day, of the sixty-five families who had been left destitute by the blight, only eight families had decided not to go, and three of those were moving to join relatives in other parts of Ireland.

There was no celebration. Declan sensed his own quiet despair in the way they went about the business of ending a lifetime of tenant-farming on their beloved peninsula. He wanted to touch every remaining bush and tree, every stream and rock as he passed.

Mam moved quietly about the cottage, picking up first one thing, then another. There was little worth packing, a few clothes, some pots and pans for cooking on board ship. Declan set aside Gran's wicker trunk for placing the few items they could not bear to leave behind. He watched as Mam carefully stored Da's old cap in the bottom. "'Tis a thing of the past," she said when she saw Declan watching, "but it reminds me of your father." In the end, the trunk was not full, for they kept discarding things after they had been tenderly placed there, then thinking better of it.

The week before departure dragged by; there seemed to be too little to do. Declan roamed the hills but came back depressed, for the stench of the blight still clung to the air. He wanted to go, to get it over with.

Mam coughed more each day. The red in her cheeks never faded. Declan knew the consumption in her lungs was far advanced. She appeared fine one day with sudden bursts of energy, but the next day would find her weak and exhausted. He worried about her taking the long ocean voyage and prayed each night that somehow she would survive the crossing.

Declan knew the events of the past year had taken their toll on her. She grew thinner before his eyes, and he winced each time she moved, the stoop of her shoulders revealing her pain. Her graying hair showed little of the red highlights, which once had crowned her beauty.

Declan decided the activity of the move was good for his mother. For the first time in months, she showed some interest. Perhaps the idea of seeing her sons again would keep her going. He convinced himself the trip would restore her health, that she would be her old self again.

The cottage looked clean and too empty. Everything had been packed. In two days' time, they would leave their home forever. Mam puttered about, touching each piece of furniture or dish with a forlorn little gesture. Declan was glad when he heard someone approaching the cottage. He opened the door to Paddy's knock. Declan eyes lit up when he saw the basket of praties at Paddy's feet.

"I thought you might be getting low," Paddy said.

"We're down to eating one potato each, morning and evening," Declan replied, unable to take his eyes from the basket.

"Then put the pot on to boil," Paddy said cheerfully, "and fill your stomachs. I had a few praties left and thought you could put them to good use." He carried the basket inside and nodded to Mam. "God bless all here," he said.

"And you," Mam replied.

"I sent a letter off to Liam explaining what has happened here," Paddy said, seating himself before the fire. "He'll surely be there to greet us."

"I just hope he has some paying jobs for us," Declan replied. "We're fifty-seven families arriving at the same time and all looking for work."

"Oh, I hear tell that ships arrive in Boston every day, and they're able to take them in. I do be wishing it was spring, though. There's more work to be had in springtime."

"Aye, winter can be long without work."

"That's true enough, lad, true enough." Paddy got up and went to the door. "We'll be gathering in two days at the green for the walk to Cork City. Ye better be there by daybreak. It'll be twenty long Irish miles. I'll be seeing ye there, God willing." He tipped his cap to Mam. "Good health to ye, Mam," he said as he went out the door.

Declan ate his fill for the first time in months. He sat with his feet up on the hearth and sighed. "Do ye know, Mam, it takes little to satisfy a man when his stomach is full."

"'Tis true, it does," she said, taking a broom and tidying up the floor. "We Irish are content with too little. Perhaps that's why we don't struggle harder for more."

"Now, Mam, don't be giving me none of your lectures," Declan chided. "And put that broom down. What matters it if the floor is scuffed? Two more days, and we'll be gone forever."

"As long as I'm here, it stays clean," she said firmly, sweeping the small pile of clutter out the door. She scattered the dust out into the night. "Looks like rain again," she said quietly. "At least there're no more crops to ruin." She shut the door and leaned against it, coughing.

Declan heard the rain start shortly after he had gone to bed in the loft. The soft patter on the roof was an achingly familiar noise. Its tapping increased as the wind picked up. He would miss the sound and wondered if they had thatched roofs in Boston. There was so much he didn't know about the place where they would be living. All that any of them knew of America came from the few letters from those who had gone before them, small references to jobs and streets and strange-sounding names. *At least I can speak English*, Declan thought, so few of them can. Thank the good Lord my mother taught us the language as she had been by her parents. How would the others manage without being able to understand the language? So many things to ponder over. He wished they could start so that it would be over sooner.

By morning, the downpour had increased. The damp, oppressing roof hung close, giving off its fumes. Mam coughed with nearly every breath. Declan held her in a sitting position as the spasms struck her, the force of them causing pain in his own chest.

All day, the rain drove against the cottage. The turf fire smoldered and spluttered. The wet air drafted down the chimney, sending clouds of smoke into the cottage, causing Mam to cough harder. Declan sat by her bed and wiped the sweat from her brow. The fever had raged since early morning. Each breath was tortured. Every cough brought up more blood. Declan wiped her mouth and chin. He held the basin for her when it was more than he could wipe away. He knew she would not be making the trip in the morning, and he could not leave her.

At times, Mam thought he was Da. She called him Tim and talked about times when they were young. Other times, she called him Liam and warned him to be careful on the raids. Declan got up to light a candle. He poked up the fire, stirring the fine white dust created by the burning turf. The fire hissed as rain found its way down the chimney.

Mam was racked with a cough. Declan dropped the poker and ran to her. He held her upright, but she couldn't get her breath. She struggled against the powerful pull inside her. She could not get air. Her face turned blue, and she gasped noisily. Declan felt his panic rise. Bright red blood trickled from the side of her mouth. The cough dragged out in a strangling noise, and Declan pulled her to him, pounding on her back. The coughing stopped, and she went limp in his arms. She did not breathe. She was dead.

Declan thought his own heart had stopped beating, so great was the pain that crushed him. He rocked her back and forth in his arms. "Mam, Mam," was all he could say. As he rocked her, he found himself softly singing the lullaby she had sung to him so long ago. "Tur-a-lur-a-lur-a, tur-a-lur-a-lie." His tears came at last. He held her and rocked her and sang as he cried.

At last, he gently laid her back on the bed. He looked at her dear face, hoping she found the peace she had longed for. At least, she would be with Da. *I can place her beside him*, he thought.

He washed her up carefully and combed out her long hair. From the trunk, he took the dress she had been married in and put it on her. The red blotches had faded from her face; but even in her paleness, she looked beautiful.

Declan pulled the feather mattress to the floor, his mother still resting on it. From the bedstead, he fashioned a rough box. He cut the mattress and lined the box, placing her on the soft feathers. Covering her with the rest of the feather bed, he made a top for the box from the table. He nailed it shut.

Declan tried not to think as he worked, concentrating on what he was doing. He had to find a way to get her to the graveyard. He remembered the webbed net of ivy vines they used to haul turf from the bog. Spreading it on the floor, he pulled his mother's coffin onto it. He strapped the vines to his shoulders and dragged the coffin from the room. He would take her to Da.

The rain still fell, and the high road was slick with mud. Declan dragged his precious burden up the hill between the dripping hedges. The load was heavy, and his breath became labored. He stopped several times to rest. He remembered the day they had brought Da up this same road to the graveyard on the hill.

The ground was soft and not too difficult to dig. The rain had slacked off, and Declan was glad it did not fill in the hole. Gradually, he uncovered his father's casket. It had already started to rot. He enlarged the space until he could drag his mother's coffin into the hole. It fit snugly beside its mate, and Declan was pleased. He left the netting beneath its load. Kneeling in the mud, he crossed himself but could find no words. Slowly, he filled the hole with the wet soil.

Declan stared at the soggy mound of fresh earth. *They're together again*, he thought, *at least I've done that much for them*. He closed his eyes but could still see the double grave. In the darkness, he saw a black figure . . . a priest . . . a stranger, who made the sign of the cross and held his hand over the grave. "May the Lord always look with favor on this family," he prayed. "There is a common spirit which binds a family together which neither distance nor death can break." He scooped up a handful of the wet soil and extended it to Declan. "Take this bit of earth, and those you love will be with you always, though your journey be far from this place."

Declan's eyes flew open as he felt the cold wet earth in his palm. He was alone. No one stood on the other side of the grave. He stared at the Irish soil in his hand in bewilderment. He made the sign of the cross and stumbled away, leaving his mother and father together. The handful of earth felt heavy in his pocket.

Declan stopped at the small beach on the way back to the cottage. Stripping the muddy clothes from his body, he dove into the waves. Quickly, he cleaned himself in the icy water and washed the mud from his clothing. He ran naked through the night to the still-lighted cottage.

He hung his clothes by the fire to dry and quickly dressed in his only other clothes. He put a kettle on to boil and added the last of the praties Paddy had brought. While they cooked, he cleaned up the mess he had made building the coffin. He swept up the shavings from the floor and piled the small pieces of leftover wood by the fire. Mam would want him to leave it clean and tidy.

From the trunk, Declan took his mother's things and placed them back on the shelves. Her pretty blue teapot looked at home there, and Gran's plates too.

In the bottom of the trunk, he found his father's cap and the small tobacco pouch he had always carried. Declan placed the handful of soil from his pocket into the waterproof pouch, sealing it carefully. He put the cap on his head and stuffed the pouch deep in his pocket.

When he had finished, he looked around. It looked strangely empty without the table and the feather bed. Declan preferred to remember his home as it had been. Eating the praties by the fire, he rolled his still-damp clothes into a bundle and took it outside to the curragh. He went back for one more look. Picking up the candle from the table, he deliberately walked around the room, touching the flame first to one thing, then another. When he was sure the fire was burning steadily, he went out, closed the door, and tossed the short stub of the candle onto the thatched roof.

From the curragh, Declan could see the blaze through the small window. He rowed toward the opposite shore and watched until the roof flared up. In his mind, he saw his grandfather as he had seen him burning in his long-ago vision. He too saw a ship engulfed in flames and a black-haired girl leaping into the sea with her clothes afire. He wondered who she was and why he wanted to run after her and dive into the sea. Before he had a chance to examine these sights, the cottage roof exploded into leaping flames and collapsed into the room below.

The curragh touched the shore. Declan jumped out and pulled it onto the landing. Shouldering his bundle, he turned the boat over and stored the oars underneath.

The rain had stopped, and the sky in the east was turning pink. Declan turned toward the village without looking back at the land that had belonged to his ancestors since time began.

PART TWO

*"May the Lord watch between thee and me
while we are absent one from the other."*

CHAPTER 1

THE SOUND OF the anchor being brought aboard the ancient cattle ship momentarily distracted Liam. He lifted another barrel of salt pork and carried his load to Aiden McLean, who lowered it into the hold of the ship for storage. Never had he seen so much food. Barrels and barrels of salted meat, flour, potatoes, and other staples were seemingly endless in the heavy sacks he carried across the deck. *Food being shipped out of Ireland while the Irish people starved*, he thought as he lifted yet another one.

Liam felt the ship lift and drop, moving with the tide from the dock. The movement threw him off balance as he passed a heavy crate to Aiden. "Easy, lad," Aiden said, "jest lean with the flow. Ye'll soon catch the timin'."

Liam stopped for a moment and felt the ship move with the tide toward the mouth of the harbour. It was a soft even rhythm, and he adjusted his stride to match. *Like edging down the cliffs of Old Head*, he thought, *tis a matter of balancing your weight*. He turned back to his work.

The Irish coastline gradually faded away, but Liam didn't glance back. There was no one there to wave him off. He wouldn't think about those he'd left behind. He carried another barrel across the deck, balancing the weight across his shoulders and adjusting his stride to match the increased rolling of the ship as it moved out into the Irish Sea. "Just stay with the rhythm," he repeated to himself, "tis only a matter of balance."

Aiden muttered angrily every time Liam handed him another barrel. "May they all rot in hell through eternity . . . may the little people cut out their tongues and use them to bait their traps . . ." Every time Liam approached, there was a new curse—each one more bitter than the last.

Aiden had led Liam aboard the ship the night before and taken him to their quarters below deck. There was little light from the whale oil lantern that swung from the center of the low overhead; and although the portholes were open, no air stirred.

Four crew members sat around an upturned barrel playing cards and drinking from tin cups. No one spoke to the pair as they stowed their belongings in small netting strung at the foot of their bunks. Liam could feel the hostility hanging in the stifling air. "Pay no never mind to them'uns," Aiden said in Gaelic. "Their puny British minds tell 'em they're God's chosen few. They take their pleasures from goadin' the likes of us, though I'll never fer the life of me figger out why. They're the dregs of the London streets if ever I saw 'em."

"Don't tell me we've got us h'another H'Irisher h'aboard," a Cockney voice spoke up, just loud enough to carry to the two men by the bunks.

"What's one more stink mixed h'in wid all the h'others," another voice said.

Liam saw Aiden's fists clench and his shoulder muscles convulse into hard knots under the tight-fitting jersey.

"God grant me control," Aiden spoke again in Gaelic. "I'll kill the bastards one of these days."

"Hi 'ope this h'un speaks the King's English, I do. I can't stand the bloody stupid look h'on their dumb mugs when ye give h'an h'order h'an they don't h'understand a bloody word." The other players laughed, and they began to tell stories about similar experiences.

Liam and Aiden moved silently to the rope ladder and up on deck. There was no sense in answering. They didn't want a fight on their hands.

Aiden pounded the ship's rail with both fists. "I jest wish it was their bloody heads," he said, his strong, wiry body shaking with his fury.

As the days wore on, Liam discovered that his new friend was always angry. There was no relief from his rage. Liam thought he must have been born angry. As the two of them sat out on deck at night, smoking Aiden's rotten-smelling, hand-rolled cigarettes made from tobacco he had bought in America, they confided in each other. Liam discovered his fellow Irisher had good reason for his anger.

Aiden was not a tall man. He was a full head shorter than Liam, but he was well built with strong wide shoulders and a fighter's shape. His arms were long, and his hands were exceptionally large. With a shock of almost white-blond hair, he was an albino, he told Liam; and indeed, in the night light, his eyes did seem to shine pinkly.

Liam learned that Aiden and his family had been put off their land in Limerick when they couldn't pay their rent three years ago. His father had been killed in a mining accident, and there was no money. His mother died from the coughing disease shortly afterward. Aiden had watched as the English soldiers burned their cottage to the ground, plowed it under, and planted grass for the newly imported cattle to graze on.

Aiden's bitterness spread within him like a disease. He hated, and hatred had become a part of his personality. There was nothing he wouldn't do to get back at the English. He made his contact with the revolutionary Whiteboys through a distant cousin in Dublin. They could help him get the revenge he desired.

At their suggestion, he got a job on the crew of the decrepit *Penelope*. Working to destroy them from within their midst appealed to his need to repay them for what they had done to his family and his homeland. From this spot, he helped men like Liam escape from English persecution and carried messages back and forth from the Irishmen in America who still wanted to help Ireland fight English control.

The organization in Boston would help Liam when they landed and find him work, Aiden told him. Aiden would also take something back with him on the next trip. The revolutionary group in America was not large, but there were already thousands of Irishmen in the new country, and they had all left their homeland because of the English persecution.

Thousands of American dollars were being raised and sent back through agents like Aiden. "And not just dollars," Aiden said, "guns too and ammunition. The day will come when there will be a revolution in Ireland, as sure as all the saints in heaven, and it will be as successful as the one in America."

Liam stared at Aiden in disbelief. He had no idea the movement had spread so far. He had thought no further than the small raids he made with the tiny group in his own village.

"If they could have a successful revolution in America, so can we,"

Aiden said with enthusiasm. "It jest takes organization and patience. Patience—that's the hardest part. But revolution will come, ye mark me words, and then we'll kill every bloody Englishman who ever set foot on Irish soil."

Aiden's anger disturbed Liam. He wanted no part of killing or even talk of it. He was done with all that. He had given up everything, even the girl he loved, to put it behind him.

As Aiden talked, he paced back and forth across the small deck space where the two remained apart from the unfriendly crew. "We'll be able to use ye well in America, Liam." He spoke in short, brisk sentences that matched his abrupt steps. "Ye have a fine way of talkin'. Ye can speak good English and even read and write. Tis a fact they trust anyone who can speak their language. Yes, we can make good use of ye there."

A pain gnawed at Liam's stomach. He wanted no part of this deception, but he knew he owed his life to these same revolutionaries. He had no doubt that if they had not smuggled him out of the country, he would have been caught and hanged from the nearest tree.

Liam said nothing to Aiden about his thoughts. He listened to all Aiden had to say and appeared to agree, but in his heart, he knew he had to find a way to get out of working with these rebels.

As the newest recruit on the crew, Liam was assigned the lowest of the lowly tasks. He was already bruised and sore from being kicked and knocked about by the first mate and crew members alike as he carried slops and garbage, scrubbed the officers' quarters, and fetched and carried for anyone who laid eyes on him.

Liam made up his mind to bear the humiliations in silence. He was damned if he was going to get himself whipped or beaten because some bloody Cockney decided he hadn't done his bidding.

"Bide yer time, Liam," Aiden advised. "Our turn will come, and then the bloody bastards'll pay and pay more than they think."

The mass of humanity Liam had watched board the *Penelope* had been confined entirely below decks. The men had been separated from the women and children. At either end of the hold, a huge compartment had been set aside for these steerage passengers. Four portholes in the entire length provided the only light and air, and these were kept closed during the bad weather, which was most of the time.

To the still lingering, putrid odor of the cattle now was added the un-deniable stench of human waste. Sanitary facilities were nonexistent, unless you could call a row of buckets at either end of the hold as sanitary. One of Liam's duties involved drawing these buckets up from the hold after they had been attached to ropes, and emptying them overboard each morning, being careful to throw the contents with the wind, he soon discovered.

As the trip went on, the stench from steerage increased. Liam was directed to go down into the hold and organize crews of passengers to clean up the worst of the filth accumulated from six hundred passengers confined for what had now been nearly six weeks. Storms had swept them off course, and they had lost several days from their schedule.

Liam climbed down the rope ladder which had been dropped into the men's compartment. The rising fumes nearly made him gag. How did they live down here, he wondered. He looked at the narrow wooden bunks built along both sides with a passageway of perhaps four feet. In this aisle, the passengers spent their daylight hours.

From the hatchway above streamed bright sunlight, spreading maybe six feet in all directions. The streaked portholes let in a thin patch of light that did little to disperse the dimness. At one end of this dismal dormitory stood a wooden partition, looking for all the world like Anne Boleyn's stall at home, behind which was the row of slop pails. The stink penetrated everything, overpowering even the pungent odor of vomit from the seasickness which still plagued the ailing passengers confined in this hellhole.

Gaunt yellow faces stared at Liam as he caught the lowered buckets of water passed down to him from above. Brushes, soap, and vinegar for disinfectant soon followed. Liam knew this sudden interest in cleanliness on the part of the captain stemmed not from concern about the comfort of the steerage passengers, but from the fact that the ship would reach port soon, and the health inspectors would come aboard to be sure they were bringing no disease into the city.

"Cleanup day!" Liam shouted in Gaelic. "Everyone is to help. Let's get this stinkin' mess smelling like the heather on the hill." He was sud-denly surrounded by fellow Irishmen, all talking at once. At last, here was someone who understood their language. They had tried to get someone to listen to their complaints since the voyage began.

Liam was bombarded with questions: When do we get to America, how many more days, can ye get us more drinkin' water, is there a doctor on board, will this ever end, and can you get us out of this stinkin' hole?

Liam held up his hands in protest. Gradually, they quieted. "I'm jest a lowly crew member. I have no authority to do anything," he began. Their protest strengthened. Liam raised his hands again. "I'm an Irisher like yerselves. No one is going to listen to me. But I do have some water and brushes here, and you need to use 'em, or we're all going to get sick. I need volunteers to start at either end." Apathetic eyes looked out at him from the bunks. The men gathered round him mumbled in protest. "We're payin' passengers. Why should we have to clean up the ship?"

Liam shouted over their voices. "Because no one is going to do it if ye don't, that's why." The voices quieted. "If ye don't want to become sickened, then ye better pitch in and clean up this pigsty," he continued. "It won't do ye any good if the ship gets to Boston Harbour, and yer all dead from the sickness, now will it?"

A gray-haired man of about fifty raised his arms. The griping stopped. "The lad's right, boyos," he said. "It's fer ourselves we'd be doin' it." He turned to Liam and stuck out his hand. "Eamon McManus is the name, from Kilkenney. Let's strike a wee bargain, lad. I'll get this workgang organized like, and ye git us some word on how our womenfolk are farin'." He looked Liam square in the eye. It wasn't a question he was asking.

Liam knew the only acceptable answer was yes. Otherwise, the hold was going to smell even worse, for there would be a riot such as only the Irish could stage. The slop buckets would be thrown over everything, the bunks torn down. There would be nothing left to the place. It wouldn't matter that they would be the ones to suffer. No rioting Irisher ever thought of consequences. A riot was a riot, and the devil take the hindmost.

Liam shook the extended hand. "I'm mighty pleased to meet ye, Eamon McManus," he said firmly. "I'm Liam O'Dwyer from Kinsale. I'll do my damnedest to find out what I can about yer women. I'm to organize the cleaning there as well." A cheer went up from the men. Eamon McManus gave a lopsided grin and handed out buckets and mops and brushes. He then directed others to clean up their personal trash, which had accumulated over the long voyage.

Eamon drew Liam aside. "Me daughter's over in the other side. Her name's Maureen. She's about yer age, maybe a mite older though she wouldn't be admitting to it. She has kind of faded red hair and a plump little figure and the sweetest smile this side of heaven. I'd take it kindly if ye kin find out how she's holdin' up." He paused and rubbed a gnarled hand over a neglected gray beard. "Tell her I'm doin' good fer an old duffer, and me knee's still servin' me, in spite of the dampness." He ran his fingers through his thin gray hair. "I've been some worried about my Maureen. She's all I got left, 'cepting me older son who we're goin' to in Providence."

"I'll see what I can find out, Eamon," Liam replied. "Tis a bad thing to keep families apart. Tell the others I'll take messages to their womenfolk if there is someone here who can write them down. I can maybe leave them with one of the women, someone who can read 'em."

Eamon limped away, favoring his left knee. He spoke to a red-bearded man who pulled out a stub of a pencil and a tattered notebook. Liam watched as the two passed among mates taking down names and messages.

CHAPTER 2

LIAM HAD NO trouble picking out Maureen from the dirty, ragged crowd in the women's section. She was trying to settle a dispute between two screaming, blowzy women who were shouting obscenities at each other. Liam had heard no worse language from the roughest of crew.

"Ye should be ashamed of yerselves, the two of ye talkin' like that. We're all in this together, and ye have no reason to jump on each other." Maureen turned to the younger of the two brawlers and adjusted the top of her bodice, which had been partially torn from her by the larger, more vocal woman. "There, now, let's forget what's been said and done, like the ladies we are." She held them apart with a stiff arm on each chest as they struggled to get in one last lick. "We're all going to be in a strange place from now on, and we'll need to stick together. No more bickering about coming from Connemara or Limerick. One place is no better than the other, and we're going to be needin' each other's support in the new country." Her rough square hands soothed the straggling hair of the younger woman as she spoke.

"I'll not be needin' the likes of this 'un when we git there," the older one spoke up. "She's a Connemara slut, and being in America ain't goin' to change that none."

"Now, Florrie, let's not be sayin' things we'll regret later," the young woman who must be Maureen of the red hair was saying. "Ye shouldn't be sayin' things when ye don't know the truth of it. Now the two of ye promise me ye'll be dacent to the other." She placed a conciliatory hand on each offending shoulder.

"Humph," said Florrie, shaking off Maureen's hand.

"Jest let her stay away from me and mine," the other woman put in before turning away.

Maureen patted her shoulder and turned to watch Florrie slouch off. As she did, she saw Liam standing in the square of light under the open hatch. She pushed the faded red hair back from her round face. All eyes followed her as she walked toward Liam. Their attention had been so focused on the fight and her attempts at resolving it that they had not seen or heard the ladder being lowered nor Liam's descent.

Liam saw that conditions were even worse here than in the men's section, for here there were children and elderly. Thin, scrawny kids—pale from the lack of sunlight and too little food—stared with only mild interest as Liam caught the lowered buckets. They looked without hope at the patch of sunlight but were too weak to venture from their bunks. They squinted at the intrusion, their eyes too accustomed to the darkness to seek out the light.

Maureen stopped in front of Liam. "I speak some English. What are ye wanting? Did ye come to help us?" Her blue eyes darkened as she struggled with the words. She was, perhaps, five years older than Liam's own twenty and was rather attractive in a motherly sort of way.

"Ye speak very good English," Liam said with a smile, "but it won't be necessary." He continued in Gaelic, "I'm Irish like yerselves." He put out his hand. "Liam O'Dwyer."

Once the women realized he could understand them, they crowded around him in excitement. Liam could not make himself heard above the din of their voices. He looked helplessly toward Maureen.

As her father had done with the men, Maureen now raised her hands. She got the same response. They gradually quieted and turned their faces toward her. Instead of her father's stern, direct approach, hers was a soft, soothing one. "Come now, let's mind our manners and hear what himself has to say."

Liam explained that the buckets and mops were for cleaning up the place, and Maureen soon had the women organized and at work. Glad of the release from inactivity, they were soon singing as they went about familiar chores.

Maureen picked up a small blond child with a blotchy red face and swung her onto her hip with a completely natural motion. Liam was reminded of his own mother. Indeed, Maureen made him think of Mam in many ways. He found it both comforting and disturbing. A wave of homesickness rushed over him.

"Yer father described ye to me, so ye must be Maureen McManus," Liam said. "I've a message fer ye, and some fer the other womenfolk as well."

Her relief was visible. Liam saw the blue eyes water with sudden emotion. "He says not to be worrying. He's doing grand." Liam pulled the scribbled notes from his pocket. "If ye kin find someone who kin read, here's messages fer them frum the menfolk."

Maureen's hand trembled as she reached for the papers. "Ye'll be in our prayers this very night fer yer kind deed," she said softly. "And if ye kin take our replies back to them, we'll be saying prayers fer a long time to come, I kin promise ye that."

Liam looked into the kind round face. It held hope and compassion, along with a kind of pleading. She looked away, and her eyes followed her companions as they worked. "They do so badly need a wee bit of hope, especially the young mothers and the children. If anything happens to their menfolk, they'll be alone entirely in a strange world."

Liam placed a hand on hers. "Take them their messages, and tell them I'll take their replies to their menfolk as soon as I kin." The smile she gave him was reward enough. He would find a way to get back into the men's section.

Maureen soon found someone who could read and write, and the messages were distributed and replies written. She handed them back to Liam as he gathered the buckets to take back on deck. "We can't thank ye enough, Liam O'Dwyer. The news ye've brought, and the work itself, have done us more good than the washin' up that was surely needed. Ye've given us all something to hope for." She looked around at her fellow passengers as though they were her own family. "Ye can see it in their eyes."

Liam watched the kind motherly face. Dulled from the lack of sunlight and too pale, it was still the most comforting face he had ever seen. He hated to leave this red-haired woman.

"Tis wrong to keep families apart like this," he said. "Maybe I can do something. I don't want to hold out any false hope, but I'll try to get you and yer father up on deck together some night, and maybe some others too."

"Surely that would be a miracle, Liam, and I'd dearly love to see me father, but don't put yerself in any danger on account of us. We've managed these many weeks, and I guess we'll get along fer another fortnight or so."

"Ye be here under the ladder just after the moon comes up two nights from now," Liam said, placing a hand on her firm white arm. "If I can, I'll let down the ladder."

"Thank ye, Liam. I'll be waitin'."

Walking on deck that night, Liam spoke to Aiden about the conditions below deck. "Ye wouldn't believe it, Aiden," Liam said. "The children are like plants dying from lack of light. Ye should see their faces. They look more like the cattle that left the ship than like Irish young'uns. They have too little food and no fresh air. The voyage has already been weeks longer than they were told. Many are already out of food."

"I know, Liam. I know." Aiden replied. "I tried to help 'em meself on one voyage and got meself whipped fer interferin'. There is jest nothin' we can do."

"What I was thinking was maybe we could sneak some of 'em up on deck late at night. At least they would get some fresh air." Liam looked hopefully at Aiden in the dark. Aiden made no reply.

"I'd be willin' to take the chance if you'd jest stand guard fer us," Liam said, refusing to give up. "Ye wouldn't have to be involved more than that, Aiden. I'll take the risk. You'd just have to give us a warning if someone was comin'."

Aiden chuckled and placed a friendly hand on Liam's shoulder. "I've been havin' me doubts about ye these past few weeks, Liam, but ye just may make a good revolutionary after all. Ye ain't talked much like a rebel, but if yer willing to take a risk like this to git a lick in at the English, mebbee I've misjudged ye." He watched Liam's reaction as he replied "I ain't much fer talkin', as ye've found out, but I don't like settin' by and seein' injustice done."

"Tis jest like I've been tellin' ye, Liam. That's what this rebellion is all about, jest rightin' wrongs what's been done to us Irish."

"Then ye'll help me git some of 'em up on deck at night?" Liam asked.

"Begod, why not?" Aiden replied with excitement. "It'll be good to git in another lick at the bastards."

With Aiden's help, Liam was able to get Eamon and Maureen together in the clear, cold nights that followed. Each time, he had them bring two other couples. For a few minutes, they were able to clear their lungs of the stench below and flex their muscles, as well as renew their faith that those they loved were faring at least well enough to last out the remainder of the journey.

Liam felt a strange kinship with the McManus family and stayed near them as he listened for Aiden's signal. He needed to feel their love and concern for each other—needed to feel part of a family circle again. He was plagued by homesickness and a longing for Maire.

A week later, Liam quietly lifted the grate from the hatch that led to the steerage below. The rising wind made creaking noises in the masts above him. A storm had been threatening all day, and he thought the dark cloudy night would be good cover for his friends to enjoy a few minutes of night air.

As he let down the rope ladder, he could picture Maureen waiting in the darkness below. He heard an unexpected sound and looked over his shoulder. He could see nothing. He knew Aiden was watching just a few feet away.

Liam gave the signal by shaking the rope twice. He felt it gripped from below just as he was struck from behind. His head erupted in pain, and he felt himself pitching forward. As he reached for the rope ladder to break his fall, he felt his ankles being grabbed from above.

His head swirling, Liam dangled in the air for a few brief moments before he was raised to the deck and jerked roughly to his feet. His arms were wrenched behind him and pinned in a vicelike grasp. He could not see who held him, but he sensed that Aiden was being held in a similar fashion. The first mate stood between his two prisoners, a club swinging from his fist.

"Take the scum to the masts and tie 'em up fer whipping," he ordered. "I'll teach the filthy papists to disobey orders."

Liam was shoved from behind. *Whipping*, he thought, *and Aiden too.*

He should never have gotten him into this. He stumbled in the darkness. A rope was tied about his wrists, and he was pulled into a standing position against a mast. The rope was lashed around a spar and his wrists pulled above his head and secured. His feet barely touched the deck. The mast rubbed roughly against his chest as it rocked in the wind. Across the deck, Aiden was strung on the forward mast in a similar fashion.

The ship began to pitch and roll as the wind increased. Lightning flashed jaggedly across the sky. As if on signal, the rain started. The heavens opened and spilled out everything at once. The masts swayed in the wind, scraping Liam's chest. He groaned in pain. His arms ached as they strained against the ropes, and his head pounded from the blow. Through the agony of the storm, he heard Aiden groan.

"Leave 'em be," the first mate shouted. "We'll git to them in the mornin'. We got other things to be doin' what with the storm worsenin'." They moved away in the darkness.

The ship rolled sideways as the waves heightened. Seawater washed over the deck. Lightning flashed again, and the thunder roared almost at once. "God save us," Liam prayed.

He caught a glimpse of Aiden as the lightning came once more. He was slumped against the mast, his arms straining from above. "Aiden, kin ye hear me?" Liam called.

"I kin hear ye," Aiden shouted over the wind.

"I'm sorry, Aiden. I'm sorry to have gotten ye involved."

"Ain't yer fault, Liam."

"I wish I could take yer lashes fer ye, Aiden," Liam shouted over the noise of the storm. "It's fine thanks ye'll be gettin' fer helping me."

"I've been whipped before, lad. Ye jest have to grit yer teeth and bear it."

There was nothing Liam could say. He raised himself to his toes to ease the strain on his arms. In the dark, he listened to the creak of the swaying masts. His chest was scraped raw, and the blood ran down his chest with each movement. Liam thought of the lashes he would receive in the morning. He had never really been hurt in his life. How would he take them? Would he scream? Strange how one wanted to appear strong, even at a time like this. What did it really matter if he cried?

The storm grew worse. Liam knew the ship was old and decrepit. He had his doubts about her ability to hold up during heavy seas. He felt a surge of adrenaline spurt through him as panic hit him. They would all drown! He and Aiden would have no chance at all, tied to the masts like they were.

He heard the cries from below deck. My God in heaven, the steerage passengers! They would die like rats! Already they were being thrown about. There was nothing he or anyone else could do to help them, for the situation was about to be made worse, as orders were shouted to cover the hatches. Heavy seas were already washing over the deck. If the hatches were left open, seawater would pour down on top of the passengers with every wave. They would soon be awash, maybe even drowned. But now, they would be suffocating in the heat and the lack of oxygen.

The ship could no longer be steered. The sails were furled, and the wheel lashed into place. The storm controlled the ship. It would simply have to ride it out. Crew members tied long ropes about their waists to keep from being swept overboard. They staggered along the deck lashing down everything in sight, and were swept off their feet and into the rails as the wretched craft pitched and rolled.

Twenty-foot waves towered over the ship before crashing down. Seawater poured over the two men lashed to the masts, filling their eyes and their nostrils and even their mouths. Liam struggled against his restraints. He didn't want to die lashed to a post. *Maire*, he thought, *I'll never see her again.*

The wind hit them broadside and carried the ship horizontally across the water. The ancient craft rose to the crests of the waves and dropped like dead weight into the troughs. The sides of the ship groaned like a woman in labor. She shrieked and gasped and moaned. She strained between the pull of the sea and the push of the tearing wind.

Lashed to the swaying mast, Liam struggled to breathe. Icy rain was driven by the gale force winds and hammered his entire body, cutting off his breath. Every third wave brought water from the raging sea exploding over the ship and raining in torrents over him. He struggled for breath between drenchings. As the ship heaved first in one direction and then another, Liam felt as if his body was being tortured on a rack as the mast tried to follow the motion of the deck to which it was attached. The agony went on through the night.

In the dim morning light, Liam saw that Aiden had passed out. His body hung from the crossbar as though crucified. From below, Liam heard the frantic cries of the passengers as they were thrown about by the storm, and his whole being cried out for them.

Suddenly, the storm ceased. The sun came out, bathing everything in a strange yellow light. The wind stopped as though on command. The ocean still raged; but without the wind, the ship rode the waves instead of bucking against them. Liam saw several crew members unleash themselves and dash to secure cargo and to tie down the huge sheets of sails that had flapped loose in the wind.

As suddenly as the storm had stopped, it began again. The startled ship pitched violently. Liam felt the strain of his arms against the crossbar as the wind lifted his body off the deck. He heard Aiden groan and saw his body extended straight out into the air as the force of the wind struck him.

A gigantic wave hit the ship. The ropes that held Aiden snapped, and he was swept away with the water that rushed over the deck. Two other deckhands flew through the air past Liam's face. He could not see who they were; he was too busy trying to keep from drowning as the salt water poured over him.

CHAPTER 3

AS ABRUPTLY AS the storm had started, the wind abated. Lashed to the main mast, Liam hung helplessly as the gigantic waves continued to toss the ship. Each new flow of salt water sent fresh pain through the open gashes on his chest, and blood washed away with the receding water.

Liam began to wish he had been washed overboard along with Aiden. He could not get out of his mind the sight of Aiden being swept out into the raging sea. There was no way his friend could survive. He was already unconscious, and his hands were still tied together. Even in a calm sea, he could not have survived. Liam blamed himself for lessening Aiden's chances.

The rain deteriorated into gray drizzle, and slowly the waves subsided to the point where the captain was once more in charge of the ship. "Cut him down," the captain shouted when he saw Liam lashed to the mast. "I don't know or care what he has done. Every hand is needed. We've lost too many to the storm to spare another."

Liam fell to the deck as his arms were cut loose. Exquisite pain rushed through his body, bringing a wave of nausea. He retched as salt water and bile filled his throat and nostrils. He let out a groan, and the first mate nudged him with the toe of his boot. "Get up, you scum," he muttered. "Ye've escaped the whip this time, and ye kin thank the storm fer that. Git on yer feet and help with those sails. We've no time to coddle ye."

Liam pulled himself upright, not knowing how he managed. He stumbled to the men who were struggling with the huge sheets of canvass. His arms felt useless, but somehow he made them move. Taking hold of the sail, he helped spread it out and held on while repairs were made. Little by little, the sea quieted and finally the sails were unfurled. They were underway once more.

For two solid days and nights, every available hand worked on the pumps in the bilge to rid the ship of water. How they had stayed afloat was a miracle. No one remembered the passengers below until after the danger was over.

Liam opened the hatch to the men's compartment and heard the sloshing of water. The rope ladder splashed as he climbed down into the hold amid the silence of the passengers huddled on the bunks. The water was stagnant and black and at least two feet deep. The stink of human waste and garbage caused him to gag. Liam took one look at the bleak faces. "I'll be back with some kind of help," he said, "but first I'll check on the women." He climbed back up the rope without another word.

The conditions were much the same in the other compartment. Maureen had already organized a crew who was attending those who had been thrown about by the storm. Broken bones were splinted with boards torn from the bunks, and they made a platform for their cookers so they could boil water. The children sat on the top bunks with silent frightened faces and huge staring dark eyes.

Liam pleaded their case before the captain. The only concessions he gained were permission to organize a crew of the passengers to bail out the compartment and to allow them additional cookers on which they could boil drinking water. The captain knew without these measures, he would have typhoid fever raging before they landed.

Liam, with Eamon's help, soon had a line of passengers strung from the hold, up the ladder, and stretched across the deck to the rail. Buckets were passed hand-to-hand until the water could be dumped back into the ocean. Once more, they scrubbed and cleaned with vinegar water. *The cleaning accomplished several purposes,* Liam thought. *It keeps the passengers too busy to worry about their sorry state, tires them enough so they can sleep, and keeps them from knowing we have been blown off course and there will be another two weeks before we reach port.*

The weather turned cold as the days went on and was probably the only thing that kept the dreaded sickness away. *Bless the good Lord for that,* Liam thought. Snow started to fall by the time they sighted Boston

Harbour. They had been seventy-five days on the water, and it was now the last week in October.

The landing was a nightmare. The passengers were required to stand for hours in the freezing temperatures while the health inspectors inspected the ship and examined each of the passengers and crew. The captain invited the inspector to his cabin for a warming drink while the passengers waited in the cold early-morning air. At last, despite what would likely become an outbreak of pneumonia, they were permitted to disembark.

No word of the arrival of the ship *Penelope* had reached the friends and relatives who planned to meet the passengers. For weeks, they waited for the overdue vessel, and no word had come. Many had given her up for lost and returned to their homes. When the weather turned cold, still more gave up hope. Only a handful gathered on the wharf to greet the weary, storm-ravaged passengers.

There was no one to meet Liam, nor had anyone been expected. His only contact had been Aiden McLean, and now Aiden was gone. Liam pushed the thought to the back of his mind during the last days of the trip. There had been so much to do that he fell into his bunk in exhaustion at the end of each shift. He pushed to the back of his mind the knowledge that now he was on his own. He knew no one; he had no money; he had no prospects of a job. He also knew, though he had not admitted it to himself, he now had no contact with the revolutionaries. While he was left with no one to turn to, he was—beneath his concern—relieved he was at least temporarily released from his obligation to the rebels.

The passengers had been gone for several hours before Liam was free to leave the ship. Dusk already threw dark shadows across the piles of goods which had been unloaded and now lined both sides of the wharf. Little could be seen from where he stood, only the city's three hills outlined against the sky to the west. He took a deep breath. The air still smelled of the tide flats and fish, but it was far better than the stinking ship he had just left. He smiled to himself. There was nowhere to go but up. The first step ashore was at least an improvement. Shouldering his small bundle, he strode down the dock toward the city whistling a tune, glad to be alive.

As darkness set in, the dockworkers thronged toward the street Liam could see ahead. They laughed and talked among themselves, happy another workday was over. Liam hung along their edge, wondering if he could get work with them. A dozen different languages could be heard, but no Gaelic and little English. He made up his mind to try his luck with them in the morning—if he could make himself understood, that is.

As he stepped off the rough wooden dock, he heard someone call his name. In his surprise, he didn't recognize the voice. "Liam. Liam O'Dwyer! Over here!"

In the shelter of a row of shadowy warehouses, Liam saw Eamon and Maureen. "What are ye doin' here?" Liam asked. "I thought ye was being met by yer son."

Eamon shifted the collar of his thin coat to keep the cold wind from his face. "He wasn't here to meet us. I guess he didn't get word of when the ship was comin' in. We were so late gettin' here and all."

"Oh, Liam, what are we going to do?" asked Maureen. "It's getting dark already and all the coaches are gone, even if we had money for them."

"Have ye no address fer yer brother a'tall?" Liam asked. "Do ye not know where he's stayin' or where he works?"

"He said he was leaving the last address we had, goin' with a railroad crew where there was more work and better pay. He said not to worry. He'd be here to meet us, and he'd have a place all ready fer us to live." Maureen shivered as she spoke, and Liam could see the large eyes dark in her white face.

Eamon spoke up. "What do ye think, Liam? Shall we try to walk in to the city and see if we can find a place to stay? We've little enough money . . ."

"But, Father," Maureen interrupted, "we could miss Tomas entirely if we leave this place, and we might not be able to find our way back."

"But it's already getting dark, Maureen, luv. Surely if our Tomas was comin', he'd be here by now."

Maureen tossed her head. Liam could see the red hair bounce on her shoulders. "What's the use of us arguing about it? We've nowhere to go anyway. We could wander the streets all night and not find a place to stay, and if we did find one, ye know full well our few shillings wouldn't be enough." She looked up at Liam with a sigh he recognized as relief that she had spoken up.

"Bad as that, is it?" Liam asked.

Maureen nodded. Liam caught a glimpse of a tear in her eye, but she didn't cry. She just pursed her lips in that determined way she had and looked straight ahead.

"I'm no better off meself," Liam began. "I worked on board fer jest me passage. I haven't a ha'penny to me name, and Aiden, who was washed overboard during the storm, he was my only contact here in Boston."

"Then we might jest as well stick together," Eamon said. "What say we find a sheltered place out of the wind? I figger we better stay here near the docks. Surely Tomas will hear that the ship has docked and come in the mornin' lookin' fer us." Liam nodded, helping Maureen with her bundles.

They moved cautiously down the street. Ice was already forming in the puddles, and the ruts made in the mud by the day's traffic were frozen into hard, unforgiving ridges.

Between two decrepit buildings, one of which leaned to the left and the other to the right, they spotted several wooden crates which had been unloaded and left for the night. Liam arranged them so they blocked the wind, and they crawled into the sheltered space. From her bundle, Maureen pulled a light blanket, dirty and smelling of the ship's hold, but it helped to ward off the freezing temperature. The three of them huddled together, sharing the warmth their bodies created. They managed to sleep a bit before morning.

The next day, Maureen and Eamon brushed themselves off and gathered their belongings. Liam watched as they stationed themselves at the end of the long wharf where Tomas would surely be able to find them.

Liam followed the ragged line of dockworkers reporting for work. He would find out where to ask for a job. His shoulders ached from the cold and from the cramped quarters of the night, but he looked no worse than the gang he followed.

"What makes ye think we'd hire the likes of you?" the foreman said with a sneer when Liam asked if there was work.

"I ain't afraid of hard work, and I've a strong back," Liam said firmly.

The burly long-armed man looked Liam over. He glowered over a long nose with a red pimple at its bridge. "Irisher, ain't ye?" he asked. "I know the accent even though ye kin talk better English than most of the rotters." He walked around Liam. "I've heard tell the Irishers have tails like monkeys."

The workers gathered nearby laughed loudly. "We don't want no dirty H'irish on our crew, Gov'na. We got no room fer no bloody, pope-lovin', idol worshippers."

Liam gripped his fists in anger but said nothing.

"Ye heard 'em," the boss said. "We got no room fer no Catholic Irish here. An' ye won't find anyone on the wharfs that'll say any different. Why don't ye go on back where ye came from? They ain't enuff work fer the rest of us, to say nothin' of givin' it to the likes of you H'irishers."

Several workers shouted. "You tell 'em, Gov'na!" "Go on back to Ireland!" "Go kiss the pope's ass!"

Liam turned away and walked back down the long wharf. There would be no sense in looking for work on the docks.

CHAPTER 4

EAMON AND MAUREEN were still waiting at the edge of the street where Liam had left them. They looked worried when Liam told them no one would hire Catholics on the docks or on the ships that were unloading. "What will ye do, Liam, if ye can't find work with winter comin' and all?" Maureen asked.

"Oh, I'll find somethin', ye can be sure of that," Liam answered with more confidence than he felt. "I'll not be giving up so quick, that's fer sure." He said good-bye once more and headed toward the city.

Near the docks, the streets were narrow and dirty. Warehouses lined both sides, leaning like drunken sailors over the crowds of horse-drawn wagons and carriages. Liam had never seen so much activity in one place. The drivers cursed and shouted at the vehicles in front of them as they made their way toward the wharves.

The whole line halted as one wagon stopped at a warehouse to complete his business, for there was no room to pull aside for the others to pass. The shouting of obscenities increased and even evolved into fistfights, while the rest cheered on one or the other of combatants.

Liam stopped to ask for work whenever one of these wagons stopped, offering to help load or unload but was driven off with angry words and sometimes even with whips.

The buildings seemed to hover over him as he approached the city. He could not understand why they had built everything so close together. Some of the buildings actually were attached to each other for a whole block, appearing to be one ugly long shapeless mass, yet they were apparently a row of separate businesses. Faded signs hung above each narrow door, identifying the type of shop and the kinds of goods available. Liam thought there was no order to it at all. A baker was next to a cobbler, and a seamstress was next to a public house.

Large wholesale warehouses offered goods from the Far East, goods Liam had never even heard of. He even saw a shop where they offered Irish lace. He tried to go in to see if anyone spoke Gaelic but was driven off by a man with a colorful towel wrapped around his head. *Surely, he never came from Ireland.*

Liam passed another wharf and could see yet another in the distance. Thousands of masts waved in the breeze, forming a maze of spires and ropes. It would be necessary to turn west if he were to leave the harbour behind. If they all had the same attitude toward the Irish as he had run into on Long Wharf, he was wasting his time in this area.

He cut across the mud-filled street and followed signs leading to the Custom House. Great marble steps led up to a grand entrance. Elegantly dressed men in bowl-shaped hats went in and out of the heavy doors. Liam moved on down the street. It was too grand for him.

The narrow lane passing the Custom House led him to a wide avenue called Broad Street. Liam turned northwest and followed it several hundred feet until he came to a street paved with cobblestones.

He had heard of these strange rounded stones placed side by side to form a covering for streets, but he had never seen them. Remembering the small lap stone Terry the Cobbler used to stretch leather for boots, he decided the stones looked like that to him. Stepping cautiously onto them, he felt their rounded tops through the thin soles of his boots. It didn't hurt exactly but felt very uneven and uncomfortable, for his large boot covered several stones at once. He preferred the dirt streets.

Liam was amazed at the immensity of the city. There were thousands of businesses here. Surely, there would be plenty of work for all. He stopped and inquired at the shops along State Street and was chased away as a vagrant. Although he had taken pains to wash his clothing as best he could in seawater, they did look dirty and wrinkled, and he realized that he had slept in them for several nights. He could not rightly blame these people for not treating him seriously. But what was he to do? He had no way to get any other clothing or even to clean up what he had. Rubbing his hand over his chin, he realized that by tomorrow, he would look even worse as his dark beard—already a day old—grew out.

Liam's spirits sunk lower as he was turned away from more doors. He walked all the way to Washington Street, which seemed to be the center of the city, and sat on the curb to rest. In the distance, he could see the tall hill toward which he had been headed for most of the day. Its height dominated the city. To the north and south were smaller hills. The whole mass of the city nestled within the circle of these three hills and the sea to the east. He wondered what was beyond the hills to make so many people huddle here so close together.

A constable nudged Liam with his stick. "Move along, son. You won't find anything for work in this part of town, if that's what you're looking for. You belong in the West End with your own kind, or better yet, in South Boston."

Liam got to his feet. He wanted no trouble with the law. Facing the afternoon sun, he moved along Washington Street. The day was getting late.

He began to worry about Maureen and Eamon. Maybe he had better check to be sure that Tomas had shown up. Taking Mill Street south, he circled back toward the docks. *Was he really concerned about his friends, or was he simply looking for warmth and companionship,* he wondered. He quickened his step. Whatever his reasoning, he had better get there before dark or he might miss them. His empty stomach growled as he searched for the streets that would lead him back to the docks.

Liam turned south on Broad Street, remembering that he had crossed a street by that name somewhere near the Custom House earlier in the day. The late autumn sun outlined the three hills at his back as he passed the impressive building. The surroundings began to look familiar, and he felt a small thrill as he realized he had found his way around on his first day in a city.

The now-familiar harbour appeared in front of him as he turned onto Purchase Street. The forest of masts swayed in perfect rhythm, rocked by the incoming tide. Ships now lined both sides of Long Wharf. At least three more had arrived during the day. Hundreds of people rushed to and fro along the street leading to the dock, and Liam wondered how he would ever find Maureen and Eamon. He kept to the side of the street, avoiding the muddy splashing of the horse-drawn drays and carriages that were all headed toward the city. Dusk crept over the area as the sun slipped behind Boston's three hills.

He spotted a large group of people at the side of the gangplank leading to the wharf who seemed to be queued up for something. He wandered over to them, edging around to see what was happening. At the other end of the line, two bonneted women were ladling out soup. The aroma hit his nose at once, and his stomach wrenched with hunger. He moved to the end of the queue, praying that the food wouldn't run out before he reached the front of the line. He hadn't eaten since morning of the day before.

The line inched slowly toward the steaming black iron pot. As Liam moved closer, he watched each time the ladle reached down into the kettle, coming up filled with vegetable-laden soup. His mouth filled with saliva. He counted the people in front of him. Fourteen. He prayed that the kettle was bottomless and there would be no end to the wonderful, marvelous food he saw being dropped into each bowl, and indeed it did seem to be so. More people queued up behind him. He could not see where the line ended.

Liam was third in line when he saw the woman tip up the kettle and scoop the last of the liquid from the bottom. His disappointment was so great he thought he would faint dead away. He closed his eyes and swayed. A cheer went up from the queue. His eyes flew open to see that a new kettle had been brought, and the aroma rose with the steam into the cold night air. The pain in his stomach gnawed beneath his knotted belt.

Holding the full warm bowl cupped in his hands, he moved away, looking for a place to sit down and enjoy the food, but there was no room. There was hardly a place to stand. He sipped at the hot liquid. Clearly, some meat had been cooked in it. He could taste the meaty roughness and that of turnips and carrots, but there were no chunks of either meat or vegetables. It was nourishing just the same and just what they all needed. At the bottom of his bowl, he discovered a small piece of potato. It tasted of home.

Noticing some women moving through the crowd collecting bowls, he moved toward the nearest one. As she turned to take his extended bowl, he saw that it was Maureen. Their eyes met over her armful of dishes. "Tomas?" he asked.

She sadly shook her head. "But we've eaten," she said with a small smile. "Thank the good Lord fer that." She took the bowl from Liam's hands. "How good the soup was," she said.

"Where's Eamon?" Liam looked around but couldn't see the older man. "Is he all right?"

"He's waiting fer me jest around the corner on Purchase Street. Why don't ye join him? I'm going to see if these kind ladies know of a place we can sleep tonight." She turned away toward the table that held the still steaming kettle.

Liam watched her go, wanting to protect her, to shield her from another night in the cold of the street. He felt responsible, as though she were his own sister. He thought of Kate at home warm in the little cottage and was glad she was not here. He walked slowly along the wharf toward Purchase Street and Eamon.

He found him leaning against a dilapidated wooden dray that rested drunkenly on a broken wheel. A weary horse stood sleeping in the harness. "I'm to watch over it till the driver gits back with repairs," Eamon said, "in exchange fer a place to sleep in a shed fer the three of us."

"Ye've done better than I have, Eamon," Liam replied, clasping his friend's hand. "I've not been able to find a spot of work, but I'll not give up. There must be somethin' fer me to do in this fine city."

"Did ye ever see the like, Liam? I didn't know there wuz this many people in all the world." Eamon's arms swung wide as he spoke.

"Tis grand all right," Liam said, "but not what I call friendly-like."

"That's true enuff." Eamon hesitated. "I wonder what's keeping Maureen. I don't like her wandering around by herself."

"I'll go to meet her," Liam said and walked back toward the wharf one more time. He heard a scuffle before he saw anything in the dark.

"Come on, lassie, give us a kiss. Ye look like ye could keep a man warm all this cold night." His voice was harsh and slurring from drink.

"Keep yer hands off me, ye big baboon!" It was Maureen. Liam broke into a run and grabbed her assailant by the back of the neck. He pressed his large fingers into the soft flesh.

"Leave her be!" he shouted. He lifted the man off the ground, and Maureen fell free of his grasp. Liam dropped him.

"Ye can't blame a man fer tryin'," the faceless man whined. "Tis goin' ta be a cold night."

"Git yerself off," Liam growled, "before I kill ye." The man fled into the darkness. Liam reached out, and Maureen came into his arms. Her body trembled against him. "It's all right, luv," he said. "It's all right." He held her close until she stopped shaking. All he could think of was that she was not hurt. She was safe. His day was not wasted after all.

"I'm all right now, Liam. Ye kin let me go. I do be thanking ye." She stepped away, not looking at him. They walked along the wharf in the darkness. There seemed to be nothing to say.

At last she spoke. "The ladies said they let people use the basement of their church to sleep in, but there was no more room." She paused. "In any case, they don't allow Catholics. She said she was sorry, but they could not let heathen inside the church." Her voice was hollow, like the sound of their echoing footsteps on the wooden ramp.

Liam put his arm around her shoulders. "Eamon has a promise of a place to sleep in a shed fer the three of us. He's watching the man's dray fer him. At least we won't be on the street."

Maureen sighed. "He's a good man, my father." They walked in silence to the corner of Purchase Street.

CHAPTER 5

LIAM WAS HALF-ASLEEP the next morning when the girl in his arms stirred. He pulled her close. "Maire," he murmured, "oh, my darling Maire." She pulled away and scurried from under the thin blanket that covered them.

Liam came fully awake. "I'm sorry, Maureen. I'm sorry," he stammered, but Maureen was already out the door of the drafty shed where they had spent the night.

Beside him, Eamon had stirred and sat up, rubbing the sleep from his eyes. Liam stared from Eamon to the door. "I didn't mean to hurt her," he said. "I must've been dreaming. I thought she was someone else."

Eamon crawled from beneath the blanket. "Yes, well, my friend," he said slowly. "I might jest as well tell ye now. Ye won't be forgiven, not fer a long time to come. There's nothin' in this world a woman hates like bein' called by the wrong name."

Liam wanted to crawl back under the covers and stay hidden in the cold, drafty, bare shed that had been provided them for the night. *Here he had gone and insulted the sweetest lass he'd ever known . . . well, maybe the second sweetest*, he thought.

Eamon opened the door and looked out. "I'll go after her and see if I can make peace, but I can tell ye now, we're in fer a long, hard day with that one." He went out into the icy morning.

Liam gathered their things, folding the blanket and packing the straw case Maureen had carried from home. He mentally kicked himself for his stupidity.

"Liam. Liam, come quick!" Eamon shouted from the street. Liam dashed from the shed remembering Maureen's attacker from the previous night. "Our girl has got herself a job! She's done it, by god, she's done it!"

Maureen stood beside a carriage pulled to the side of Purchase Street. The middle-aged woman who had been ladling soup from the iron kettle the night before leaned from the window. A liveried driver stood stiffly by. "Now, Miss McMahan, if you will just get your things, we can be off," the lady said.

"Oh, thank you, Mam." Maureen picked up the lady's hand. "You're so kind. I'll be jest a moment." She dropped the gloved hand and turned back toward the corner. Maureen had recognized the lady from the night before and remembered her kind words. She stopped to thank her once more for the soup. When Mrs. Pendleton introduced herself and asked where she had stayed the night before, Maureen told her of the night she had spent with Liam and her father. Mrs. Pendleton was overcome with concern and immediately offered Maureen a position in her household.

Maureen picked up her skirt and seemed to be poised to run when she spotted the two men. "Oh," she cried in a startled voice. She dropped her skirt and stared. Liam saw her square her shoulders and turn back to the carriage. "Please, Mam, can ye use me father and his friend too somewhere around the place? They're good workers and do need some place to go." Her strong voice carried back to Liam and Eamon in the crisp morning air.

The woman looked at the two bearded, wrinkled men on the corner. She looked back at Maureen. "Oh, my dear, I'm so sorry, but I really couldn't."

"Please, Mam. I couldn't jest leave 'em here not knowin' where they'll be and all."

Liam and Eamon moved at the same time. They reached the carriage together and stood in front of Maureen. "Please, Mam, don't pay any attention to her a'tall. She'll be glad of the job, whatever it is." Eamon spoke up. He turned back to Maureen. "Now let's have no more of this nonsense, girl. Up into the carriage with ye." He lifted his daughter to the step.

"I'll get your things," Liam spoke up. "They're all packed." He ran back to the shed and grabbed Maureen's bundles. He hurried to the carriage and handed the bundles to her.

He father spoke up, taking her hand. "We'll be jest fine now. Don't you worry none about us. Ye jest go with this kind lady. Ye know ye can't stay out in the cold another night."

Liam looked at the woman's concerned face. "If you would please tell us where we can send a message to let her know when we find work, Mam, we'll send word so she won't be worrying."

Maureen's blue eyes looked from her father to Liam. "I can't leave ye. I can't."

The lady took Maureen's hands in hers. "There now, lass," she said patting her gently. "Everything is going to be fine." She took a small pencil and notebook from her handbag and wrote on the paper. She tore the page out briskly and handed it to Eamon. "This is the address of my husband's livery stable. Tell them Mrs. Pendleton said to find work for you both."

Maureen gave her a look of adoration. Liam and Eamon snatched their caps from their heads and murmured their appreciation as the driver jumped up into his high seat and slapped the horses with the reins. Maureen leaned out and waved until the carriage turned the corner.

Liam and Eamon were nearly two hours finding the livery stable. They had to ask directions at every corner. As they neared the center of the city, a constable asked them what they were doing in that part of town. "It's a livery stable we're looking for, sir," Liam said. "There's work for us there, waiting."

The constable looked a bit skeptical and said abruptly, "Move on then, and don't be stopping anywhere else." He pointed out the way and watched until they were out of sight.

"It ain't exactly the friendliest town ye've ever been in now, is it?" Eamon asked as they moved away.

"But there's work, Eamon, work for all three of us." They walked on with more spring in their step.

The Pendleton Livery and Stage Company was located behind a large hotel. The building was made of weathered wood and in not much better condition than the warehouses near the wharf. Liam smelled the familiar odor of horses and hay. "We'll do fine, Eamon, don't you worry."

"I'm not worryin', lad." Eamon looked around uneasily. "But there don't seem to be much goin' on now, do there?" The yard was empty of both vehicles and horses, but the ground had been churned to mud by recent comings and goings. Liam led his friend through the heavy wooden door held in place by sturdy leather hinges. The cold wind tugged as he pulled it closed behind him. They walked past several horse stalls which had been divided with widely spaced slats. The place stunk of droppings and urine.

They nearly ran into a little man wearing a business suit and a bowler hat. "Now where in tarnation did you two come from, and what are you doing here?" he thundered at them. "Haven't I got enough troubles this morning without dealing with the likes of you?" He planted himself in front of them and glared. "Well, speak up. I asked you a question."

Liam swallowed hard. He extended the piece of paper Mrs. Pendleton had given them. "Please, sir," he said, "Mrs. Pendleton said we were to come here and there would be work for us."

The pudgy man grabbed at the paper. "Oh, she did, did she? Why doesn't that woman keep her nose out of my business? She's always bringing home some stray or other." He studied the paper in his hand. "I don't interfere with her house, why does she insist on interfering with the livery stable?" He looked the two men over carefully while he spoke. "Women!" he muttered almost under his breath. "They never know when to leave off."

Liam held his breath and said nothing. The bandy little man studied them, holding their eyes steadily. "Either of you ever work with horses before?" he asked. "Ever harnessed one up?"

"No, sir," Eamon said.

"Yes, sir," said Liam.

"Well, which is it, yes or no?" He looked from one to the other.

"I've worked in a stable, sir," Eamon said, hat in hand, "but mostly cleaning up."

Liam spoke up. "I know repairing harnesses and such—and shoeing, that I can do."

Mr. Pendleton grabbed Liam by the coat collar. "You mean you're a blacksmith? Holy god, why didn't you say so?" He dragged Liam to an open doorway. The heat from the farrier was almost a living barrier. A team of horses stood restlessly in a stall. "One of 'em threw a shoe this morning and I've no smithy. Can you help out, lad?" He dropped Liam's collar and smoothed it carefully.

"I'm only an apprentice, sir, but I've shoed many a horse."

"Good. Good. You're hired. Let's get at it. The stage is already an hour late."

"And my friend, Mr. Pendleton, sir?" Liam spoke up. "Have you work for him too?"

Mr. Pendleton looked at Eamon. He shook his head. "Aw, what the hell, why not?" He pointed to a pitchfork standing in the corner near the stalls. "You can clean up this place. Horses can't thrive in a pigsty." He stomped toward the door then turned and said, "If you've no place to stay, you can sleep in the haymow." He motioned with his head to the loft above them. "But no smoking now, ye hear?" He thundered out to the yard.

Eamon grinned at Liam, grabbed a pitchfork, and headed for the stalls. Liam dropped his bundle in a corner and went to the forge. God was good. They had work and a place to sleep. He blessed Mrs. Pendleton and Mr. Pendleton too. He picked up the tools and remembered the last time he had shoed a horse; he touched it with a red-hot iron, and his father had been thrown through the stable door. He closed his eyes against the sudden memory of the blood pouring from Da's head.

CHAPTER 6

THE NEW ENGLAND winter was long and difficult, but Liam had found a strange sense of contentment. As the days settled into the routine of long hours of work and exhausted sleep, he discovered he liked the lack of responsibility and the sameness of the days.

Maureen had brought blankets and heavy greatcoats for Liam and Eamon from a collection Mrs. Pendleton organized for the benefit of the immigrants who roamed the city streets, hopeless and hungry. *The lady was a saint*, Liam thought, *though a Protestant*.

Maureen held the quilt-lined greatcoat for him to slip on. "Tis a grand fit," she said, smoothing her hands across his shoulders and down his back. "Mrs. Pendleton said I was to have the best of the lot fer the two of ye. I picked the one with the broadest shoulders fer ye. I knew twould fit the likes of you." She ran her hands across his shoulders again. "It'll keep ye warm as a fire-roasted pratie all winter." She moved around in front of him, adjusting the lapels slowly, admiring the fit of the coat.

Liam put his hands on her elbows. "Ah, Maureen, what would we ever do without you?" he asked. "You've saved us time and again. You're a real blessing." She lifted her face, her lips parted. Before he knew what was happening, she was in his arms, and he was kissing her. Appreciation for her kindness had nothing to do with the kiss, for it was not gentle at all, but a wild, passionate thing filled with all the emotion that had been bottled up inside him for months.

Several seconds passed before he realized that Maureen's body was pressed close to his, straining to get even closer, and she was returning his kisses with abandon.

Liam came to his senses. He pulled back, dropping his arms from her. *What am I thinking of? This is Maureen. Dear motherly Maureen.* "I'm sorry. I'm sorry." He stepped away from her. "I don't know what I was thinking a'tall," he stammered, turning away. "Forgive me."

Maureen stood where he had left her. "I'd rather think ye did know what ye were doin', that it wasn't an accident. Ye don't need to apologize."

Liam turned back to her. Her face had turned pale, and her eyes held a pleading question. "But I am sorry, Maureen. It should never have happened. You're the sweetest, most thoughtful woman I ever knew, and I wouldn't hurt you for the entire universe. I . . . I guess I've been by meself fer too long and missing those at home."

"What yer tryin' to say is that ye have a girl back in Ireland. Do I have that about right?" Her voice sounded dry and brittle.

Liam took a step toward her and took her hands in his. "Maureen, I do beg your forgiveness. Yes, there is someone back home." She pulled her hands away. He saw tears spring into her eyes and the sadness there, and he reached for her hands again. "I'd like you to be my friend, Maureen, my very dear friend. You and Eamon have been like father and sister to me. Can't we keep it like that, Maureen, and forget what just happened?"

She looked into his eyes. "A sister. Yes, of course, Liam." She pulled her hands away and turned back to the box filled with wool socks and blankets. "I'll jest be leavin' this with ye and be back to me work." She patted the box slowly then turned to the door.

Why am I thinking of all this now? Liam asked himself. *That was months ago at the beginning of winter, and May is already here.* He led out the fresh team of horses he was to deliver to the Bensen Stage Company for their early-morning run to Providence and shook the unwelcome thoughts from his mind. He had been over it enough times before, and he still could see the hurt in Maureen's eyes.

The fog washed in off the harbour and the smell of the salt and the dampness made him think of home with a longing that was still with him after the endless winter months in America. He was beginning to doubt he would ever be free of it. He led the team into the Stage Company yard, pulling them into position in front of the waiting coach.

"And would ye be a kind lad, Liam, and hook the beasties up fer me?" Casey O'Hara, the stage driver asked. "It's running shorthanded I am this mornin'."

"Shorthanded, are ye?" a disembodied voice asked from the fog behind them. "Then I'm jest the boyo ye've been hopin' fer. Even in this fog, that is surely blanketing the entire ocean frum here to County Cork, I kin see that ye need a good strong back and a pair of willin' hands to help ye git this marvelous vehicle all the long way to the good town of Providence."

Liam stared into the fog. There was something about the voice, not just the accent, which was pure County Cork, but the ring of it, a wonderful, funny, beat-around-the-bush way of talking that could only be… "Morgan!" he shouted. "Morgan O'Shaunessey! What are ye doin' in Boston?" He rushed to the burly man and grasped him in a huge hug.

"Unhand me, ye big baboon, and let me have a look at the face on ye, fer ye sound, fer all the saints in heaven, like Liam O'Dwyer!"

"Tis me, Morgan, and I've never been so happy to see anyone in me whole life!" Liam lifted Morgan off his feet and swung him around while they both hooted and hollered like two kids in a hayloft.

"Put me down, Liam. Put me down!" Morgan shouted. "Here I'm trying to strike a bargain with this handsome coach driver what needs a willin' hand to help git him to Providence, and yer treating me like a wee lad in knee britches."

"He's right," broke in Casey. "Put the lad down and get these horses hooked up. I'm without a helpmate this very mornin', and I'll be late pullin' out fer sure. Give him a hand, laddie, and I'll hear what ye have to say to me."

Morgan and Liam beamed at each other and maneuvered the horses into place, hitching them to the stagecoach while they exchanged information about themselves and their families.

The two natives of Ringrone Peninsula stood back to admire their finished work in the manner of all Irishmen, their hands in their trouser pockets and beams of pleasure on their faces.

"And yer brother, Donal," Morgan said, "he's up and married Maire Foley, and none of us even suspecting that he'd been a'courtin' her. And all the rest of us boyos a'wonderin' how he had snapped her up ahead of us."

Liam stared at Morgan. *Could I have heard right?* Morgan couldn't have said what he thought he had said. "Would ye say that again, Morgan?" he asked quietly, all hilarity and pleasure gone from his voice.

"What's ailin' ye, Liam?" Morgan asked, sober now too. "I jest said Donal had married that pretty little Maire Foley, and none too soon either. It looks like they had been rollin' around in the heather a bit, and the wee one should be comin' a bit early."

"Donal and Maire?" He grabbed Morgan by his coat sleeves. "Yer sure? Donal and Maire, married?"

"That's what I said. Three, maybe four months after ye left home. Surprised us all, like I said, but she'll make him a right fine wife. Ye should be glad fer him."

Liam dropped his hands from Morgan's coat. "Yes, of course. Yer right, Morgan. I'm sure they'll be very happy." He turned away from his friend and checked the fittings on the harness once more. "I'll speak to Casey about takin' ye on to help in exchange fer the trip to Providence, Morgan. I have to be getting back to the Livery. Good luck to ye, Morgan, and I thank ye fer the news of my family. It was good to see ye agin'." He shook Morgan's hand warmly.

"I hope the news didn't upset ye none, Liam," Morgan said. "I know ye were courtin' her yerself at one time."

"Oh, no no. It was jest sudden like." Liam shook his hand again and turned away. He stopped to talk to Casey as he grasped the reins of the replaced team. "He's a good lad, Casey, and a hard worker. If ye can use him on the trip today, he needs to get to Providence." Casey nodded and clapped him on the back. Liam led the spent horses back to the livery stable, hardly aware of what he was doing, his thoughts on Maire and Donal.

Liam was at a loss for what he should do. His mind refused to function in a logical manner. He decided he must write a letter and enclose whatever money he had saved. It was the least he could do. He had left Donal with the full responsibility of the family. Now Donal had his own wife and baby to care for. Liam's whole being ached at the thought. The idea of Maire in Donal's arms—in Donal's bed—was almost impossible to bear.

God in heaven, help me, he prayed. *I must not hate my brother. I must not blame him for loving her. She is easy enough to love; the Lord above knows that. Didn't I love her myself? Didn't I do more than that; didn't I make love to her? How could she have forgotten so soon? How could she?* Remembering what Morgan said about the babe, his thoughts turned in another direction. The babe would arrive early, he said.

Oh my god, could it be true? Is it possible the baby is my own? Had Maire married Donal because she was carrying my child? Had he married Maire to protect her? Didn't I ask him to take care of her?

He might never know the true way of it, but he would do what he could to help them. Liam knew that he still loved Maire, and he loved Donal too. And he loved the child, whether it was his own or his brother's.

After weeks of debating it in his mind, Liam had, finally, been able to write the letter and enclose passage money for Donal and Maire. There would be work here for both of them, and the baby would have a better chance than any of them had.

Liam stepped off the wooden dock into the muddy street and turned west, making his way through the maze of wagons and horses and the numerous stacks of lumber, barrels of sweet maple syrup, and pungent beaver pelts being loaded on the waiting ships.

In one of these same ships was the letter he had just sent off to Ireland. The news that Maire had married Donal had shocked him beyond belief. Inside his chest, a cold hard lump had formed, and the pain was a constant reminder. His Maire, his sweet Maire, married to someone else—to Donal, his own brother. Liam's mind kept refusing to accept the truth, yet it was true. There was nothing to be done; Maire would never belong to him. She was Donal's wife, and marriage was forever.

One thing Liam knew was that he could not be in Boston when they arrived. Perhaps he could learn to bear the thought of their marriage, but he realized he would not be able to stand the sight of its reality.

Later that night, after their work was finished, Liam and Eamon decided to go for a pint or two at a pub on Ann Street. The walk was long, but Liam felt desperately in need of a drink, and Eamon never refused an opportunity to mingle with fellow Irishmen who gathered there.

The neighborhood deteriorated fast as they moved along Ann Street where the rows and rows of ramshackle tenement houses lined both sides of the narrow street. Thousands of immigrants lived in crowded, dirty flats overrun with rats and cockroaches. In the small courts hemmed in on all four sides by buildings, outhouses served the tenants, their rank odor smothering the neighborhood.

Liam tried not to breathe as they walked along. *Strange that the smell of human waste was more offensive than that of the animals*, he thought. He had gotten used to the smells of the stables and even found the odors of the horses pleasant in a primitive sort of way.

The small pub was wedged comfortably between a warehouse and a particularly weather-beaten, grayed tenement building at the corner of Ann and Fleet streets. Here, the thirst of dockworkers and immigrants alike was quenched with cheap, homemade brew.

They heard the sounds of singing and the raised voices before they reached the door. Liam recognized the familiar melody of "Greensleeves," a song Niall was always singing. Homesickness enveloped him again. Most of those who came to this ugly small place were Irish, with a smattering of Portuguese and Italian dockworkers. The sounds of the familiar Gaelic language was like being home, but tonight, it only emphasized his feeling of separation from his family.

The two made their way to the wooden bar at the far end of the room. "Rum!" shouted Eamon to the round balding man in the dirty shirt behind the bar. He placed his coins on the counter, knowing that he would not be served until his payment was in sight. A tin mug was placed in front of him.

"Porter for me," Liam said. The strong beer was the closest he could come to the poteen brewed at home. He savored the familiar bitter taste.

They carried their mugs to a long table in the center of the room, and several scruffy-looking men shoved themselves along the bench to make room for them. Liam took a long draft and felt the drink ease down his throat. "Ah," he said and gave Eamon a satisfying look.

"Aye, a good way to top off the day," Eamon replied.

The middle-aged man across the table was swinging his mug in the air as he spoke. "And the salmon swim all the way up the Bandon this time of year, and at Innishannon ye kin see them shinin' all silver in the water. They hurl themselves up over the dam, some of 'em four, five feet long. Ah, tis a grand sight. Ye'll niver see a purtier one if ye live to be a tousand an' one." He took a swig from the waving mug.

Homesickness mixed with the beer in Liam's stomach. The Bandon River—Innishannon. He caught the man's eye. "Are ye from Innishannon then?" he asked.

"I am," the man replied, "and sorry I am I ever left it."

Liam extended his hand across the table. "Liam O'Dwyer from Kinsale."

"Well well, we're practically neighbors, my boy." He grasped Liam's hand. "Dinty McLean, and I'm mighty pleased to meetcha."

"There was a lad on the ship we sailed on named McLean, Aiden McLean," Liam said. "He got me a job on the crew fer me passage."

The man on Dinty's left looked up from his mug. He gave Liam an unreadable look. "Then ye came over on the *Penelope*?" he asked in a cold voice.

"Aye, I did, and glad I was to set foot on land," Liam said still trying to puzzle out what the man's steely look meant. "Ye knew Aiden?"

"Aye." The man's eyes never left Liam's face. He took in every detail, as though he were memorizing each feature. "Aiden seems to have dropped out of sight. He was nowhere to be found after the *Penelope* docked in October."

Liam returned the man's steady gaze, but a cold feeling had returned to his stomach. He had made a mistake, and he knew it. He had been careful never to mention his name or the ship he had sailed on if there were strangers around. Now in his homesickness, he had betrayed himself. He showed none of his emotion as he spoke. "Aiden McLean was washed overboard in a storm. I saw him with me own eyes."

The man's gaze did not flinch. "And why wasn't ye washed overboard too, Liam O'Dwyer of Kinsale?"

The cold lump in Liam's stomach hardened. So he was right; they had caught up with him. Perhaps this man even suspected he had killed Aiden. He did not allow his glance to waver. "I reckon I would have gone over too, 'ceptin' I was lashed to the mast." He paused. "Aiden was my friend," he added. "He was mourned."

The man rose from his seat. "Let me buy you a drink, Liam O'Dwyer, and we'll drink to the soul of Aiden McLean and to all other Irish patriots."

Liam followed him as he went to a table in the far corner of the dark dingy room. The nondescript man swiped his arm across the littered table. Empty bottles and tin cups crashed to the earthen floor and settled in the corner. He turned toward the bar. "Two mugs of porter," he shouted. The bartender immediately nodded, grabbed two cups, and pushed through the crowd to their table. "Yes, sir, Mr. Connors. Here ye are, sir, compliments of the house." He scuttled away.

Liam noted the respectful glances from the other men in the room. *So he is someone of importance*, he thought. Accepting the fact he was now reconnected with the revolutionaries, he sank into the chair opposite his host.

The man called Connors was of average height and build. There were no distinguishing features, except for the cold blue eyes and strong nose. His sandy hair grew close to his heavy eyebrows and hung from its center part to cover his ears. His hands were long and slender but looked strong, powerful even.

"We've been looking fer you," he said, looking straight into Liam's eyes.

"I expected you would be," Liam countered. "I had no contact after Aiden was drowned. I didn't want to speak to the wrong people, so I waited." He did not allow any emotion to show in his voice.

"Yes." Conner's look was one of judgment now. Liam waited. "Yes," the man repeated, "it makes sense."

They spoke in English. Liam knew there were few in the room who could speak more than a few words of the language and those with difficulty. The din of the many voices in the crowded room left little chance of being overheard.

"Can ye move on from this place sometime soon?" Connors asked Liam.

"You mean leave Boston?"

"Aye. Have ye made ties that can't be broken?" Connors took a deep draft from his cup.

"I don't make ties easily," Liam said, raising his own cup. He thought of Eamon and Maureen. He would be sorry to leave them, but he was ready to move on. He would have gone soon anyway, though he hadn't planned it in quite this way.

"Good. Doesn't pay to get too close to people in this business." Connors leaned over the table toward him. His voice was low, and Liam strained to hear. "We can use you in Connecticut. Make yer way to Farmington where they're building a new canal. Report to Colin McCarthy, the foreman on the job. He'll take you on. You'll get orders from him." He shoved back his chair, and for the first time, extended his hand to Liam. His grip was firm and strong. Liam felt the pull way up to his shoulder, and nodded, further sealing his commitment. Connors rose and made his way out of the smoke-filled pub.

Suddenly, the singing that had been going on in the background penetrated Liam's consciousness. It was another of Niall's favorites. He could picture his brother roaming through the fields, pouring out in clear crystal tones the songs of ancient Ireland. The vision overwhelmed him. How he missed his brother. He wished he were back home now with them all in the thatched roof cottage.

Liam finished his drink alone and went to find Eamon. The walk home was long and cold. He paced himself to Eamon's limp, lost in thought, Niall's singing ringing in his ears.

CHAPTER 7

NIALL'S TENOR TONES rang out over the audience, filling the New York Park Theatre with love and longing for Ireland and those left behind. Every eye focused on this new singer who could sway their emotions from laughter to tears with a voice sent straight from heaven. For a whole month, Niall's silvery tenor voice had entranced the Park Theatre audience as the opening act for various popular entertainers.

The nearly 1,200 music lovers had come this night to hear the lovely voice of the beautiful Clara Fisher. The tiny sixteen-year-old soprano, appearing for the first time in New York, had been a resounding success at the Drury Lane Theatre in London. The opening act of about twenty minutes was scheduled to allow latecomers to settle down before the main performance. According to the playbill, the new Irish tenor would "transport you to the Emerald Isle in a wave of heartwarming nostalgia."

Niall's dark curls gleamed like polished bronze in the glow of the stage lights. His wide white smile flashed across his handsome face, bronzed from his recent voyage from Galway. The ladies in the audience, both married and unmarried, clutched their hands to their breasts as their enthrallment made them breathless.

The applause thundered as Niall made his final bow. They stood and would not stop clapping. "More! More!" they shouted. It was atypical of the Park Theatre patrons. Niall held up his hands, smiling widely. As the sound died down, he began to sing again. His voice carried a quiver of longing, of homesickness. He sang of soft rain, of the mists, of the heather on the hills.

The bud on the gorse glowed gold in the sun
And the stream flowed soft to the sea,
The heather smelled sweet in the heat of the day
And the fields were all copper and green.
No matter how far as a traveler I roam
Twill always be home to me.

A hush fell over the audience. Niall made a sweeping bow and left the stage. The avalanche of applause followed him. They did not want him to leave. They stood and clapped and called for more.

In the wings, Niall beamed with pleasure. They loved him! They loved him! He caught the annoyed look on the face of Clara Fisher, the evening's main attraction. He decided to take another bow. Out of the corner of his eye, he caught a nod of approval from Roxanne. He strolled with nonchalance to center stage and bowed gracefully, allowing his smile to include every aisle of the barely seen audience. He threw two kisses at them and bowed again. Applause followed him as he walked off stage. *The beauteous Miss Fisher will have trouble quieting them down after that*, he thought with smug satisfaction.

Niall had been upset with Roxanne when she told him he would be the introductory act. He wanted star billing, but Roxanne insisted that as an unknown, they wouldn't draw a great enough audience—better to use Clara Fisher for the opening. She had been right, of course. He had played to a packed house. And they loved him!

Niall rushed to Roxanne and grabbed her, kissing her on the lips with enthusiasm. She threw her head back and laughed with delight. Over her shoulder, Niall saw her husband watching without expression. Only his eyes showed his disapproval. Niall dropped his arms from Roxanne's waist. "You're a wonderful manager, Roxanne. You and Sean really know your business."

He turned away from Roxanne's fallen face and went to Sean and grasped his hand. "A thousand thank-yous, Sean. I won't let you down. You can be assured I'll keep my end of our bargain." Sean hugged him around the ribs while the stage crew beamed.

The orchestra finished their piece and paused while the audience settled down. Clara Fisher walked onto the stage. Niall noticed the applause was considerably less than should be expected. He knew he had made it so. They were still hearing his voice.

The excitement of his reception kept Niall awake far into the night. He relived his few moments on stage over and over. He smelled the makeup; he felt the heat of the lights; he heard the sound of applause. It was everything he'd ever wished for. He wanted to shout, to sing. He could not believe his luck.

Niall had been in America exactly sixty days. His voyage across the Atlantic had been quite different from that of his older brother, for Niall traveled first class. He was completely unaware of the steerage passengers. He knew only that the weather was clear, the sea was gentle, and a good breeze carried them along at a fast clip.

Every day on board, he listened as Roxanne and Sean lectured about the New York theater, the makeup of the audiences, their likes and dislikes. Niall knew they were talking as much for themselves as for him. They had to make some decisions on how best to present him and the songs he would be singing.

The long afternoons on shipboard they spent in the passenger's lounge where a surprisingly good piano poured forth music under Sean's capable hands. Roxanne drilled Niall on ballad after ballad.

"It's the sad ones that will get them," she said. "They're all filled with longing for home, longing for their loved ones left behind. They don't want to forget. They're afraid they will forget. That's what will bring them back over and over. They want to keep their memories fresh, even though they are painful."

"But that doesn't make sense," Niall protested. "Why would anyone pay to come to the theater to be made miserable?"

Roxanne laughed. "Ah, but we Irish love to suffer," she said dramatically. "We like nothing better than to weep and gnash our teeth." She shook her coppery curls and rolled her green eyes in exaggerated tragedy.

"I don't believe it," Niall replied. He could not comprehend such a thing.

"But tis true, to be sure, Niall," Sean interrupted. "The Irish believe in suffering. The worse things are, the more justified they feel. That's how they have been kept cowed by the English and by the Church all these many years."

Niall shook his head in disbelief.

"And we're going to take advantage of that, Niall. We're going to appeal to their sorrow, their tragedy. We're going to wring their hearts, and we're going to do it with your grand, pure, heartrending, tenor voice," Sean said, accompanying himself with a dramatic tremor of the keys.

Every day they worked, both for the sixty-day journey and the thirty days that followed. They dug up all the old songs from their memories. They rewrote them to serve their purpose, and they composed new ones, incorporating the idea of emigration and settlement in a foreign country far from home.

Niall felt drained of emotion at the end of each day. As satisfying as the work was, he found it exhausting. He was thankful for the fact as he lay on his bunk at night remembering the posturing, curvaceous body of Roxanne. Niall had tried his best to keep his distance from her, but she was always there under his nose, tempting, tempting. Sean's eyes, too, were always there, daring him, challenging him.

Niall decided to bide his time. He needed them both, and he was not going to do anything to interfere with this opportunity. For now, he would keep his hands off his desirable boss. He found a not-so-appealing lady from County Clare two cabins down who was more than willing to appease his needs.

At last they sighted land, and an excitement spread over the ship like applause. After weeks of nothing but sky and water, Niall feasted his eyes on the dull shore. The land was flat with low, sandy beaches, and in the distance were pine forests. There was no enchantment, certainly not when compared to the land they had left, but it was land—the land of promise.

As they doubled Sandy Hook they found themselves in the outer bay, formed by the shores of Staten Island and Long Island, which Sean called the Narrows. The beauty was unexpected. On the left was Staten Island with bold and lofty heights covered with dark green wood to the very summit. Its cool, shady valleys were covered with rich vegetation which hung out over the water, touching the lapping waves. On a high bluff commanding a view to the sea stood a gleaming white lighthouse, and Sean pointed out a tall signal post used to telegraph the arrival of vessels to the city.

Farther on, Roxanne called Niall's attention to the brick building of the Seamen's Hospital, for which every passenger entering the Port of New York was taxed one dollar. At the foot of this edifice stood the village, its pitched, roofed houses scattered in all directions.

The harbour pilot boarded the ship and guided them toward the shore with energetic command. The crew took on new life and sprung quickly to follow his orders. The ship moved with a style she never knew or had hinted she possessed. Here, a brace was tightened; there, a halyard pulled. The sails sheeted home, and the ship moved proudly and majestically toward its destination.

Roxanne waved enthusiastically to the men on the newsboat which pulled alongside as they requested information about the ship. A statement would appear in the newspapers the next morning under the heading, "Shipping Intelligence," containing the name of each newly arrived vessel, the number of passengers, the length of the voyage, the freight carried, and any other facts the newsmen could gather. Roxanne hoped there would also appear an item that Mr. and Mrs. Sean O'Flaherty, owners of several New York theaters, had arrived from Galway.

An order was shouted from the quarterdeck and the ponderous anchor plummeted to the bottom. The ship swung round to the tide as the health officer boarded for his inspection. The next morning, Niall joined his companions on the sloop sent to escort them to shore.

For all his pretended sophistication, Niall was awed by the confusion, the noise, and the bustle near the wharves of this seaport town. The streets were filled with a continuous succession of carts pouring from side streets, laden with merchandise of every imaginable sort. These discharged their cargo onto towboats about to start for the interior. Other wagons were being loaded with materials taken from the newly arrived ships to be delivered to warehouses and shops.

Niall watched as confusion reigned. Wheels jammed against wheels as drivers fought for a place in the crowded street. Horses fell, loads were thrown off, and drivers cursed and shouted. Steam ferryboats crossed and recrossed the river to Brooklyn glittering on the opposite shore.

As far as they could see, the length of the huge river was filled with shipping. Sloops were trailing gay streamers, and splendid packet ships plowed stately through the dark water. Roxanne excitedly called Niall's attention to the other side of the quay where the town lay spread out before them. Rows and rows of houses of red, green, yellow, and white pushed inland, their upper-story shutters flung wide to catch the sun and the breeze from the sea. Colorful awnings stretched from shop to street in an uninterrupted line.

Sean and Roxanne ushered Niall along the quay and onto the sidewalk crowded with shoving, bustling humanity. Niall had never imagined that so many people could be jammed into so narrow a place, all intent on different purposes.

Cleverly painted signs hung swinging from over the doors of the shops that lined the walkways. Niall was embarrassed to admit he did not know what some of them meant. As skilled as he was in English, it was like a whole new language. "Domestics" did not mean help but "dry goods." The sign "bakery," he discovered, meant a place to purchase bread. "Storage" signs were displayed from every third or fourth building, and "taverns" were everywhere.

A man in black distributed Bibles, and a "carman" offered to take him to a first-rate boardinghouse that would charge only three dollars a week.

"Pay no attention to them," Roxanne advised, pushing her way through the mass of people. "We already have a place to stay, and we'll get rooms for you nearby. You can't trust those hackers."

Niall lay back on his soft bed and looked around at his cozy room. *I've come a long way*, he thought. *Here I've been in America exactly two months, and I have a neat little room and a position in the New York theater.* He relished again the sound of the applause. "They loved me," he said aloud, "and they're going to keep on loving me." He blew out the candle and settled under the warm blanket. *Next time I want top billing*, he thought as he dropped off to sleep.

CHAPTER 8

NIALL BRISKLY STROLLED along Fifth Avenue basking in the sunlight as well as in his continued success at New York's Park Theatre. Gentlemen now tipped their hats in recognition, and ladies lifted their eyes, showing soft, hopeful smiles when he touched his stylish hat in response to their admiring glances.

Niall enjoyed his new position in life. He loved being admired by men and women alike. He was good at what he did and he knew it, and best of all, they knew it. He carried his handsome, broad shoulders proudly, and held his richly bronzed head high, flashing his appealing smile at everyone who glanced in his direction.

Needing to impress the London songbird, Niall invited the lovely, shy Miss Clara Fisher for lunch at the Regency Hotel. He could not really afford the price of the expensive menu at the Regency but thought of it as an investment in his future.

He had been quietly courting the star since the second night of their performance. Roxanne had flatly refused Niall's request for equal billing with Miss Fisher. She would not jeopardize her contract with the popular soprano. Besides, she said, he needed the exposure, and Clara Fisher could draw large audiences. Niall had given this statement some thought. Miss Clara Fisher could do more than that for him, Niall concluded. She could be the means to hurry him along the way to top billing.

By the next evening, Niall's carefully planned campaign was under-way. He started with a delicate small bouquet of deep purple violets. His note said simply, "Violets for Beauty." It was signed, "An Irish Admirer." The next night he sent a small pottery container of shamrocks. His note said, "Shamrocks for Luck" with the same signature. She smiled at him for the first time as she left the stage.

Each night for a week, Niall left his token in her dressing room with the scrawled signature. On the seventh night, he placed a delightfully carved leprechaun on her dressing table. He stood back to admire his gift. Clara stepped from behind a screen. "I've caught you," she said with a delighted smile.

"Ah, and I thought ye'd think twas the leprechaun himself who brought ye all the tokens of admiration," Niall said in his most Irish accent.

Clara laughed with delight. "So you really did leave the flowers and things. I knew it had to be you." Her smoke-gray eyes sparkled. "I do thank you, Mr. DeCourcey."

"Ah, now, Miss Fisher, now that we're friends, couldn't ye be callin' me by me given name?" He laid the accent on thickly. "I'd really be enjoyin' that."

"Why, yes, I guess that would be all right, Niall, since we're working together every day. And you may call me Clara." She placed her small hand on his sleeve. Niall saw the blush rise to her cheeks at the contact.

"Thank you, Miss Fish . . . , I mean, Clara." He smiled down into the innocent eyes. "I really did mean that about being friends. I do enjoy working with you. You have a wonderful voice, and you're a truly beautiful lady." Her blush flushed darker.

For two more weeks, Niall paid her the most courteous attention whenever they met. At rehearsals, he quietly slid into the chair next to hers and paid her compliments. He was careful never to be alone with her for more than a few minutes. He kept in mind that she was only sixteen years old and inexperienced. She was also well chaperoned. He set out to win over the chaperone as well. Sensing that Clara was more than half in love with him by her admiring glances and the way she squeezed his hand when she thought no one was looking, he pressed on.

Niall had been careful to be most respectful and never to see her alone. But today he had suggested that they sneak away from the chaperone and have lunch together. He suggested the Regency, knowing it to be a respectable place for a lady to meet a gentleman for lunch. He also knew the theater columnists gathered there. They would be seen and mentioned in the press.

They arrived at the steps of the Regency at the same time. Clara, having successfully slipped away from her chaperone, wore a light gray outfit that matched her eyes. It fit close to her body and bound her tiny waist with bands of black satin. A matching hat, also trimmed with black satin ribbons, which tied beneath her pointed chin, framed her small face. She was a very attractive young lady.

He escorted Clara into the dining room with his hand under her elbow. He noted that she trembled. Could it be the first time she had been out alone with a man? *By this time at home*, Niall thought, *I would have her tumbling in the heather. But there are different rules here, and I have a different goal in mind.*

All eyes followed as the maître d' led them through the elegant dining room to a white damask-covered table. They made a handsome couple, and he was pleased they were attracting so much attention. Only after he had graciously seated his companion did he acknowledge the looks of recognition from the newsmen seated at a corner table.

"Would you like me to order for the both of us?" he asked as the gray eyes looked up from the fancy menu in confusion. Niall had taken advantage of the opportunity to study the menu and get recommendations from the maître d' when he made reservations the night before.

"Yes, Niall, please," she answered quietly.

"My pleasure, Clara." He appeared to study the menu briefly. "The steak and kidney pie is delicious here and will make you feel at home. How does that sound, with, perhaps, some asparagus tips? They're in season now and very tasty. A light red wine would be nice with that."

She nodded and gave him a grateful little smile. Niall placed their order and turned his full attention to his very pleasant companion.

During the meal, Niall saw that the newsmen watched them with interest. He casually reached over and picked up her hand as he paid her a compliment on last night's performance. "I shall be so sorry when you return to London, Clara. I can't believe a whole month is over, and your last performance is tomorrow night." He squeezed her hand gently and watched the faint color rise once again to her cheeks.

Clara tried to pull her hand away, and Niall pretended not to notice.

He gave her an intimate smile. "We work so well together," he said. "I wonder how we would sound singing a duet. It would be fun to try, don't you think?"

"Oh, Niall, what a delightful idea! Our voices would blend beautifully, and you make a wonderful appearance on stage."

"Let's!" Niall answered excitedly. "Let's surprise everyone, even Roxanne and Sean! I'm sure we could keep it a secret."

Clara giggled with delight. "What fun! Somehow they make so much work of everything. I just like to sing. Sometimes I think that if they'd all stop working so hard and just let us sing, the performance would be much better."

"My thoughts exactly. There's nothing like the feeling you get from singing in front of an audience." He pressed her hand again. "Let's put the fun back, Clara. Let's surprise everyone and sing together tomorrow night. You could make the announcement at the end of your program, and I'd come out and we'd do our number. What a grand finale to your tour! The audience will love it!"

"But we should rehearse, Niall, shouldn't we? How can we surprise them if we can't practice? I'm not sure it should be that unplanned."

"But wouldn't that take out the fun, Clara?" Niall looked deeply into the gray eyes.

She held his look for a moment then lowered her lashes in confusion. "Perhaps we could find a way to rehearse a number together," she said quietly.

"It would be an honor for me to sing with you, Clara. You're already so famous. Imagine playing in Drury Lane Theatre! I always dreamed of playing there, and now to sing with someone who has. Twould be such a grand thing for me."

"I'd enjoy singing with you too, Niall. You have a marvelous voice. I know you'll soon be a star in your own right."

Niall appeared deep in thought for a moment. "I have it!" he said. "I know how we can rehearse without raising any questions. You'll be rehearsing last, as always, this afternoon. I'll stroll onto the stage just as you finish, as though I had something to discuss with Sean. As I approach him at the piano, I'll be humming." He paused. "Do you think 'Greensleeves' would be a good number? I've heard you sing that, and it's one I have done." She nodded in agreement. "So I'll be humming 'Greensleeves,' and you'll hear me and start humming too. We'll smile and start singing together."

Niall watched Clara's expression play over her face. He had success within his grasp; he knew it. "We'll get Sean to play it, and we'll do the whole number. If we're excited and act pleased, we can get Sean to play it again to be sure we can do it well from the beginning." He sat back and folded his arms. 'What do you think, Clara? Do you think it will work? I can hardly wait to try."

Clara laughed. "I love the idea, Niall. Let's do it."

As they passed the table where the newsmen sat, Niall pretended he didn't notice, put his arm around Clara's waist, and gave her a familiar small hug.

Clara's performance went splendidly. Her final aria was perfect. The audience knew they would not have the opportunity to hear her again, and they gave her a warm, enthusiastic ovation. She bowed with grace and threw grateful kisses to them. As their applause grew thinner, she held up her hands to quiet them and poised to give her farewell.

"Thank you so much. You've been such a wonderful audience here in this lovely city, I've planned a little surprise for you as a farewell gift." She paused while the audience ruffled their anticipation.

"It has been a pleasure for me to work with the marvelous voice of Niall DeCourcey. You have shown how much you've enjoyed his wonderful tenor renditions. Mr. DeCourcey and I have decided to present you with a duet as a parting gift." Niall strolled onto the stage, and the audience broke into a pleased response. "Bravo!" a voice called out. The applause increased.

Niall bent over Clara's hand, touching it lightly with his lips before he bowed to the audience. He looked at the orchestra leader. "Could you give us the introduction to 'Greensleeves'?" he asked. The audience applauded their approval once more. They settled down as the orchestra picked up the familiar melody.

Their voices blended in perfect harmony. Her lilting soprano filled the air and flew out over the enthralled audience. His rich, warm tenor caressed them and assured them that love was forever. Her young, slim

body unconsciously leaned toward his tall, strong frame. His dark flashing eyes filled with desire. Her innocent red lips drew closer to his. Niall's gleaming smile shone in the circle of light that enclosed them as their voices rang out with the longing and passion of the music.

The audience went wild as they made their bows. Niall hugged her to him, letting the wave of sound sweep over them. "I told you they would love it," he whispered.

"You were wonderful! We were wonderful!" she replied.

Niall stepped back and took Clara's hand, bowing low. He then bowed once more to the audience and stepped toward the exit. The audience rose to its feet, and the applause thundered. Niall gave them one more bow and disappeared behind the curtain. The applause continued for several seconds.

Clara's final bow was anticlimactic. Niall had stolen the show. As she left the stage, she looked into his face with puzzlement. She saw his look of satisfaction. "You knew it would be like that, didn't you, Niall?" she asked. He threw out his hands in a helpless gesture, but he couldn't prevent the look of success in his eyes. She turned away and walked slowly to her dressing room.

Roxanne watched the little scene with pleasure. She rushed to Niall and threw her arms about his neck. "Niall, darling, you were wonderful!" she exclaimed. "The idea was strictly genius. I couldn't have come up with a better one myself. Starting Monday, you get top billing." She kissed him with enthusiasm and not a little desire. After a moment, Niall let her go. He looked at Sean and made the same helpless little gesture he had given to Clara.

CHAPTER 9

WITH EACH PERFORMANCE, Niall's success gathered momentum. New York's elite thronged to the theater and filled it to overflowing every night. The critics, to a man, praised his voice, his presentation, and his charisma. They also kept their readers informed of his attendance at social affairs throughout the city. His charismatic personality allowed him to be accepted by the city's theater crowd and the moneyed class alike.

Niall loved the attention and the acclaim. As his popularity grew, he sought out the city's most accomplished tailors and haberdashers and became a fashion plate, as well as an artist.

There was one other field in which he became well known, although this one did not appear in the press. One evening, Sean O'Flaherty invited him to come to his private club for a game of cards. The two had played a bit on the long voyage to America, and Sean had discovered that his fellow Irishman was a natural gambler.

Niall was pleased to be invited to the Gentleman's Club whose membership was made up of successful businessmen and investors in the growing area. Sean, through the success of his theaters, had earned his place with these prominent men. To be accepted into this group would mean success indeed, and Niall craved success in every field. He played the role of a rich Irish landholder to the hilt.

Dressing carefully in his newest gray frock coat and darker, tight-fitted trousers, he arranged the cravat of deep wine paisley which set off his russet hair. He carried a gray umbrella, a fashion of the men of the upper class. Niall felt a nervous excitement at the potential of the evening, but he was enough of an actor to appear at ease.

The elegance of the interior of the Gentleman's Club shouted in a quiet way as the two men entered the foyer. A dark thick Oriental rug covered the floor, and gleaming oak tables demanded their attention. The many-faceted crystal chandelier swung musically as the air from their entrance caressed it. The atmosphere held a faint odor of pipe and cigar.

Sean registered his guest at the desk where an elderly white-haired gentleman instantly recognized Niall and complimented him on his performances. Niall bowed his head briefly in acknowledgment.

They were led to a second-floor sitting area. Heavy overstuffed chairs were clustered in small groups, and a large fireplace, unused in this early autumn weather, dominated one end of the room. Here, too, the floor was covered with imported rugs and rich oak furniture. Gas lamps threw a soft light over the room.

Several men greeted Sean or came forward to be introduced. Each was identified by not only his name but by his business identity as well. Niall was impressed by the affluence represented. They were the most recognizable names and businesses in the city. They were the top lawyers, politicians, the most prominent landowners, and shipping magnates. Niall recognized and was warmly welcomed by Charles Hammond, the industrialist he had met and played cards with on board ship.

The group soon gathered around two beautifully polished gaming tables. Green-shaded gas lamps hung over each, highlighting the area. Niall found himself seated opposite Hammond, and he remembered the telltale look that appeared in Hammond's eyes which revealed his intentions. Niall knew he was more than a match for at least one of his opponents. He watched the others carefully as they played. They were a shrewd bunch, applying their business acumen to the game.

Having neither won nor lost heavily, Niall was invited to return. Twice a week for the next few months, the same group met. The same money changed hands over and over as they all had their good and bad nights.

Niall was careful not to win or lose too much, though his winnings grew steadily. A quiet excitement also grew in him. His scrutiny of his fellow gamblers had given him clues to their game.

He discovered that their business dealings were directly related to their card playing. When business was good, they were confident, forging ahead with a definite plan and nearly always ending the evening with success. When their business dealings were going badly, their card playing suffered too. They were unsure in their betting. They hesitated in their selection of cards. The way they moved both the cards and their money betrayed their day's activities.

Each night Niall watched beneath his thick long lashes. The first few hands told the story of the business day. Niall's winnings started to pile up, and he began to invest in the companies that he knew through his observations of his gambling associates were doing well.

Niall spotted early in their association that Charles Hammond was in trouble. He was losing heavily nearly every time they played. Niall decided to find out more about the newly industrialized textile mills he knew were Hammond's source of income. *Perhaps*, he thought, *there might be a hidden opportunity there. Sometimes, one man's failure could be another man's success.*

After the evening's game, the men often hung about the club, drinking and talking until the early-morning hours. Niall deliberately sought out Hammond, and they became quite friendly. Niall knew from their acquaintance aboard ship that Hammond loved to tell stories about his youth in Sussex. He encouraged him and listened attentively, throwing in a few stories of his own younger days, although they were far from the truth. In a few weeks, he was invited to Hammond's home for dinner. He was pleased with the progress he had made.

Niall was ushered into the fashionable brownstone mansion by a white-gloved butler who took his hat and cane and hung them on the oak hat tree in the long entranceway. Heavy doors lined the hallway, but he was led to an open doorway at the end of the intricately patterned carpet where he could see a fire glowing in an enormous fireplace.

He took in the room's elegance. Oak wainscoting ran around the almost square room, reflecting the fire's soft light. The room contained a variety of textures, all pleasing to the eye. Niall reminded himself that the wealth of this family came from the textile industry. The wallpaper was of a raised patterned texture entirely new to him, although he had been in many homes of New York's most wealthy personages. The upholstered chairs and settees were covered with brocaded flowered materials, which appeared both rich and practical. Even the scarves and runners covering the tops of the heavy golden oak tables were of textiles unknown to him.

Niall approached the group seated around the fire. Charles rose and extended his hand, grasping both of Niall's in his own. His grip was warm and sincere. "Come, come, my friend, and meet my family." He was led to an older woman whom he took to be Mrs. Hammond, and who sat with a coverlet covering her legs. Over the fireplace hung an oil painting of a beautiful lady whom Niall recognized at once as this woman in her youth. Her dark hair had faded now to a steely gray, and her mouth was drawn in, showing the pain she endured; but her eyes held the same bright intelligence and appeal.

She extended a small white hand to Niall. "I'm absolutely delighted to meet you at last, Niall DeCourcey. All New York is talking about your marvelous voice. Charles was gracious enough to take me to one of your performances, which I thoroughly enjoyed. Thank you for coming to New York."

Niall bent over her startlingly warm hand. "If for no other reason than to meet you and Charles, the trip was worth it," he said.

The young lady in the chair on the opposite side of the fireplace smiled at Niall. "I hope you will include me in that comment as well, Mr. DeCourcey."

"Our daughter, Mary Margaret," Charles interjected.

Niall crossed to her and took her hand. She was not as young as he thought at first glance, nor did she have the beauty of her mother. She was not ugly, but instead, simply plain. Niall could think of no other word. She was uncommonly plain.

"I'm sure you will be named first when I've had the opportunity to know you better, Miss Hammond. An opportunity I look forward to." He lingered a fraction of a second over her hand. Charles beamed with delight. Mary Margaret's colorless eyes studied Niall without expression.

The butler arrived with a tray of drinks. "Shall we have a small cocktail before dinner, Niall?" Charles asked. "I have persuaded the ladies to join us."

"A wonderful idea. Thank you, Charles." Niall's polished smile encompassed the two ladies. Mrs. Hammond motioned him to a seat next to her.

"English sherry for my favorite ladies," Charles said as he served them from an extended silver tray, "and scotch for our guest and myself." He seated himself beside his daughter.

Mrs. Hammond looked contentedly about her. "It's such a pleasure to have my family seated around me in the evening. Do you have a family, Mr. DeCourcey?" She sipped at her small glass of sherry.

"Ah no, I'm afraid not," Niall said with a sad shake of his handsome head. "My parents are long gone. I have no one but some cousins in Ireland. I do envy Charles for the comfort and pleasure this home and family must give him." Niall included the whole room in his expressive gesture. *What a polished liar I have become*, he thought.

"You'll be welcome whenever you wish to enjoy it, Niall," Charles said. "We're a small family and have room to include more."

"Thank you, Charles. I'm fortunate to have a friend like you," Niall replied. Mary Margaret studied him but did not add to the conversation. Niall gave her a warm look over his glass. Except for a questioning raise of her eyebrows, her expression remained placid.

The butler spoke from an adjoining doorway. "Dinner is served, ma'am."

"I'll not be joining you for dinner," Mrs. Hammond said. She looked squarely into Niall's face. "I've not been well lately, so I must go to my room. It's been a pleasure to meet you, Mr. DeCourcey." She extended her hand to Niall. He pressed his lips to it, feeling the feverish heat once more.

"My pleasure, Mrs. Hammond. I hope you will be well again soon." She gave him a sad little smile but said nothing. The butler moved behind her chair, and Niall realized that it had been placed on casters. Charles bent over and kissed her cheek as the butler rolled the chair from the room.

"I'll be up later, Mother," Mary Margaret said. "Shall we go in for dinner?" she asked, extending her arm to Niall as the door closed behind her mother.

The conversation at dinner was light and entertaining. They spoke of their enjoyment of Niall's performances. Charles and Mary Margaret had seen several of them. They also spoke of the Boston area where they had a summerhouse. "Most of the textile mills are in the Boston area, you know," Charles said.

"I should like to see them sometime," Niall said casually.

"We'll have to arrange that," Charles answered.

"Perhaps when we get settled at the summer house, you can join us for a few days," Mary Margaret rejoined.

"An excellent idea, an excellent idea," Charles added.

"I'd be delighted," Niall said. "I'll arrange my schedule to get away whenever you suggest."

"Wonderful, wonderful," Charles said. He pushed back his chair and rose. "Shall we have coffee and cigars in my study, Niall?"

Mary Margaret rose too, and Niall scrambled to his feet. "I always have my coffee upstairs with Mother," she said. "So I'll say good night, Mr. DeCourcey."

"I do so hope I'll see you again, Miss Hammond. It's been a pleasure." Niall pulled her chair out of the way and took her hand. "You have been a most pleasant hostess." He kissed her hand slowly and saw the guarded light in her eyes.

"I would enjoy having you call again, Mr. DeCourcey," she said formally. She gave him no time to answer but moved from the room with surprising grace. Niall knew she was leaving any further contact up to him. *A girl as plain as she had little other choice*, he thought, *if she were not to be embarrassed by refusal*.

During the next few months, Niall was invited often to the Hammond home after his performances, though he saw little of the plain daughter. Mrs. Hammond grew weaker and weaker and seldom left her room. Mary Margaret spent her evenings reading to her mother.

Gradually, Niall discovered the extent of Hammond's holdings in the textile mills in both Waltham and Lowell in Massachusetts. Charles owned a large amount of the stock in both Boston area mills. He was also the treasurer of the Lowell Mills. Niall was a good listener and encouraged Charles to talk about his business affairs.

Hammond's twice-weekly card games suffered as his wife's condition deteriorated. The Waltham mills were going downhill, Niall discovered.

This knowledge helped him win heavily against Charles. Night after night, his winnings grew, and he invested all he could afford in Charles's Lowell mill.

Mrs. Hammond slipped into a coma. She had not long to live. Charles lost interest in his business and spent more and more time at his wife's bedside. Mary Margaret encouraged him to continue his games at the Gentleman's Club for he needed to get out of the house. He lost heavily.

Niall knew the night was coming when Charles would give himself away entirely, and he would have to be ready. He had to find a way to get more cash, for he had invested most of what he had won and his cash was low.

In his room, Niall fingered the brooch Jocelyn Winters had given him as a parting gift. *Were the stones real,* he wondered. *Were those truly emeralds and diamonds?*

The next day, he approached a jeweler on Madison Avenue. He had purchased several pieces of jewelry for his lady friends there and asked for an appraisal.

"Are you sure you want to part with this, Mr. DeCourcey?" the jeweler asked.

"For now, I just want to know the value," Niall replied. "The brooch has been in my family for generations. I don't think it has ever been appraised. I'd like to know its worth today."

"Stones like these are always a good investment, my friend," the jeweler said, adjusting his eyepiece to a new angle. "These are some of the finest emeralds I've seen in a long time." He studied the piece again. "And the diamonds are flawless as well." Niall felt his excitement rise. *God, bless dear, sweet Jocelyn*, he thought; *she had parted with the family heirlooms.*

Two days later, Niall sold the brooch to another jeweler. He knew he received less than its real value, but the roll of large bills in his pocket was more money than he had known existed a few short months ago. There was enough to give him a stake anywhere. He thought of Charles and his vast holdings in the textile industry. *There is a lot more to be had than what I have now*, he thought. He would be ready when Charles was ripe for the picking.

Charles was in trouble before the night's play was hardly underway. He bet heavily. One by one, the others dropped out as Niall won steadily, but Charles would not give up. He kept raising his bets, and Niall decided his friend no longer cared whether he won or lost.

They were the only two left in the club by two o'clock. Niall asked before every hand if he wished to stop, but Charles indicated he wanted to go on. Niall continued to win.

At last, Charles drew a slip of paper from his waistcoat. "This represents my interest in the Lowell Mills," he said. "I will wager this against everything you have won tonight."

Niall swallowed hard. This was the opportunity he had been waiting for. He shuffled the cards slowly. He looked across the table at the man who had befriended him. "You're sure you want to do this, Charles?" he asked. Charles nodded his head. Niall dealt the cards.

He knew from his first look at his cards that he had won. Charles drew one card, then another. Niall took one and stood pat.

Charles laid his cards on the table. "Two pair," he said slowly.

Niall placed his own hand face up. "Full house," he said. He didn't offer to draw in his winnings. Charles took a sip from his glass of scotch. Niall watched him carefully.

At last, Charles raised his eyes. He looked his friend full in the face. "I have one more offer, Niall. I will resign as treasurer of the Lowell Mills and support your candidacy, which would be almost automatic with my support." He hesitated. "I also include my daughter's hand in marriage. Take both or neither. If you win, it's all yours. If you lose, I take the whole pot."

"You can't be serious, Charles," Niall protested.

"I'm very serious, my friend. The treasurer's position is worthless to me without the stock. It could mean a great deal to you. And as for my daughter, she is nearly thirty years old. She has no prospects for a husband. She is, as you know, no raving beauty. It would give her mother and me a great deal of pleasure if she were to be married to a man like you."

"Mary Margaret is a wonderful person. Any man would be fortunate, indeed, to have her for a wife, but I have no plans in my future for a wife," Niall spluttered.

Charles studied him. Niall shifted uncomfortably. *He's neither as drunk nor as desperate as I thought,* Niall realized.

"You should not forget, Niall, my entire fortune goes with my daughter. Her mother and I have no other heirs. You could do a lot worse."

Niall studied Charles's face. He looked at the pile of money on the table in front of him. He wet his lips. The slip of paper representing the Lowell Mills fluttered as his breathing increased. He extended his hand to Charles. "Agreed," he said.

Charles took his hand. "There is one stipulation only," he said. "Mary Margaret is never to know of this. You will propose marriage in the usual way." Niall offered his hand in agreement, and they briefly shook.

Charles picked up the deck. "The hour is late," he said. "Shall we decide on a draw of the cards?" Niall nodded in agreement. Charles dealt one card to Niall, face up. The jack of spades. He dealt himself one card, face down. He placed the pack on the table to his left and took a sip from his glass. He turned the card over without looking. Niall stared at the five of hearts.

Charles Hammond extended his hand across the table to Niall. "You've won fair and square, son," he said. Niall stared at the pile in the center of the table and all it represented. Elation swept over him. Everything was his. He smiled broadly at Charles. "Thank you, Charles," he said.

"I'll tell Mary Margaret you'll be calling tomorrow evening, shall I?" Charles asked.

Niall swallowed noisily. "Yes yes, of course," he said slowly. Charles left the room as Niall collected his winnings from the table.

Niall went directly to Roxanne's flat. He knew that Sean was in Boston. Roxanne's face showed both surprise and pleasure as she opened the door. Her voluptuous figure showed clearly through the sheer garment she had hastily drawn over her nightclothes. Niall swept her into his arms without speaking and kissed her with the passion that had built up over the past months.

"I wondered how much longer it would take for you to come to me," Roxanne said as she gently closed the door.

CHAPTER 10

AT THE SAME moment that Niall sold Jocelyn's emerald-and-diamond brooch to finance his gambling, Kate opened the door of Jocelyn's room in their London home. She gasped at the sight of Jocelyn and Sidney Atkinson entangled in the rumpled bedclothes. The two sprang apart at the sound, their naked bodies exposed to her view.

Jocelyn slid from underneath Sidney's white body and threw her arms up over her head. Her long blond curls tumbled about her sheepishly smiling face. "Wait! Wait, Kate!" Jocelyn called out as Kate tried to back out the door.

"I'll come back when you are dressed—both of you," Kate called and pulled the door quickly shut on the scene. She closed her eyes, her breath rapidly increasing. She could not believe what she had seen. Kate knew her employer was prone to ending up in bed with nearly every man she met, but this was the first time she had actually walked in on them.Kate leaned heavily against Jocelyn's door. She would see that no one else in the house discovered what had been going on inside that room.

Jocelyn knew she was doing wrong. She also knew that her father had been terribly upset over her escapade with Niall at Kenmare. Jocelyn had sworn it would never happen again and had begged to be allowed to go out socially once more. After all, now she had a companion who would look out for her.

Jocelyn's father had given in after a few weeks of cscorting his daughter and Kate about by himself. He was a kindly man with a huge potbelly and a fringe of white hair around his bald head. He loved his only child with a passion and could deny her nothing. Jocelyn took only a few days to convince him that everyone but herself had been to blame. It was what he wanted to believe. He kissed the top of her head and told her he knew she would never allow herself to be compromised again.

Kate sighed. Mr. Winters would never believe his daughter enjoyed these escapades. In his eyes, she would always be innocent. Kate also knew if Jocelyn was caught by anyone else, the blame would fall on her. It was her job to keep Jocelyn out of trouble. Then what would she do? She had left everything behind in Ireland.

Kate heard the doorknob turn behind her. She stepped away. Sidney opened the door and came out. He glanced at Kate, cleared his throat uncomfortably, and moved quickly to the stairs. Kate heard his footsteps cross the foyer below and the sound of the heavy door open and close. She sighed and opened Jocelyn's door and went in.

Jocelyn sat in front of her dressing table. She was fully clothed and was arranging the mass of curls on top of her head. Her deep blue eyes looked into the mirror and caught Kate's disapproving glance. She swung around, laughing at Kate's expression.

"Don't look so shocked, Kate darling," she said, swinging the silver hairbrush toward the still rumpled bed. "Sidney's not so bad. I might even marry him some day."

"That's ridiculous, Jocelyn," Kate said sternly. "You won't marry Sidney, and you know it."

"Sidney would make a good husband, if one wanted a husband," Jocelyn said slowly. "He's a successful barrister, and his father's in Parliament. Besides, he's not so bad in bed."

"Jocelyn! Stop that!" Kate exclaimed.

"Do I shock you, Katie, luv?" Jocelyn turned back to her mirror and began to brush her hair again. "You know, Kate, you're still a prim little Irish Catholic even after living with me for six months. The blessed Lord and all your Irish saints only know how that can be."

Kate sat in the small lavender chair by the window looking out over Hyde Park. "You can do as you like, Jocelyn. I know you will anyway, but it's my duty to see that you stay out of trouble. Your father will dismiss me if you are caught. You know how poorly I lie. I just can't cover up for you and be convincing." Kate's large, innocent, dark eyes held Jocelyn's in the mirror.

"Oh, Kate, I'm sorry. I never think about anyone but myself, do I?" She lowered her eyes and hung her head.

Kate knew it was an act and ignored the remark. "Why don't you just give Sidney up?" she asked.

"Oh, I could give up Sidney easily enough, luv. He's just for fun, after all. But surely you don't expect me to be entirely celibate? I'm not one of your nuns after all."

"That's true enough," Kate replied with a sigh. "But what are we to do? Your father is going to hear about this, or if not this time, then the next. You really must start acting like the lady you are, Jocelyn."

"But, Kate, life is so boring without men. I can't bear afternoon teas and recitals and 'Good morning, Mrs. Smythe, how are you this morning?' and all that rot."

"We must think of something, Jocelyn. If your father dismisses me, you know he'll get some older woman to be your companion. You're not going to like that. She won't put up with all the things I do."

Jocelyn rushed to Kate, dropped to her knees, and threw her arms around her. "Oh Kate, you've been such a darling. You really have, and I do appreciate you, and I don't want to lose you. I would hate having anyone else underfoot all the time. I'll be good. I truly will."

Kate returned her embrace. "Oh Jocelyn, you know you won't be good. You promise that every time. But couldn't you be more careful, at least? I mean, after all, having a man in your bedroom in the middle of the morning—with all the maids scurrying around the upstairs and all. You really must use more sense. Anyone could have opened that door. You're lucky twas only me."

"I will, luv. I will be more careful." She rose to her feet. "You won't leave me, will you, Kate?"

"Of course I won't leave you, Jocelyn, not until your father says I have to go."

Kate left Jocelyn to finish arranging her hair. She went to her own room and put on her coat and hat. The autumn day was brisk, and a walk in the park would clear her head.

As she buttoned her high-collared coat tightly around her neck, the cool air struck her. She crossed the cobblestone street to the fenced park that stretched as far as she could see. It was a marvel that such a wonderful area had been saved in the middle of the huge city. She loved the park and walked there most days.

Nearly all the dried leaves had fallen from the trees, and she kicked at them as she walked along. The smell reminded her of home. *How I miss them all back at the little cottage. Why haven't I heard from them? Why have my letters been returned? What has happened to Mam and Declan?*

Kate had received only two letters since she came to London six months ago. She had written to explain that Niall went to America, and that she was coming to London with Jocelyn. Declan had written back after Gran had died and Maire's baby was born. It had been a sad little letter. It hadn't sounded at all like Declan.

His second letter told her that Liam had sent passage money for Donal and Maire and their baby daughter. The rain, he said, had been falling for weeks; and a whole field of potatoes had rotted. But she was not to worry; there was still the other field. There would be enough with only him and Mam there. But Kate was worried when there was no further word.

What had happened? Had the only other field of potatoes rotted as well? Were they starving? In her last few letters, Kate had enclosed money she had saved, but they had come back to her. "Unclaimed," it said on the smudged and tattered envelopes. What had happened to her family? Where were they?

If only she could go back for a few days, just to be sure they were all right, Kate thought. But there was no way. How would she get to Liverpool by herself? And then she would have to get from Cork City to Kinsale. Even if she had the money, she wouldn't know how to make the arrangements, and there was no one to go with her.

Could she ask Edward for help? Kate was not sure what she should make of Edward's attention. He watched her with interested eyes and was most attentive. He searched her out at the social events she attended with Jocelyn, and he had called at the house often—so often that Jocelyn said he was a nuisance.

Still Kate treated him with cool detachment. Her attraction to him made her feel uncomfortable. She did not trust her own feelings and imagined he saw her as some kind of curiosity. He obviously had not remembered their first meeting in the fort at Ringrone Peninsula. She was glad of that, but he had made an impression on her that day which she would never forget. She apparently had not made the same impact on him. Perhaps that was what bothered her. No, she could not impose upon Edward for help. She did not want to be obligated to him for anything. There could be no future for their relationship. She was a nobody, and he was an English gentleman. She would not encourage him, however deeply she felt.

Kate walked through the falling leaves and the cold autumn sunlight without seeing or hearing anything around her. She fought off a sense of depression. If only she could go back home. If only she could see her family again, then she would be content. The old familiar feeling of homesickness made her weak with longing. She decided to rest for a while.

As she approached the bench, a priest rose and turned to leave. He stopped directly in front of her. "Kate! Kate O'Dwyer!" he shouted. His arms flung out in welcome.

"Father McBride?" Kate questioned. "Is it really you?" She stepped into his embrace. *Someone from home*, she thought. *Twas a miracle!*

"Oh Kate, Kate," he said, his arms encircling her and drawing her close. "How wonderful to see you!" His hands rose to stroke her hair; his body pressed against hers.

Kate drew away, uneasy at his overfamiliar welcome. "Whatever are you doing in London, Father? Do you have news of my family? All my letters have been returned. What has happened over there?"

"Oh, Kate, it's good to see you. You look wonderful, just the way I remembered." He held her at arm's length, his hands still on her shoulders. He studied her. "Except you're quite the fashionable young lady now, aren't you?"

"Father, please, where is my family? Tell me."

Father McBride led her to a bench and sat her down beside him. He took her hands in his. "They're gone, Kate. All of them. Every family on the peninsula."

"Gone?" Kate asked in bewilderment. "What do you mean, gone? Gone where?"

"Gone to America, Kate. All of them. The blight hit every farm. There was nothing but a sickening black mass in the fields. There was nothing to eat. They would have starved if they had stayed."

"But how did they get to America? What did they do for passage money?" Kate could not understand how they could have money for passage if they had none for food.

"Squire Atkins paid passage for them. They didn't want to go, but he said he wanted to clear the land for grazing cattle. I told them they had to go, that they would starve if they stayed." He paused and dropped Kate's hands. He clasped his own hands between his knees. "They blamed me for not standing up for them—my own parishioners. They said I had deserted them." His eyes raised to Kate's. "But I was right. I know I was right. Squire Atkins would have let them starve. I did what I thought was best for them."

He looked away from Kate's stricken face. "In the end, your mother spoke up for me," he said in a bewildered voice. "Isn't that strange? She was the only one who spoke up for me."

They sat in silence for several minutes. Kate's mind tried to sort over all she had heard. She could not image the whole village gone, the ground empty. "Gone," she said. "Mam and Declan. Gone to America."

Father McBride picked up Kate's hand once more, rubbing it between his own. "Declan left with the others, Kate, but not your mother." Kate's eyes sprang up to meet his in sudden panic. "She's dead, Kate. The consumption finally caught up with her. She died the night before they were to leave."

Kate gave a cry of pain. Father McBride gathered her into his arms. She wept on his shoulder, unaware when he began to stroke her hair and kiss her cheek, holding her close. His lips traveled to her white neck, exposed as he stroked the long black strands away while she sobbed. Suddenly, he was kissing her lips, not gently, but with a passion out of control. "Oh, Kate, oh my love, how often I have dreamed of this."

Kate struggled to get away, realizing all at once what was happening. "Please, Father! Stop!" She twisted her body away from him, but he pulled her closer.

"Don't pull away from me, Kate. We're all there is left. Just you and I. We need each other. You need me, and I need you." He placed his lips on hers again, demanding, trying to force a response.

Kate struggled against him. "You don't know what you're doing,

Father! You don't know what you're saying!" She broke free of his grasp and jumped from the bench.

He took a step toward her then dropped his arms. "I'm sorry, Kate. I don't know what took hold of me." He could not look into her eyes. "I guess it's just being so far from home and . . . and . . ."

"Yes, Father," Kate broke in. "That's it. Homesickness is a terrible thing. I've felt so alone sometimes. Yes yes, that must be the reason." She rushed the words, anxious to accept any excuse for his action. She turned away from him, pulling her handkerchief from her pocket and scrubbing her mouth. She wiped away her tears and sat down on the bench stiffly. He was her parish priest; she would not think of what had happened.

After a long awkward silence, Kate cleared her throat and said tentatively, "You didn't tell me, Father McBride, what you are doing in London."

He sat at the opposite end of the bench. His face was white and his square chin quivered despite his clenched lips. Kate closed her eyes as she thought of those lips pressing against hers. *How could he have done it?*

Father McBride leaned over his clasped hands, which hung between his knees in dejection. "I . . . I was sent here to train for duty in a mission church. I'll be sent to America soon. They don't have enough churches now that there are so many Catholics immigrating."

Kate turned her mind off to everything but his words. She would not permit herself to think or feel anything. "Will you like that?" she asked.

He didn't look at her. "It won't be Ireland, but at least I'll have a parish again."

"Yes," she said, "that will be good." She heard the words and made the appropriate replies, but all she felt was a numbness.

There was nothing left to say. Silence settled between them. Finally, she rose and faced him. He got up from the bench and shook her hand briefly, letting it drop between them. "Thank you, Father, for the news of my family," she said quietly.

"Can I call on you, Kate? To bring you any news I have? After all, I am your parish priest and your only contact with home."

"No, Father, I think it would be best if you didn't." She saw that his eyes were stricken with pain. "Let's make this our good-bye," she said. "I wish you luck with your mission."

"Thank you, Kate," he said. "I hope you will be happy."

"Good-bye, Father." She turned away and walked briskly down the path toward home.

CHAPTER 11

KATE WAS BACK in her room and had taken off her coat before the traumatic events of the day caught up with her. She began to shake and could not stop. The actual sight of Jocelyn in bed with Sidney had been a jolt she had not admitted even to herself. She thought she had become very adult since she left the tiny village in Ireland and moved into Kenmare Castle and then on to the huge Georgian mansion in the elite part of London.

The truth was that she was accepting this new life only on the surface. She had not allowed the reality to seep into her subconscious. Having been raised in an Irish Catholic community, she was still innocent. She accepted without question the strict dogma she had been taught concerning the sins of the flesh. The unexpected sight of a naked Jocelyn under an equally naked male body had been a brutal shock.

Before the truth of what she had seen was fully accepted, the news of her mother's death and Declan's departure for America was thrust upon her. The idea that her home and her entire village had been wiped off the surface of the earth was still more than she could grasp. Her mind was too full of the other catastrophes. She could not even consider the possibility.

Kate went into shock. She did not remember that Father McBride had taken her into his arms and had kissed her with a fiery desire to possess her entire body. Her mind shut it out, and there remained only the encompassing feeling that she had committed a grievous sin for which there was no forgiveness.

Jocelyn found her in her room wide eyed and trembling, a blanket wrapped around her body. She could not speak. Every time Jocelyn asked a question, Kate mumbled incoherently and tears rolled down her waxen face.

Jocelyn put Kate to bed and summoned a doctor. Upon examination, he could find nothing wrong with the girl except for what appeared to be a chill. "She seems to have had a shock of some kind," he said. "Has something happened recently to upset her?"

Jocelyn immediately remembered the scene that morning in her bedroom but dismissed it. Kate was certainly more sophisticated than that. *Hadn't she known since the beginning that this kind of behavior was a part of my life?*

"She seemed to be fine when she left for her walk in the park. We had a minor disagreement this morning, but she didn't appear unduly upset."

The doctor held a candle close to Kate's eyes. "Definitely a shock of some kind," he said again. He looked up at Jocelyn on the other side of the bed. "She went for a walk in the park you said. Hmm . . ."

"My god, you don't think she was raped?" Jocelyn exclaimed.

"Well, I didn't want to suggest such a thing to you, but there's always that possibility . . . er . . . ah, perhaps we should have one of the older maids come in while I examine her."

"Oh for God's sake, Doctor. I'm not a child. Examine her. We need to know."

He pulled back the bedclothes. Kate's body flinched under his touch. The doctor examined her carefully. "No, she hasn't been raped. She's still a virgin." He ran his eyes over her legs, her stomach, and even turned her over and looked at her buttocks. "No sign of bruises even." He covered the trembling body, tucking the covers gently around Kate's shoulders. "We can rule out a physical attack."

"Thank God for that favor," Jocelyn said with a sigh.

"Yes, but that leaves only an emotional crisis. Who could she have met in the park?" The doctor packed his instruments into his bag. "Who were her friends? Does she have a young man she's interested in? Sometimes, these young girls take casual attention from men very seriously."

Jocelyn's mind flew instantly to Edward. She knew Kate was in love with him, and she suspected that Edward was half in love with Kate, though he didn't know it. He had been their constant companion since they arrived in London. But Edward was not the kind of person who would cause anyone so much as a headache, let alone a trauma like this. She was puzzled. There was no one else she knew whom Kate could have met. "She has no real friends here," she said. "Of course she has met many of my social circle, but there is no one who paid her any special attention."

"Her family then?" The doctor asked, picking up his bag.

"They're all back in Ireland or in America. She doesn't talk about them much." Jocelyn watched the white face with the enormous black eyes. *Even in this condition, she is beautiful,* she thought.

"Well, Miss Winters, have someone keep an eye on her for a few days. I'll be back on Friday to have a look at her. No doubt she'll be recovered by then." He opened the door and hesitated. "Keep her in bed, and I would have someone with her at all times, if that is possible."

"Oh yes, I'll stay with her myself. Thank you, Doctor," Jocelyn said, closing the door behind him.

For more than a week, Kate lay without speaking, without interest in what was going on. Jocelyn was faithful in her promise to look after her and sat by her bed, holding the small white hand, talking away about all the everyday little happenings. Kate watched her animated face with large eyes, without reacting.

Edward Graham came to sit beside his beautiful Irish friend. He talked in soothing tones, reassuring her that she was loved and needed. "Indeed what would we do without you? Jocelyn would be completely wild by now, and I would be lost. Since the first time I saw you with your face streaked with tears in that tumbled-down keep at the end of Ringrone Peninsula, your dear sweet face has haunted me."

Kate's eyes did not acknowledge she heard him.

"Whatever are you talking about, Edward?" Jocelyn asked.

"She never told you?" Edward looked from the white face on the bed to the blond beauty of his cousin. "I didn't think the two of you had any secrets."

"Well, obviously the two of you have been keeping something from me. I thought you met for the first time at the Kilarney Horse Show."

Edward turned back to the girl on the bed. He picked up her hand and held it to his cheek. "I didn't recognize her at the time, but there was something about her that kept nagging at my memory. I could not possibly have forgotten so interesting a face." He moved his lips to caress the hand he held. "It wasn't until I saw her lying here with those haunted eyes that I remembered."

"Remembered what? For heaven's sake, Edward, tell me."

Edward watched the face on the pillow. "I thought she was an apparition when I saw her," he said softly. "She was lying in a pile of straw in the corner of an abandoned fort. She was frightened when she discovered I was there. She jumped up, those dark eyes all startled and innocent."

Edward paused, studying the cameo face before him. When he spoke again, it was as though in a dream. "She wore a quaint dark skirt and a white bodice wrinkled from her sleep. Her wild black hair was tangled, and she pulled back the long strands with that graceful gesture she has, twisting them into a cascade at the back of her neck. She was the most beautiful thing I had ever seen." Edward's eyes lingered on each feature as he talked. "She had a strange way of speaking, but her English was fair and her brogue thoroughly delightful." Edward pushed a few strands of black hair from the delicate face. "I was completely enchanted."

"But what happened? Why didn't you recognize her?" Jocelyn asked.

"I saw her only that once. She looked nothing like your composed companion. I found nothing of that wild Irish girl in her when I met her in Kilarney." He paused. "Yet there was something . . . something that I couldn't forget . . . but could not remember . . ."

Jocelyn studied her cousin's face. "I do believe you're in love with her, Edward."

Edward rose and took Jocelyn's hands. "I do believe I am," he said.

One morning as Jocelyn sat down on the edge of Kate's bed, ready to feed her from the breakfast tray the maid had placed before her, Kate brushed her hair back from her face and said, "Why is everyone waiting on me? I don't need to be waited on."

Jocelyn swept Kate into her arms, tears streaming down her cheeks, "Oh Kate, luv, you're better. Oh, I knew you'd be all right." She hugged the thin body to her and rocked her back and forth.

"What are you doing, Jocelyn? Of course I'm all right." Kate replied.

Jocelyn sat back and examined her friend. "I'm so glad, Kate. You must be hungry. See, we've brought a tray for you."

"I'm starved," Kate said, "but you needn't have brought a tray." She reached out. "How good it looks." She smiled her old familiar smile.

Jocelyn beamed at her. "I've missed your smile, Kate. I'm glad to see it again."

Kate studied her face as she devoured a slice of toast. "I guess you'd better explain to me what's happened, Jocelyn." She looked down at the food on her tray. "I'm not sure I remember. Snatches of things keep coming to my mind." She pushed the breakfast tray away.

Jocelyn moved the tray back in place. "You eat your breakfast first, and I promise I'll tell you everything."

Kate returned her smile. "All right. I agree. I'm hungry."

Kate could not believe at first she had been unaware of anything for more than two weeks; but slowly, as Jocelyn talked, events began to slide back into her memory. She had heard everything that had been said, but only now did they reach her conscious mind. "Edward . . . ," she said, "he remembers that day at the fort."

"Oh, he does," Jocelyn said with excitement, "every detail." Kate smiled.

A silence followed at the thought of Ringrone Peninsula and her home. Memory came flooding back. Her huge eyes looked up at Jocelyn. "She's dead, you know. Mam's dead. From the consumption, he said. And Declan's gone to America. The whole village is gone."

Jocelyn held Kate's hand as she talked. It all came out, sometimes tumbling in a rush and at other times, hesitantly, painfully—all but the unacceptable scene of Father McBride taking her in his arms and forcing on her his hot, passionate kisses. She could not talk about that, not yet—maybe not ever.

Kate's recovery was slow but steady. Edward was attentive, stopping by every day. He brought her funny little gifts she could not refuse. He brought her books to read that explored more fully the ideas they discussed. It was a stimulating time, and Kate began to accept that life was still good, and these were her friends. Except for the empty space within her left by her mother's passing, she could not remember being so happy.

One evening as Kate and Jocelyn sat talking with Edward, Mr. Winters came home bursting with news. "What is it, Father?" Jocelyn asked. "You look like you can't wait to tell us something."

"How would you like to go to America, my dear?" he asked, stopping in front of his daughter and looking anxiously into her face.

"America? When? I'd love it!" Jocelyn squealed with delight.

"We'd leave in March or April. I've decided to open an office in Boston. We'll be shipping lumber from there."

"Boston! How wonderful!" Jocelyn exclaimed. Her eyes flew to Kate's. She would be able to see Niall! What marvelous luck!

"I'm leaving the London operation in Edward's hands. We've worked out the arrangements, but we didn't want to tell you until everything was settled." Mr. Winters went on, strolling to his favorite chair and lighting his pipe.

Jocelyn glanced at Edward. "You mean you knew and you didn't tell me? Edward, how could you?"

Kate glanced anxiously from Jocelyn to Mr. Winters. *Was she to go with them? Would she really be able to see her brothers again?* She held her breath, but then she remembered that Edward would be staying in London. Did he really love her? Could she leave him without knowing?

Mr. Winters smiled. "Of course you'll come with us, Kate. You're part of this family now."

Jocelyn flew to Kate and flung her arms around her. "Of course you will, Kate. I wouldn't go without you. Father knows that."

Mr. Winters smiled at the two girls as they danced around the room, their arms about each other. "It's settled then. Good." He left the room as they grabbed Edward's hands and included him in their celebration.

CHAPTER 12

THE CROWD OF peasants moving toward the gangplank shoved Maire and Donal along the quay. The great double-masted ship rocked gently with the swell of the incoming tide. Maire clasped the heavy bundle of clothing under one arm and the sling, which held her baby, tied under the other. Brigid slept contentedly, unaware they were literally being shoved from Irish soil.

Behind her, Donal protected them as best he could from the press of humanity straining toward the ship. He too was loaded with bundles. He had used the last of their money to purchase potatoes, hard-crusted loaves of bread, and two slabs of salt pork. This, along with water, would be their diet for the two-month long voyage.

Fares could be purchased on these ships either with provisions, which meant the captain would provide meals for fifty to seventy-five days; or one could purchase a fare without provisions, in which case, it was necessary to bring food on board. The captain supplied only water, fuel, and a place for sleeping.

Most ships sailing from Ireland required passengers to provide food for themselves, except for the small first-class section. Fare without provisions cost four pounds sterling, double that if it was to be provided. Steerage passengers were fortunate to scrape together enough for the fare alone, and many boarded without adequate food.

Donal gripped tighter to his load as he was pushed from behind. "Sorry, mate," said the heavily laden man beside him. "Didn't mean to crowd ye. Tis a mite like being in a herd of cattle, ain't it? Ye must move with the rest of 'em or be trampled."

Beside him, a woman holding a crying infant spoke up. "The babe is hungry. How am I going to feed her in this unholy mess?"

The man leaned over and kissed her on the cheek. "Let her be, luv. She wouldn't be true Irish if she wasn't able to fight off a bit of the hunger. We'll be on board soon." He looked back at Donal and gave a small helpless look.

Donal recognized the worried expression in his eyes. He had seen the same one in his own as he had shaved earlier in the day, using the small piece of tin that Maire had polished for him.

The woman was pushed from behind and stumbled forward. Maire put out her arm to steady her, even as her husband reached out. The two women looked into each other's faces, and then each looked down at the other's baby. They were of the same age and coloring. Brigid slept peacefully unaware; the other screamed with hunger. The two young mothers smiled at each other.

"Ain't motherhood grand?" the carroty-haired woman said.

"Just grand," Maire replied, laughing. The two shifted the weight of their slung burdens and moved along with the crowd. "I'm Maire O'Dwyer, and this is my daughter, Brigid," she said with a smile.

"Pleased to meetcha, Maire. Excuse me if I don't shake your hand, but I don't seem to have a spare one." She gave a grimace. "My name is Enid McFarland; my husband's Joe. This noisy one is Teresa. We're headed fer Boston, wherever that is."

"Us too." Maire turned her head back to indicate the men behind them. "Joe McFarland, say hello to my husband, Donal."

The two men sized each other up. Donal noted Joe's freckled face and shaggy red hair. He saw a broad, pleasant smile that displayed crookedly spaced teeth and recognized in his eyes their common problems and common goals. "What do you say we stick together, the four of us? The women would have the talk of the babies to share."

"Good idea, Donal. Enid would like that, and I could use a fellow sufferer to talk to—someone who's been kept up by a squallin' infant." They all four laughed as baby Teresa howled louder.

As they approached the planks that led to the ship, a seedy looking crewman shouted into a makeshift cone to amplify his voice. "Ye'll be in separate quarters!" he shouted. "Men in one, women and children in another. Ye'll have to divide yer food and other needs before ye get on board. Hurry it up now. Men over to the left, women to the right."

Maire looked at Donal in panic. She was carrying all the clothing; he had all the food. They would have to unpack everything.

"Move aside with yer bundles if yer splittin' 'em up." The crewman called out. "Give others a chance to get on board."

Joe McFarland drew his wife and Donal and Maire into a tiny circle. "They'll get all the best spaces if we stop to unpack. I've got clothing and blankets fer two, and Enid's got food fer two plus the baby's things. I see the two of ye have split the loads just the opposite way. What say we share what we have and get on board now?"

Maire looked to Donal. The plan sounded all right to her. They would both have food and blankets, and she had the baby's things. Donal nodded. "Sound's fine to me," he said. He leaned over to kiss Maire. She turned her face so that it landed on her cheek. "Try to get a lower bunk near a porthole so you have some air," he said. "The baby will need it, and you too."

Joe was also giving advice to his wife. "Uncle Joe, you remember he went to America two years ago, says to take the lower bunks opposite each other. That way, you have the use of the space between without disturbing others." He kissed his wife's lips slowly, lovingly and rubbed his cheek against the baby's head. "God bless ye both," he said.

Maire and Donal's eyes met over the couple's heads. Maire's eyes pulled away first. Donal leaned over and kissed the sleeping Brigid. "Take care of her, and yerself, Maire. I love you both." He turned away and joined the queue of men filing onto the ship.

Maire and Enid shifted the weight of their infants in unison, automatically moving toward the swaying double-masted ship.

The nine-hundred-ton brig was licensed out of Liverpool to carry five hundred forty passengers, but through alterations could cram seven hundred into the steerage area. The square-rigged ship was less roomy than the liners of the day and was low between decks and poorly ventilated. She was required by law to carry fifty gallons of pure water for each passenger, but this law was often broken by last-minute loading of goods for which room had to be made. Even as the passengers of the good ship *Ebbtide* made their way to the crowded wooden platform on which they would live for the next sixty or more days, the crew was rolling barrels of recommended drinking water back to the docks where they were left in the sun.

Maire's heart sank as she descended the ladder leading down into the dark steerage section. Three whale oil lanterns were spaced out along the overhead, throwing a dim light over the long narrow line of two-tiered bunks. The top bunks, she noted, had less than three feet of clearance, and the lower ones not more than four. The aisle separating them was perhaps four feet wide.

Hastily, Maire and Enid agreed on lower bunks opposite each other, one of them beneath a small round porthole that was open to the sea air and showed a small patch of light. Nearby was an area that had been boarded off for cooking, above which was a narrow open vent to carry off smoke and fumes from the cookers.

Brigid woke immediately upon being placed on the hard bunk. Maire looked at Enid with a sigh. "I guess we'd better feed these two and leave the settling for later or we'll never get any peace."

"Aye, yer right, Maire. We might jest as well have 'em on the same schedule. That way, maybe there'll be some quiet in between." She flung her pack on the bunk and unslung the crying baby, making cooing noises as she worked. On the other side of the aisle, Maire undid her bodice and held her baby to her aching breast. Enid sat down beside her, placing the nipple of her generous breast into Teresa's mouth. The crying stopped immediately.

A steady line of women and children filed by them to the bunks farther down the dismal dark dormitory. A frowzy-haired woman gave the two nursing mothers a disgusted look. "Babbies! Jest me luck. There's nottin' in the world like squallin' babbies in a crowded place. Let's hope there's after being some beds on the other end from this." Mumbling, she shoved her way along the bunks.

Maire and Enid watched solemnly as the women filed past. Without exception, they were poor and ragged, wearing several layers of clothing to lessen their loads. Tin pots and cups dangled from their packs. Net bags of potatoes and turnips and fat round loaves of hard-crusted bread were slung over their shoulders. Eyes red from weeping showed their suffering. Thin children were pulled along, stumbling, their skinny arms sticking out of ragged sleeves. Some cried, some shouted and laughed with each other, but all had eyes filled with fear of the unknown.

The two babies were satisfied at last and slept, mouths slack against their mothers' nipples, dribbles of milk running down tiny chins. "Let's put them both on this bunk to sleep," Enid said, "then we can unpack things on the other without disturbing them."

The young mothers took out only the essentials for the children and stored the rest under the bunks, leaving room for whomever would occupy the top bunks. It was the only storage space. Maire looked over the cooking area as she sat on the bunk to rest. "At least they've provided cookers. We decided not to buy one, thinking to pay someone for using theirs."

"I see they've bolted 'em down," Enid said. "I guess otherwise they'd slide around and be dangerous in a storm." Their eyes met in apprehension. Maire looked down the crowded aisle. The wooden bunks were old and dry. The partitions at each end were of wood too. She looked at the rope ladder and the small square of light from which they had descended. She saw no other exit. If there were a fire, they would never get out. She trembled with the thought.

"It doesn't do to expect trouble," Enid said, putting her arm around her new friend. "We'll be all right. The ship will get us there. It helps to keep telling yerself that."

"Yer right, of course," Maire said and trembled again. She leaned across the aisle and looked at the babies lying on the bunk. She had to be strong for their sakes.

Across the way, two small boys clambered into the bunk over Enid's head. They chattered to each other and looked apprehensively about. Their mother climbed into the top bunk with them without a word.

Maire moved aside for an elderly woman who stopped and looked at the top bunk overhead. Because of the infants, it was the last to be chosen.

"If ye kin help me git up there, I'll try not ta be any trubble to ye, sweet," the woman said in a trembling voice.

Why, she must be at least seventy years old, thought Maire. Her face was so thin that the bones pressed against her papery cheeks. She had no teeth, and her long bony chin nearly met the narrow nose that reached down over the sunken mouth. As Maire helped her up the widely spaced boards that made up the makeshift ladder, her heart was torn out of her. *Why, she weighs no more than a child*, she thought.

"I wish I could offer you the lower bunk, but I have to tend the baby so often it wouldn't be possible for me to be up there," she said, feeling guilty.

"Not to worry, luv," the old woman mumbled. "I don't move around much. I'm better off up here out of harm's way. Ye'll jest have to help me down to git to the necessary."

"Of course. Ye jest let me know," Maire said, patting the thin blue-veined arm. "I'll be glad to help." The woman was already nodding off. Maire stored the old lady's belongings beneath the bunk, wondering at the meager supply of food.

A group of women already crowded around the cookers, bickering about who would get the first use of the six oil-fired burners. "We'll have to have some kind of system," one woman shouted. "There's only six cookers, and there's more than three hundred of us." There was more shouting. No one was in charge, and everyone had her own idea of how it should be done.

In the end, a tall big-boned woman took over. She allotted twenty minutes a day for each family. They would team up with others and cook their food in the same pot if they needed more time. They would have to prepare enough food for the day in their one-time period. The water would be kept boiling for the next one to use in order to save time.

Enid whispered to Maire behind her hand. "She reminds me of Mother Superior giving us catechism lessons at the convent." The two friends snickered.

The women grumbled among themselves but eventually agreed it was a fair arrangement. There was more difficulty deciding who would be the first each day. Mother Superior decided they would start at different ends of the rows each morning.

The cookers were lighted, and the first of the six women dug out their pots, filling them with water from the barrels which had been placed beside the cooking area. The water could be used for drinking and cooking only. The contents must last for twenty-four hours. There would be no more until the next day.

Dusk had fallen by the time the ship began to move. The motion sent them staggering between the bunks. Pots and pans clanged and banged, and their belongings had to be rearranged under the bunks so they would not slide into the aisles.

There is so much to learn, Maire thought, *so much adjusting to an entirely new way of doing things. How will we survive—all women, together in this crowded place?*

Brigid awoke and began to cry. Maire picked her up and cuddled her close. The ship rocked with more pitch as they left the harbour. The open ocean lay ahead, though they could not see it, nor could they see their homeland dwindling in the distance.

CHAPTER 13

MAIRE THOUGHT SHE would never be free of the odor of seasickness. Old Maggie in the upper bunk was green before they left Cork Harbour and vomiting by the time they hit the first roll of waves in the Irish Sea. Maire held her washbasin under the old lady's chin every time she gagged. Maggie's skin felt alternately dry and crackling, damp and clammy. She kept nothing down, not even the sips of water Maire painstakingly spooned into her foul-smelling mouth every couple of hours.

By the second day, nearly every third person in the crowded quarters was suffering from seasickness. Enid's baby, Teresa, had refused to suckle and whimpered day and night. Neither Maire nor Brigid seemed to be affected. Each morning, Maire felt the tiny forehead with dread, but the infant remained cool and content.

The stench grew by the hour. The offending odor hung in the air like fog over a beach. The few women who were not affected tended the others and cooked pots of thin gruel to spoon into their suffering neighbors. Four-month-old Teresa fussed constantly; and the boys in the upper bunk hung listlessly over the edge, spewing vomit over the aisle, while their mother moaned, her aching head in her hands.

By the end of the first week, most of the victims had recovered. There were, perhaps, only twenty or thirty who could not get about to tend to their own needs. Old Maggie was among those who still suffered, and Maire watched anxiously as she realized the woman would not recover. She was now burning with fever, her skin a dry, parched red. Each day, Maire swabbed the hot face and tried to force water between the clenched lips.

"If she does not have water, she will die," she said to those who kept telling her to leave the old woman alone.

It was the day the wind died that Old Maggie too gave up her last breath. Early that morning, she asked Maire to send for a priest. But there was no priest to be had. There was a sudden silence when she died. The ship stopped dead in the water. Maire made the sign of the cross on the wrinkled forehead and bowed her head. She could not pray. She could only remember Gran's death and the priest who came too late.

The women in the hold were allowed up on deck for Maggie's burial at sea. There was little more air on deck, for not a waft of breeze stirred. The sun's rays were blinding after the dimness of the steerage compartment, and the glare on the smooth flat water made their eyes ache. The only relief was from the lessened stench.

They prayed briefly for their dead companion and gasped in unison as the tightly wrapped body slid down the tilted plank into the motionless water. Maire was the only one with tears in her eyes for the old woman. She wept at the small insignificant indentation in the sea and at the suddenness of its disappearance.

For eight days, the ship did not move. The sun glared from the sky, and the heat and the stench were unbearable. The small portholes let little air into the still motionless ship.

After the fourth day of stillness, groups of twenty people from each section were allowed on deck for ten minutes at a time. Maire and Enid were among the first to go up. A small part of the deck had been roped off, confining them to the small area. Maire breathed deeply of the hot still air. Even the stillness smelled heavenly. She fanned the fresh air into Brigid's face, making her coo and laugh. This small relief brought new hope.

Twenty men from the other section emerged from the steerage. Maire spotted Donal among them. An adjoining roped-off area confined them to their own space, but they all rushed to the ropes and reached across to embrace wives and children or to ask about them.

Donal held out his arms and Maire leaned into them. "I've been so worried. Are ye all right, luv? And Brigid, how is she?"

Maire was surprised at the sudden protected feeling she had as

Donal's arms enfolded her. She let down her guard for the first time and returned his embrace.

"Oh, luv," he said, "I've been so frightened for you." He kissed her neck. Maire pulled away and placed Brigid in his arms. She caught only a glimpse of questioning hurt in his eyes before he turned to the child.

"She looks grand," he said as Brigid smiled up at him, reaching for his weeks' old beard. "And you do too, Maire," he said, feasting his eyes hungrily on the two of them.

Enid rushed to the rope. "Joe, is he all right?" she asked anxiously.

Donal turned to her. "He's fine now, after a long bout of seasickness. He's worried about you and the baby."

"You're sure he's all right? Why isn't he with you?"

"The line was cut off just at his turn. He'll be up on deck with the next group."

Enid turned away. "But I won't," she said slowly. "Jest tell him we're fine, and that we love him," she called back.

Donal turned back to his family. "Her baby doesn't look too good," he said quietly, looking Brigid over carefully.

"Poor Teresa hasn't been doing too well and doesn't suckle properly. She cries most of the time." Maire hesitated. "But I wouldn't tell Joe. He can't help, and there's no sense in worrying him."

"I won't tell him," Donal replied with concern, "but I'd want to know if something was wrong with you or Brigid."

A whistle blew, and there was no time for more words. Donal kissed Maire quickly. She was aware of his look of love, as they were led back to their dismal dark quarters.

Maire looked forlornly through the small round porthole. There was nothing but ocean as far as she could see, calm, motionless water with a pale thin colorless line marking the horizon.

Water had been rationed since the first day of the calm. One pint of water per person, per day, was the allotment. Besides this, one barrel of water was provided for cooking. The women used this over and over for the boiling of the praties that made up the bulk of their diet, until the meager supply boiled away. The small bits of salt pork which were occasionally buried in the cooking pot were no longer used. It would only make them thirsty. They ate the potatoes plain and chewed noisily on the now-dried bread loaves.

On the morning of the ninth day since the calm began, Maire awoke to a slight rocking of the ship. The wind had freshened. She listened to the sounds of the crew above deck rushing to raise the sails as she put her face to the porthole and breathed in the stirring air. Holding the fretful Brigid up to the open space, she wished she could make her understand that she should breathe deeply.

Brigid whimpered softly, making sucking noises. Maire offered her breast, and the tiny mouth grabbed hungrily. There was nothing there to nourish her. Maire had known for days that her milk was drying up. Each day, the rationed water left her with less milk for the growing child. Brigid cried again and sucked harder, pulling at the unyielding source of food.

Maire winced in pain. She uncovered the other breast, knowing it was hopeless. Brigid screamed in anger. Maire could not hold back her own tears. She hugged her child to her and cried. "I'm sorry, darling. I'm sorry," she crooned over and over between her sobs, rocking the baby back and forth in her arms.

"Here, Maire, let me." Enid held her arms out for Brigid. Maire looked up at her friend with eyes turned almost violet in the dim light of the lantern. "I've plenty of milk, and Teresa doesn't seem to want much," Enid said. "Let me nurse her for you."

Maire looked down at her screaming infant. *My child must eat*, she thought. *I must do this*. Her own need to give was as great as the baby's to receive, but she knew she had nothing to offer. With an overwhelming sense of worthlessness, she passed Brigid to Enid, placing her in the outstretched arms. She turned away as Enid placed the infant to her overflowing breast. *At least, Brigid is being fed*, Maire thought as she curled herself into a ball on the hard bunk and wept.

The next day, three women in steerage became ill. Vomiting and diarrhea struck simultaneously. They rushed behind the wooden screens that shielded the malodorous slop pails. The cause was not seasickness, though they vomited in the same way. The odors of food being cooked and the stench of the oil cookers and lanterns added to the reeking smell from behind the screens. Many took to wearing cloths tied over their mouths and noses.

By the third day, six more women came down with the mysterious ailment. The first three could no longer walk to the screened pails at the end of the compartment. The added foulness penetrated everything, even their food and water.

Baby Teresa barely nursed, crying sickly while Brigid consumed her mother's milk. Maire held her and tried to tempt her to suck a rag soaked in water. *The baby must get liquid*, she thought. *She must.* Enid watched anxiously as Brigid sucked noisily at her breast.

Each day, more women contracted the disease. Abdominal cramps convulsed their bodies without warning. On the ninth day, two women died, their bowels flooding the bedding with a murky liquid. They were both young, perhaps in their middle twenties.

The women were not let up on deck for the burial of the two victims as they had been when Old Maggie died. The ship's health officer came down into the hold, his nose covered with a white handkerchief. He looked briefly at the dozens of sick women and ordered the entire steerage sealed off.

"The men in the other compartment? Are they sick too?" Enid asked a nervous crewman as he nailed boards over the portholes.

"About the same as you in here; some of the crew too," he mumbled. He would answer no more questions.

Maire was seriously frightened for the first time. She held Brigid close to her breast as she watched the crewman ascend the ladder and draw it up after him. The women sat silent and motionless as they heard the heavy grate fall into place and the hatch hammered down. It would be opened only to draw up their waste materials and to lower the water barrels. They began to fear that they would never see the light of day again.

CHAPTER 14

NOW THAT THE area was sealed off, the unfortunate steerage passengers had nothing to breathe but their own infected air. More women took to wearing cloths over nose and mouth. Maire helped Mother Superior move all the sick women to one end of the compartment. They cleaned them up the best they could with the limited amount of water. Those who were well enough began to sleep on the bare wood of their bunks rather than use the bedding, which retained the odor if not the germs of the illness.

Every day, there were more dead, and every day the crew dropped down canvas bags for the bodies to be wrapped in. The women knelt and recited the rosary as their companions were unceremoniously hauled up through the square opening one by one and dumped into the ocean. They worried constantly about their husbands and sons in the other compartment. Were they all right? Had they too contracted the sickness? There was no way for them to know—no one to answer their questions.

The day came when there were no more canvas bags to be used. The bodies were then wrapped in their own soiled blankets and hoisted on deck. Anything that could be found was used to weight them down before they went to their rest at the bottom of the sea.

Maire anxiously watched Brigid for any sign of sickness, but her child thrived on Enid's rich milk. She carefully boiled their drinking water, and since she was located near the cooking area, she also kept a pot boiling all day for use by the sickened women. The ailing Teresa still nursed weakly.

Maire lay down beside her daughter and stared into the dimly lit compartment. All was quiet except for the groans of the ill. More than thirty women had been taken up to the deck wrapped in their blankets that morning. The total count was now over one hundred. More sickened every day. Maire was now convinced they would all die.

She tried to pray, but each time she repeated the words, she grew angry. God, if there was one, had forsaken them. He had allowed them to be confined in this hellhole and was crucifying them one by one. How could she believe in so cruel a god? She had no need of such a one.

Maire looked at her own beautiful daughter sleeping beside her. Her reddish curls were damp against her forehead, and the long dark lashes, so like her own, rested on the white cheeks. If you are there, God, don't take my baby. Let her live. Let her live.

"Maire! Help me!" called Enid from across the aisle. "It's Teresa!"

Maire jumped from her bunk. Teresa had gone into convulsions. Her tiny body jerked forward and backward without control. Her mouth hung open, and her blue eyes rolled back until nothing but the whites could be seen. Her body suddenly arched back and would not release itself. Her back extended until it looked like her spine would break. The tiny legs stiffened and convulsed back toward her buttocks. Enid screamed, "Help her! Oh god! Somebody help her!"

Maire grabbed the child from the bunk. She thrust her into the kettle of cooling water waiting by the cookers and immersed the stiffened child several times. The tiny body convulsed once more then went limp. Teresa gave a small sigh and stopped breathing.

Maire looked up at Enid's stricken face. She rose from her knees and placed the dripping baby in her mother's arms. Enid clutched the still form to her without a sound. She sat on the bunk holding her until dawn came. Maire wept as she saw her offer her breast to the child, opening the dead baby's mouth and inserting the nipple into it.

Maire tried to take Teresa from her mother, but Enid would not release her. At last, Maire sat beside her friend, her arms about her shoulders; and they both rocked back and forth on the hard bunk.

Maire had to pry the stiffened body from her mother's arms when the time came to wrap the dead for what had become their morning ritual. There were fewer bodies than yesterday, and some of the sufferers seemed somewhat better. Despite their mourning, there arose a faint hope that the disease was lessening.

Enid sat motionless and unseeing on her bunk as they raised Teresa's wrapped body to the square of light above. Maire sank to her knees and recited the words of the rosary along with her fellow passengers, but the prayer was automatic. Her whole being shouted, "Why? Why? Why?" She was conscious of a feeling of thankfulness that her own daughter was not the one being dropped into the sea, and a faint feeling of guilt rumbled there, disturbing her grief.

Brigid screamed for her morning feeding. Maire tried to shush her, but the child's hunger would not be quieted. Maire looked anxiously at Enid, but the grieving mother still sat staring into space. She did not offer to take Brigid to nurse.

Maire tried to ignore the sudden leap of fear that gripped her throat. She carried Brigid to the cooking area and spooned some of the thickened water from the bottom of the cooking pot into Brigid's mouth. The baby slurped hungrily then spit it out. Maire walked the length of the narrow passage trying to quiet her demanding cries.

She paused in front of Enid. Her friend did not stir. Enid's arms were wrapped tightly around herself, and her body moved back and forth in a small rocking motion. She did not see Maire standing there nor hear Brigid's cries.

Maire smoothed the stringy carrot-colored hair back from Enid's sweating forehead. "Oh, Enid," she cried, "please forgive me, but I must do this." She forced the arms away from the grieving mother's shoulders and placed Brigid in them. Enid's bodice still hung open from when she had tried to feed her dead infant. Marie nudged Enid's breast toward Brigid's searching mouth and watched as Brigid grabbed on to the nipple with desperation.

Enid looked down at the child at her breast. "Teresa," she said with a long sigh. "Oh, Teresa." The tears rolled down her cheeks. She watched Brigid suck hungrily and smiled up at Maire, her tears already drying.

Maire was not comfortable with what she had done, but she knew she had no other choice. Without milk, Brigid would starve. Enid had plenty of milk and no child to nurse. They needed each other. Maire watched the two on the opposite bunk with a small growing fear inside her.

That evening, Maire had no appetite. Even the smell of the food made her stomach squirm. The heat-enclosed area was suddenly unbearable. She jumped from her bunk and grabbed the large metal spoon used to take potatoes from the boiling pot. Running to the porthole, she pried loose the boards that covered it. The rotted boards fell, and she pulled the round covering open. Fresh air poured in on her. She coughed, nearly gagging when it hit her; her lungs had been too long without fresh air.

When the other women saw what she had done, they ran to the other portholes and ripped away the boards. A brisk wind was blowing, and fresh sea air rushed into the compartment. The women cheered. They crowded around the four portholes and talked excitedly.

"Maybe with fresh air, we can survive," Maire said. She felt a sudden exhaustion. She lay down on the bunk, and immediately her body convulsed with pain. Her insides seemed to be tearing loose. Nausea struck. She jumped up and ran to the reeking pails behind the partition.

Back in her bunk, she lay waiting for the next cramp to take hold. *Not now*, she thought, *now when we're almost there*. "Enid," she called out to her friend. "Enid, promise me you'll take care of my baby."

"Hush now, Maire. You'll be all right," Enid responded. "Aren't some of the women getting better? You're strong. You'll be all right."

"Promise me, Enid. Promise me."

"I promise you I'll always take care of her," Enid said slowly.

Maire had been sick for four days when they heard shouts of excitement from the deck above them. "Land!" They had sighted land. They had made it. For twelve weeks, they had lived in this stinking hellhole, and now it was over.

The women crowded around the portholes for their first look at their new homeland. An hour passed before they saw the dark gray patch on the horizon. It jumped out at them all of a sudden from the colorless sea.

A new excitement took hold. They had survived! They would soon be off this filthy ship and with their loved ones once more. Maire groaned in her pain and made another trip to the end of the aisle.

Maire did not know when the ship slowly moved into Boston Harbour. Nor did she realize the ship had stopped for the health officer to come aboard for his inspection.

It was the sudden silence among the women that registered in Maire's consciousness. She tried to pull herself into a sitting position but was too weak. She had kept nothing in her system for a full week, and her mind would not focus on what was happening.

"Enid," she whispered hoarsely.

Enid stood next to her bunk with Brigid in her arms. "Yes, luv, I'm here."

"What's happening? Everyone is too quiet."

"It's nothing fer ye to worry about, luv," Enid returned. "Ye jest git some rest."

"Tell me," Maire croaked through her dry throat.

Enid moved away and returned with a tin cup of water. "Try to sip this, and I'll tell ye," she said. Placing Brigid on the bunk, she held Maire's head so she could drink.

Maire sipped and swallowed with difficulty. She took two, then a third swallow before pushing the cup away. "Tell me, Enid," she said, trying not to consciously follow the path the cool liquid was taking to her tortured stomach. She braced herself for the firelike pain that would follow.

"We have been refused landing in Boston," Enid said slowly. "They think the disease we have on board is cholera."

Cholera! Maire sank back on the bunk. The fire in her stomach began to burn. Cholera! No wonder so many have died. She pulled herself up on her elbows. Enid sat with her hands folded in her lap.

"If we can't dock in Boston, where will we go? What other place will take us?" Maire asked weakly.

Enid silently pushed her back. "We don't know, Maire. We don't know."

CHAPTER 15

AFTER THE BRIEF period of hope that followed the sighting of land, a new desperation took hold of the entire ship. Maire lay on her bunk, her knees pulled up against her stomach in an attempt to lessen the excruciating cramps. She tried to think of home and the hills she had roamed and the sight of the sea crashing against the cliffs of Old Head. Sometimes, she walked with Liam there, and she knew she called out his name in her delirium. Liam became confused with Donal in her mind, and even Declan sometimes was in her tortured dreams, breathing life into Brigid's limp body.

Enid forced fresh, sweet water between Maire's clenched lips. "It's barrels of clean water they've given us," she said, "and fresh fruits and vegetables, but they still refuse us landing. And we're not to dump our garbage into their harbour or allow anyone to go ashore." She spooned the cool, clear water into Maire's mouth as she talked. "We're to be gone by tomorrow. Canada, they say, will put us on an island and hold us in quarantine till there's no more sign of the sickness."

Maire tried to raise herself. "But Liam is in Boston!" she cried out. Enid gently pushed her back. "I know, luv, but yer not to worry. It'll work out."

They felt the ship move out on the morning tide, and their hopes fell further. They were headed away from Boston, away from those who planned to meet them, away from the only contact they had with friends and relatives or the possibility of work.

A new kind of silence gripped the pale, light-deprived passengers. The fear of the unknown gripped them with a new ferocity. What would they do? How would they survive? Even if they escaped the dreaded cholera, how could they escape the cold and hunger of the coming winter without work, without homes? They cried out in the night in their sleep, possessed by frightening nightmares, and they dreaded the knowledge of who and how many had been taken by the disease in the men's quarters.

The heat of the summer and early autumn had gone and a crisp, fresh breeze blew in through the small portholes, cleansing the putrid air. The crew lowered water, heavily laced with vinegar for cleaning the compartment; and those who were able scrubbed the bunks and washed the bedding. They were also allowed to pass the slop pails and other wastes up the ladders to be emptied every two hours, and these were cleansed with vinegar before being lowered to them.

There were fewer new cases of cholera every day and fewer deaths. The new procedures and the fresh, clean water were paying off. Faint hope began to stir once more.

Maire was still gripped with cramps, and the headaches continued to be violent, but she was able to keep down the water, and she slept without the moans of pain and the torture of the nightmares. Still too weak to rise, Maire was hardly aware of what was going on when the day came that there were no new dead. Six weeks had passed since the first death, and every day had seen bodies raised up through the open hatchway. The disease was, at last, abating. Maire wet her dried lips and tried to speak but could not get the words from her constricted throat.

The ship rolled and tossed as they moved farther into the North Atlantic. The air from the portholes turned cold. The small patch of visible sky was gray and threatening. They had been six days out of Boston, sailing parallel with the coastline.

Maire heard the heavy iron anchor slipping noisily into the sea before she realized that the ship had stopped. Darkness had already fallen, and there was no sign of light. She had no idea of where they were. The scurry of footsteps and shouts on the deck above her told her the sails were being lowered.

The hatch cover was drawn away and the rope ladder thrown down. The women rushed to gather round as it hit the deck. Maire raised herself on her elbows to watch. A crew member held a lantern through the square hatch. "Yer all to gather yer things and come up on deck. Hurry, now. We haven't much time."

"What about the sick? They can't climb the ladder," Enid called out.

"Yer each to pick a sick person to help. We'll lower a rope seat fer 'em to be placed in. Ye will be responsible fer that person until ye git ashore. Ye'll have to decide fer yerselves how to team up."

Enid held Brigid tightly in her arms. She walked slowly to Maire's bunk. "We'll manage, don't worry," she said. "I'll take care of Brigid, whatever happens. I want ye to know that."

Maire smiled. "You've been a good friend, Enid. I'll never be able to thank you enough." Enid patted her hand and turned away.

Hastily, Enid packed their few belongings. She dressed Maire in warm clothing and wrapped a blanket around her. Placing Brigid in the sling, she tied it under her arm. When their turn came, Enid picked up Maire and carried her to the lowered rope chair.

Maire's head swung weakly. She grasped tightly to the ropes as she felt herself being raised. Her stomach cramped, and she prayed the diarrhea would not return. Enid climbed the ladder with Brigid swinging to and fro in her sling.

Of the two hundred and ninety women and children who had entered the compartment when they sailed from Ireland, seventy-four waited on the deck to be put ashore. Of these, thirty-two were still suffering the effects of the disease. Brigid O'Dwyer was the only child who had not been touched by cholera.

Conditions were as bad in the men's section for they had not thought to boil their drinking water until it was too late. Of the original four hundred, only one hundred and sixty eight survived, eighteen still too weak to walk.

Enid searched desperately in the dim light for some sign of her husband and Donal. The men stood in a group behind a roped-off area similar to the one that confined the women on the other side of the deck. She could see neither of their husbands. Maire tugged at her skirt and kept asking if she could see them. They prayed that the two men had survived.

"I can't tell. They all look alike," Enid replied, "but there are so few, so few of them." They watched the pitifully small group with fear constricting their hearts.

They heard rather than saw the lifeboats being lowered in the dark night. There was a half-moon in the black sky, and a few scattered stars showed here and there amid the heavier clouds. A cold wind blew from the east, and the ship rolled as the ground swell pitched them against its force.

The first mate shouted into a cone-shaped object. "We'll take twenty men and twenty women in each boat. Each couple will be responsible for one sick person. Ye'll have to climb down netted ladders so watch yer step. The rope chairs will be used to lower the sick one to ye in the boat. Step lively now and be quiet, so's we kin hear what's goin' on."

There was no time to team up with someone you knew from the men's section. They were counted off from the line crowded against the ropes. Maire and Enid hung back and watched anxiously for their husbands. At last, Enid spotted a familiar figure. "Donal! Donal!" she shouted, waving her arm in the air. "Over here!"

Donal worked his way to the rope opposite them. "Maire?" he shouted. "Where's Maire and Brigid?" Enid motioned to Maire seated on the deck beside her.

"Where's Joe? Is he all right?" she called back.

Donal shook his head and made the sign of the cross. Enid cried out in protest. "No!" she shouted. "Oh, no no!" She leaned against the rope, her face in her hands. Brigid awoke and cried out. Enid clutched the child to her and wept in great sobs. From the deck Maire cried too, though she knew that part of her tears were those of relief that her own husband had survived.

At last they reached the rail and Maire was strapped into the rope chair that had been raised from the lower deck. She reached for Brigid, but Enid shook her head. "She'll be safer with me," she said. "You might drop her." Maire nodded in agreement. The chair swung out over the pitching lifeboat and was lowered toward the dark tossing ocean while she clung dizzily to the ropes.

Maire landed in Donal's arms. He pulled her to him weeping almost hysterically, even before she was released from the chair. "Thank God! Thank God you're alive! Oh Maire, Maire, my love. I'm so thankful you're alive. I've prayed every day that you would be spared." He covered her thin small white face with kisses. "I love you so much, Maire. I love you so much." He held her in his arms, and they rocked with the rolling boat.

Enid took a place at the opposite end of the boat. She waved at them and held the blanket protectively around the child. Maire tried to talk through her tears. "Teresa . . . ," she began, her cracked voice choked with sobs. "Brigid . . . ," she began again. She could not talk.

Donal strained his eyes to see the quay, but he could see nothing. The moon dodged in and out of the racing clouds. He thought he saw a nearby lifeboat beach itself against a stretch of sand. There was no quay! They were being put ashore on an empty strand!

Donal glanced quickly at the sailors who were rowing their lifeboat. As they drew in their oars, one of them called out, "Everybody out! Take yer belongin's! Come on now, everybody out!"

Donal grabbed the nearest oarsman. "You bastard!" he shouted. "You're abandoning us! You're putting us ashore on a deserted beach!" He shook the sailor with all his strength.

"Unhand me, ye big baboon! No one would have ye anywhere. What else were we to do with the lot of ye?" Donal shook him again. "At least yer off the stinkin' death ship," the sailor shouted back at Donal. "Ye ought to thank us fer that!"

Donal did not let go of the man's arms. "There're sick people here. What are they supposed to do? Where will they go?"

The sailor shook his head. "Go ashore, mate. Yer lucky to be alive. What happens from here on is up to you."

Donal dropped his arms, strapped their belongings to his back once more, and turned back to Maire. Her sunken eyes looked up at him in the moonlight as he jumped over the side of the boat into the thigh-deep water and gathered her into his arms. He waded to the black shore through the ice-cold pounding surf, making his way toward the darker line of forest that met the strand. She was feather-light in his arms; and even as he plodded onto the deep wet sand of the beach, he relished the feel of her head on his shoulder. He gently placed her on the sand beneath a huge pine tree. She was asleep by the time she touched the cold earth.

CHAPTER 16

DONAL LOOKED AT the sleeping Maire, and his heart overflowed with thankfulness. God was good after all. Despite what had happened, he would bless God all his life for sparing her. He would nurse her back to health and make her love him as he loved her.

Arranging their bundles to shelter his wife from the cold wind that blew from the pounding ocean, Donal looked around for Enid and the baby. She was nowhere in sight; she had not followed them up the beach. Which child had survived? He had seen only the small head covered by a blanket, and he could only pray it was Brigid.

The moon skittered in and out of the clouds making vision difficult. Donal looked around at the unbelievable scene. The strand was littered with the shadowy forms of his fellow passengers and their ragged bundles of possessions. Some were already huddled in their blankets against the bitter cold. Others stood bewildered, turning to stare into the night.

Donal knew their thoughts were the same as his own. Peering into the dark sea, he wondered if the ship was still there, or if they had been abandoned completely. He stared toward the dark forest and at the towering, threatening cliffs which loomed over them at either end of the half-mile-long stretch of sand and was as dazed as the rest at what had happened.

Donal could see no one who looked like Enid, no one who appeared to be carrying an infant in a sling as Enid had done. Donal felt his heart constrict with a sudden, sharp pain. Was the child she carried Brigid? Or was it her own Teresa? Maire had mentioned both names as she struggled to communicate what had happened. Fear churned his insides. Was his pain the dreaded cramps of cholera?

A new fear tore at him. What if he contracted the disease now—now when he was so desperately needed to care for Maire? He could not—he would not—allow himself to get sick. He swallowed with difficulty as the fear constricted his throat.

Donal searched frantically among the people huddled on the beach. He shook their shoulders, asking desperately, "Have ye seen a young woman with a babe? Has anyone seen a child—a woman with a child?"

Others searched too, not knowing if those they hunted for were dead or alive. There had been no chance to search out their loved ones on the deck before they were forced into the lifeboats. Now in the dark, they ran about the beach, stumbling over the dark forms, asking in desperation if anyone knew if they still lived. "Did he know them? Had they been sick? Were they still alive?"

Donal's anxiety grew as he tried to answer their questions, searching his mind for the names of those who had been sick or died. His empathy with them was so great his mind seemed paralyzed. "Dermot McTeague? Yes yes, I think he survived. I'm not sure. I think he was the one in the last bunk. Yes, he was all right. He should be here." The questioner embraced him and burst into tears of joy.

Donal prayed he had been right. He could not be sure. Everything that had happened in the past three months was jumbled in his mind.

The other answers were even worse to give. "Teddy Hogan? I'm sorry, but you don't need to search for him. He was one of the first to go." Donal wept with them and felt the fear and the grief once more.

His own desperation was making him weak. No one had seen Enid. It was as though she had never been in the lifeboat at all. Was the baby she carried her own, or was it Brigid? Maire would never forgive him if he did not find her baby, nor would he be able to forgive himself. He remembered his tiny daughter's sweet face, the soft reddish curls wet against her round head. He felt the small fingers curled about his own and ached for her touch.

At the far end of the beach near the cliffs, he saw the lifeboats pull ashore with provisions. The crew carried barrels of water and nets filled with potatoes and some of the squash that had been supplied to them in Boston Harbour. As soon as the supplies were unloaded, the boats pushed off and the crew rowed into the dark of the ocean.

Donal rushed to the pile of provisions. At least they had not been left to starve. He had stowed everything with Maire and had nothing with him in which to put either food or water. Quickly, he stuffed his pockets with potatoes. Realizing he would not be able to get enough even to keep them alive for a few days, he took off his coat and filled it with the vegetables. He tied the arms, making a loop he could carry over his shoulder. He thought of the sling that swung from Enid's shoulder as she climbed into the lifeboat. Whichever child rested there, he must find her. He remembered his promise to Joe McFarland on his deathbed that he would care for them.

The air turned colder as daybreak approached. The cold wind quickly penetrated the sweater Mam had knitted for him last winter. But Donal knew that the potatoes wrapped in his coat were more important than keeping warm. They could survive the cold; they could not survive the hunger.

Dawn came quickly out of the eastern ocean. The sun rose like an angry red ball, almost bouncing out of the sea. The light was blinding, and the shadows caused by it, deceiving. The dark shapes Donal saw floating in the surf were not debris, but bodies.

The tide had been coming in strong all night, and the wide beach they had landed on was now a narrow strand. The sick and the weak had been flooded and drowned, or swept into the strong surf and carried into the undertow. Donal felt his own knees weaken as he remembered the strong pull of it against his legs as he had struggled ashore with Maire in his arms, his bundles weighing him down. Had Enid and the babe been swept away?

The survivors were now crowded together on the narrow strip that stretched between the towering cliffs. Many were soaked from the tide that had wakened them with a frigid wetness. They shook and shivered as they huddled together in their desperation. Hurriedly, Donal moved among them, searching the strand's entire length for Enid, but she was not there. She had disappeared, she and the baby with her.

Donal wearily picked his way back to the tall tree where he had left Maire. He did not know what he would tell her, but further searching made no sense. Enid was not there.

He began to panic as he saw survivors searching the pockets of the helpless. They were robbing the sick and the dead. *Maire*, he thought with a sudden hopeless fear. She was alone with no one to protect her. Donal ran, shoving his way through the wretched crowd. He wished them all dead. He wished them all floating in the angry sea with the pathetic bundles of humanity that had been washed out into the pounding surf. He wished he had never left her, that he had never searched through the night for Enid and the child. Maire was all that mattered. She was his life.

He stumbled up the last few yards through the deep sand, his breath coming in noisy gasping sobs. At first, he did not see her; and then he remembered he had placed her so that she was protected from the wind by some low-growing shrubs. He fell and crawled on his hands and knees toward the clump of short scrub pine that grew up to the giant tree.

Maire still slept, sheltered by their tattered bundles, her white face turned like a morning glory to the sun. He gathered her into his arms and wept.

Donal must have slept briefly there in the sand with Maire cradled in his arms. He woke as something cold and wet hit his face. It took him a few seconds to realize where he was and what had happened. He looked down into Maire's eyes staring up at him. Large white snowflakes landed gently on her face.

It was snowing! God help them, it was snowing! Donal sat Maire up and climbed to his feet. "We've got to get moving, Maire!" he said. "We've got to find shelter before the snow gets heavier, or we'll freeze to death!"

"Where's Enid? And Brigid?" Maire looked anxiously about. "Where are they, Donal?" Her voice panicked. "Where are they?" She struggled to her feet, her eyes searching the beach.

Donal placed both hands on her shoulders and turned her to face him. With the few words she had spoken, he knew that it was her own daughter he had searched for. He spoke slowly and softly. "I could not find them, Maire. I searched all night. But they are not here. I don't know what happened to them."

Maire shook her head back and forth in disbelief. Her eyes were huge and dark violet in her white face. "No. No," she said. "I don't believe you." She struggled against his hold, but she was too weak to pull away.

"She's gone, Maire," Donal said. "She's disappeared."

"She can't be. Enid said she'd look after Brigid. She said she would always look after Brigid. She kept telling me that . . ." Maire's voice trailed off. Her eyes took on a wild look. She began to shake.

Donal placed her gently on the ground, clasping her in his arms. "I searched all night, Maire. I talked with every group on the strand. No one has seen them. No one has seen a woman with a child in a sling."

Maire began to talk quietly. Her voice seemed to come from a distance. "When Teresa died, it was as though Enid was in a stupor. She did not even seem to hear what I said to her. She would not believe her baby was dead."

Maire stopped and wrapped her arms around herself as Enid had done when Teresa was taken from her. "When my milk dried up, Enid offered to nurse Brigid along with Teresa. After Teresa died, Brigid was hungry, and there was nothing to feed her." Maire's voice faded away. She swallowed noisily and cleared her throat before she started again. "I placed her to Enid's breast. She called her Teresa." Maire's huge eyes looked vacantly into Donal's. "She thought Brigid was her own child brought back to her."

Maire slumped with exhaustion against Donal's chest. She was quiet for several moments, and then she spoke again. "I think I sensed, even then, she would never give her back to me."

Donal held her closer to him. They wept together. At last, Maire laid her head on the sand and he covered her with the blanket as she fell asleep.

The snow fell faster and faster, whipping around in swirls as the east wind drove in from the ocean. Donal gathered their things into a pile. Maire would be too weak to walk, he knew, but they could not wait until she grew stronger. He would have to carry her. He packed what he could into a bundle that he could strap on his back and made another packet to drag behind. He fastened a pot and their tin cups to his belt, and then he wrapped Maire in the two thin blankets.

Donal knew he could not follow the path at the end of the strand as his fellow passengers were already doing. He guessed that route led to the nearest settlement, but they would not be welcome when they arrived. Word would spread quickly that they had been put ashore because they could not land anywhere else. The villagers would have no choice but to drive them away. They could not take a chance with the dreaded cholera.

Donal tied his load to his back and picked up the girl who was his wife. He shoved his way through the thick undergrowth that led into the forest.

CHAPTER 17

DECLAN CAME INSTANTLY awake from a deep sleep, the vision still clear in his mind. "Donal!" he shouted, sitting up quickly and bumping his head on the bunk above. "Donal! Stop her!"

Christopher McCarthy stirred beside him. They had been assigned to the same wooden bunk in the steerage compartment of the English brig, *Tudor*. "What is it, Declan? What's the matter?" Chris asked, still half-asleep.

The images were still sharp before Declan's eyes. "She's taking Brigid away," he declared. "Stop her! Stop her!"

"Ye've been dreamin', Declan," Chris said, shaking him. "Wake up!"

Declan looked at Chris in confusion. The abrupt awareness of his whereabouts jolted him. He looked around at the crowded lantern-lit compartment. Two, sometimes three to a bunk, his fellow passengers slept. The greasy, pungent smell of the whale-oil lantern caused a nagging ache in his stomach. He looked at his bunkmate. Chris was staring at him as though he had taken leave of his senses. "I saw her, Chris. I saw her leave with Brigid."

"Whatever are ye talkin' about, Declan? Ye've been sleeping like a babe. Ye didn't see anyone. Ye've been dreamin' . . . a nightmare, most likely."

"No no, it wasn't a dream," Declan said slowly. "I saw a strange woman. She had Brigid in a sling under her arm. Donal carried Maire up the strand." Declan wiped the sweat from his brow. He looked around in desperation. "While Donal's back was turned, the woman went to the end of the beach and disappeared into a forest by a tall rocky cliff. She kept looking over her shoulder to be sure Donal wasn't watching. I tell you, she's taken their baby!"

Declan moved to the edge of the bunk and let his legs hang down. In this position, he could sit up without hitting his head on the bunk overhead. Chris crawled over and joined him.

They were silent for a few moments, each busy with his own thoughts. Chris's blond, strawlike hair stood up in spikes, and he made a futile effort to flatten it. His rough, work-worn hands appeared too big for his slight frame. He peered at Declan from under bushy brows, which nearly met at the bridge of his overly large nose and rubbed his hand over his pointed chin, following the line to the tip. "Jest what do ye mean, Declan, when ye say ye 'saw' this woman?"

Declan had come to feel very close to this lad from Skibbereen in the four weeks since they left Ireland. They were of the same age, both to turn sixteen in a few weeks. But Declan knew there were few people in his life he could talk to about this uncanny ability he had of seeing things that hadn't happened yet, or that were happening a long distance away.

He had the feeling, in this case, that what he had seen was actually happening at the same moment of his vision. When he shouted out, he had tried to warn Donal—tried to make him stop the woman. He returned his friend's worried look and decided he must tell him. He had to tell someone.

"Gran said I had the 'sight,' whatever that is," he said slowly. Declan watched Chris rub his hand over his arms and knew the words had caused the hairs to rise there. "It's an odd kind of thing to explain, but sometimes I see, as though they were happening right before me, things that will happen in the future, things that haven't happened yet."

"Holy god, Declan!" Chris exclaimed, making the sign of the cross repeatedly.

Declan sighed. He knew Chris would never really understand what he was trying to tell him. The village Chris had lived in all his life was a tiny cluster of thatched shacks, and the inhabitants had little contact with the outside world. Chris could neither read nor write and could speak very little English. All his life, he had been fed tales full of superstition and legends of half-truths by the storytellers who roamed the country and by the elders of the family whose purpose was to entertain rather than relate truth.

"Tis nothing to get excited about, Chris. Tis nothing weird or frightening. I jest see something, that's all." Declan knew he was trying to convince himself as well as his friend.

"But, God in heaven, help us! Declan, ye see things that ain't there! Tis the work of the devil, surely."

"I don't think so, Chris. Father McBride said it was, but he really didn't listen to me explain it. He said if I was going to have visions, I ought to try to see Jesus and the Blessed Mother. What he didn't understand is that I don't try to see anything. They just come to me. It's not anything I do or don't do."

"Mebbe the wee folk have got to ye. Ye know about the wee folk, don't ye? Fairies and such?"

"Ah, Chris, that's just superstition. I know better than that, and ye do too."

"I've heard about 'em, though," Chris replied slowly. "Some of 'em are good and some are bad. Mebbe a bad 'un got into yer mind."

"What makes ye think the visions are bad? Seems to me they try to do good. If I could warn people in time, I could stop the bad things from happening to 'em." Declan knew he was justifying. He wanted Chris to believe him. He wanted to know it wasn't his imagination playing tricks in his mind.

"But how could ye warn yer brother what's in America about somethin' that's happenin' right now, if that's what ye were tryin' to do?" Chris asked, getting off the bunk and pacing back and forth in the narrow aisle.

"If I jest wasn't so stupid," Declan said. "If I was smarter, I'd figure out a way to know these things sooner and be able to help people. I jest need to figure out how."

Chris stopped in front of him. "Gosh, Declan, that surely would be a grand thing. I kin see it can't be the work of the devil, not if ye could do that. Mebbe ye have a real gift from God."

"No, I don't think that's true either," Declan said slowly. This idea seemed to Declan to be the same kind of superstition as the other. He didn't want to examine the idea; maybe it was heresy he was thinking. "Seems to me if God gave me something special, I'd know what to do with it. I think maybe some people are able to do these things but have to learn more about them somehow. You know, like playing the fiddle. Some people have a natural flair for fiddling, but before they can play real good, they have to learn the fine points."

Chris sat back on the bunk beside Declan. "That makes sense, I guess. Ye sure are smart, Declan, to figger out these things. I would'a been scared out of me britches if I'd seen somethin' in the dark, especially some strange woman stealin' a poor babby." Chris crawled into the bunk and was instantly asleep.

Declan sat with his long, slim hands folded between his knees, thinking about what he had seen. His heart ached. *Poor, darling Brigid*, he thought. He remembered the last time he had held her soft sweetness in his arms, and the feeling he had that he would never see her again. *Did I, at the time, know what would happen? Could I have prevented it*?

He tried to reach Donal with his mind. Maybe it wasn't too late. Maybe Donal could still catch the strange woman and take Brigid back from her. *Donal! Donal! Do something!* He strained with his effort to reach him, but he had no feeling of success. He wiped the sweat from his forehead.

At last, he lay down next to Chris on the hard bunk. He lay awake staring at the widely spaced boards, a bare three and a half feet over his head, trying to find some good in his strange ability, some way to recognize the warnings sooner. *If I can't use it, what good is it? Why doesn't the whole thing go away and leave me alone? I'd rather not know these things if I can't do something about them.* Pushing the thoughts out of his mind, he tried to keep them away from his consciousness, back with the memory of Mam dying.

Declan had steeled himself against thinking about his mother's death. He had not allowed himself to think of her on the long walk to the harbour in Cobh. Underneath his consciousness, it nagged at him—prodding him to remember, to accept her death as fact. Aware he was shaking it off, he told himself he would examine the events later. Plodding through the rain with the sad, hopeless line of tenant-farmers who now had no farms and of villagers who now had no village, he refused to remember that she was dead.

As he walked, Declan felt as though he were on a narrow strip of land from which everything behind him had been cut off and everything in front of him was too unreal even to be speculated about. Putting one rain-soaked boot after the other, he followed the person in front of him wherever it led. He tried not to remember that the priest had not been summoned when Mam died, that she had not had the last rites of the Church. He pushed away the truth that he had not even thought of fetching Father McBride.

Declan's hand kept straying to the hard lump in his pocket, which was the handful of damp soil wrapped in his father's pouch. He did not understand how he got it. Pushing the disturbing memory out of his mind, he concentrated on the rain dribbling down his face as he walked along.

On the quay, Declan teamed up with Chris McCarthy and his sister, Peggy. The two were traveling alone, and Declan preferred their company to that of his own neighbors. He had not yet sorted out his feelings of their shunning Mam and their treatment of Maire. These two new companions would keep him from having to examine those feelings.

Peggy was a year younger than the two boys. She had a small pixie-like face and large almost-black eyes. Her hair was also black and had been cropped straight around her small head just below the ears. Her skin was tanned a dark brown from working in the fields. She clutched her brother's hand with a kind of desperation.

They were joined at the quay by other peasants like themselves, many of whom had also been wiped out by the black rotting of their crops. The blight seemed to have jumped from one area to another—sometimes skipping whole counties, then wiping out entire villages without reason or plan. Together the group boarded the weather-beaten two-masted ship that waited at the dock.

Declan had seen similar ships in the distance from the top of Old Head Point. They had looked exciting and romantic from that vantage point. Up close, this one looked as though it might sink at any moment. Her wooden bulk was ancient and rotted.

As they boarded, Declan saw everything on board was dried and salt encrusted. The small opening to the lower deck gave him an uneasy feeling, as more than four hundred men, women, and children descended the ladders to the steerage.

When the time came for the women and children to go into separate quarters, Peggy begged to stay with her brother. "I can pretend to be a boy. I've done it before. You know I have, Chris."

"It's not possible. Peggy. You have to stay with the women," Chris implored. "The voyage will last for weeks. "Twouldn't be safe fer ye in with the men." He turned to Declan for reassurance. "Tell her Declan. Twouldn't be fittin'."

"He's right, Peggy. It would be better fer ye to be with the women-folk. Ye'll be fine, and I'll look after Chris." Declan patted her shoulder. "Look for Brigid O'Malley. She was our neighbor. She'll be a good friend to ye."

Peggy turned away after giving both boys impulsive hugs. Declan shouldered his pack and turned to the queue of men, and then on impulse he shouted after her, "Peggy, take a place near the hatchway. You'll be safer." He didn't know why he said it. He had no way of knowing if what he said was true.

CHAPTER 18

EXCEPT FOR A cold wind that kept the ship rolling and pitching, the crossing was quite uneventful. Declan decided his feeling of wariness when he boarded the sea-battered craft was only that of his own fear of the unknown. They had made good time, crossing the Atlantic in fifty days, thanks to a brisk wind which had stayed with them most of the way.

The cry of "Land Ho!" was heard throughout the ship, and it was as though someone had turned on warmth and light at once. Cheers rang through the steerage compartment. Even those who were still seasick perked up with new hope.

From the portholes, they could see nothing that had the slightest resemblance to land, but the one cry had been enough to assure them the voyage was nearly over. Declan looked over his bundles of clothes. They certainly would win him no favors from man or spirit. He wondered if he would be able to find work and how he would locate Donal and Maire and Liam.

Chris sprawled across the bunk with his face pressed against the porthole. "I see her!" he shouted. "I see America!" Declan jumped onto the bunk and looked out. The sun was just slipping behind the horizon, and outlined by its red glow was an uneven stretch of dark. As the color spread, the dark shadow took shape, and as far as they could see was land, beautiful solid land. After nothing but rolling water for seven weeks, anything would have looked good to them, but this was the land of promise—America!

A thrill of excitement rose from his chest. Surely, there was opportunity here for him. He prayed that all the wonderful stories he had heard about this new world were not false. He would make them come true. They had been through enough tragedy. They watched the land come closer, each filled with his own dreams, until it was too dark to see.

At daybreak, Declan watched for the first sign of the harbour; and as the day wore on, he could see the city itself nestled in a semicircle of three hills. The town extended out almost into the sea with long wharves, like fingers, reaching out into the water, ready to grasp the ships.

In the harbour and along the wharves were hundreds of ships—ships of all shapes and sizes. Declan never knew there were so many seagoing crafts in the entire world. The immense forest of masts swayed in unison, dancing to an unheard fiddler.

They sailed parallel to the shore just beyond the shipping lanes. There seemed to be no end to the long line of wharves which flanked the city. The colored roofs of the houses marched upward to the surrounding hills, the tallest of which supported a golden dome glittering in the October sun, topping off this wonderful city, sheltering it in rays of light.

It was nearly dark when they, at last, turned to the narrow end of the harbour and toward the wharves. Declan dashed to his small bundle of belongings and took out the letter Liam had written. At the bottom of the sheet was the address of the livery stable where he worked—Pendleton's Livery, 304 Somerset Street, Boston, Massachusetts. What a strange name, Massachusetts. Declan wondered if he was pronouncing it right. There was so much to learn. What a wonderful thought! So many new things to experience!

As he stared at the words on the paper in his hand, they began to twist and turn. Flames shot from them, leaping into the air from the page. There was no smell of smoke, and Declan felt no heat; but as he watched, fear rose into his throat, and he sensed a distinct warning. *"Get out! Get out now!"* Declan dropped the letter onto the deck. It fluttered whole and unscorched to his feet.

Declan pulled Chris from the bunk. "We've got to get out, Chris. Now!" he said, his voice filled with urgency.

"What's going on, Declan? What do you mean, get out?"

"Don't argue. Jest come with me." Declan grabbed his friend's hand and pulled him toward the hatchway. The hatch above was open, but the rope ladder had been hauled up. "Wait here, Chris. Don't move. I'm going to get Padraig Fitzgerald."

Padraig was nearly seven feet tall and had shoulders that spanned at least three and a half feet. Declan rushed to the big man who stood near the cooking area, stooping so that his head would not touch the overhead. "Can ye do me a wee favor, Padraig?" Declan asked. "I have need of a good, strong back."

"Then ye've come to the right man, lad," Padraig replied with a wide grin. "What is it ye need doin'?"

"Can ye give me a boost up to the hatch? Me and Chris have a hankerin' to watch while the ship docks."

"Sure, lad. I kin do that, but ye might be getting yerself in trubble."

"Everyone's busy with the docking. They'll never be noticin' the likes of me and Chris on deck." The urgency Declan felt nagged at his mind, but he tried not to hurry. He had to have Padraig's cooperation or they'd never get on deck.

"Ah, come on then, lad," Padraig said with a shake of his head. "I was a frisky lad once meself. Let me give ye a bit of a boost, like, and ye'll be on deck before ye know it."

Padraig was at the opening in three long strides. Declan scurried along beside him. He lifted Declan to his shoulders and balanced him steadily. Declan's head protruded through the hatch opening. He reached for the ladder coiled just beyond the edge. Even as he pulled the rope toward him and dropped it to the compartment below, his mind noted the fibers were dry and flammable. Panic seized his throat. He grabbed the ladder, and removing his feet from Padraig's shoulders, he stepped onto the swinging rungs. "Come on, Chris. Let's get out of here." He turned to Padraig. "Come with us, Padraig." He could not explain the feeling he felt; and despite his conviction they were in danger, he knew the other passengers would not listen to him.

Padraig shook his head. "Ah no, lads. Ye go ahead an' have yer fun. I'm too old fer adventures." He gave his booming laugh and boosted Chris up the ladder as if he were a wee one.

Declan scrambled on deck with Chris close behind. "Thanks, Padraig.

We'll leave the ladder in case ye change yer mind." Padraig smiled and turned away.

Declan and Chris hid behind a huge coil of rope and strained in the darkness to see if anyone was about. Forty feet along the deck was the opening to the women's compartment. The hatch stood open. "We have to get yer sister out of there," Declan whispered.

Chris grabbed Declan's sleeve. "Will ye tell me what's goin' on, Declan? What are we doin' up here, and why do we have to get Pegeen out?"

Declan locked eyes with Chris. "It's a warning; one I can't ignore. We have to get off this ship. Now!"

Chris's eyes widened. Declan knew his words were being weighed. He sighed with relief when he saw the acceptance in his friend's face. "I'm with ye, Declan. Let's get Peggy."

Thank God he didn't give me an argument, he thought. Declan grabbed his sleeve, and they scrambled across the deck. They dropped flat, holding their breath as a member of the crew passed close by them in the dark night. He suspected nothing and moved quickly out of sight calling to an unseen mate, "Keep yer britches on. I'm moving as fast as I kin!"

Declan made a dash for the rope ladder coiled exactly as the other had been and threw it into the opening. The sound of the women's chatter instantly ceased. Chris descended and dropped to the lower deck, and Declan followed. He heard Peggy's quick shout of recognition before his feet touched the bottom.

"Chris! Declan! Whatever are ye doin' here?" She ran eagerly to them. As Declan reached out for her, he saw the lantern at the end of the steerage fall. Oil and fire flew across the planking. There was a sudden flash, and flame sucked up oxygen from the stuffy overcrowded compartment. Even before he heard the scream of alarm, Declan grabbed Peggy and boosted her up the ladder. "Hurry, Peg," was all he said and shoved Chris to the rope behind her.

The skirts of the woman standing next to him burst into flames. Declan reached for her, beating at the fire that raced up to her hair. He pulled the burning skirt from her and wrapped what was left of it around her blazing head. He picked her up and shoved her onto the smoking ladder. She scrambled to the top ahead of him.

It was strangely quiet below after the screaming of the moment before. They were all dead. Most of the oxygen had been consumed in the brief flash of the fire. Declan felt bile fill his throat and forced it back down, the taste clinging to the roof of his mouth.

He saw the smoke rising from the open hatch of the men's section. "Chris, get the women to the rail," he shouted. "Try to get a lifeboat into the water." He dashed for the open hatch. The ladder was already ablaze.

At the bottom of the ladder, Padraig Fitzgerald was lifting his fellow passengers, one after the other, onto the burning rungs. Declan reached down to help them to the deck. Up through the small square they came, their legs afire, screaming and gasping for breath. They threw themselves to the deck, rolling to beat out the flames.

Declan heard the clanging of the alarm. The fire had been discovered, but it was too late. He already could see flames shooting up through the deck in several places. Smoke curled around the sides of the ship, and even as he watched, the forward sail exploded into brilliant orange.

Declan reached down to grasp the arms of the man struggling up the burning ladder. Suddenly, the rope let go. The ladder fell, the man with it, to the deck below. Padraig's clothes were ablaze, and Declan could see that his great long arms were black and blistering. Still, he lifted another passenger up toward the open hatch. Declan reached down and grabbed his arms and pulled him to the deck. The boy gasped and fell motionless to the deck. Declan turned back for the next one, but no one was there. He looked down into the compartment. There was nothing but raging fire. Padraig Fitzgerald had collapsed. Next to Padraig, Paddy the Smith fell to the planked floor as the flames consumed him.

The whole ship was ablaze now, both sails throwing flames into the air, the complex of ropes outlined black against their orange outrage. Declan ran to the rail beating his arms against the bits of burning canvas that rained down on him. He saw Chris and Peggy scramble over the rail and jump, their clothing ablaze. Declan dove into the water behind them.

CHAPTER 19

DECLAN WAS A strong swimmer, having played in the Bandon River since he was old enough to toddle about. Surfacing in the cold, murky water of Boston Harbour, he looked around for Chris and Peggy. He could see Chris's blond head, his spiky strawlike hair for once plastered to his head, but he could barely see the small white face beneath the dark cap of hair bobbing next to Chris.

Declan quickly swam to their side and set the pace for the quay more than six hundred feet away. The icy dark water nearly took his breath away, and already he could feel the ache of the cold seep into his legs.

The water smelled of garbage and sewage and of the peculiar rotted wood odor of ships just in from the sea. Declan kept his eyes on the lanterns now moving about on the wharf and on the crowd which had been attracted by the fire in the harbour. He was beginning to doubt they could make it to the quay.

Already several small skiffs had set out from the wharf to rescue the swimmers, and Declan saw a couple of lifeboats being lowered from the docked ships. *They had better hurry before the cold water drags us down,* he thought.

The burning ship threw out weirdly colored lights across the water, casting fingers of moving shadows in the waves of the incoming tide. As the cold crept through his body, it became harder and harder to lift his arms. He shifted to a sidestroke, but the lesser motion made the cold penetrate even deeper. Chris was tiring, and Peggy had dropped behind.

Declan swam back to her, reaching her side just as her head went under. She didn't cry out. She simply slipped beneath the water. Declan grasped desperately for her. He felt her cold arm in his hand, and the weight pulled him down. Water filled his nose and mouth. He struggled for the surface, refusing to let go of her. She rose with him, struggling against his rescue.

Declan gulped air into his bursting lungs as he reached the surface, pulling Peggy's head above the water. He shouted for help. Chris appeared at his side. Peggy's head sagged, and Declan turned her onto her back and put his arm around her neck in an effort to keep her head above water. Chris grabbed her under an arm and prayed aloud. "Don't give up, Pegeen. Don't give up. Oh, God, don't let her die."

A rowboat loomed in front of them. Declan called out, and it swerved to miss hitting them. The two men in the boat reached down, and Declan and Chris lifted Peggy up to them. "Get the water out of her!" Declan shouted as they pulled her aboard. "We'll get in by ourselves."

The two men placed Peggy over the center seat, her head hanging down toward the deck. One of them forced the water from her by pushing on her rib cage. The other lifted her arms awkwardly. Declan and Chris hoisted their tired bodies over the side with their last bit of strength and lay on the floorboards in exhaustion. Declan heard the water gush from Peggy's lungs and the sound of her vomiting. She would be all right.

The cold hit them all at once. The temperature was near freezing, and they were drenched with seawater. Their bodies shook uncontrollably, and their teeth chattered so loudly they could not talk. Both men stripped off their coats, tossing one to the boys and gently wrapping the other around Peggy's heaving shoulders. One of the men sat in the bow as the other placed the girl in his arms before taking his seat and rowing for shore.

Declan suddenly became aware of the other sounds around him. From the water, voices called for help, and screams resounded from the burning ship. On shore, loud anxious voices shouted orders.

Hands grasped the side of the boat, causing it to list dangerously. An old man whose face was covered with black blisters hung over the gunnels. "Help me!" he pleaded in Gaelic. "My legs won't move. I can't swim anymore." The oarsman pulled him into the boat. The legs of his britches had been burned away, and his skin was a mass of blackened open flesh. He collapsed on the floorboards without another word.

Declan concentrated on the sound of the oars as they dipped faster and faster into the dark water. He felt the boat hit the quay, and even before they tied it off, hands reached down for them. Declan lifted Chris with the last of his strength. He saw Peggy being raised gently into the arms of two waiting men.

"We'll need a stretcher for this one," the oarsman called. "He's badly burned and out cold." A makeshift stretcher was lowered for the rescued swimmer, as Declan felt himself being boosted to the wharf. He reached out to grasp the hands stretched out to him. Immediately, he was wrapped in a waiting blanket and ushered forward along the dock toward shore. Ahead, he could see that Peggy was being carried swiftly down the quay, and Chris was struggling to keep up. Declan hugged the warm blanket closer and hurried his step, not wanting to lose sight of his friends.

He looked back at the blazing ship. Its bow rose into the air as he watched, and she sank stern first into the freezing water of Boston Harbour. There was a gasp, then silence, as the people on the quay watched in horror. Blackness descended. The light of the fire was gone. Declan crossed himself beneath his blanket. "God rest their souls," he prayed. He was the sole survivor of the fifty-seven families who had left Ringrone Peninsula.

Declan stumbled in the sudden darkness. His companion placed a steadying hand under his elbow and held firmly until they entered a warehouse, which had been opened to shelter those who had been rescued.

There were, perhaps, two dozen people huddled around the hastily lit iron potbellied stove. Seawater dripped from their clothes making puddles where they stood. Their wet hair clung to their heads outlining skulls obscenely. On a bench sat three women, Peggy among them. Her eyes looked large and sunken in her small pale face. The woman beside her was the one Declan had saved as her hair caught fire. The other was even more badly burned. She had no hair left at all, and her scalp was red and already blistering. Her eyes stared blankly. Declan wondered if she had been blinded.

Chris stood behind Peggy, his hand on her shoulder. She reached up and grasped it as they both trembled from the cold. Declan felt his hands tingle as he held them close to the heat of the stove. He could smell the smoky pitch as it sparked. The heat reached out, and the steamy odor of drying wool rose from their blankets. He could not think beyond the moment, nor bear to think of what had just happened. They huddled around the warmth of the fire without speaking, gradually warming and drying, allowing themselves to rest in the cocoon of their shock.

Declan did not know how much time had passed. He roused from his exhausted sleep and gradually became aware of the sounds of voices nearby. He stretched to look through the door through which they had entered the empty warehouse.

A small cluster of people talked loudly. One man tried to make himself heard over the group, holding his hands into the air to quiet them. "The hearse is outside to take the dead to the morgue and the seriously injured to the hospital," he said. The group murmured approval. A man in black stepped into view. He was obviously a preacher, but not a priest, Declan decided.

"I can take ten survivors to the church, but I don't want anyone who is seriously burned. We have no way of dealing with them. And no Catholics," he added firmly. Declan watched as the heads nodded in agreement.

Declan moved to stand beside Chris. Peggy leaned back against him, sleeping. They watched as the badly burned women and two men were escorted to the waiting hearse, which would drive them to the hospital. Chris swore in Gaelic at the Reverend Mr. Baker as he led away a group of dazed survivors, identified as Protestants.

Declan saw that in addition to the three of them, two older men were left around the now-reddened stove. One of them clutched a rosary, the beads moving nervously through his fingers. The other glared at the floor.

The group by the door dwindled to three. They held a hushed discussion, glancing toward the remaining survivors with annoyance. At last, one left and the other two approached the group by the stove. "Father McNair from St. Mary's has been sent for. He'll know what to do with you all," one of them said and gave a sigh of relief.

"We'll be leaving now," said the other. "You may stay here until the priest comes for you." His nose lifted as he spoke, his distaste obvious.

None of the group commented as the two men left, closing the door behind them. One by one, the exhausted survivors stretched out on the floor near the potbellied stove and slept.

Declan heard the click of well-shod shoes striking the dock outside the warehouse. He opened his eyes as the door was opened, and an early-morning sun threw a splash of light on the worn floorboards. Two black-clad nuns stood in the doorway. They cleared their throats noisily. Declan jumped to his feet as his companions stirred awake.

"Good morning, Sisters," he said respectfully.

The two stood with their hands hidden in their wide sleeves, their heads covered with black veils, while starched white-edged wimples stiffly framed their faces. The older one stepped forward. "I understand there is a young Catholic female here who needs protection," she said firmly, not looking at Declan's face.

"She's with her brother, ma'am, and I'm her friend," Declan replied, a dry distaste filling his mouth. "It's not protection she needs as much as a place to sleep and some food."

"She cannot stay here among men." The two moved as one toward the bench where Peggy was just rising. They gave her no greeting. "You're to come with us," the older nun said. "You'll have a bed to sleep in and enough food to eat and work to do." She nodded to her companion, and the younger one took Peggy's arm.

"Hold on a minute." Peggy's voice echoed in the empty warehouse. "Don't I have somethin' to say about this?"

Chris stepped forward. "Hush, Pegeen," he said gently. He turned to the two sisters. "My name is Christopher McCarthy, and this is me sister, Peggy. You are surely right when ye say that she can't stay here with us men. She's needing yer help, to be sure, and 'tis a blessing that ye can give it. But I'll be wanting to know where ye'll be taking her and when I kin be coming to fetch her, or at least, come to see her."

The elder sister nodded in agreement. "I'm happy to hear you're a man of good sense, Mr. McCarthy. Your sister will be in good hands. We are Ursuline Sisters from the convent in Charlestown. You may call in one month's time. She may, of course, leave with you, or if she prefers, remain with us as a novice." She turned to Peggy. "Come, my dear. We must not tarry. It's not proper to be in such a place in male company." She made a complete about-face and marched for the door. The younger one followed.

"Do I really have to go, Chris?" Peggy asked.

"There's no other way, Pegeen. The Lord only knows where we'll be. And ye'll be safe there."

Peggy flung her arms about her brother. "I'll die in a convent altogether," she said.

"Ah, ye won't now, Pegeen. And I'll be coming after ye in a month's time, ye can be sure of that."

Peggy removed herself from Chris's arms. She went to Declan. "Thank you for my life," she said solemnly. She planted a quick kiss on his cheek and ran to the waiting sisters.

CHAPTER 20

ONLY THE CLICK of the rosary beads moving consistently through the old man's hands marred the silence after Peggy left with the two nuns. Declan wished he had more faith to draw on, but instead he felt a desperate dread of the future and an undeniable concern at the sight of Peggy walking down the long wharf flanked by the two dark-clad figures. He saw her arms swinging free, but he could not shake the impression that she was somehow bound, boxed in, unable to communicate.

He shook off the feeling. Peggy certainly would be better off in the convent until Chris found work and a place to stay. Declan thought of the willing, even eager, response when the preacher said he would take no Catholics. If the rest of Boston had the same prejudice, it would not be easy to find work or even shelter.

The elder of the two old men spoke for the first time. Declan thought he must have read his mind. "I should have told them I was a Protestant," he grumbled. "I can't think of a thing I owe the Catholic Church."

"Surely ye wouldn't deny yer faith?" Declan asked. "What do we have left, if not that?"

"And what good is faith, if it doesn't provide?" the man said morosely, studying his work-worn hands.

"Will the two of ye stop?" Chris shouted. "'Tis not the time to question God. Seems to me now's the time we need him most." He looked around at the three faces. "Each one of ye has more brains than me, but I'm not dumb enuff to desert God now. Didn't he send the sisters for Peggy? Isn't she safe now because of them?"

Declan watched his friend's face. He would not destroy Chris's faith by voicing his own feelings of dread. "Yer right, Chris. There is that. Thanks be to God."

The old man with the rosary spoke up. "The best thing God can do fer us now is to let us die. That's what I pray fer."

"The way I look at it, if he wanted us to die, he's had plenty of chances lately," the other man said. "I figger he's not through with us yet."

Declan's mind flashed back to Mam saying those very words. She had been so right. God was not through with them. He was glad that Mam hadn't had to go through the fire. The smell of the burning flesh was still with him. The thought of it being hers would be more than he could bear.

The old man's voice brought Declan back from his thoughts. "I am not waiting around fer God, whatever he's got in mind. I'm getting out of here and finding me a job, and ye kin jest bet I'll not be mentionin' being a Catholic." He rose from the bench and hitched up his britches. "And I don't reckon it'll spoil the pope's day none."

They said nothing as he left. The other old man kissed the cross on his rosary and crossed himself.

Declan and Chris went outside to see what the day was like. They watched as a carriage pulled up at the end of the wharf. The breath of the horse was clearly visible in the cold morning air. Two priests stepped down from the wagon, lifting their long black skirts.

Declan watched as they walked toward them. Their shiny black shoes caught the sun as they moved in and out from beneath the swinging cassocks. Both men were young with pleasant smiling faces. They seemed to be enjoying their morning stroll, watching the seagulls circling above the sea of waving masts in the harbour. Declan felt none of the apprehension he had felt with the two nuns.

The two boys nodded respectfully as the priests stopped in front of them. "Are the two of you from the burned ship then?" asked one of them in a thick Irish brogue.

"Aye, Father. We are," Declan responded.

"Are there others inside, then?" asked the other, his accent a match for the first.

"Only one old man left. The Protestants came for the rest of 'em," Declan explained. He would not hope. They had taken their time in coming. But he could not deny the feeling that had risen at the familiar lilt of their voices.

"And two nuns from the convent in Charlestown came fer me sister," Chris added.

The taller of the two priests looked the boys over from head to foot. "Yer a scrawny twosome, tis true," he said, lapsing into the rustic English that matched that of the two arrivals from Ireland, "but I reckon they'll take 'em over at the Bishop's Basement, don't ye think, Sean?" He turned to the other priest.

"God save us from the bishop's wrath if they can't read or write," the other replied. He watched the two boys' faces but did not ask them a direct question. Chris threw an anxious look at Declan who gave him a minute shake of his head. The priest turned away as though he had not seen the brief exchange. "I'll be seein' to the old man inside then," he said, opening the heavy door to the warehouse. "We can be leavin' him at the Rescue House until we can find him some work."

Declan and Chris looked at each other with satisfaction. *Perhaps God still had plans for the old man too*, Declan thought.

The Bishop's Basement turned out to be exactly what they had said— a lower floor beneath an abandoned storefront that had been taken over by the Church for use as a chapel.

They had driven in the carriage over a low long bridge to what was known as South Boston. Here, Catholic families clustered in neighborhoods of ramshackle warehouses turned tenements. Enterprising landlords had converted worthless, weather-beaten firetraps into housing for hundreds of families. A single pump was the water supply for four or more buildings housing up to five hundred people. Two flimsy outhouses served the same number.

There were already lines forming at the pump and outhouse alike as Declan and Chris rode through the miserable streets of South Boston. The tall buildings cast dark shadows onto the street as the priest stopped the horse before the open door of the makeshift chapel.

"Father Murphy will have a good breakfast fer ye, my friends," the priest called Sean said as he jumped from the carriage.

"That sounds grand," spoke up Chris, "then maybe me insides will stop the grumbling."

"Let's hope so, Chris," commented the other priest. "It's kept me awake the whole trip from the harbour." They all laughed as they descended from the carriage.

Mass ended as they entered the crude, candlelit chapel, and the priest was ushered off the altar. Declan wondered if it was Sunday, or if this was simply an everyday morning mass. He had lost all track of the days.

The congregation consisted entirely of young men. Declan watched them with curiosity as they filed out through a side door. *They're an odd lot*, he thought, *dressed strangely in homespun trews and knitted shirtlike coats*. But they were clean, and they looked well fed.

The two priests led Declan and Chris down the center aisle. They all four stopped to genuflect before the glowing red light on the white draped altar. Declan felt a sudden wave of homesickness.

They went to the side door, through which the priest and his attending altar boys had disappeared. The priest was removing his vestments in the small barren room which served as the sacristy. The two young men who had escorted him from the altar were nowhere to be seen. The priest folded his garments carefully and crossed himself before turning to them.

"Ah, good mornin' to ye, Robert, Sean." He nodded to each in turn. "And what have we here? Where did ye find these two? They look like they slept through an incoming tide." He walked around Declan and Chris as he spoke.

"They're from the ship that burned in the harbour last night," Father Sean said. "They seemed like good prospects for the bishop."

Father Murphy stopped in front of the two boys and stuck out his hand. "Welcome to the Bishop's Basement, lads," he said, shaking their hands in turn. "And how is it that you're not burned up with the rest of them on board?"

Chris spoke up quickly. "Declan, here, saved us all." Declan poked him in the ribs. Father Murphy looked from one to the other. "Sounds like a long and interesting story. What do you say we have some breakfast first?"

"That sounds grand, Father," Declan said with relief.

"Will you join us?" Father Murphy asked the other two priests.

"Ah no, thank you, Father. We've eaten already, and we must be getting back to work." They shook hands all around and left with Declan's and Chris's thanks.

Father Murphy turned back to the newcomers. "Declan and Chris, is it? Let's go downstairs and get something to eat before the other lads eat everything. If you're as hungry as I am, you won't want that to happen." He led them down dark shaking wooden steps to a room below that held four long tables. About thirty young men and boys sat on wooden benches eating noisily. They rose to their feet as the priest entered the room followed by the two refugees.

Father Murphy marched to a chair at the head table, which was facing the room, and indicated they were to be seated. He motioned Declan and Chris to seats on either side and signaled two serving boys to bring their food. Crossing himself quickly, he mumbled a brief blessing. Declan and Chris did the same.

The bowls of porridge were steaming hot, and there was rich creamy milk to pour over it. Plates of crusty bread were passed down the table with round dishes of deep yellow butter. The two boys' stomachs rolled and growled at the heavenly aroma. Father Murphy smiled and urged them to begin. "I guess it's been a while since you ate," he said bending to his own bowl.

The two nodded in agreement and dug in. Mugs of strong tea were set in front of them. They smiled at each other in appreciation but were too busy eating to talk.

The others had finished their meal and were talking quietly among themselves. Father Murphy rose and dismissed them. They filed from the room in two lines. Declan watched the orderly rows with interest and wondered what they had gotten themselves into.

Father Murphy leaned back in his chair. He had eaten every scrap of his food. "There's nothing like a good breakfast to start off the day, as me old Irish Da used to say, though he got one seldom enough," he said, pulling a pipe from beneath his cassock.

Declan and Chris scraped their bowls and chewed the last crusts of bread. "We do be thankin' ye fer the food, Father," Chris said, swallowing the last gulp of tea.

Declan looked at the tanned square face of the priest who was study-ing him with interest. His face seemed familiar, but Declan did not believe he had ever met him. *He is about Liam's age*, Declan thought, *maybe twenty-two or twenty-three*. His rugged face was newly shaven, and he had a strong, broad nose. His dark hair sprung back into curls, still damp from a morning wetting. The blue eyes were relaxed and friendly as he sat back with his pipe held loosely between full red lips. A good face, Declan decided, and an intelligent one too. Where could he have seen it before?

Declan's experience with priests had been limited to Father McBride and his aged predecessor, Father McBain. Neither had left any lasting impression on him, other than a faint dislike and a combination of fear and resentment.

"Now then," Father Murphy said, "what are we to do with the two of you? I take it you have no friends or relatives to turn to in the area. So how did you come to be sailing to a strange city in a foreign country?"

Slowly, the two boys told their stories—stories of hunger and dispos-session, of dead parents and lost brothers and sisters. Father Murphy leaned back and smoked his pipe without asking questions. He let them talk.

"And then Declan knew the fire was coming, and he got Peggy and me off the ship," Chris finished up. "And he saved lots of others too. None of 'em would be alive if it wasn't fer Declan." Father Murphy studied Declan's face as Chris spoke.

"He exaggerates, Father," Declan interrupted. "He's a typical Irish storyteller, anything for a more interesting tale."

"Tis true, Father, every word," Chris spoke up quickly. "He knew the fire was going to happen, and he got us out."

Declan glowered at his friend, but he spoke to Father Murphy. "There were too many. And the fire happened too fast, especially in the women's section. They died too quickly, the breath sucked right out of them." He saw the flames again in his mind and smelled the sickening, scorching smell of burning flesh. "I couldn't save them. I didn't have enough warn-ing." He held out his hands in a helpless gesture, his eyes stricken. For the first time, he realized that his hands were burned. Even as he looked down, the hurting began.

CHAPTER 21

DECLAN WINCED AS Father Murphy cleansed his burned hands and applied an evil-smelling ointment to the blackened skin. The priest's outsized hands were gentle and awkward at the same time. "Smells terrible, I know," Father Murphy said. "It's bear grease—a trick I picked up from the Indians I worked with when I first came to this country."

He wrapped clean cloths loosely around Declan's hands, taking pains not to let them cling to the open burns. "Interesting people, the Indians. They have a special kind of spirit, a sensitivity to nature and the world around them that few people seem to have, a kind of openness to what's going on around them." He paused, still holding Declan's bandaged hand.

Declan studied the man as he talked. He seemed to have an openness of his own. Declan felt he could trust him, could talk to him about his innermost thoughts. He knew he had to talk to someone about what had happened. The underlying excitement had been threatening just below the surface of his consciousness since the first inkling of warning had come. He had actually made use of this strange sense of foresight which had been nagging at him since he was seven years old. *Had it all been chance? I really don't know, but what I have done once, I can do again.*

"I knew about the fire before it happened," Declan blurted out. He watched Father Murphy's face carefully for some sign of shock or disbelief. *Maybe he'll think I'm crazy,* Declan thought with a note of panic.

"I thought as much, Declan," the priest answered calmly without looking up.

"I didn't smell smoke or anything like that. I didn't see the fire either." Father Murphy looked into his face, and Declan knew this young priest was trying to read the truth of what he was saying. "The fire hadn't started yet," Declan continued, "but I knew it was going to all the same."

"Like I said, that kind of thing is common among the Indians. I've known only one other white person who had that ability. It's very rare, but a wonderful thing, nonetheless." Father Murphy's voice was calm and even toned. "A special talent should be used, as you used yours to save the people on the ship."

Declan felt relief run through him at the words. A burden had suddenly been lifted. He felt a lightness and exhilaration. At last, he had found someone who understood. "I'm glad you don't think I'm possessed, Father. Most people have thought so." He was reassured by the sudden grin that brightened Father Murphy's face. "Father McBride, back home, said I was possessed by the devil, and I should pray to be redeemed."

"Most of us are fearful of things we don't understand. I've always tried to understand all I could before I made a decision, rather than condemning something because of my own lack of knowledge."

Declan held up his bandaged hands and examined them. *They were going to be pretty useless for a while*, he thought. He remembered the woman who was burned all over, the one they carried off to the hospital in the hearse. If only he had been able to save her and all the others who were now dead and drifting in the sea.

"Father Murphy," he said slowly, "do you think I could learn to make better use of these warnings? They are such fleeting things, and mostly so few details I can't catch the sense of them—not in time to do anything."

"It seems to me you made very good use of the warning you had, Declan. You saved yourself, your friends, and several more besides."

"But so many died!" Declan cried out. "If I'd known more, I could have saved them!"

"Perhaps we're not meant to save the world, Declan, only little pieces."

"But if I had known which lantern would fall and when, I could have prevented the fire altogether."

"Still, you did save some, and surely that's a blessing," the priest said. "I would say that's a step in the right direction."

"You're right on that, Father," Declan replied, rising from his chair. "This is the first time I've been able to save someone else from harm. Mostly I recognize what I've known only when it's too late to act."

Father Murphy rose too and placed his hand on Declan's shoulder. "Open yourself up to it, Declan. Don't ignore the slightest twinge. The Indians call it communing with nature. The ancient Celtics said they were waiting for the spirit. The Church might say you were meditating on God. Whatever it's called, Declan, be alert and aware. You've proved you have a power to do good."

Declan felt a lightness in his head. He wanted to jump and sing. He was no longer an outcast. Someone believed in him and his visions.

Father Murphy's acceptance left Declan free to open himself to other things, other beliefs. The Church no longer threatened him. He found that beneath his skepticism, his faith was strong, stronger than ever.

During the months that followed, Declan became an integral part of the Bishop's Basement. He discovered that the fledging school was meant to teach young men and boys, to select those who would, with proper training, become priests, or at least workers for the Church. It was the pet project of Bishop Benedict Fenwick, the second bishop of Boston. Frustrated that there were no training schools for priests in the northern states, the bishop was laying the groundwork for his dream.

In the early nineteenth century, the Catholic Church in America was centered in Baltimore, and most of its priests came from Europe. The few seminaries that had been founded by the Church for the training of badly needed priests were clustered around that city and the surrounding states.

The Catholics were not exactly welcomed with open arms in the northern cities, and Boston was still a Puritan community and intended to remain such. The bishop, however, had other ideas. He dreamed of a city built around a university and a seminary, and he would build it with the immigrating Irish.

The Bishop's Basement, nicknamed by the priests who worked there, was to be the foundation for his dream college and the surrounding city. Here, he would select the few who had the ability and the inclination to become his future priests. Here, he would also find those who would build and populate his city. Around his city would be a farming community, and he would plant his Irish farmers where they could grow the potatoes that made up their diet. They would be at home and content. He would create an American Ireland and make it the best of both, for this was the opportunity to bring out the best of the Irish—the love of the land and the love of God.

Declan attended classes every day, perfecting his English and learning the history of the world by learning the history of the Catholic Church. He became Father Murphy's right hand, assisting at mass each morning and listening to his informal, rambling talks in the evening, talks that were always open for those eager to learn. Thus they selected those who were to be favored, and the bishop stopped by to observe and encourage those who had picked themselves for this honor.

Declan saw less and less of Chris, for Chris was unable to read and seemed impossible to teach. Declan searched him out among the group who would be the farmers in Bishop Fenwick's dream.

As spring came, Chris went to the plot of land in Charlestown where they grew potatoes and other vegetables for themselves and for the city's poor. Chris complained to Declan that every day he was within sight of the convent where Peggy had been taken, but he was unable to gain entrance. He rang the bell outside the gated wall, but they would not admit him. No one would answer his questions. He did not even know if Peggy was still there.

Declan remembered his apprehension when Peggy had been led away by the two sisters from the convent. He decided he would talk to Father Murphy. Perhaps he could find out what had happened to Peggy.

Declan had no visions in the days he spent in the Bishop's Basement. He was relieved that they had left him, at least for a few months. They had always signaled a danger of some kind. Perhaps no visions meant his family was all right.

Declan tried to locate Liam, but in the confusion of the fire and all that followed, he could not remember the address that had been written at the bottom of the letter. When he tried to remember, he saw only the flames licking at the page. He took every opportunity to inquire about livery stables and those who worked there, but no one had heard of Liam.

He followed Father Murphy's suggestion and put up notices in the Catholic churches asking anyone knowing the whereabouts of Liam or Donal or Niall to contact him. He heard nothing. They had disappeared in the huge city.

Declan realized he had attached himself to Father Murphy to fill the emptiness left by his brothers. He had come to love the young priest and was able to talk to him about his most private thoughts, but the void was still there. He had accepted that his Da and Mam and Gran too were gone for good, but he could not accept that his brothers and Kate had disappeared from his life.

The terrible ache of homesickness gripped him when he went to his hard cot in the dormitory of the Bishop's Basement. The loss of his family gnawed at his stomach and his joints and caused a painful, tight feeling in his chest. Often, he clutched the handful of Irish soil he had brought with him, hoping to ease his aching heart with the smell of home.

He crept from his bed and into the study room when he could not dismiss the thoughts from his head. He would light his small candle and read the books Bishop Fenwick brought every week for his favorite students. Lost in the world of history, the pain of the present faded and left him in peace.

CHAPTER 22

KATE'S VOYAGE TO America was quite unlike that of her brothers. Jocelyn's father had special quarters built aboard his fast new clipper ship for his daughter and her companion. The luxurious oak-trimmed cabin reflected the warmth of the colorful shaded lanterns, and the beds were covered with down-filled quilts.

The fast ship rode smoothly over the rolling waves. There were neither steerage compartments nor other passengers, Irish peasant or otherwise. The Wellington-Winters private craft carried only the family and their household belongings, and some specially ordered Sheffield china and delicately cut glassware from Waterford in Ireland. Mr. Winters would realize a fine profit on these items, which were in great demand in the cities of America.

The sea blessed the London travelers, and they arrived in Boston Harbour early in May of 1830 after only forty-five days on the water. Kate stood on the deck of the *Jocelyn Winters* and let the warm fresh wind blow through her hair. She watched the three hills of Boston draw closer and felt an excitement build in her that had not been there when she had approached the docks in Liverpool. Her family was here. Her future was here.

The umbrella of rooftops unfolded from its golden dome atop the central hill, shielding its houses from the glaring sun. Only the weather-beaten warehouses and sea-softened gray shacks protruded from its protection. The swaying masts extended into the morning sky, lining every wharf and quay, shifting in cooperation with the incoming tide.

The ships in the crowded deepwater harbour moved smoothly aside to make room for the polished clipper, as though prearranged, as she glided skillfully into a reserved berth.

Kate replaced her Parisian bonnet, smoothing her unruly hair in place. She clutched Jocelyn's hand as they stood together at the rail. Their trunks stood ready to go ashore. They had only to wait for the gangplank to be put into place and they would step foot on American soil. "We're going to love it, Jocelyn. I know we will!" Kate exclaimed.

Jocelyn's face held a faint frown. "I don't know, Kate. It's smaller than I expected, and so . . . so . . . wooden." It was true. Boston was a city made of wood, a sharp contrast to London—at least the London the affluent knew. Stripped of lumber long ago, the newer sections of London no longer used wood to build. They constructed everything of brick. The buildings of fashionable London glowed red and warm and had a continuity that wooden structures lacked.

Mr. Winters signaled the young ladies he was ready to debark and led them down the hastily laid gangplank. On the wharf, the workers paused in their duties and watched admiringly as they passed—some whistling with appreciation, others shouting ribald comments. The two women carefully kept their eyes straight ahead and clung to Mr. Winters' arms.

An elaborate carriage waited at the end of the dock. A footman stood by two shining black horses holding them immobile as the two attractive arrivals were handed into the carriage by Mr. Winters. "We'll drive by the Wellington-Winters warehouse before we go to the residence," he said to the driver as he stepped into the carriage and placed himself opposite the girls.

They moved smartly along Commercial Street as most of the heavy traffic of carts, wagons, and small one-horse chaises headed toward the wharf area they had left behind. Mr. Winters leaned out of the carriage to watch for his new place of business. "There it is," he called out. "Just there on Lewis Wharf. The new one." The fresh unfinished lumber stood out among the line of grayed, sagging buildings. The girls leaned out to see the new home of Wellington-Winters Shipping Company. They could not read the sign, but the new white paint glistened in the morning sun.

The driver stopped the carriage. "Did you wish to stop and go inside, sir?" he asked.

Mr. Winters waved his hand. "No no, drive on. I'll get the ladies settled first, then return." He leaned contentedly back in his seat, assured that his new venture was indeed a reality.

Kate watched as the carriage cut up Fleet Street. The tenements hung out over the narrow lane. She hastily put a lace-trimmed handkerchief to her nose as she recognized the offensive odor of the outhouses. As she did so, she became aware of how far removed she was from her own native way of life. She knew without being told that behind those walls were her fellow Irish—crowded, dirty, and penniless. She removed the dainty white cloth from her nose.

"Oh, Kate, do cover up," Jocelyn said. "Be careful not to breathe the air. We could get some kind of disease from that terrible smell."

Kate laughed. "It takes more than bad smells to kill an Irisher," she said.

Jocelyn looked at her over her own handkerchief. "I keep forgetting you're Irish, Kate. You're so normal."

Kate said nothing. She looked back out at the depressing tenements. *These people could appear "normal" if they had been given the advantages we have*, she thought. The carriage moved away from the crowded slums and onto Hanover Street, a wide cobblestone avenue leading straight through the city toward the highest hill.

The elegant house on Beacon Hill sat close to the street, which sloped sharply toward the city center. Kate drew in her breath at the view from its vantage point atop the hill. The whole city lay spread out before them. Although they sacrificed something in the way of front gardens, Kate could understand why the elite of the city had chosen the hill for their own. No doubt there was room for a garden in the back.

Inside, the house possessed a certain elegance, though its furnishings were too stiff and stately for Kate's taste. High-quality English carpeting covered the floors, but otherwise there was little in the way of ornamentation. They had brought most of their own furnishings with them on the ship, and the two girls decided where their paintings were to be hung.

The collection of porcelains, which had been Jocelyn's mother's, would be placed about the room. It would soon look like home.

Left alone in her room, Kate looked out the window at the city. She liked the place, she decided. It was not as frightening as London had been. The warm colorful houses had the look of a village rather than a city. She felt the familiar draining of strength she recognized as homesickness. How far away home seemed. She shook away the thought. Her family lived here now. This was home. She wondered which of the thousands of buildings spread out before her housed her brothers.

Where could she begin to look for them? She had no idea where Declan would be. She had no single clue to start from. Would the whole village have settled together? Surely one of the few Catholic churches would know if a whole village of people started attending mass. Perhaps that was the place to start. She would find out where Catholic churches were. She could attend mass each week at a different one.

The door burst open, and Jocelyn rushed in. "Kate! Kate! You'll never guess! Niall is coming to Boston! Look here!" She waved a small newspaper. "It says right here that he's coming to Boston!"

Kate grabbed at the newspaper. "What do you mean it says in the newspaper? Why would it say in a newspaper Niall is doing anything?" She craned her neck to read where Jocelyn was pointing. "The sensational new Irish tenor, Niall DeCourcey, will be appearing at the Tremont Theatre on Friday next," she read. Tears ran down her cheeks. "Oh, Jocelyn. It's true. He is coming to Boston." The two clung to each other and wept, then shouted for joy and danced around the room.

Several minutes passed before they went back to read the remainder of the article. "Mr. DeCourcey has been a tremendous success at the Park Theatre in New York where he has been appearing for several months. He has graciously consented to appear at the Tremont Theatre during his stay in this city while visiting his fiancée, Miss Mary Margaret Hammond, and her father, financier Charles Hammond."

"Oh, Kate," Jocelyn wailed. "He's engaged to be married!" Her face turned from sorrow to anger, to resolve. She swung her supple body around indignantly. "Well, if it's marriage he wants, we'll just see who wins out." She flounced to the door. "I'll bet I have just as much money as she does." She slammed the door as she left.

Kate stared after her. Jocelyn hadn't even considered Niall might be in love with this Mary Margaret Hammond. Kate was aware Jocelyn was probably right about Niall's reasons for marrying. It was too much like Niall for it to be a coincidence that his future wife was an heiress. Kate stared at the door Jocelyn had slammed.

Was she really in love with Niall? Would she seriously consider marrying him? Kate didn't think so. She loved Jocelyn dearly, but she also was aware of her shortcomings. Jocelyn would not marry beneath her. Of that, Kate was certain. The idea of class was too much inbred in her. And she certainly would consider Niall beneath her. It was the idea that someone else would have him as a husband that was bothering her.

Kate and Jocelyn sat in the box seats just to the left of the stage in the newly opened Tremont Theatre. Mr. Winters had been wheedled into escorting them when told that Kate's brother would be performing. He had no reason to suspect that Niall was the same individual who had been involved in Jocelyn's escapade at Kenmare Castle. He had seated the young ladies in their box and excused himself to have a Spanish cigar in the lobby.

Kate was so excited she took no notice of the admiring glances they were receiving from the men in the audience. They did indeed look charming. Jocelyn postured in her peach-colored, fitted outfit with the short matching cape, her blond curls peeping out of the tasteful headdress trimmed with feathers.

Kate wore the newest London color of Terre d'Egypte trimmed with rows of bright gold buttons in the shape of tiny hearts. The matching beret encircling her dark curls was also trimmed with matching gold hearts. The three handsome young men in the next box nearly fell from their places in their effort to get a better look at these bewitching creatures. Jocelyn fluttered her long eyelashes as she pretended not to hear them asking each other who the lovely newcomers might be.

At last, the orchestra started and the curtain went up. Filled with anticipation, Kate could barely sit still. When they announced the program for the evening, she realized they would have to sit through a two-act play called *Wild Oats* or *The Strolling Gentleman*, before they would hear Niall sing. Jocelyn explained the best acts were always last, giving time for latecomers to arrive for the main attraction.

Kate thought the play would never end. Although not particularly well acted, some of the lines were funny, and she relaxed enough to laugh at the comedian's antics.

At last, Niall stood on the stage in front of her. How handsome he looked! Jocelyn squeezed her hand. "I'd almost forgotten how absolutely devastating he is!" she whispered to Kate. *Oh, he is*, Kate thought. *He is wonderful.* His clear tones flowed up to the loft, sending shivers of delight over them.

Kate could not take her eyes off her brother, nor could she stop the memories that flowed out of the sound of his voice. He sang of home, of the hills, of the villages and the sea. She looked at the audience who sat with their eyes glued to his face. They were from every country of Europe, and they were transported home by his poignant voice. *No wonder he is a success*, she thought.

Kate sat back in her chair and closed her eyes. She could see the familiar countryside and the river flowing by. Once more, the warmth of the open hearth and her family surrounded her. She opened her eyes to see that Niall had looked up and recognized them. Jocelyn was throwing kisses, and as Niall's eyes held hers, Kate felt the tears of joy flow down her cheeks. She had found the first of her four brothers. Together, they would find the others.

When the performance ended, Kate and Jocelyn waited at the stage entrance on School Street with a reluctant Mr. Winters. He was faintly disapproving as, at last, the stage door opened and Niall appeared. Niall took Kate into his arms and held her close. "It's so good to see you, Kate. So good." He held her away from him and looked her over. "What a beautiful, fashionable woman you've become!" He turned her around admiringly. Kate giggled and turned to Jocelyn. "You must meet Miss Winters and her father," Kate said, enunciating the last word so that Niall would realize the identity of this elderly gentleman who escorted them.

Niall instantly extended his hand to the older man. "How nice to meet you, Mr. Winters. Thank you for being so kind to my sister." He turned to Jocelyn, placing his back toward her father so that he could not see their exchange. Niall leaned low, pressing his lips to Jocelyn's hand and lifting his eyes to hers. "When can I see you?" he asked softly. Jocelyn smothered the instantaneous, satisfied look that appeared on her face. "We loved your performance, Mr. DeCourcey," she said. "Wasn't he wonderful, Father?" she asked, turning away from Niall.

"Yes, quite," her father replied stiffly.

Niall invited them to accompany him to the Boylston Hotel, a favorite place for performers and theatergoers alike for a light repast after a performance.

While Niall and Kate brought each other up to date on their news, Mr. Winters excused himself and went to the bar for something stronger to drink. Niall immediately turned to Jocelyn. "I'd forgotten how beautiful you are," he whispered. Jocelyn's laugh rang out, causing her father to pause as he made his way through the crowded room. "When can I see you, sweet?" Niall asked, taking Jocelyn's hand in his.

"When can you get away?" Jocelyn asked innocently. "I understand you're visiting your fiancée."

"Well well, you haven't missed much in the short time you've been here, have you?" Niall said.

"We saw it in the theater news column, Niall," Kate broke in. "Do tell us about her."

"Not much to tell. She's a very nice person. You'd like her, I think."

"Would I like her too, Niall?" Jocelyn asked, pouting.

"Perhaps not, Jocelyn, though she is very rich and very much a lady."

"I thought as much," Jocelyn said.

Talk turned to family and the missing brothers. Niall did not know of their mother's death nor of the desecration of their village. Nor did he know Donal and Maire had come to America. He had not seen any of them. "Let me know how I can help to locate them, Kate," he said as they parted. "I'll do anything I can."

He bent over Jocelyn's hand again as they said good night. "Meet me here tomorrow night at seven?" he asked when her father turned to the door.

"Of course," Jocelyn replied with a satisfied smile.

CHAPTER 23

SEVERAL HUNDRED MILES north of Boston, Donal found that he had to rest often as he made his way through the thick undergrowth of the Canadian forest, carrying his sick wife and all their possessions. Maire was pathetically light in his arms, for the sickness had taken all the flesh from her. He became aware as he pushed deeper into the woods that his own strength had been lessened by the long weeks of inactivity aboard ship.

Donal lost track of time as he forced his way inland. The sun at his back held no warmth, for the thickly grown trees shaded him. From the position of the sun, he judged the time to be about noon when he stumbled upon the deer path. Although narrow and tangled with roots, it made a clearing through the undergrowth he could follow without having to force his way forward.

A clear fresh spring sparkled at a point where the path turned south. Donal placed Maire gently nearby and after drinking from the icy water, he carefully washed their cups and cooking pot. Maire awoke, and he gave her some of the water. She asked where they were but went back to sleep before he could answer. Donal rested beside her for about an hour, trying not to think of anything but the present moment. He touched Maire's face, softly brushing the dark hair away. "Please love me, Maire," he whispered. "I can do anything if only you will love me."

Two deer came to the spring to drink. They watched the intruders cautiously with huge brown eyes. They drank slowly, not moving their eyes from the reclining figures, and with a sudden leap, disappeared into the brush.

Donal began to think of how he could make himself a weapon. They would need food. Where there were deer, there would be other animals as well. He would have to find some way of capturing them—a snare, perhaps, or a trap of some kind, if he could not make a weapon.

He had watched the clouds forming overhead all afternoon, and the temperature dropped sharply as the sun disappeared. Darkness followed quickly in this northern clime. He found an undergrowth of thick bushes and pushed his way into them, flattening the center to make a place to sleep.

He lay Maire down and tucked the blankets around her. Dragging their bundles into the thicket, he pulled two small potatoes from his supply. Deciding against making a fire, he ate the praties raw and drank from the cool water he had brought from the spring.

Donal lay down beside his wife and cradled her in his arms, arranging the blankets. She stirred but did not waken. The night was cold, but they were protected from the wind, which whistled through the great trees towering over them. He prayed no animals would discover them and that they would find shelter tomorrow. He soon fell into an exhausted sleep.

By morning, snow was falling. Even through the overgrown bushes, Donal could feel the wet flakes landing on his face. The day was gray with low clouds hanging close to the treetops. Maire awoke, and Donal gave her water to drink and fed her some of the red berries he had found near the spring. They were somewhat dried, for the season was late for berries, but he knew these would be safe to eat. They were like their own blackberries back home, except these were a dark red.

Donal loaded his bundles on his back and, picking Maire up once more, followed the deer path south. Without the sun, he knew he would not be able to tell direction or time. He decided to take note each time the path turned but soon lost track of its twistings. The snow swirled down through the trees, filling the indentations of the deer tracks in the path and outlining the branches extending out from each side.

By afternoon, the path beneath his feet was invisible. Donal placed his boots carefully so as not to stumble on unseen roots and rocks. The branches bent low from the weight of the snow. He opened his mouth as he walked steadily along to let the cold wet snow melt on his tongue. *At least we won't have to worry about our water supply*, he thought as his thirst lessened.

It was nearly dark when Donal noticed the trees seemed to be farther apart. They were thinning out with every step he took through the three inches of snow. Did it mean a clearing was ahead? His heart pounded at the thought. Of course it could mean danger or the loss of shelter from the trees in the storm. He forced himself to consider this.

Donal stood at the edge of the woods in the gathering dusk. A wide stream cut a path through the forest, tumbling over huge rocks and fallen tree trunks. Bits of ice clung to its edges and around the snow-covered rocks. The bank of the stream was no more than three feet wide on the east side, but he could see more land on the west a little farther downstream.

Balancing himself carefully, Donal crossed the stream on a fallen tree with Maire clutched in his arms. He gently set her down on the far bank and returned for their belongings. She sat up and watched fearfully as he took a wrong step and teetered back and forth on the dead tree. Panic seized him before he regained his balance, and he ran quickly across and jumped ashore. Maire hugged him thankfully as he dropped down beside her. Hope surged up in him. "Feeling better?" he asked, noting that her eyes were clearer.

"I'm hungry," she said, nodding her head. "I guess that means I'm better." Donal dug a potato from their pack and handed it to her.

"Can you chew on this as we walk along? We had better see what's around that bend before dark." Maire nodded, and Donal helped her to her feet. He picked up his packs and put his arm around her waist to support her. She walked slowly and weakly, but she was walking. Donal felt new hope. She was going to get well. It was good to see her walking and showing some interest in eating. Everything would be all right. She was going to get well.

Maire stumbled and fell just as they moved around the curve in the stream. Donal knelt to help her up, dropping his bundles on the ground. As he tried to get her to her feet, something caught his eye—a break in the trees that grew down to the bank of the stream ahead. It was gray and improperly shaped, out of place in the forest. It did not belong.

Donal took several seconds before he realized what he saw was a shelter of some kind—a manmade structure—a building. "A cabin!" he shouted. He left Maire where she had fallen and rushed forward.

There was no smoke coming from the chimney of the small cabin made of peeled logs. Even as he dashed toward it, Donal was aware the house was deserted. He pounded on the door, knowing no one was inside and stepped back to get a better view. Snow covered the roof and clung to the crevices between the layered logs.

Donal had never seen a house of this construction before. No one used logs to build with in Ireland. Wood was much too precious. He examined the structure carefully. Moss grew up the sides, and a kind of lichen he didn't recognize crept out from between the weathered logs. He saw that dried animal skins had been stretched across two high windows.

Donal went back to the heavy, wooded door. It hung from leather hinges, which appeared to have been cut from a horse's harness. Another piece of leather had been looped through a wooden block and fastened with a peg. Donal loosened the peg and pulled the strip of leather from its place. The door opened noisily on its stiff hinges. He caught the odor of animals emanating from the dark interior.

Donal went inside cautiously. Nothing stirred. He made his way across the earthen floor and pulled the dried skins from the windows. Enough light came in for him to see there was an open hearth at one end, and a bunk had been built into the wall on the far side. A wooden table and two benches stood in the center. "Thank Mary, Joseph, and all the saints," he said aloud.

"Amen," said Maire from the doorway. She clung to the open door. "I walked by myself," she said proudly. "I am going to get well, Donal." She gave him a weary smile and promptly collapsed to the floor.

Donal ran to her and scooped her into his arms. He carried her to the bunk covered with a thick bearskin, still carrying the scent of its original owner. Donal placed Maire on the bunk, tucking the warm pelt around her.

There was much to do before darkness thickened. Donal searched for matches and found a tightly covered tin near the hearth. He made use of a small pile of split wood in a corner. The chimney belched smoke a couple of times before beginning to draw. The fire blazed up. They would have light and warmth.

Deciding it was safe to leave Maire, Donal checked the chimney once more and went back to the head of the stream where his packs made a white hump on the snow-covered ground.

Their pot was soon filled with snow and hung over the fire. When the water boiled, he added four small potatoes and a turnip from their meager supply. They needed to eat.

The aroma of the cooking vegetables filled the cabin. Maire stirred and woke. She sat up in the bunk. "What smells so good, Donal?" she asked, looking around the room. "How welcoming the fire is. It will make a fine house, Donal, at least until I'm well again."

Donal felt a warmth grow in him, glowing like the blazing fire. He helped Maire to sit on the bench by the hearth. He mashed the vegetables for her and they ate together, tired but strangely content. Donal knew he would remember this moment forever.

Maire's head nodded over her emptied cup, and Donal carried her to the fur-covered bunk once more and tucked her in, thanking God she felt better and that they had found shelter from the storm. He looked out into the night. Snow fell heavily and was driven hard against the cabin by a rising wind. Carefully, he banked the fire with the last of the wood and lay down beside her. He was instantly asleep.

CHAPTER 24

THE NEXT MORNING, Donal explored the cabin. Rough boards had been nailed in place for shelves, and on these he found more matches in a tin box and three half-burned candles. Tucked in the groove where the shelf attached to the wall he discovered a long narrow, paper-wrapped packet. He unwrapped it carefully and gasped in amazement as four lead pellets rolled across the shelf. A small bag of powder fell to the floor.

Why would anyone wrap ammunition so carefully, he wondered. And why hide them wrapped in paper? He looked again at the curling sheet of parchment. Something had been written there. Donal read the scrawled English words.

> *My wife and child are buried near the large oak tree behind the cabin. There is no reason for me to stay any longer. I cannot bear to be here without them. Whoever finds this is welcome to what I have left behind. I take only what I can carry. The gun can be found buried under the right end of the woodpile. I did not want Indians to discover a weapon.*

The note was signed *Angus MacDonough.*

Donal blessed the Scotsman for his thoughtfulness. He hastily pocketed the pellets and powder and went outside. The large oak tree had lost its leaves. They lay brown and moldy over the mound of frozen earth exposed by the blowing snow. The crudely made wooden cross leaned over the grave drunkenly. Donal brushed the newly fallen snow away and set the primitive crucifix properly in place. He made the sign of the cross and bowed his head. "God rest your souls," he murmured.

Donal found the neatly stacked woodpile nestled near the edge of the encroaching forest. A large pine tree extended its branches in protection. The night's snowfall had hardly touched it. Suspended from an inner branch of the pine, a skin-wrapped object swung back and forth in the wind. Donal stared at the long thin bundle. Using a fallen branch, he reached up to pull the object down. Snow fell from the branches, landing on his face and sliding down his neck. He grabbed the end of the swinging packet and knew by the touch it was an axe.

How clever this MacDonough was, Donal thought. Hung like this, his axe would never be buried in the snow. Only a clever man could survive in this climate. Donal vowed he would learn from this man who had been kind enough to think, even in his sorrow, of the person who would come after him.

The axe was still sharp to the touch. Donal split the chunks of wood as he took them from the right side of the pile. In a few minutes, he had uncovered a section of disturbed soil and knew that he had found the gun. The ground was still soft under the woodpile, and he easily dug out the gun that had been wrapped in several layers of deerskin.

He undid the skins carefully. The smell of mold and fungus reminded Donal of the odor that clung to the storage bin on the side of the hill on Ringrone Peninsula. He shook off the memory.

The ancient weapon lay on its bed of skins. *Heavily oiled and in good shape, the gun could not have been buried more than three months ago,* Donal thought. He blessed the man who had lived here and his foresight. With it, they would be able to survive. "God bless Angus MacDonough," he said aloud.

Donal rushed to show Maire his find. She had risen from her bed and stirred up the fire. A kettle was hanging over the hot flames, and she sat beside the hearth. Her eyes were clear, and she had attempted to free the tangles from her hair. "It's a gun," he shouted. "We can get meat!" He knelt before her. "With this, we can survive the winter! With meat, you can get well and strong again!" He grabbed her and kissed her on the lips. He was too excited to note that she did not respond, but neither did she turn away.

Donal banked the fire after they had eaten sparingly of the potatoes and turnips. He helped Maire to the bunk to rest and assured her he would return before dark. He loaded the cleaned gun and went out to hunt for game.

The winter of 1829 was bitterly cold in the Newfoundland area of Canada, but the snowfall was less than usual. Donal and Maire had plenty of wood to burn to keep the small cabin warm. They hoarded the meat that Donal was able to kill with the little ammunition he had, or trap with snares, but they were used to eating little. Donal found a small cache of potatoes, squash, and turnips that MacDonough had hidden in a root cellar near the bubbling spring. They wasted nothing; and while they did not gain weight, they survived, and the red meat gave them strength.

The wind howled through the long winter days and nights, and they huddled by the fire wrapped in the malodorous bearskin. Maire's health improved slowly but steadily. They became friends during their long time together, but still Maire would not allow him to make love to her.

"You're my wife, Maire," Donal reasoned. "You cannot hold me off forever."

"I know, Donal, but you're like a brother to me. I can't make love to you. I can't."

Donal cursed Liam for staying in her mind. She would not think of him as a brother if not for Liam. But he could not bring himself to force her. It wasn't enough that he loved her; she had to return his love.

Often, they talked of Brigid and wondered if she still lived. Maire asked over and over how he had searched for her child on the beach where they had last seen her. Was he sure he checked with everyone? Was there no one with a child?

Donal's guilt at his failure to find Brigid grew in his mind as the winter dragged by. He imagined that Maire blamed him for her disappearance. He blamed himself. He should not have given up. He should have stayed in the area and hunted in every house and behind every tree and rock. How could he have left without knowing?

Every time they talked of the child, Donal's guilt grew. He would look at Maire and know he had saved her, and he would be glad he had carried her away from the sickness and the crowds and had brought her to this cabin in the woods. In the long dark nights, his feeling of relief that Maire was alive and well added more guilt to his mind.

He came to believe he had sacrificed Brigid for his wife's life, and began to question whether he had lost Brigid deliberately. *Did I resent the child because it was Liam's and not my own?* He could not bear the thought. He left his bed and paced the floor in the darkness of the nights and left the cabin during the daylight hours, roaming the woods that surrounded their cabin.

Spring came late, but it did come. Donal and Maire left the cabin that had saved their lives and followed the stream south. Eventually, the stream flowed into a river. They had no idea where they were other than that they had gone west and south from the shore where they had been abandoned.

They followed the stream for two days before they heard the rushing of the river ahead of them. The spring rains and melting snow had caused the river to rise and overflow its banks. Huge trees had been uprooted and left still resisting its strength, as they lay half-submerged in the rushing water. Giant-sized boulders had been undermined along the banks and hung precariously on the edge of the swiftly running water.

Donal and Maire skirted the riverbanks, following the sound of its path as they forced their way through fallen trees and newly grown underbrush. He often had to chop their way through dense thickets with the axe he had brought from the cabin.

On the fifteenth day, they heard the sound of human voices. As they rounded a bend in the river, they saw a crew of nearly twenty men dragging huge newly cut trees into the river. The water was jammed with them. Hundreds of trees flowed out into the rapidly running water and were carried downstream in the rush of rapids, bumping against each other and jumping up on end as they collided with the force of the raging river. The men shouted and swore at each other and at the giant logs they shoved into the rapids.

Donal and Maire stood nearby and waited until the men took a rest from their labors. They watched a team of four immense oxen being led from the surrounding forest, dragging behind them a load of huge logs which had been bound together with heavy ropes. As soon as these beasts were released from their loads, they were led back into the woods for yet another.

A roaring fire had been built in the protection of a small knoll. The aroma of coffee drifted on the wind, and Maire and Donal were drawn to the fire. A small wiry man poked at the blaze with a long peeled stick. He wore a red knitted cap, as did most of the men who worked on the river's bank. His feet were covered with boots laced to the knees, and his deerskin pantaloons bloused out above them. A bright colored coat hung loosely about his narrow shoulders. He had a beard of several day's growth and fiery black eyes. He called a greeting to them as they approached, but in a language they did not understand.

Donal raised his hand and shouted, "Hello!"

"Welcome!" the man shouted in return. That seemed to be the extent of his English. He motioned to the steaming pot on the open fire, and Maire and Donal nodded their agreement with eagerness. They extended their tin cups, and a thick brown liquid was poured into them. Heat spread through the metal cups, and they quickly set them on the ground before it could burn their fingers. The man roared with laughter, and they joined him tentatively.

The smell of the coffee carried to the workers, and they cast hungry looks toward the fires. They soon finished disposing of the load of logs and walked toward Donal and Maire with curious glances.

"English," said the coffee server, pointing to the newcomers.

A giant of a man stepped forward and extended his large calloused hand. "I am Gerard. I speak English. You are welcome," he said haltingly.

Donal felt his hand enveloped in the giant's paw. He tried not to wince. "O'Dwyer's the name. This is my wife. We make our way south to Boston."

The man poured coffee from the pot into the tin cup the cook handed to him. He did not flinch at the heat. Donal watched with admiration as he drank the scalding liquid. The man spat on the ground. "The first thing I will do when we get to a village is get a good cup of coffee. This chicory is like mud." He went back to the pot and poured himself another cup.

Maire sat on the ground and sipped the bitter drink. She did not speak and avoided the curious glances of the men. Donal pointed to the logs in the river. "What happens to them?" he asked with a sweeping gesture.

"Ah, my friend, if luck is with us, they flow down the river to Kilburn, where we join the St. John River. From there, we tie them into rafts and sail them to America."

"Can ye use another worker?" Donal asked. The man looked at Maire. "She stays with me," Donal said. "She could give the cook a hand. We'd work for our food and a stake at the end of the trip."

"Ye'll have to keep her in hand. I'll not have me men upset by no woman."

"And ye'll keep the men in hand," Donal answered.

"Done," the giant said, extending his hand. Donal steeled himself against the grip.

Donal had never worked so hard in his life. He was half the size of most of the men and thin from undernourishment, but he soon developed the shoulder and arm muscles needed to handle the heavy logs and found the rhythm that made the work enjoyable. They rode behind the logs in bateaux—long leather-covered boats—leaving the river to camp at night, catching up with the logs the next day. At times, the logs jammed up and piled on top of each other, causing a tremendous puzzle of a dam against which the swiftly flowing water pounded and leaped like the surf of the Irish Sea. Donal found he was adept at balancing himself on the floating trees and skillful at selecting the right logs to remove to dislodge the jams. The work meant danger, but he found it exhilarating.

Maire was glad to see the log drive ended. The trip had been rough. The men rose before dawn and started the day with a mug of strong rum before breakfast. She knew that Gerard had given orders to the men to leave her alone, but she kept out of their reach, keeping to herself and speaking only when spoken to. The rides through the rapids frightened her, and she thought they would never reach the end of the great river.

At Kilburn, the logs were hauled from the river by teams of oxen and taken to the St. John River. They lashed some of the logs together with tough peeled vines, making huge rafts. Several of these rafts could be tied together to make a mile-long platform, and several sheeted sails were planted in their midst. The men were kept busy keeping the rafts clear of the rocks and pushing them along in the calm water when the winds refused to fill their sails.

At last they reached the mouth of the St. John at Calais. Several of the logs were laced together to form a linked "boom" across the river to keep the logs in place. Here, they would stay until they were loaded onto ships to be taken to England.

Gerard praised Donal for his work as they said good-bye, paying Donal twenty American dollars for his two-month's labor. Donal had never had so much money in his possession at one time before. He bought Maire a homespun dress and a bonnet to match, and for himself new britches and a shirt from a small shop in the harbour town of Calais. They booked passage on a packet boat for Boston and rented a room where they could take a bath and spend the night in a real bed.

Maire was sound asleep before Donal crawled in beside her. She smelled sweet and clean. Her hair was long and hung in damp curls around her face. Donal kissed the wind and suntanned cheek but did not expect a response. He had grown used to her indifference. Nevertheless, he lay awake beside her filled with longing. He tried not to think of what lay ahead for them. They would be in Boston in ten days' time. Would Liam be there waiting for her?

CHAPTER 25

DONAL REFUSED TO allow himself to go directly to Liam for help. He was not ready to meet his brother just yet. Fellow passengers on the packet from Portland had told him that work would start soon on the Boston-to-Lowell Railway, and they would be hiring laborers.

Catholics found it difficult to find work in Boston. Prejudice against papist immigrants had taken a firm foothold, he was told, not only against the Irish, but against the Italians and Portuguese as well; although there were more Irish and more arriving every day.

Donal and Maire stepped off the packet boat onto Lewis Wharf. Maire trembled against his arm. She expected to be turned away at each step. The horror of their first entrance to Boston Harbour was too fresh in their minds. At least there were no health inspectors to come aboard this time, no one to turn them away. They made their way up the wharf and onto American soil unchallenged.

Donal watched Maire with growing concern. The undulating sea had brought all the suppressed memories of her missing baby flooding over her. Dark circles appeared once more under her eyes, and Donal felt the accusation in them as she talked of her lost child. He was sorry they had taken the packet boat. He wished they had stayed in the snug little cabin in the Canadian woods where she would be his and his alone.

Donal stopped to ask for work at each of the warehouses along the dock, even the newly constructed one with "Wellington—Winters Lumber & Shipping" written in bold letters across the front. He had no way of knowing of its connection with Kate. The sign in the window read, "No Papists Need Apply."

Donal had not expected this kind of rejection in America. Everything he had heard about this new country promised a land of opportunity. Opportunity for whom, he wondered, the English? Were the Irish never to get away from their influence? After all, who were these Americans but displaced Englishmen? He should have realized they would have brought their prejudices with them.

Door after door closed on him. There was no work for Catholics. Am I to deny my faith, Donal wondered. Of course the thick Irish brogue was an instant giveaway. When an Irishman opened his mouth, the words came out green, the English said. Maire was the only person Donal knew whose speech sounded more English than Irish, and he could thank his mother's lessons for that.

Hot and tired, Donal found a room for them in a cheap boardinghouse on Ann Street. The dirty, dark walls smelled of cabbage and urine. The room held a rope-laced bedstead and one rickety chair. A washbasin and water pitcher had been placed on a small table. Its one window stood open, allowing flies to come in on the stilted air. The odor of the outhouses lining the narrow strip of dirt separating them from an identical building rose like smoke, stopping to drift through each open window of the ancient buildings.

They dropped their bundles on the floor, and Maire spread their blankets on the bed and lay down. "What are we going to do now, Donal?"

"I'll go find some Irishers to talk to. They will know if there's work about. I'll find out where to apply for the railroad work the man on the packet told me about. There'll be something. Just rest and don't worry."

Donal hoped he sounded more reassuring than he felt. The signs in the windows had shaken him. *Why did anyone care what you believed as long as you could put in an honest day's work?* He walked along Ann Street. Tenements and rooming houses leaned out over the street.

The July heat hung in the air, causing rainbow waves to rise from the hard packed street. Donal had never felt temperatures this high. He wiped the dripping sweat from his forehead with the colorful scarf he wore around his neck, a habit he had picked up from the river men.

Donal spotted a tavern sign near the corner of Foster Street. Two drunks staggered from the doorway singing in Gaelic. He would find Irishmen inside, there was no doubt. He hoped some of them would be sober enough to talk.

Donal stood just inside the door, letting his eyes adjust to the change from the bright sunlight. The smell of homemade poteen filled his nostrils, and his hunger for the drink overtook him. Except for the heavy, sweet rum the loggers had shared with him, Donal had not had a drink since his father's wake. Was it only two summers ago? Where had the time gone? So much had happened, it seemed more like a lifetime.

Donal made his way to the bar of bare, widely spaced boards. The familiar sound of Gaelic voices drifted over him and mingled with the smell of the liquor. He put his coins on the bar. "A pint of poteen," he said in Gaelic.

"A newcomer, are ye?" the bartender asked, filling a mug from a spigot in a nearby barrel. "A tousand welcomes to ye." He placed the mug in front of Donal. "Though this is the only place ye'll be hearing it, like as not."

Donal nodded to the man, raising his mug in salute. He drank the thick dark liquid without raising it from his lips. The brew burned its way down his chest and hit his stomach, making a small explosion. He closed his eyes and let the fire spread through him. "Ahhh!" he sighed, letting the word draw out as pleasure filled him. He replaced the mug on the bar and fished more coppers from his pocket. "The same," he said, pushing the mug toward the barman.

"Ye have a grand thirst, lad," the barman said as he opened the spigot. "'Tis a good day fer it out there, I'm told."

"Oh, it tis. It tis," Donal replied, drinking more slowly this time. *What a beautiful drink*, he thought, *a beautiful drink. How I have missed it!* He let the feeling of it flow through him, mingling with the sound of Gaelic voices, the friendly bickering and the singing. *Twas a bit of home*, he thought. He hadn't realized how long he had been without the companionship of others like himself. He drank his poteen and looked around at his fellow immigrants.

They were a sorry looking bunch. Dirty and sweaty, most had beards that had been left to grow untrimmed. Donal had let his own beard grow through the cold winter and on the long spring log drive. He had groomed it neatly in Calais before boarding the packet. The growth was thick and showed patches of dark within its rich sandy color. He had left a moustache too and rather liked the look of it in the tin mirror.

He carried his third drink to a table where five disheveled Irishers were singing a song of the heather and the hills, one that he had heard Niall sing a thousand times. He lifted his mug and sang with them, a little off tune, his voice slightly slurred with drink.

Donal remembered little of what happened by the time he stumbled into their dingy room late that night. Maire was angry and frightened. She shouted that he was a thoughtless, blighted Irishman and couldn't handle his drink. "For the first time since we've been married, ye sound like a wife," he said. Maire's mouth fell open, but she could not think of a word to reply. Donal grinned mindlessly and toppled into bed. The next morning, he tried to sort over in his mind the scraps of conversation he had had with his fellow drinkers. There was little of value, and that was mostly discouraging.

There was no work in the city for the Irish. All the other workers had banded against them and threatened to walk out if Irish were hired. The Irish would work for lower wages than anyone else, and the other workers were afraid for their jobs. Only the lowliest of labor was available, and the starving immigrants snapped that up quickly. It was a dog-eat-dog situation, with only the scraps of that going to the Irish.

The new Boston-to-Lowell Railroad would not begin construction for another month, and rumor had it there would be plenty of ditch-digging work; and few but the Irish would be interested, for the harbour terminal was to be built in the middle of the tidal flats. Twas sure to be stinking, filthy work. His fellow drinkers agreed that it was, nonetheless, work, and their families had to eat. But that was a month away. They had another mug of poteen while they considered.

"We have to find Liam," Donal told Maire. "In his letter, he said there was work. Of course that was a year ago. Things have changed in that time, according to all the talk I heard." He watched Maire with interest. She showed no sign of excitement at the idea of finding Liam; instead, she looked alarmed.

"How can we face Liam, Donal?" she asked. "How can I tell him that Brigid is lost?" Donal saw the anguish in her face, the dark eyes violet in the dim light of the room. "I cannot face him," she cried out and buried her face in her hands.

Not find Liam? Donal felt the streams of pleasure spread through him. *I thought she was only waiting to find Liam; that her life would begin again when she found him.* He held her against him. She did not cry, but her body trembled with tiny convulsions. "It'll be all right, luv," he said soothingly. "Liam will not blame you. He'll understand."

"I cannot go," she said.

"We must, Maire. We have nowhere else to turn. I must have work. People are starving here, right here in the tenements. We must get out of the city."

Finding Liam was not easy. Donal and Maire made their way to the address on Somerset Street, but a blackened, empty space was all that remained. The livery had burned several months ago, they were told when they inquired at neighboring shops.

"Twas a terrible thing," one woman said. "The horses were trapped inside, and the screaming was like hell itself. Everything was lost. An old man who worked in the stables was never found. He slept there at night. He must have perished in the blaze, God rest his soul," she added crossing herself. "He was lame, they said." She turned back to her house and shut the door, wiping her eyes on her gigantic white apron.

Donal found the owner's home address. He went around to the kitchen entrance and asked after Maureen. A middle-aged woman appeared at the door, her arms covered with flour to the elbows. "She ain't here no more," she replied to Donal's questions. "After her father was killed in the fire, she went to Providence, I think. She had a brother there, or someone like that."

"Did ye know her father," Donal asked quickly, "or the young man who worked with him, Liam O'Dwyer?"

She paused, her back still turned to him. "Maureen used to talk of them. She was kind of sweet on the young one. But he up and left one day without tellin' her as much as a fare thee well." She paused, facing him now. "He wasn't burned in the fire, if that's what yer askin'."

Donal nodded. He spoke up quickly before she could close the door. "Ye don't know of any work around, do ye?" She looked him over carefully. Donal smiled his best smile. He was thankful he had resisted stopping by the pub this morning for a bit of courage.

He saw he had passed her inspection. "There's nothing around here altogether, lad. Mr. Pendleton, he's got his own problems. I did hear from the butcher that his nephew was making his way to Lowell where they're building a canal of some kind. I don't know any more, but ye could seek it out, like."

Donal grabbed her hand and kissed it. "I do be thanking ye, ma'am. That I do." She pulled her hand away quickly, but Donal saw a bit of a smile cross her reddened face before she closed the door. He knew she'd be telling her friends of the brash Irisher before the hour was up.

It took three days to walk the twenty-five miles to Lowell. Their cash was already running low, and the weather was fine. The stage passed them on its run between the two towns the next morning and again returning in the evening. "Aren't we lucky," Donal joked, "that we have two good legs each and did not have to spend money to ride?" Maire threw him a rueful look, but she laughed all the same. She had been more like her old self since she had been able to put off meeting Liam and telling him of Brigid's disappearance.

They saw the smokestacks of the factories of Lowell before they saw the town. Stinking black smoke poured from several dirty tall yellow brick chimneys. As they climbed the hill from Chelmsford, they saw the ugly cluster of rectangular brick buildings, and the noise of the machinery rushed up to meet them. Donal knew the town had been built around the textile mills, and the canals had been built by Irish laborers. They could see the canals cutting like streets from the Merrimack River to the mills more than a mile and a half away.

To the east, they could see that work was underway on a new canal. The route would no doubt continue to the smaller river in the distance. In the flatlands at the edge of the oldest of the canals was a collection of shanties with the same look as the tenements in the slums of the city. *That's where we'll find the Irish*, thought Donal. *It's the same everywhere.*

"How ugly the factories are," Maire said, her eyes still on the stinking smokestacks.

"They may be ugly, Maire, but they mean jobs," Donal replied, shouldering his pack and starting toward the dingy town below them.

CHAPTER 26

DONAL AND MAIRE went first to the settlement of Irish laborers to find out if they knew whom to see about work. They circled the complex of noisy textile plants and followed the river. Beyond a small stone bridge across a tributary, they could see the shacks that housed the laborers. In little more than an acre of land were more than a hundred crude huts and cabins. Built of slabs and rough boards, they stood seven to eight feet in height. The chimneys were topped out with two or three stacked flour barrels or casks. Small holes had been cut high in the sidewalls for air and light.

As Donal and Maire approached, more than a hundred children rushed from a central building of similar construction. They decided it must be a school of sorts, and Donal thought the schoolteacher would be a good person to answer his questions.

The schoolmaster's name was Walsh who spoke with a broad Dublin accent. "You could talk to Hugh Cummiskey or Pat McGinnis about canal work," he said. "But they're not hiring right now. Got all the laborers they need. There's been an influx of newcomers lately. Not much work in the city for them, so they come to the outlying areas hoping for jobs."

"Is there anything else in the area?" asked Donal, trying not to show his disappointment. "I see there is a lot of building going on."

"That's true enough, but they won't take on any Irish. Feelings are running high right now because of the Church, you know."

"What's this about the Church?" Donal asked.

"One of the mill owners has given some land to the bishop to build a church here. There are nearly a thousand Catholic souls here and no church. But the townspeople don't like the idea." He turned away and mumbled, "They'd have to admit we're Christians, like themselves, if we have a church." He tucked his books under his arm and marched off.

Maire and Donal left their bundles with one of the women who clustered around the pump from which the entire area got their drinking water. Maire helped her carry the large wooden bucket to the dark shack. *Our cabin in the Canadian woods was better than this*, Maire thought.

Maire asked questions about work in the textile mills as they rested. The two dirty children climbed into their mother's lap. "If they find out yer Irish, they'll be no work fer ye, lassie." The woman studied Maire with tired eyes. "But ye have a fine way of talkin'. Ifen it was me, I'd not tell 'em I was Irish, nor Catholic neither. Ye cud jest not tell 'em . . . I mean, not lie, but not tell 'em. Ye know what I mean?"

"That's a grand idea," Maire said, as though she hadn't been thinking along those same lines herself. "Ye don't know what kind of women they look for mostly, do ye?"

"They take country girls fer the most part. They come here straight from the farms. They do have to live in the dormitories that the company owns, though. Yer husband ain't goin' ta think much of that, I'll wager."

Maire smiled. "Well, he'll have to put up with it if I can get work. He hasn't had any luck, and we have to eat." She rose and smoothed the wrinkles out of her dress. "Do you think I could wash up a bit," she asked. "I want to look neat and clean when I ask for work."

"Of course, dearie, use some of the fresh water ye helped to carry. If I didn't have these two young'uns to care fer, I'd go fer a job meself. We surely could use a little extra comin' in."

Maire presented herself at the Lowell Manufacturing Company office. The manager looked her over from head to foot before settling his eyes on her tanned face. "So you're looking for a position with us, Miss Foley?" he asked, taking in her auburn curls and deep big blue eyes. "Have you been in the area long?"

"My brother and I just arrived today. We have come from Nashua in New Hampshire." Maire silently begged forgiveness for the lies she was telling. "Our father passed away a few months ago, and it was necessary for us to sell the farm. We both have to find work." She noted he was sympathetic to her words. "I've been told your mills here are a nice, respectable place for a woman to work. I'm a good worker, though I must admit, it's been mostly farm work." When he showed no reaction, she hurried on. "I do read and write a good hand, and I'm willing to learn." She smiled at the bearded face without looking into his eyes.

"Well now, Miss Foley, you sound exactly like the type of women we have here at Lowell Manufacturing. You can start tomorrow morning in the spindle room." He scribbled something on a piece of paper. "If you'll go to this address, the housekeeper will assign you to a dormitory for our girls. You'll be expected to follow her rules and make yourself useful. All the girls help with the work in the dormitories."

Maire took the paper from him, hardly able to keep her excitement in check. She had a job! It had been easy! She could hardly wait to tell Donal.

"Thank you, Mr. Johnson. Thank you very much. You've been very kind." She rushed from the office and into the street. Clutching the paper to her chest, she leaned against the building. She couldn't believe her luck. It was the first good thing that had happened to her in her life. *And I didn't even have to lie about being Irish or Catholic*, she thought. Of course she had told him her name was Marie Foley. But that wasn't exactly a lie; she had just omitted the O'Dwyer part and pronounced her name a bit differently. There was that bit about the farm and her father dying. *Oh well, a job was worth lying for*, she thought as she walked along Pawtucket Street toward the ugly three-story, box-shaped building that was to be her home.

Maire knew by the way Donal walked as he crossed the stone bridge that he hadn't had any luck. What was he going to say when he found out what she had done? She watched with growing apprehension as he walked up the lane to sit beside her outside the wooden shack where they had left their bundles.

"There's nothing, nothing at all," he said, wiping the sweat from his forehead with the kerchief tied around his neck. "We've come all this way for nothing." Maire was not sure how to approach him with her news. She sat quietly and said nothing.

"We can go back to Boston in the morning. There's a barge that brings raw materials for the mills and takes back bolts of cloth for the Boston market twice a week. They'll let me work our passage by leading the oxen that haul the barge along the Middlesex Canal." Donal's voice held no expression.

Maire looked at him anxiously. She had never seen him so discouraged. "Why go back to Boston? What is there for us in the city?" she asked.

"At least there are more possibilities for jobs. There's nothing here." He gestured at the dirty wooden shacks.

Maire sat silent for another moment. "I went to one of the mills while you were gone," she ventured. Donal looked at her without interest. "I'm to start tomorrow in the spindle room, whatever that is," she said with a smile.

"You mean you found work? Why didn't you tell me?" Donal asked excitedly.

"I wasn't sure you'd approve, but there are other women there, Donal, lots of them. And they're respectable too, from nice homes and farms around." She knew she was talking too fast.

He gave her a skeptical look. "You don't sound too sure, Maire. What's wrong?"

"Well," she said and paused, "I had to tell them I wasn't married, and I have to live in the workers' dormitory with the other women."

Maire steeled herself against the look of hurt on his face. "How could you, Maire?" he cried out. "How could you?"

"It's work, Donal. You said yourself we had to do anything necessary to get work or we'd starve."

"But living apart!" She saw anger spread over his face. "You've just been waiting for an opportunity like this, haven't you? I should have known!" He got to his feet shouting. "I should have known you'd take the first chance you got to get away from me!" He grabbed his pack and put it on his shoulder. "I'll tell you this, Maire Foley. This hasn't been much of a marriage for me either, and I don't expect it would have gotten any better. You just go to your women's dormitory. Maybe that's where you belong!"

"But Donal! I didn't mean . . . ," Maire shouted, but Donal was already striding toward the bridge. "Oh, Donal," she said softly, "I didn't want to hurt you." But of course, he couldn't hear the words or the regret in her voice.

Donal bought a bottle of whiskey from the barge attendant. They drank it together, commiserating with each other about the unfairness of life that had brought them to the edge of this muddy canal in the middle of nowhere. They both fell into a drunken sleep on the flat barge which would carry the bolts of wool to the city.

The next morning, Donal plodded along the path at the edge of the canal urging the pair of oxen along. He nursed his aching head and cursed all women, whipping the oxen when they stalled along the muddy path. At noon, he bought another bottle from the attendant. He drank just enough to dull his thoughts, but no amount of drinking could remove the ache in his gut.

In Boston, Donal went back to the same room he had shared with Maire the night of their arrival in the city. The tavern was nearby, and he spent more time there than in his room. He drank the cheap beer the bartender brewed himself. The taste was rotten, but it kept Donal from thinking of his wife working in a woolen mill and sleeping in a dormitory for single women.

Donal's money ran out in the matter of a week. He could not afford to pay for the room. He was sorry to give it up, for it was his only link with Maire. Sleeping on the street in front of the tavern, he dribbled the remains of his bottle on his already filthy clothes.

Hunger caught up with him by the time another week had passed. Left with no money and no place to live, he swept up the tavern and spread clean straw on the earthen floor for the price of a vile-tasting beer. A street cleaner let him work for an hour while he went for a drink inside the tavern. Donal swept the horse dung from the street into a flat dustbin and received eight copper pennies, just enough for a pint of poteen.

The sudden rush of the alcohol into his empty stomach sent him reeling. The room spun and darkness closed in. He did not know when he hit the floor.

CHAPTER 27

IN CONNECTICUT, LIAM found work well underway on the Farmington Canal. The new waterway began at the basin in New Haven and cut through the state northward, a projected total of fifty-eight miles. There it would join the Hampshire and Hampden Canal, traveling another twenty miles to end at the Connecticut River in Northampton, Massachusetts. The canal would have lockage of two hundred eighteen feet, each of which was twelve feet wide and eighty feet in the clear.

Liam immediately started work in the forge making parts for these locks. Although the work was hot and intense, he thanked the powers that be he did not have to join the digging crews. The labor gang, made up almost entirely of Irishmen, dug the four-foot depth through rock and granite-packed twenty-foot wide path. At the surface, the canal would measure thirty-six feet. The workday started before daylight and lasted until dark. It was backbreaking, pick-and-shovel work.

These heavy laborers could expect to live no more than twelve years, the straw boss told Liam, a fact he had little trouble believing. The extreme climate, which fell below freezing in winter and reached into the eighties and nineties in the summer, took its toll on the immigrants who were used to a constant, more moderate climate. They suffered malaria from the mosquito-infested, muddy water they stood in every day; tuberculosis was also their enemy, as well as the meager, unfamiliar diet. Add to this the loneliness and the unsanitary living conditions of the "Paddy Camps" that lined the current stretch of work, and the short life expectancy could be understood.

Liam found he was in great demand to write letters and other documents for the illiterate canal workers. From their meager earnings of eight dollars a month and their housing and meals, such as they were, these men sent money from their pay every month to their families in Ireland.

Liam collected money every month as well for the revolutionary cause. They all had stories to tell of their harsh treatment by the English and were anxious to do what they could to free their homeland from these tyrants. Oftentimes, Liam insisted on taking less money than the men wanted to give, knowing they would be broke and begging before the month was out.

He found that he was given whatever time he needed to travel the length of the canal to collect monies for the revolutionary cause. It was, after all, the reason he had been given the position. He found that sometimes, paydays were postponed, waiting for him to arrive to collect from the men before they could drink up their wages.

Liam hated doing this kind of thing. He hated the pep talks he had to give the men to get them fired up about the injustices being done in Ireland. Each month, he was given all the gory details of events happening back home. He didn't doubt they were true; he could hear worse any day from the workers themselves, but he felt they should be allowed to leave all that behind and concentrate on starting over.

Another thing Liam was uncomfortable with was the growing store of arms hidden in the back room of the forge. On any given night, he would be awakened by a signal against the wall over his makeshift bed. Out of the night would come three or four dark-clothed figures with their cache of weapons. Sometimes, they brought only two or three guns wrapped in sacks; other times there would be heavy, wooden boxes that took two men to carry.

These weapons were being hidden until the time came to ship them to Ireland. There was talk it would be soon. Liam hoped so, for he wanted them out of his shop. The activity was dangerous, and he did not want to be the one to get caught with the guns.

Liam had been in Farmington for more than a year, and things hadn't changed much. The news from Ireland was still of scattered crop failures and starvation. The English continued to evacuate families from their lands and to clear them for their new love affair with growing cattle. First, the English had implanted Ireland with Englishmen, then Scots, and now with cattle. *Maybe that was progress*, Liam thought grimly.

He watched Brian O'Shea's wife cutting across the field toward his forge. The woman wouldn't take no for an answer. *Why do I always attract either the motherly types or the married ones*, he thought grimly. I wonder what I would be thinking if that was Maire coming to me across the field? *Where is she now? Have she and Donal come to America with the baby?*

Liam had trouble thinking of the baby as his own, though he accepted the idea as the truth. The child would be more than a year old now. He wished he could put them from his mind. Maire was Donal's wife and always would be. The memories nagged at him, sapping away his energy the way the revolutionary movement sapped the coppers from the workers.

Aileen O'Shea stood in the open doorway and leaned against the supporting post. Liam knew she was aware the sun was shining through the thin cotton dress she wore and outlining her generous body provocatively. She smiled, fluttering her dark long lashes. "Brian says he's after sending ye to Boston on an errand. He says maybe I'll stop hanging around the forge when yer gone. Could be he's right."

Liam reminded himself yet again that this was his boss's wife as her ample breasts pushed against the thin fabric. He said nothing. If Brian wanted him to go to Boston, he'd tell him in good time. He tore his eyes from her breasts and went back to his work.

"Seems a shame to waste good time, if ye'll be leaving soon," Aileen said. "Brian won't be back from Hartford till evening, and I ain't against goin' into the back room."

"Go home, Aileen," Liam said firmly, hitting the sledge against the lock form a wee bit harder than necessary. "I've told ye before, Brian's me boss and yer husband, and I ain't about to cause trouble about either state."

"Ye'll be sorry, Liam, when yer up in Boston and the nights are cold, and ye won't even have a good memory to warm ye." She switched her fanny at him.

"I'll manage, Aileen. Don't worry yerself about me. Now you go along home. Ye shouldn't be hanging around here."

"Ye ain't the only good-looker around here, Mr. High and Mighty! There's plenty who'd jump at the chance, and that's the truth of it."

"I'm sure it is, Aileen," Liam said, turning away. She swished herself from the doorway and turned toward the path. Liam watched her go with regret. He didn't know why he hadn't taken up her offer, except there was so much betrayal involved. He was so tired of betrayal and the guilt that went with it.

Two days later, Liam found himself on the road to Boston. He drove a team of two horses and a heavy wagon loaded with nearly two hundred rifles and several boxes of ammunition. In his pocket was the money he had collected for more than a year from the laboring immigrants, converted to a bank draft payable to Michael Connors, the man who had sent him to Connecticut. The money would be used to ship the arms to Ireland.

Liam would not go directly to Boston with his load but would head, instead, for Lowell on the pretense that the wagon contained parts for the new canal under construction there. The arms would be loaded onto the barge, which would be towed by oxen down the Middlesex Canal. His cargo could be easily transferred to a ship in Boston without arousing suspicion.

Liam arrived in Lowell in the late afternoon. The industrialized town was small compared with its counterpart in New Haven, but he recognized the grim rectangular factories. *How I would hate to work in them,* he thought. *What kind of person could take the dreary work and the heat and noise that went with it?*

The sound of the machinery followed him as he drove his team down Pawtucket Street and out toward the Middlesex Canal. He looked with interest at the maze of waterways. *How many Irishmen died to build them,* he wondered.

The barge was unloading gigantic spools of cotton and wool threads which would be wound onto spindles and woven into cloth in the mills he had just passed. The barge master, whom Liam knew was a fellow revolutionary agent, acknowledged he would be taking Liam and his wagon and horses on the return trip to Boston. "Ye'll have to wait a while to load 'em though," he explained. "I have to unload this stuff and take on the bolts from the mills. Ye can tie yer horses up here til I'm ready.

I'll get 'em aboard fer ye. We'll be leaving at six in the mornin'. Jest be here on time."

"I'll be thanking ye fer that," Liam said. "Is there a lodging house in town? I'm fer getting the dirt of the road washed off and a night's sleep."

"Aye. There's the Washington Hotel on Central Street. Ye kin git a good meal there too, so they say."

"A thousand thanks," Liam said. "I'll be here by half five of the mornin'." He made his way through a concentrated settlement of square wooden houses. The route took him to Merrimack Street, which seemed to be the commercial area. Here he found the Washington Hotel, in reality a large boardinghouse.

Dusk had gathered by the time he had taken a leisurely soak in the canvas tub that was brought to his room. He dressed quickly and went out to enjoy the evening before eating his supper.

Lowell was a strange town, he decided, for it had grown around the cluster of mills and the intersecting canals. He found at its center a carefully sculptured green and next to it a small library with a sign, which announced that the donor was the Lowell Manufacturing Company. On the opposite side of the street, he saw the ugly two-story gray buildings that housed the mill workers.

As Liam watched, several women in long cotton skirts and high-necked bodices descended the steps of one of the dormitories. They laughed and talked together as they crossed the street, lifting their skirts delicately as they sidestepped the horse droppings. They approached the spot where Liam was standing and filed up the library steps.

One of the women slowed her steps after they passed. Liam watched as she stopped. She did not turn her head, but he knew there was something familiar about her. The other women passed on into the library. She turned toward him. "Liam?" she gasped, and again, "Liam?" She tipped her head just slightly to the left, and her auburn hair caught the light from the library window. Liam's heart lurched.

"Maire!" he exclaimed. "God in heaven, it's Maire!" She rushed to him as he extended his arms. He felt her body against him, and he could not believe she was real. "Oh Maire, is it really you?" He could not think; he could only hold her to him and feel the pleasure of her presence.

Maire threw her arms around his neck and lifted her face. He kissed her as though he'd never kiss her again. All her wonder flowed out to him. He remembered every sight of her, every word spoken, every touch, and the one unforgettable time they had made love. "Oh, my Maire," he said and could say no more. They clung to each other right there in the middle of the street. He kissed her again and wept with her and looked into her dear remembered face.

The intrusion of thought brought him to reality. He remembered that she was his brother's wife. They were no longer the innocent children they had been a few short years ago. Liam looked at her treasured face. He reached up and wiped away a runaway tear. "Donal?" he asked. "Where's Donal?"

Maire pulled away from him and tried to calm herself. She looked nervously about. "We can't stand here in the street, Liam. Let's walk along." She moved ahead of him to the edge of the street. He paced himself beside her. They did not speak until they reached the center of the town.

"Donal is in Boston," Maire said at last. "At least that's where he was the last I heard."

"What's he doing in Boston? Why isn't he here with you?"

Maire slowed her pace. "Donal could not find work here. I was able to get a job in the Lowell Mills. Donal was angry because I have to live with the other women at the dormitory. He went back to Boston." She bit at her lower lip. She would not say anything against Donal unless she was asked a direct question. "Someone said he was working on the new Lowell to Boston Railway."

"But he's your husband," Liam protested. "His place is with you,"

"He doesn't see things that way." She turned to face him. "Liam," she said softly. "Aren't you going to ask about our baby?" Her large eyes looked black in the dim light of dusk, but Liam knew they would be a deep violet color as they always were when she was upset. "You do know you have a daughter, don't you?"

He took her in his arms once again at her words. He could not bear the sight of those dark eyes accusing him. "Oh, Maire, luv, I wasn't sure. I knew you and Donal got married, and the baby was coming, but I didn't know . . ."

Maire's head rested in the curve of his shoulder. Liam shook at the achingly familiar feel of it. "Her name is Brigid," Maire said quietly. "She has your dark hair and my eyes."

"I'm so sorry you had to go through that without me being there, Maire," he whispered against her soft curls.

Maire pulled her head away from its resting place. "She's lost, Liam," she said firmly. "I don't know where she is. When we got off the ship, I was sick with cholera and a friend was carrying Brigid. Donal was helping me ashore. When he went to get Brigid, she was gone . . . disappeared. Donal searched and searched, but the woman had taken Brigid and gone." She wept for their lost child. Liam held her to him and wept too for the daughter he would never know. He smoothed Maire's hair away from her face and wiped the tears from her cheeks, kissing her trembling lips. He cried for their lost love as well as their lost child.

When at last the tears were over, they walked toward the bridge in the distance, their arms intertwined. Silently, they stood leaning over the bridge, looking into the dark water below.

Maire's voice sounded hollow when she spoke. "Take me away, Liam," she said. "Take me away and love me. I do so need to be loved."

"Please, Maire, don't say such things." Liam's mind could not encompass the words she had spoken.

"I love you, Liam. I've always loved you." Maire turned to face him and took his hands in hers.

Liam's heart leaped like a salmon at her words, and as quickly filled with pain. He pulled away. "Don't, Maire. You're . . . you're Donal's wife."

"Yes," she said sadly. "I'm your brother's wife. At least, that's what the Church says. But that's the only way I'm his wife, Liam. He's . . . he's never touched me. You're the only man who's made love to me."

"Stop, Maire! I don't want to hear it!"

"Why not, Liam? Why don't you want to hear that I've been married to Donal for nearly two years, and I'm still in love with you?"

"Please don't, Maire. He's still your husband. Nothing can change that."

"No, nothing can change that," she said bitterly. "The Church finds a way to tie a woman's life into knots no matter what she does. We're all victims of men's rules, men who resent women." Her voice rose in the darkness. "I'm through with the Church, Liam. I don't owe it a thing. What did it ever do for me? Or for any woman?"

"Hush, Maire, you don't know what you're saying." Liam was shocked at her ranting.

"Oh yes, I do," she interrupted. "First, the Church told me I was a sinner for loving you. Then it told me I had to get married or be branded a harlot for the rest of my life. It didn't care who I married as long as I was married. Then it tells me I have to stay married for the rest of my life. It doesn't care how miserable I am, or that I don't love my husband, as long as its foolish rules are obeyed. Well, I'm sick of the whole thing. Who needs a god who ruins your life? Not me!"

Liam grabbed her by the elbows and shook her. "Stop, Maire. Stop that kind of talk. You've had a shock seeing me again and talking about our baby." He gathered her into his arms. "You mustn't talk like that. You mustn't even think like that."

She pressed her body close to him. "Love me, Liam," she whispered. "Love me. Right here. Right now."

Liam felt her yielding body. He ached for her to his very toes. "I can't, Maire. I can't. You're my brother's wife." She did not say anything. She stood for several seconds still pressed against him before she moved away.

"Take me back, Liam," she said quietly. "We have a nine o'clock curfew in the dormitory. I mustn't be late." They walked the long way back without speaking—without touching—their hearts breaking.

CHAPTER 28

THE MORE NIALL found out about his new financial business, the more intrigued he became. He knew he had been outmaneuvered by Charles Hammond into a marriage with his daughter, but that was fine with him. The advantages of suddenly becoming part of the moneyed class outweighed the disadvantage of being married to Mary Margaret.

In fact, he had become quite fond of his new wife. Mary Margaret realized she could interfere with his lifestyle only so far. Niall preferred the city life, and Mary Margaret would rather summer in the country; and in winter, she enjoyed staying at home. She didn't object to Niall's way of life, and the time they spent together was pleasant and rewarding.

At the end of their fourth month of marriage, Mary Margaret became pregnant. At first, Niall was annoyed at the thought of becoming a father, but in time, the idea grew more appealing. He realized his son would be able to have many of the advantages he himself had been denied, and all because of money. The idea that he would be able to provide his son with more pleased him, and he began to plan his son's future. The possibility that the child would be a female never occurred to him.

Niall's interest in his son's prospects aroused a deeper interest in the business he was now a part of. He discovered his father-in-law was a major stockholder in the A. A. Lawrence & Company. This company was the selling agent for the Lowell Manufacturing Company, which had been incorporated two years before with operating capital of $600,000. In addition to its two mills, which handled six thousand spindles of cotton and 152 looms, they operated twenty-seven boardinghouses for their workers.

When the Lowell Manufacturing Company found itself in financial trouble, the selling agents offered to furnish the money and credit needed, provided Hammond would become treasurer. Without this aid, the Lowell Company would fail. They had no choice but to accept the new treasurer.

This was the point at which Hammond decided Niall would make a good husband for his daughter. Hammond resigned, and Niall was named treasurer of the Lowell Manufacturing Company. In this position, he could approve the figures on cost and suppliers of goods Hammond obtained to the advantage of both. They could keep the manufacturing company solvent and add to their own coffers at the same time.

The time had come for Niall to visit his holdings in Lowell. He was interested on two levels. First, to see for himself the extent of the industrialized area; and second, to study the methods they were using in the Lowell Mills in order to incorporate them in his other mill in Waltham which needed modernizing. These holdings would belong to his son someday, and he would ensure they were worth owning.

Niall took the three o'clock stage from St. Wildes on Elm Street in Boston to Lowell. He enjoyed the twenty-five miles of countryside. Such room for expansion, he thought, as they went through the villages of Medford, Woburn, Burlington, and Billerica, and all so close to Boston and its harbour. He thought of the railway and the canals already under construction. *The area is a gold mine*, he thought. He sat back in the comfortable carriage and marveled at how far he had come in his thinking. *All it takes is a bit of money. With money, you can do anything in a country like this. What a future my son will have*! He felt a love he had never known before surging through him.

Niall arrived in Lowell just after dark and went immediately to his reserved room in the Washington Hotel, which he had discovered was also in his stock holdings.

The next morning, he called on Ned Johnson, the manager of the Lowell Mills. He explained his position and his interest in studying their operations.

"You're most welcome, Mr. DeCourcey," Johnson said. "If there is anything you need, please speak up. We'd be most happy to escort you around the place, or if you prefer to just walk about by yourself, you're most welcome to do so."

"Perhaps if I could have someone accompany me to take notes and jot down some figures for me," Niall suggested. "I'm sure I'll be so engrossed with the proceedings I'll forget to take down the facts."

"Of course, Mr. DeCourcey. I know just the young lady who can handle this. She's just recently been promoted to a supervisory position and she knows the operation from beginning to end. She writes a nice, clear hand too. I'll send for her."

Mr. Johnson left his office, and Niall could hear him speaking to an assistant. "Ask Miss Foley to come to my office, please," he said, "and find someone else to take over for her. She'll not be available for the rest of the day."

Niall sat back in the comfortable leather chair. The name he had heard brought back conflicting memories. He wondered where Maire was now. But of course, she was no longer Miss Foley. She was Mrs. Donal O'Dwyer. Niall was still bewildered at how Donal had pulled that off. She had been such a beauty, such a beauty, and he had never been able to get past the buttons of her bodice. He sighed with regret and got up from the chair, crossing the office to stare out the smoky window.

Niall heard the door open behind him, but his reverie still held him. "I was told to report to you here, that is, if you're Mr. DeCourcey," a young woman's voice said.

Niall wasn't sure the voice was not a part of his fantasy. There was a certain lilt he had heard before. He swung around and faced her. She gasped in amazement. Niall's smile spread across his delighted face.

"Niall!" Maire shouted with delight. "Whatever are you doing here?"

Niall stepped forward and hugged Maire to him. He kissed her lightly on the cheek. "I might ask the same of you, my dear sister," he said with a smile in his voice. He let his hand slide down her back before he released her.

"I . . . I didn't expect to find you here. Mr. Johnson said a Mr. DeCourcey would be expecting me."

A devilish light appeared in Niall's eyes. "And I was expecting a Miss Foley," he said. Maire giggled. The sound delighted them both.

"We're two of a kind, Maire," Niall said. "I tried to tell you that a long time ago." He caught the skeptical but interested look on her beautiful face. "Apparently we've both found a slight variation of our names to be more useful."

Maire laughed. "Oh, Niall, I am so glad to see you. You look wonderful. How good to see a real Irishman who has been successful. They're all so . . . so . . . I guess 'destitute' is the word."

"You look pretty wonderful yourself. Married life must agree with you. How is Donal, by the way?"

Maire's sparkle immediately disappeared. "I haven't seen Donal for several months. The last time he came here, he was disgustingly drunk. I guess he is drunk most of the time, from what I hear."

"You mean you're not living together?" He read acknowledgment in her face. "Well well, what an interesting turn of events."

They talked for several minutes about the things that had happened in their lives during the past three years. "Let's get the pretense of this tour over and get out of here," Niall said.

"But I'm expected to go back to my duties when we're finished," Maire said.

"I heard friend Johnson tell his assistant that someone was supposed to replace you for as long as I wished. Don't fight it, Maire. You're all mine for the day."

"You're sure?" she asked. "I wouldn't want to lose my job over this."

"Of course I'm sure. Don't I practically own this company?"

Maire laughed. "You're amazing, Niall."

"You should have listened to me a long time ago, Maire, my luv," he said looking into the violet eyes.

Maire looked away. "Come, Niall, let's tour the plant, and then we can catch up on the news from home."

"Exactly what I had in mind," he said, taking her arm.

They walked quickly from one operation to the next through both mills. Niall asked pertinent questions, and Maire jotted notes she thought he would need. Neither could concentrate on the task at hand. They were exceptionally polite with one another, calling each other Miss Foley and Mr. DeCourcey. They enjoyed their little game, and every time they closed a door behind them, they looked at each other and laughed at their deceit.

At noon, Maire sought out Mr. Johnson. "Mr. DeCourcey has suggested that I accompany him to lunch and go over the notes I have," she explained. "I thought I should check with you first. I mean, I wouldn't want to do anything that would appear improper."

"Oh, that's fine, Miss Foley. Whatever he wants. He's a very important man, and I'm sure he's a very proper gentleman. You just go along."

They lunched at the hotel, and Maire kept her notebook and pencil on the table to justify being there in the middle of the day. The rules for the women workers were very strict. They had to have an escort or visitor approved by the housemother after a proper introduction.

Maire knew she would be promptly reported if she were seen in the company of a gentleman. Mr. Johnson would, of course, stand behind her; but it would be unpleasant nonetheless. She was careful to keep her eyes from Niall's face and her head discreetly bowed as they talked.

After lunch, Niall hired a small two-wheeled chaise for a drive in the country. The covered vehicle was of the type hung on a C-spring, and it was drawn by a sleek brown horse. Niall took the reins as Maire sat back sheltered by the drawn soft leather curtains from the view of passersby.

They drove through the town and to a hill west of the busy industrial complex where they left the chaise and sat on the grass overlooking the area. Except for the smoking chimneys of the factories, it was a peaceful scene with interwoven canals gleaming in the early spring sunshine. "Rather like sitting on the hill above the Bandon River at home, wouldn't you say?" Niall asked.

"I don't even like to think about home, or Ireland, or anyone I ever knew there," Maire said without expression.

"There were good times too, Maire. You don't want to forget that."

"Maybe for you," she said, plucking a spear of grass from the ground, "but not for me. I don't want to remember any of it."

Niall picked up her hand, rubbing it gently. "And have things been better here, Maire?" he asked.

"No, not much," she answered, brushing away an unwanted tear that suddenly appeared. "I try not to look back at that part either."

"The future will be better, Maire. Now that I've found you, things will be better. I promise you."

"Oh, Niall, it's so good to see you," she said raising her dark eyes to his. "I've been so lonely."

Niall pulled her into his arms, encircling her tiny waist. She did not resist but came to him willingly, trustingly. He kissed her eyelids, her forehead, and then found his way to her lips. The kiss started softly, slowly, then, all at once, they were both stirred with excitement. Their kiss became desperate. They could not stop. They could not get enough of each other.

Maire clung to him, returning his kisses with abandon. "Oh, Niall, Niall, don't leave me," she whispered.

He unbuttoned her starched white bodice and pushed aside the soft undergarment, exposing the perfection of her breasts. Maire sighed with pleasure as he lowered his lips to the dark circle of her hardened nipple. She could not resist. She did not want to resist. She needed him so. She pressed his head to her breasts with both hands.

They made love on the new spring grass, overlooking the village with its shining canals and its stinking smokestacks.

CHAPTER 29

KATE HAD GIVEN up any hopes of locating her brothers. She had gone to each of the two Catholic churches in the city, even hiring a chaise to go to Charlestown to inquire at St. Mary's. Neither Holy Cross on Franklin Street nor St. Mary's had heard of an entire Irish village that had settled in Boston, nor had they heard of any of the O'Dwyers.

One morning, Kate sat beside Jocelyn as she interviewed a prospective maid. Cluny McCune was an Irish girl from County Kerry, now living in South Boston. "Oh my, yes, miss, there are thousands of Irish in South Boston," she said in answer to Kate's question. "There's more Irish than anythin' else. And a shame it is too that we don't have a proper church to hear mass of a Sunday. We have to go to the cemetery to the Little Chapel of St. Augustine, and a right dreary place it is too."

When Cluny McCune left to return to her home, Kate accompanied her, hiring a chaise, much to Cluny's delight. She had never ridden in a chaise before. "Won't my friends think I'm grand!" she said to Kate as they rode across the Turnpike Bridge to South Boston. "And won't they all be so jealous that I've gotten me a position with such an elegant family!"

Kate dropped Cluny off at the front steps of a two-story building made of widely spaced gray slabs of wood. Her parents, two brothers with their wives and three children, all lived in the place, she told Kate. "It's no better nor worse than anyone else around here," she said with a sigh, "but it surely will be heaven to have a room by meself on Beacon Hill."

Kate promised Cluny she would stop by for her in an hour and asked the driver to take her to the burial grounds. The cemetery was a dreary place, as Cluny had said, surrounded by a broken wooden fence and a wide gate that hung loosely from its rusty hinges. The driver got out and swung the gate wide, stopping after they had driven through to close it again. Twas such an Irish thing to do that Kate felt a pang of homesickness. She watched with discouragement as narrow paths wound their way between grayed, weathered gravestones and tilted wooden crosses.

"If ye could tell me which part of the graveyard yer lookin' fer, miss, maybe I could help ye," the driver ventured.

"I'm looking for the chapel," Kate replied. "I've no one here, thank the good Lord." She prayed that her words were true.

"Ah, ye shoulda said so, miss. I know it well. I go to mass there every Sunday meself." They took several turns, and Kate saw a small gray stone building, not much bigger than some crypts she had just passed. Weeds grew around and through the dirt path that led up to its three worn steps. A large stone cross loomed at the top, casting a shadow over the door.

"Father O'Shea should be somewhere about, unless there's a burial or a sick call or some such," the driver volunteered. "I'll be waiting fer ye til yer ready to go back," he added, curling up in his seat.

Kate walked up the steps and opened the heavy door with some apprehension. She heard it creak as it ground against the stone floor. The inside was very dark, and there seemed to be nobody about. As her eyes adjusted to the dimness, she made out the red sacrament light hanging over the bare altar. She decided to say a prayer and walked slowly down the aisle, her footsteps echoing loudly. *Surely if there is anyone here, they will hear me*, she thought.

She knelt in front of the altar and lit a candle, dropping a few coins into the box provided. "Please let me find my brothers," she prayed. Reciting a Hail Mary and an Our Father quickly, she rose and looked around. Hard, wooded benches lined either side of the aisle in stiff, dark rows. On the walls were hand-carved wooden figures representing the Stations of the Cross. She moved closer for a better look.

"They're really quite nice, aren't they?" a voice asked from the back of the chapel. Kate turned quickly, startled at the suddenness of the sound. "Sorry if I frightened you, miss. I didn't realize anyone was here." An elderly priest moved across the stone floor, his shoes making a hissing sound. "I'm Father O'Hara. May I help you with something?"

"Oh, Father O'Hara, I do hope you can," Kate replied. "I'm Kate

O'Dwyer, and I'm looking for my brothers, or for anyone from Kinsale in County Cork. Do you, by chance, know of them?"

"There are a great many Irish who come here. It's the only Catholic Church in South Boston, you know, not that it's much of a church, but tis all they have. I'm afraid I don't get to know many of the newcomers too well. They come and they go." He rubbed his gnarled hand over the stubble of beard. "I don't recall any O'Dwyers, and they soon stop talking about where they're from. They're too busy trying to keep body and soul together."

"I'm so afraid I'll never see them again, Father. Boston is such a big city, and there is no central place to get information. So many of the Irish move on. Only God knows where they have gone."

The old priest put his hand under her elbow. "Let's take a peek at the notice board in the back. Sometimes they leave messages to let people know where they've gone, or how they can be contacted."

He led her to a wide board attached to the wall. Scraps of paper of all kinds covered the rough board. Messages were scrawled in both English and Gaelic. They were poorly spelled and nearly unreadable. Kate's eyes devoured each one, searching for a familiar name or place. She was about to give up when she saw a scrap of brown paper sticking out from under another sheet. She carefully removed the top one so she could see the message below. Declan's name jumped out at her.

"Oh, Father," she cried out. "It's here! It's a note from Declan!" She grabbed the paper and read, *If anyone knows the whereabouts of Liam, Donal, or Niall O'Dwyer from Ringrone Peninsula, Kinsale, County Cork, please notify Declan O'Dwyer at the Bishop's Basement on W. Tenth Street, South Boston.*

Kate closed her eyes and let the tears fall. He was alive. She had been so afraid she would never see Declan again. Maybe he had found the others. "Oh, thank you, Father O'Hara," she said through her tears.

"I'm glad I was here, Miss O'Dwyer. God works in strange ways, doesn't he?"

"Yes, he surely does," Kate agreed.

Father O'Hara took Kate's arm and walked her to the waiting chaise. "Wake up!" he shouted to the driver. "Wake up, ye lazy Irisher! The lady wants to be taken to see her brother."

The driver sat up abruptly and grabbed the reins. "Where to, miss? Where to?" he called down, still half-asleep.

"Ye jest hold yer hoss still, and I'll be handin' her in, like ye should be doin' yerself, Tommy Kincaid," the priest answered.

"Yes, Father, yer surely right, that ye are," the driver countered. "Tell me when yer ready, miss, and where we're off to," he added to Kate.

Kate gave him the address, and they drove off with Father O'Hara's best wishes. Kate pondered on what the Bishop's Basement could be, and what Declan could be doing in such a place. She watched the passing tenements and the ragged children playing in the street. *It's even worse than the slums near the waterfront*, she thought.

At last they drew up in front of what looked like a deserted shop. The driver stopped his horse. "This is it," he said.

Kate looked at the peeling paint on the leaning building with the boarded-up windows. "Are you sure this is the proper address?" she asked hesitantly. She looked at the driver in desperation as he nodded. "What exactly is the Bishop's Basement?"

"It's kind of a school fer them what wants to be priests," the driver offered.

"A school for priests? In there?"

"Well, not exactly a school. It's kind of a training ground. The bishop, he takes boys in off the street, and, well, he makes something out of 'em, sometimes priests, at least he hopes they'll turn out that way."

That doesn't sound so bad, Kate thought, *but what could Declan be doing here? He wasn't a candidate for the priesthood! Not Declan!* She got out and asked the driver to go pick up Cluny and come back for her.

Her knock was answered by a scruffy-looking boy of about sixteen. His face was a pasty white and had a spattering of pimples. His strawlike hair stood in spikes. *Not exactly priest material*, Kate thought, or maybe he was, she reiterated quickly, thinking of Father McBride. "I'm looking for Declan O'Dwyer," she said loudly. "Is he here?"

"Declan? Sure, he's here. Where else would ye be expectin' to find him?" The boy said, studying Kate for several seconds without expression. "Ye kin wait inside if ye want, miss. We don't get many women visitors here. I better tell Father Murphy." He left Kate standing by the door and disappeared down the hallway.

A few seconds later a young black-haired priest poked his head around the corner. Kate heard him shout, "Declan! You better come quick! I don't think you're going to want to miss this." Kate smiled to herself. Her heart was beating so fast at the idea of seeing Declan again she could hardly stand still.

Declan's head appeared at the same point where the priest's face had disappeared a few seconds before. His eyes opened wide with surprise, and he nearly fell as he rushed toward her. "Kate! Kate! Is it really you?" He held out his arms and crushed her in a gigantic hug. Swinging her off her feet, he danced around the room. "Oh Kate, luv, wherever did you come from? How did you get here? How did you find me? I thought you were in London!"

Kate laughed. "Put me down, and I'll tell you, Declan. I'll answer every one of your questions, if you'll answer mine."

Stopping his twirling dance, he placed her feet on the floor. He stood back and looked at her, holding her hands. "What a lady you are, Kate! You're the prettiest thing I've ever seen. And here I've been thinking about you as the wee lass I used to run with in the fields."

"You've grown up too, Declan. How did you get so tall? You were shorter than me when I saw you last." Kate studied her brother.

Declan sobered as she looked at him. "Did ye know that Mam is dead, Kate?" he asked. Kate nodded her head. "There's so much to tell, Kate, and so much for you to tell me. Wherever shall we start?"

"First of all, I've seen Niall," Kate said. "He's doing grand. He's married a wealthy American lady."

"Wouldn't you know Niall would find himself a rich woman right off?" Declan replied, laughing. "What about Liam? And Donal and Maire? Did you know they have a baby? Her name is Brigid."

"Oh yes, isn't it wonderful! I was hoping you could tell me where I could find them," Kate replied. "I don't know where to look."

"I haven't been able to find them either. It's like they were swallowed up by the earth." He led Kate to a corner where they could sit and talk. They laughed and cried and held each other when the reality was too painful to talk more. When the time came for Kate to go, they were afraid to leave each other and set a definite time and place to meet, promising that nothing would keep them from it.

Kate looked forward to their weekly meetings, and they became the highlight in her life. She brought him to Beacon Hill to meet Jocelyn and invited Niall to come too. It was a grand reunion. Kate went to the Bishop's Basement too and gradually became great friends with Father Murphy, who often sat and chatted with them, renewing Kate's faith in God's representatives. How to locate Donal and Maire and Liam was often the subject of their conversation, but they were no nearer to a plan of how to start their search.

CHAPTER 30

ALTHOUGH KATE WAS content living with Jocelyn in the spacious Beacon Hill house, her family ties were strong, and she longed for the old life. Declan was her link to the past, and she looked forward to their weekly meetings.

Kate also saw Niall occasionally, but he was entirely wrapped up in his new life. It was as though the past had never existed for him. *There is nothing wrong with that*, she thought as she walked along Franklin Street toward Holy Cross Church. Perhaps one shouldn't tear oneself apart with memories too painful to bear, but part of her did not want to forget her heritage. She wanted to remember Mam and Da and Gran, and also the little thatched cottage overlooking the Bandon River. The visits with Declan allowed her to keep the memories alive.

Kate had decided to attend the late mass at Holy Cross Church before meeting with Declan at Boston Commons, a large area in the city center which had been set aside for a park and was not far from Beacon Hill. Surrounded by a white picket fence, its many paths through open fields and treed areas reminded her of home. Until a few years ago, goats and cows had been allowed to graze there, but the city had grown so fast an ordinance had been passed forbidding animals to graze.

Kate missed the open spaces of the Southern Ireland hills and the fresh sea breezes. Once out of sight of the city's buildings, she pretended the paths through the Commons were those of home. With Declan at her side, it was easy to slip into the old patterns of life. She could let herself be a child again. *If the afternoon is nice*, she thought, *maybe we can rent a chaise and drive out Western Avenue to see the view of the open country toward Longwood. It's such a lovely drive along the river, especially at sunset.*

The late mass was always crowded. People liked to sleep in on a Sunday since they had to work the other six days of the week. The late mass too brought out those who wanted to show off their fashionable clothing. Kate had never thought much about what she wore until she had come to work for Jocelyn, but now it was a major part of her new life. Her closets were nearly as full of stylish outfits as Jocelyn's, for her employer bought things and then decided she didn't like them. These she passed on to Kate, and with only minor adjustments, Kate found she was as fashionable as any other woman in the city, and at very little cost to her.

She thought it was a bit silly to put so much emphasis on clothing; but in Boston society, a lady's appearance took up the majority of her day. Kate found she enjoyed looking attractive, and it had not been difficult to adjust to this custom. Having both men and women cast admiring glances in her direction made her feel good about herself.

Kate walked thoughtfully up the church steps. She found there was less pressure going to mass in the city than there was in the small parish church at home where everyone knew everyone else. The sermons were thought provoking and not as personal as those at home. How often she had thought Father McBride was talking to her or one of her family. He, of course, knew every detail of their lives since he heard their confessions every week and attended every family event. Here, she could feel she was one of hundreds. It allowed her to get more meaning from the mass and to sort out her personal beliefs, bringing a new kind of peace.

Kate stayed a few minutes after mass was over to light candles for her brothers. She still had no word of Liam or Donal. Kneeling in front of the candles, she prayed they were safe and the family would be together soon.

The church was empty when she walked up the aisle. She pushed at the heavy double doors just as someone pulled them open from the outside. She stumbled and was caught by a man just entering the church. She saw his white collar, but the light from behind left his face in shadow. "Kate?" he asked. "Kate O'Dwyer! Is it really you?"

Kate recognized his voice at once. Hadn't she heard it echoing in her frenzied dreams for weeks after she last saw him? "Father McBride! Whatever are you doing in Boston?"

He was clean shaven, and his face looked thinner than she remembered. He held his black wide-brimmed hat in his hand and stared into her face. Kate saw that his long mousy brown hair still held the indentation of the hat just above his oversized ears. The wide smile he gave her did not lessen the intenseness of his black eyes, but it did give him a younger look. *Why, he is not old at all*, Kate thought, *probably not more than six or eight years older than Liam.* His square chin held a definite cleft when he smiled. *I really should try to like him*, she thought.

"I can't believe it's you, Kate." Father McBride held her by the arms into the light to get a better look at her. "You're even more beautiful than the last time I saw you."

Kate freed herself from his hands, which had moved down her arms. "I didn't know you were coming to Boston, Father," she said politely. "Are you going to be attached to Holy Cross Church?"

"No, I'm going to have a mission church, somewhere north of here where there's no Catholic Church at all. I told you I was training for a mission, but I didn't know where." His eyes had not left her face. "Oh, Kate, I've been so homesick! You don't know how good it is to see someone from home."

"I guess we're all homesick at first, Father," Kate said. "It's not easy to leave everything behind."

"Come with me, Kate, and have a cup of tea. All the others have gone to the Blessing of the Fleet at the harbour. We can talk as long as we want." He tucked her arm under his elbow, patting her small white hand.

"I'd really love to, Father McBride, but I'm on my way to meet Declan. I really have to go." Kate tried to pull her hand from his arm, but he held it fast.

His dark eyes pleaded, "Oh, Kate, one cup of tea won't take so long. Declan will wait for you. You don't know what it's like, Kate, to have absolutely no one."

"Well, all right, Father,' Kate said. "Just one cup, and then I really must be going." She followed him down the steps to a path that led around the church and through its small burial ground. They passed through a wrought iron gate and up a lane to an old three-story building which had to be the rectory.

"Aren't these old wooden houses ugly?" Father McBride asked. "The priests all live here. There are six of us waiting for assignments to missions, and of course, the pastor and his curate. We've been crowded and uncomfortable. Thank God they're all gone to the ceremony at the harbour. They left directly after mass, and I have to stay in case someone needs a priest while they're gone." He led the way up the wide steps and opened the door.

A red-faced, bosomy housekeeper met them at the door. "I left yer tea on the study table, Father," she said in a rush of breath. "I didn't know you'd have a guest. I'll jest set another cup and be off. I'm late now fer me lift to the harbour."

"You run along, Annie. I'll get Miss O'Dwyer a cup myself. You enjoy your day off. We'll be fine," Father McBride assured her. He gave Kate's hand a pat before letting it go.

"Bless ye, Father," Annie said, pushing past them and hustling down the steps. "You'll find some soda bread in the bread box, Father," she shouted over her shoulder. "Get some fer yer guest," she called as she disappeared behind the hedge.

Kate hesitated before going through the open doorway. "I really should be getting off," she began.

"Nonsense, Kate. Come along. When have we ever had a chance to talk this way together? It'll be just grand to hear all you've been doing." He took her arm and urged her forward. "And you say you've seen Declan? What about your other brothers? You'll have to catch me up on everyone."

Father McBride seated Kate in a stiff chair in the parlor and went to get the refreshments. Kate looked around at the wide room darkened by heavy drapes. An ancient overstuffed horsehair sofa took up one wall, and a massive library table stood in the exact center of the faded oriental carpet. The rug had worn spots in front of each of the three stiff chairs like the one she was seated in. At either end of the table piled with old books and pamphlets was a large kerosene lamp. A covered teapot and an earthenware cup had been placed on a small table beside one of the stiff chairs. Next to them sat a small dish with three lumps of sugar.

Father McBride stood in the doorway with a large tray. Kate jumped to her feet. "Let me do that, Father. You sit over here, and I'll pour your tea." Kate took the tray from him, placing it on the table in the center of the room.

Father McBride sat in the chair while Kate poured his tea into the earthenware cup. "Would you like sugar, Father?" she asked, picking up the small silver tongs next to the sugar pot.

"Yes, please, Kate," he said, watching her every move. "Two lumps."

Kate handed him the sweetened cup and brought him a plate with two slices of soda bread from the tray. "You're such a dear, Kate, to wait on me like this," he said.

"Well, now, Father, twouldn't be right for you to be waiting on me, now, would it? Aren't you an old friend of the family, after all?" she asked, helping herself to a cup of tea and a slice of soda bread from the tray. She sat down in the chair opposite him.

"This is really nice, Kate." His eyes took in the picture of her sitting there. "Just like an old married couple, aren't we, sitting in the parlor and sipping our tea?"

"Hardly that, Father," Kate replied. "My folks never had a parlor to sit in. For them, twas the old bench around the family board, or a stool in front of the hearth."

"Ah, but life is different now here in the new country, isn't it?" he suggested. "I guess I could get used to the better things in life." He looked around at the room. Compared to what they had in Ireland, it was luxury itself. "I might never have become a priest at all, if I had known such things existed."

"But surely, Father, you've never regretted becoming a priest. Why, you're the ideal sort of man for a priest," Kate said.

"Do you think so, Kate?" he replied, watching her sip daintily from the heavy cup. "Sometimes I wonder." He sat back in his chair, extending his long legs out onto the worn carpet. "Sometimes, I think it would be grand to have a family of my own." He paused and looked Kate over from head to foot. "Having a wife like you," he added.

Kate saw the black eyes smolder. She shuddered. Replacing her cup on the tray, she rose from her chair. "I really have to be going, Father. It's been nice seeing you again, but I have to meet Declan."

Father McBride rose quickly, upsetting his cup as he placed it on the table. "Don't go, Kate! Please don't leave me now." He rushed to her and grabbed her cold hands. "I've been so very lonesome. You're the first good thing that's happened to me for months." He tried to push her down in her chair. "Couldn't we just talk for a little longer? I don't want to be alone all day. Please, Kate."

Kate allowed herself to be seated in the chair. "All right, Father, just for a few minutes then. I know what it is to be missing home."

"Thank you, Kate," he said, gathering the tea things onto the tray. He paused in front of her. "Would you like to see some of the things I brought from Kinsale? I have a lovely old chalice which came from the destroyed abbey at Sandy Cove. Do you remember the ruins there? All the children thought it had a ghost who appeared in the fog. Come, I'll show you."

He did not wait for her to reply but led the way out of the room and up the rickety stairs. She felt as though the narrow walls were closing in on her. They passed the landing on the next floor, and he led her up another flight. It was dark and musty smelling. "Just a bit more, Kate," Father McBride said. "We mission priests don't live in much luxury up here, but we must be thankful for what we have."

Kate followed him into a small room. One bare beam ran across the length of the ceiling, and the slope of the eaves showed they were near the top of the building. A wooden crucifix hung on the whitewashed wall over an iron bedstead. There was one straight, wooden chair and a small table with a washbasin and water pitcher.

Kate went to the chair and started to sit down. "No no, not there. Sit here on the bed, Kate. It's softer, and I'll need the chair to get my things from the top shelf of the closet."

Kate hesitated then sat down stiffly on the rough blanket covering the single bed. Father McBride dragged the chair over to the closet.

"I keep my things up here out of sight," he explained, taking down a small wooden box and placing it on the floor beside Kate's feet. He sat down beside her and opened the box. Inside, nestled in soft paper, was a heavy silver chalice, filigreed with ivy and grapes. On one side was a raised, heavy Celtic cross. The chalice must have been at least a thousand years old.

"Oh, how beautiful!" Kate exclaimed. She took the silver vessel from its bed, caressing the design. "How heavy it is! It must be solid silver! How wonderful to own such beauty!"

Father McBride watched her expressive face. It's beauty reflected in the silver chalice. He placed his hands over hers. "Your beauty is much more precious, Kate," he said softly. He reached out and touched her cheek. Kate looked up with startled eyes. "To have you here, Kate, in my room, is more than I dared dream." He put his arms around her before she could move. "Don't you know how much I love you, Kate? How much I've always loved you?"

Kate dropped the chalice from her hands. It rolled into the dust under the narrow bed. She struggled to get away from him. "Father, please don't!" she cried out, pushing at his arms.

But the priest was not about to let her go. He forced her back onto the bed and began to kiss her. She struggled against him, her anger rising. "Stop it, Father. Stop it. Now!"

"Love me, Kate," he pleaded between kisses. "Don't you understand that we were fated to be together? You've been in my mind ever since the day of your father's wake. Since you became a woman."

He pulled her head back and placed his lips against hers, forcing her lips apart. She was repelled to feel his tongue, hard and pointed, dart into her mouth. She became more frightened. She kicked at him, but he held her in place.

His lips moved to her neck, pressing on the pulse that pounded there. "Oh, my Kate. You're my wife, just as I always dreamed. You're here on my bed with me."

He did not hear her protests. He pulled at her thin bodice, and it opened under his hand. He lowered his mouth to her breast and groaned with ecstasy. "Oh, Kate, you belong to me now. Say you belong to me." He ripped at her skirt.

Kate screamed and tried to claw at him, but his hands pinned her arms, and the weight of his body kept her beneath him. She kicked at his legs, but he would not yield.

He pulled up her skirt, and she felt his fingers tearing away her undergarment. She screamed again, but he seemed not to hear and would not stop. "You're a priest!" she yelled. "How can you do this? Stop it! Stop!"

He lifted his priest's skirt, and she felt his bare legs against hers, and he was inside her. She screamed as a searing pain tore through her. His body pounded against her again and again. She could not believe what was happening. Pain clouded her vision.

Kate threw her head back to get away from his wet mouth. From the wall above her, the figure on the crucifix stared without compassion. She could not think. She could not feel. She could only hear the horrible groanings as he fell against her.

He gave one last cry, and Kate felt the pressure of his hold released, even as his seed spurted into her. She shoved him away. "Get off me, you filthy beast!" she shouted. He slid off her body to the floor. Kate pushed him out of the way with her foot and rose from the bed.

She pulled down her skirt and tried to straighten her torn bodice. He watched with horror-stricken eyes. "Oh my god, Kate! What have I done?" He scrambled to his knees and clutched her skirt. "Forgive me! Oh, Kate, please forgive me!" he begged.

Kate threw a look of disgust at the groveling figure. "Take your hands off me," she said firmly.

He drew them away quickly. "Forgive me, Kate," he begged again.

Kate looked at him for several seconds before speaking. "It is not me whom you should be begging forgiveness from, Father. It is God who must forgive you."

A new horror came into the black eyes. He gave a stricken cry. "Oh dear God!"

"Yes, you'd better pray to your god. Beg his forgiveness—that is, if he is still listening to the likes of you. You, who call yourself a representative of God! May he allow you to rot in hell for what you have done this day!"

Kate ran from the room and down the two flights of stairs and out of the rectory. She rushed through the little cemetery and down the path beside the church, clutching her torn bodice together. There was no one in sight on the street in either direction.

She hesitated a moment, then ran toward the Commons. Declan would be waiting there. Declan. Oh, thank God for Declan! He would take care of her. He wouldn't let anyone harm her. He would take her out of this terrible nightmare.

CHAPTER 31

DECLAN PACED BACK and forth between the wooden bench and the duck pond in Boston Commons, where he had been waiting for more than an hour. *Where is Kate?* he asked himself over and over. *It is not like her to simply not appear. She would have sent somebody to tell me if she were not coming. What could have happened?*

These meetings had become important to both of them, somehow reassuring them they still belonged to a family. Declan felt a wrenching inside every time Kate left after a visit, a vague fear that he would never see her again. He knew Kate felt the same. Where could she be?

He walked back to the pond again and watched two pair of white swans approach each other in a kind of fencing duel. He turned back to the bench, wondering if he should go to the house on Beacon Hill.

Declan paused at the end of the path and watched the street, straining to see around the corner. He spotted her as she came running over the cobblestone, clutching her chest as though she could not breathe. He gasped, "Something is wrong! Something has happened to her!"

As he rushed to meet his sister, her black hair flew behind her like ruffled feathers. Her long full skirt looked thrown on, and her bodice was soiled and rumpled. "My god, your clothes are torn!" he exclaimed in alarm as he reached out for her. Her white face was frozen in an expression of horror, and the dark eyes were glazed.

Kate stumbled the last few steps before flinging herself into his arms and let out an anguished cry. "Declan! Oh, Declan!" she sobbed. Her body shook like a pine tree in a gale. He held her tightly to him, making soothing noises like Mam did when they were children.

"Hush, hush, Kate. It's all right. You're safe now. I'm right here."

He didn't know what she was safe from or if, indeed, everything was all right; but he needed to get her calmed down before he could find out. "There now, Kate. Declan's here," he said, his face in her hair.

Gradually, the trembling stopped. Her breath came in sobs, but they were no longer racking her whole body. Declan led her to a bench, his arm still around her. He let her lean against him as they sat and cradled her head on his shoulder. *Darling, innocent Kate*, he thought as he gently pushed the damp hair away from her face.

"Oh, Declan," she gasped. "He raped me!" The trembling started again. Tightening his arm around her, he silently prayed, *Oh God, please don't let it be true.*

"What! Who raped you?"

"Oh, Declan, whatever shall I do? I feel so . . . so . . . exposed . . . so dirty."

Declan's mind whirled with the impossibility of believing what he was hearing.

"Please, Kate, tell me what happened. Who did this?" His mind raced. *I'll kill him, whoever he is! The fiend deserves to be killed!*

Kate began to cry again. "He did rape me, Declan. He did!" she cried out. "I tried to fight him off, but it was as though he didn't hear. He was a madman, like someone possessed. Oh, Declan, how could he? What shall I do?"

Declan turned his sister to face him. "Slowly now, Kate, tell me what happened. I'm sorry to make you talk about it, but I must know who did this to you." His anger was raging inside him. He had to know. He'd kill the bastard.

Kate nodded her tearstained face, swallowing hard. "I went to mass at Holy Cross. I stopped to light a candle. When . . . when I came out . . . everyone was gone. Father . . . Father . . ." She could not go on.

"Please, Kate, tell me," Declan urged.

"Father McBride . . . Father McBride was just coming into the church. He . . . he was so happy to see someone from home. He said he'd been so . . . so lonely . . . so homesick . . ." Sobs tore at her throat.

"But Father McBride is back in Kinsale!" Declan interrupted.

"He said he's going to a mission church," Kate whimpered.

"Kate, please, what does this have to do with you being raped?"

"Don't you understand, Declan? He is the one! It's Father McBride who raped me!"

Declan stared at his sister with his mouth hanging open. "Father McBride! How could he do such a thing?" But even as he spoke, Declan remembered the troubled dreams he had after Kate left home. In his dreams, the shadow of Father McBride hung over her. He had not understood the priest was a danger to his sister. *I should have known,* he thought. *I should have known it was a warning. Damn these feelings that don't make themselves properly known!*

He held his sister in his arms until her new tears were quieted. He remembered all the things he hated about the beady-eyed priest who had destroyed Mam's last days. He also recalled the scene after Da's funeral when Father McBride had raved at Kate. *Why, even then, he must have been tortured by Kate's beauty! That's what his anger had been about! He must have been going through hell trying to keep his hands off her all these years! The man must be mad! Yes, he did it all right.* Declan had no doubt now the priest was capable of raping his sister.

"You do believe me, don't you, Declan?" Kate asked, wiping the last of the tears away. "I know you don't believe he could do something so horrible, but it's true. I don't understand it myself, but it happened."

"Yes, Kate, of course I believe you. Father McBride is a man, a weak man, but a man, just like the rest of us. Priests have the same weaknesses as everyone else."

Kate hiccupped. "No one else will believe me," she said quietly.

"No one else has to know," Declan said, "just you and me." He hesitated as a thought struck him. "And Jocelyn, I think. You'll need someone to be close to you."

"Jocelyn, yes. Take me home, Declan. Jocelyn will know what to do. I feel so . . . so invaded. How can I face what he has done to me? Father McBride—a priest—our own parish priest! Oh, Declan, how could he?" The tears threatened again, and he saw the battle she fought in her pale face. *She is so lovely,* he thought. *She must have been driving Father McBride mad for years.*

They walked together, arm in arm, to the edge of the park where Declan hired a chaise to take them to Beacon Hill. He left her in Jocelyn's care and returned to the chaise. "Take me to Holy Cross Rectory," he told the driver.

Declan paid the driver and stepped out of the chaise in front of the old rectory building. He knew before he went up the steps that something unusual was going on. The front door stood wide open, and he could hear loud excited voices. *Well, they would have something else to get excited about before he was through*, Declan thought, taking the steps two at a time.

At the foot of the hallway stairs a plump, bosomy woman stood, wringing her hands and wailing. "What's going on?" Declan asked. "Where is everybody?"

The woman motioned toward the stairs with her head, without missing a beat of her wailing. Declan dashed up the narrow, dark stairway. The first landing was empty, but he could hear voices above. He ran up the worn steps. Three black clad priests stood on the landing at the top of the stairs, nervously shuffling from foot to foot.

"Father McBride?" Declan asked.

"In there," one of them said, pointing to a doorway where two more priests waited. Declan pushed his way into the room.

There, suspended from an oak beam, hung Father McBride, the cord from his habit tied tightly around his neck. Bare white feet dangled limply beneath the black frock, in sharp contrast to the purple face with its protruding tongue. His bulging, lifeless eyeballs stared vacantly down upon the upturned straight, wooden chair.

Two other priests filled the doorway, staring at the swaying figure. Declan walked to the side of his parish priest. He caught Father McBride's legs in his arms to stop the swinging. "Someone cut him down," he said without expression.

One of the priests placed the overturned chair on the floor and stepped up on it, much as Father McBride must have done. Reaching up, he cut the cord.

Declan felt the weight of the dead body slump in his arms. He carried it to the rumpled bed and lay Father McBride down. Declan closed the staring eyes and folded the hands across his chest. He knelt beside the bed and crossed himself. "May God rest his soul," he said.

From beneath the bed, the silver chalice pushed against Declan's knees. He picked it up, not realizing what he held. He placed the precious vessel on the bed beside the priest, rose from his knees, and left the room.

Declan was in a daze. He could not concentrate on his studies or his other duties. At last, he confided in Father Murphy. "Burdens are sent to strengthen us, Declan," he said when Declan cried out his why.

"But I can't believe desecrating an innocent young girl can be justified for any reason," Declan protested.

"We're not meant to judge, Declan," Father Murphy said calmly.

"Well, somebody ought to judge such things!" Declan shouted.

"Someone will, Declan, in the end."

"That's not good enough," Declan said, pacing the room. "What good is a Church that can allow a priest like him to go on? There must have been some sign of his disturbance. Looking back, I can see it."

"Don't blame the rest for the sin of one, Declan. He was a weak man, a man driven to desperation by a vow of celibacy that he could not handle. Weak men are in every profession. The priesthood doesn't have an exclusive on them."

"But his act reflects on the whole Church!" Declan declared.

"Yes, that it does. Weak links always do."

"I've heard that the whole is no stronger than its weakest link," Declan said defiantly.

"Ah, but when that link is removed, the whole is stronger than ever," Father Murphy said, placing his arm about Declan's shoulder. "And it seems to me that, in this case, it has been very effectively removed."

"That's true, Father, but the damage has been done." Declan's eyes met those of his friend.

"Yes, I'm afraid that's true too. Now we must concentrate on helping Kate to survive this ordeal."

"I'm going to see her this evening. Would you come with me, Father?"

"I'm not sure she's ready for that yet, Declan. The sight of a priest coming to her door may upset her even more. When she has had enough time, I'll be glad to go. Why don't you take a few days off to spend with her? Take your books. You can study while she's resting. Tell her I send my blessing."

Declan spent three days with Kate and Jocelyn. Kate was pale and drawn looking, and she spoke quietly of everyday things and listened while Jocelyn and Declan told stories to cheer her. She even smiled once in a while and didn't cry as much at night, Jocelyn told Declan. She was eating too and paying more attention to how she looked, but the eyes held a haunted look, as though she could not shake a nightmare that had shocked and frightened her. "She'll be all right, Declan," Jocelyn reassured him. "It just takes time."

Declan went back to the Bishop's Basement, but he could not get his sister out of his mind. There was something else bothering him, something he ought to do something about. He spoke to Father Murphy. "I don't want to neglect another warning, Father," Declan said, but the two of them could not think of a thing to do.

Dreams bothered Declan's sleep every night, but he could make no sense of them. The baby, Brigid, was often in them, and he would wake feeling her tiny fingers grasping his own.

For several weeks, Declan went out to the fields with Chris to take his mind off Kate. The day was grand for working, and they could always use an extra hand with the September harvest. The two lads worked side by side, getting properly tired.

One evening, after a long day's work, they rode toward South Boston in the hay wagon that had been donated to the project. The other young men sang and joked. One leaned over to Declan. "Ye know, Declan, I met a man on Sunday last, whose name was O'Dwyer."

"Is that so," Declan asked. "And where was that?"

"I was visitin' me brother near the Basin. He's workin' on the new Boston-to-Lowell Railway. He works with this O'Dwyer. Donal was his name."

"Donal!" Declan shouted. "You saw Donal?" He shook the lad by the shoulders. "Where? When? How is he?"

The lad pulled himself free of Declan's grasp. "Well, if the truth be known, he was drunk . . . roaring drunk."

"What did he look like?" Declan asked

"Kind of brown hair, shaggy beard, not too tall." The lad shook his head. "He was pretty well into his cups and staggerin' all over the place."

Declan sat back in the wagon. "Could have been him, I guess. Donal always did like his drink. Where can I find him?"

"They're working in the mud, building right out into the basin of the Charles River. They live in a shanty town just off Leverett Street."

"I do be thankin' ye," Declan said, already deep in thought and slipping into a natural peasant accent. *Donal! At last! This news will be just what Kate needs. We'll go together and find him. We'll go tomorrow. I sure hope he's sobered up by then.*

CHAPTER 32

DECLAN CALLED AT the mansion on Beacon Hill late in the afternoon of the following day and was met at the door by Jocelyn. "I'm so glad you came today, Declan. Kate is in shock. We have just come from the doctor." She hesitated and looked at Declan with apprehension. "She's pregnant, Declan! Damn that priest!" She turned and pounded the wall with her fists.

"Oh god no!" Declan exclaimed. "Is she all right? Hasn't she been through enough?"

"To make matters worse, Edward is arriving from London soon. Has she told you about Edward?"

Declan nodded. "I think she's in love with him, has been since she first saw him up at the old fort."

Jocelyn took Declan's hand. "It's so sad, Declan," she said. "Her first reaction today when she found out about the baby was of what Edward would think of her. Come, you can cheer her up. She's in her room."

"I have good news," Declan said. "I think we've found Donal. He's right here in Boston. I had thought to take her to see him today."

"Oh, Declan, that's wonderful! It's just what she needs to get her mind off this new complication."

Kate looked pale and thin. Declan wondered if she had been eating. She'd have to take care of herself now that a baby was coming. Declan thought of Maire and the long months before Brigid arrived. He had been so in love with her. Now he was going to see her again. He pushed the thought to the back of his mind.

Declan rushed to Kate and grabbed her hands in his. "Come on, Kate! We're going to see Donal! He's right here in Boston!"

Kate sat up quickly. "Donal! Oh, Declan, are you sure? Here in Boston?" She jumped from the bed, a new light shining in her eyes. "I'll be ready in two shakes."

She already looked like a new person. Jocelyn and Declan exchanged pleased glances. "Wear something old and some walking shoes, Kate," Declan said to his sister. "Donal's living in a pretty rough area."

"I don't care where he is. I just want to see him and Maire and . . . and the baby." She threw a desperate look at Jocelyn but said nothing to Declan.

They decided to walk. It was a beautiful late afternoon, and they didn't want to arrive before Donal finished work. They strolled along Hancock Street, crossing Cambridge and jogging across to Lynde Street, which would lead them directly out to Leverett. Declan wasn't sure where on Leverett Street he would find the workers' quarters, but he was sure he would know when he saw them. There was nothing quite like the hurriedly constructed wooden shanties that were always built for Irish laborers.

Declan and Kate saw the workers as they came to the corner where Leverett turned toward the Canal Bridge. They streamed from the Charles River Basin covered with mud, all of one color from top to bottom, looking like walking clay figures and smelling worse. Stinking tidal mud clung to them, sloshing in their boots as they walked and drying like plaster to their clothes, their skin, and their hair.

The workers laughed and shouted to each other as they filed toward the shacks that Declan and Kate now saw through a narrow alleyway. "How will we ever know which one is Donal?" Kate asked. "They all look alike."

"I'm sure the mud washes off, Kate," Declan said with a laugh. "Remember when we used to work in the peat bogs? It's about the same, I expect."

The two followed the strange-looking laborers as they filed across Leverett Street. Several of them stopped in front of the tavern on the corner. A pretty carroty-haired girl poked her head out the door. "Ye can't come in till ye wash up!" she shouted. "Git on over to the pump and clean off first!" She slammed the door in their faces.

"Hey Kitty! Come on out and scrub our backs like ye do fer someone we know!" one of the men shouted, drawing loud guffaws from the rest.

Declan put his hand on Kate's arm. "You wait here, Kate. I'm just going to ask after Donal. Don't move from this spot now," he added.

"I'll be fine, Declan. You go find Donal," Kate answered. Declan approached the dozen or so men as they went toward the pump across the street, and the others went on through the alley.

Declan spoke to the man at the end of the line queued up for washing. "Excuse me, but can ye be tellin' me where I could find Donal O'Dwyer?"

"Sure, lad," the man said with a laugh. "Everyone knows where Donal is right this very minute."

"And don't we wish we were in the same place, Fitz!" someone shouted.

"And where might that be?" Declan asked.

The man rolled his eyes and his face lit up with an expression of what might be called bliss, at least, that's what Declan decided it was beneath all the caked mud. "The fortunate Master Donal O'Dwyer is sittin' right this very minute in a tub of hot water, having his back scrubbed by the very desirable, redheaded barmaid of the establishment across the way." He paused to lick his lips. "But I wouldn't be disturbin' him, lad. Donal won't be fittin' to talk to till he's had at least three jars."

Declan had to laugh at the man's expression. "I do be thankin' ye, friend," he said and gave a salute to the eavesdropping queue.

Declan walked back for Kate and they went into the tavern. There were no windows inside, and except for lanterns hanging over either end of the bar, there was shadowed darkness. Sawdust covered the dirt floor, and a mildly unpleasant odor of stale beer clung to the air. Behind the bar a beefy, red-faced man in a dirty white apron was wiping mugs with an equally dirty towel.

Declan approached, placing his hands on the sticky surface of the bar. "I'm lookin' fer Donal O'Dwyer," he said. "Would ye be kind enuff to tell him his brother, Declan, is here?"

The man looked Declan over with speculation and then glanced across at Kate. He lifted one eyebrow in appreciation. When he spoke it was to Kate. "Ye ain't Donal's wife, are ye?"

Kate laughed, and the music carried through the room. "Oh no. I'm not his wife. I'm his sister." She looked up to see Donal standing in the open doorway behind the bar. He was wrapped in a large yellowed towel, and his mouth hung open. His hair was wet from recent washing, and water dripped onto his face and from the scraggly beard that hung almost to his chest. Behind him the carroty-haired girl peaked over his shoulder.

"Kate! Declan!" Donal shouted. He scrambled around to the end of the bar, tripping over the long towel. Declan grabbed him before he fell. "Declan!" Donal shouted again, grasping his brother in a gigantic bear hug. He moved to include Kate, and the three of them hugged each other, laughing and crying and shouting each other's names.

The newly rinsed-off men began filing into the room. "Let's get out of here," Donal said, "where we can talk, private like."

"Ye better put some clothes on first, Donal," spoke up Kitty from behind the bar.

Donal looked down. The towel had nearly fallen off during his excited greeting. He grinned sheepishly. For the first time, he looked like the old Donal.

"Come in the back while I get dressed." He led the way behind the bar and into the back room. On the way, he patted Kitty on her fanny and said, "Bring me a jar, will ye, luv, while I get me clothes?"

A folding canvas tub stood in the middle of the floor of the dingy room, which was piled high with crates of bottles. A puddle of water ran from the spot where Donal had gotten from the tub. "Grab a box and seat yerselves," Donal said. "I'll jest get me clothes on." He went behind a stack of crates. "I can't wait to catch up on the news."

Donal's voice had a scratchy sound, and he cleared his throat with a catchy little cough every few words. Declan wondered how long his brother had been drinking heavily.

The girl with the carrot-top hair came into the room. She had three mugs of beer on a tray. "Hullo!" she said. "I'm Kitty. I thought ye might be thirsty too, so I brung ye a jar along with Donal's." She smiled tentatively, first at Declan and then at Kate. She made a kind of curtsy. "I have to git back. It's our busy time." She turned to the door. "Yer drink's on the tray, Donal," she called to the stack of crates as she passed.

"Thanks, luv," Donal said, coming from behind them fully dressed.

"She's a good girl, Kitty," he said, nodding his head in the direction she had gone. "She took me in when I ran out of money and had no place to go."

Declan looked at Kate. *Where was Maire*, he wondered. *Should they ask about her?* He decided he must. "Where's Maire, Donal? And Brigid?"

Donal threw him a look of such pain that Declan was stunned. *What had happened? Where were they?* His mind raced with the possibilities.

Donal cleared his throat again. "Let's go where we can talk, and I'll tell you all about it." They followed without speaking.

The three walked up Leverett Street to the bridge. Off to the left was a small square of green grass where a bench had been placed overlooking the wide river. They sat down with Donal between them, and he told them of the voyage and the cholera and of Brigid's disappearance. They sat in the dark by the swiftly flowing river and wept as the pain of loss swept over them.

"When we got to Boston, there was no work, especially for Catholics," Donal continued. "We heard they were hiring at the reconstruction of the canals in Lowell, so Maire and I walked the twenty-five miles. The canals were not hiring."

He paused, getting up from the bench and paced in front of them. "But the mills were," he continued in a dead voice. "Maire got taken on in one of the mills. All the women workers were assigned to dormitories. They had to live in the company housing, she said. She had settled everything before I even knew. My wife was going to live in a single women's dormitory."

He paused again wringing his hands. "I was angry. It seemed like she had taken the first opportunity to get away from me. Oh, I knew she didn't love me. She's never loved anyone but Liam. But we could have had a good life together if she had tried."

He sat down again between his brother and sister. "I think she blamed me for Brigid getting lost. She kept asking me for months if I had looked everywhere."

"Oh, Donal," Kate interrupted. "You mustn't believe that! That's not like Maire at all. She couldn't blame you."

"I don't know, Kate. The baby was Liam's, of course. She probably thought I resented her. But I loved that child. I loved her the same as if she had been my own."

Kate was shocked. She had not known the baby was Liam's. "But, Donal, are you sure the baby was not your own?" she asked.

"Of course I'm sure. That's why she married me, to have a father for Liam's child. Besides, she never was a wife to me," Donal said.

"Do you mean to tell me you lived with Maire for more than two years and never touched her?" Declan burst out. He realized what he had said. "I'm sorry, Donal. It's none of my business."

"That's all right, Declan," his brother said sadly. "We never really had a marriage, even though the Church says we're man and wife forever."

"My god, Donal, you must be a saint!" Declan blurted.

"Still in love with her, yourself, are ye, Declan? You never could keep yer eyes off her," Donal said with just a taste of bitterness.

"What did you do then, Donal," Kate asked, trying to change the subject.

"Well, first off, I got good and drunk," Donal said with his old sheepish grin. He sighed. "I've been pretty much that way since. Kitty took me in when I was at my worse."

Donal was silent for a few seconds. "I went to Lowell to see Maire a few times, but she wasn't particularly glad to see me. I guess I'd had a few too many to get up my courage to go. I haven't seen her in months."

They sat as the moon rose, and Declan and Kate brought Donal up-to-date on what had happened to them. They wept again for Mam and for the razed village. Kate didn't mention Father McBride, so Declan said nothing of her troubles. Donal had enough of his own, and Kate could tell him in her own good time.

They were walking back from the park when Donal mentioned he had seen Liam. "He told me he had seen Maire," Donal said quietly. "He was on his way west someplace. Said he couldn't stand collecting money for the revolutionaries any longer.

"How did he look, Donal?" Kate asked. "Just think, now we know where everyone is. We told you how well Niall is doing, didn't we?"

"I'm glad he's doing well. I always knew we didn't have to worry about Niall. He always finds a woman to give him what he wants," Donal replied.

Donal took several steps before he continued. "Liam looks fine. He told me my place was with Maire, either in Lowell or here. Can you imagine him telling me how to run my life? He reminded me she was still my wife. I'll just bet he's reminded himself of that more than once." Donal's voice held a new bitterness. After a few minutes, he spoke again. "So Liam's on the go again, running away so's he won't have to face things."

"Perhaps it's for the best," Declan said.

"Perhaps it is," Donal echoed.

CHAPTER 33

DECLAN WAS NOT sure why, but he could not shake the feeling of desperation that enveloped him like fog for days after he had seen Donal. Perhaps Kate's pregnancy was disturbing him, he kept telling himself, but he really didn't think that was it. For some unknown reason he felt that, as difficult as it was for Kate, the coming child would be a blessing, something of value to hang onto which would help her survive her tragedy.

He could not put a name to his feeling about Donal. He kept hearing the words Donal had said to him over and over. "So you're still in love with her yourself, Declan? You never could take your eyes off her."

Declan realized the words were probably true. He had worshipped Maire ever since he could remember. What he had not known was that Donal knew it. Declan thought he had covered up his admiration for his brother's wife very well. He still didn't believe Donal seriously thought he would ever consider anything but worship from afar.

Still, there was that note of accusation in Donal's voice, a bitterness Declan had never heard before. Of course after what Donal had been through, he had a right to be bitter about a lot of things.

In Declan's visions, he saw Donal as though he were behind a barrier that couldn't be broken through . . . as though he had been encased in the mud of the river basin, dried and cracked, and it could not be washed away. He feared Donal had deliberately closed himself within the barrier to separate himself from his family. Declan could not escape his great sense of loss.

A few days later, Father Murphy called Declan into his office. Bishop

Fenwick had asked him to select two of his top students to accompany him to Lowell for the dedication of the new Catholic church on Independence Day. "Would you like to go, Declan? I think you have earned the right," Father Murphy said.

Lowell! Maire was in Lowell! Declan's throat suddenly dried at the thought. He swallowed noisily. "Yes, Father," he said. "I'd be honored to go."

"Good," Father Murphy said rising from his chair. "I shall ask Timothy Ryan to go as well. The two of you will be serving mass and assisting the bishop with confirmation services." He looked at Declan with concern. "Maybe a change will do you good. You've been going around like a lost leprechaun for days."

Declan rose too. "You're right, Father, and I really do look forward to going to Lowell." Declan went out of the office and back to his studies. *Maire,* his mind kept shouting. *I'm going to see Maire!* He completely forgot his concern about his brother.

On the Saturday before the holiday, the bishop's entourage journeyed to Lowell, Declan among them. Bishop Fenwick had engaged every seat on the six-passenger vehicle for the trip. He was accompanied by his assistant and another priest, a Father O'Flaherty, as well as Father Murphy and the two students.

Bishop Benedict Fenwick took the opportunity to acquaint his prize students with his plans, for they were to be a part of them. "This new church is a wonderful example of what this country can do for the Irish Catholics," he said. "Attracting them to the country with jobs, we can build a community around them, and then provide them with a church and a resident priest. The next step is a school for the children. In Lowell, we'll start with a school in the church basement, and in another year, we will build a separate school building for them. This will attract more Catholics. It's a marvelous country!"

When the bishop got started on his favorite topic, there was no stopping him. Father Murphy winked at Declan as the bishop continued.

"We need priests and an educated laity. We also need native priests, educated right in this diocese. I intend to build a seminary and a college, a college where vocations to the priesthood will be fostered and where young Catholics can be prepared for the professions in American life."

He stared at the passing countryside without seeing. Instead, he saw his dream. "I want a seminary that is staffed by an American faculty, one that understands the American temper and the New England mind, one that will train my seminarians for work in New England communities."

Bishop Fenwick had been much concerned for years about the poor immigrants, both Portuguese and Irish, who came by the thousands to the port of Boston each year. They tended to stay in the overcrowded poorer sections of the city rather than go out into the country because the city was their only source of spiritual contact. There were no Catholic churches outside the cities. Those who did leave the Church's protective wings in the city often succumbed to the dominant pressures of a Protestant culture.

"I shall not only erect my college and seminary, but I shall build a farming community around it," the bishop announced to his captive audience. "This will solve many of my problems at once. I can educate both my priests and those who would join the professions, and I will have a farming community for those immigrants who are more suited for the rural life. And they will have a magnificent church of their own." He sat back against the cushion and folded his white hands across his ample paunch with a satisfied smile.

Declan saw the two priests exchange knowing glances. He gathered that the bishop held forth on this subject at every opportunity.

Bishop Fenwick looked at the two students. "You, my fine studious friends, will be the first of my seminarians. You are going to help me build my village, my church, and my college. You will be my first priests."

Declan and Timothy looked at each other and back at this remarkable man who sat opposite them. Did he really think they were worthy of being priests? Declan was not quite prepared for the announcement, nor was he quite ready for a commitment of this sort.

Bishop Fenwick watched the two young men carefully. "Of course I don't expect you to accept this idea on the spot, lads. There will be a few years yet before we have our town built and settled, and more still before the seminary can be started."

"I'm sure we'll give it careful consideration, sir," Declan said. "Won't we, Tim?"

"Yes, sir," said Tim, swallowing hard.

"We'll start our first expedition to lay out the land in the spring. You will be working closely with Father Murphy, here, to get everything ready," the bishop continued. "The land is already set aside for the Church to begin the project. The town will be called Benedicta."

He looked out the window of the coach at the passing countryside. "It's almost like having a son." Bishop Benedict Fenwick's words were barely audible.

The bishop's party lodged that night at the Stone House at the head of Fletcher Street on Pawtucket. On Sunday, he would dedicate the newly constructed, wooden, gothic church with its gilded globe and cross gleaming from the tower.

The next day was unusually warm as nearly two thousand people attended the ceremonies. More than a hundred people had traveled from Boston for the affair, at which the Boston choir sang. Declan assisted as thirty-nine souls were confirmed during the afternoon ceremony following vespers.

Declan was glad when the events were over. The church was hot and stuffy, and his long robe was very uncomfortable. The bishop had taken every opportunity to preach to him and Tim about his Benedicta project. As interested as Declan was, he could not keep his mind focused, knowing Maire was here in this same town. He yearned to get away to find her.

There had not been a minute of free time all day Sunday, and the bishop's party was scheduled to return to Boston during the evening. Declan went to Father Murphy at the first opportunity. "Could I stay over in Lowell another day?" he asked. "My sister-in-law lives here, and I haven't seen her in two years. I could take the packet boat, the *General Sullivan*, back to Boston Monday evening. I would dearly love to see her and take news back to Kate."

Father Murphy agreed. "Don't miss the boat back, now," he cautioned. "It'll be crowded with the holidaymakers."

"I won't, Father, thank you." Declan was already out of his vestments.

Father Murphy looked at his beaming face. "You're sure this is a sister-in-law you're going to see?"

Declan blushed. "Oh yes, Father. She's Donal's wife."

"Enjoy yourself," Father Murphy called as he dashed out the door.

Declan had heard the parishioners talk of a celebration to be held at the Paddylands, or New Dublin, as the shantytown was starting to be called. He knew every Irishman and Irishwoman for miles would be joining the merrymaking. He would look for Maire there.

The single acre of land where nearly five hundred Irish lived was easy to find. He simply followed the crowds spread out over the streets and fields beyond. All were headed for the Irish fair.

He could hear the music before he actually saw the sorry bunch of shacks. Even in this wide-open country, the Irish were herded together behind an invisible fence on the poorest land available. *Are we our own worst enemy*, Declan thought, *allowing ourselves to live like this when vast lands exist to the west?* He recalled what the bishop said about the immigrants clustering together in the city slums just to be near the Church. Surely, the bishop's new project was the answer. Benedicta would be just the first of many communities to follow.

Declan joined the laughing, dancing crowd and spent a few of his saved coins for familiar pastries and a mug of very fine poteen. Whatever else they had here, he thought, they had a fine still hidden away somewhere.

He asked everyone he met if they knew of a Maire O'Dwyer. No one seemed to have heard of her. "She works at the Lowell Manufacturing Mill," he said, "and lives in one of the company dormitories."

Finding no one who knew her, he wandered through the crowd, tasting the food that reminded him of home and listening to the music that took him back to the village fairs in Kinsale. How long ago it all seemed.

Declan had another mug of the strong drink and felt his head whirl. The music swirled around in his mind. He felt as though he were dancing but knew his feet were not moving. Wandering into the field beyond the settlement, he found a place to sit down in the grass. It still held the warmth of the sun. He dreamed Maire came and sat beside him, and they talked of going to a town called Benedicta where the Irish owned the land and could not be driven away.

The sun was high when Declan awoke the next morning. His mouth tasted of mud and straw, and his head objected to the faint noises of the waking village. He brushed himself off and went to the pump near the stone bridge. Putting his head directly under the spout, he pumped hard. The icy water poured over him. He gasped but held his head in place until he could bear it no longer. Taking his spare shirt from his pack, he dried himself off and ran his fingers through his hair in an attempt at combing it.

Declan felt better able to start the day. He should have known better that to drink homemade poteen. A few people were stirring about at several of the huts. He approached somewhat apprehensively and asked about Maire. At the third cabin, a woman with several children swarming about her skirts looked at him curiously. "Yer her brother, ye say?" she asked.

"I am," Declan replied. "I've been searching for her. Do you know her by chance?"

"I do. She calls herself Marie Foley. She lives at the Lowell Company House on Dutton, opposite the library." She picked up one of the small children. "I sure hope she won't mind me tellin' ye. She's been a good friend ta me and mine. I wouldn't want to do anythin' to hurt her."

"I'm sure she won't mind, Mam. I know I'll be real happy to see her, and I hope she will be happy to see me."

"Good luck, then," the woman called. "Tell her I said hullo." She went inside with her brood following her.

Declan waited stiffly in the parlor of the rooming house. The housekeeper had looked him over with a stern eye and begrudgingly sent a girl to find Maire. "We don't get many gentlemen callers during a weekday," she grumbled. "But then, it isn't every week we have a holiday, I don't suppose." She moved on heavy legs to an adjoining room, leaving the door ajar.

Declan heard Maire's footsteps. He would never forget the sound of her moving about in a room. He rose and faced the door. The look of surprise and pleasure on her face was worth all the effort he had made to find her. "Maire!" he called out, opening his arms. She came into them without hesitation.

"Oh, Declan. How wonderful to see you!" Her voice was full of happiness. "I've wondered so often where you were and what happened to you."

"And I've been almost crazy trying to find you." Declan kissed her cheek and lay his head against her hair, breathing in the heavenly scent of her.

She pulled back and smiled up at him. "How did you know where to find me?" she asked.

"I ran into Donal a few weeks ago, and he told me you were here." He still held her by the arms, and he looked down into her upturned face. *She is so beautiful*, he thought, *so perfect*. He had trouble following her questions. "And where is Kate? And Mam? Oh, Declan, there's so much to catch up on."

"Yes, so much," he said, swallowing with difficulty. He had not expected to be so overwhelmed by seeing her, by touching her.

"Let's sit down over here, Declan, where we can talk." She led him to a stiff horsehair settee. "We have to entertain our callers in this parlor," Maire said. "They're very strict about hours and who we see and all. I'm surprised the housemother let you in. It must be your innocent Irish look." They laughed together.

Declan sat beside her and held her hand, watching her face while she talked. "Donal told me about Brigid," he said at last.

Maire's eyes filled with tears. "I miss her so, Declan. I relive every sweet moment I had with her. I remember how you saved her life by blowing your breath into her the night she was born." She raised her huge violet eyes to his. Tears wet the dark lashes and hesitated there. "Oh, Declan, I can't believe I've lost her." The tears dropped onto her cheeks.

Declan reached out and pulled her head to his shoulder. "Don't cry, Maire. I can't bear it." He stroked the auburn curls so close to his face, hardly daring to believe she was in his arms.

The door to the hall opened. They looked up at the same moment. Donal stood in the doorway. Declan was shocked at the look of hatred on his brother's face.

"Well well, isn't this a pretty sight. My wife in the arms of yet another O'Dwyer brother! What is there about the O'Dwyers ye can't resist,

Maire? We seem to hold an unholy fascination for ye. All except the one ye married, of course."

Declan jumped to his feet. "You're mistaken, Donal. This isn't what it seems."

Donal walked around his brother, looking him over in an exaggerated manner. "It didn't take ye long to git yerself to Lowell, did it, Declan, once ye found out where she was?" he sneered. "I knew ye hadn't gotten over her. Ye still had that hangdog look every time someone mentioned her name."

"Donal, please!" Maire interrupted. "You're wrong about this."

"Well well, Little Miss Innocent is going to speak up to defend my baby brother. As I remember, ye always spoke up fer Liam too."

"You must be drunk, Donal, as usual," she said, turning away from him.

"You'll be surprised to learn that I'm sober as a priest at early mass, maybe more so," Donal responded.

He does look sober, Declan thought, *and his beard has been trimmed*. In fact, Donal looked very respectable, quite handsome. His sandy hair was neatly combed, and his cool blue eyes were clear. He wore a neat tweed suit with a white shirt. *He must have been sober for days*, Declan thought.

"I had in mind to present myself to you and offer a reconciliation," Donal said with just a hint of sarcasm. "But I can see ye have no need fer the likes of me." He turned toward the door.

"Don't go, Donal," Maire said quickly. "You really have misunderstood things here."

"Oh, I'm always misunderstanding things," Donal said, walking around the room with his hands in his pockets. "I really thought when I married you that we could make it work. Oh, I knew you still loved Liam, but I thought you'd at least try to make a good marriage."

"I did try, Donal . . ."

"Be honest, Maire. You had no intention of trying. You still believed Liam would come back and take you away with him. Well, it didn't work out that way, did it?" Donal's temper was rising as he talked. "Liam came to see me a while ago. He has no intention of taking you away, Maire. He doesn't ever want to see you again."

"Donal, don't . . ." she cried out.

"And after today, I don't ever want to see you again either. You don't know what being faithful means, Maire. You thought you were being faithful to Liam. You forgot what it is to be faithful to yourself." He turned to Declan. "And if you know what's good for you, Declan, you'll stay away from her too. She'll only ruin your life."

Declan could not be angry at his brother despite the truth of what he was saying.

Donal looked at Maire once more. "That leaves only Niall. He told me he'd seen you. As far as I'm concerned, you deserve each other."

Maire was angry too. "Niall is helping me," she said defensively. "He's gotten me a better-paying job in his mill in Waltham. I'm to work in an office, writing a newspaper for the women workers."

"Ain't that grand, now!" Donal said sarcastically. "And I can just bet that Niall has other advantages to offer too, as every woman he ever met found out."

"That's not fair!" Maire shouted, but Declan saw the guilty blush creep up her beautiful neck.

"What the hell," Donal said. "He's an O'Dwyer, isn't he?" He laughed a terrible, bitter laugh as he left the room.

With a desolate feeling of reluctance, Declan followed his brother. He knew he could do no less.

CHAPTER 34

NIALL HAD NEVER known such agony. He paced back and forth on the sculptured carpet outside his wife's bedroom door and listened to her moans. Mary Margaret was having a difficult time giving birth to his son. Niall had not known having a baby was such a complicated affair. He had supposed they simply dropped them, with maybe a bellow or two, as a cow or mare would do. Her pains had been going on since the early-morning hours, and it was now past midnight.

At first, there had been the excitement of knowing the time had come. His son was arriving. He visited Mary Margaret and held her hand as they waited for the midwife. Niall watched as the contractions caused his wife's body to shudder as regularly as the waves against the shore. There had been several minutes between the spasms, and they laughed and joked about how strong their baby must be to make such a fuss about being born.

As the hours went on, her labor was no longer something to joke about. Mary Margaret's body was racked with pain. Sweat poured down her face, and her hair hung limp and lifeless. Her hands clenched every few seconds as she anticipated the next wrenching of the child within her.

The doctor banished him from the room at six in the evening. Niall was surprised by the feeling he had of being left out of one of the most important events in his life. The babe was his too, and he should be there to greet him. He was also surprised at the strength of his feelings of concern for Mary Margaret.

Their marriage had started with little more than friendship, and he was surprised to find the months of their first year brought admiration and affection. They had spent more time together during her pregnancy, and new warmth had grown between them out of their desire for the child to come. As he paced the carpet outside her door, Niall discovered that his affection had turned to a kind of love. Every agonized sound from his wife's lips sent a fear through him. He didn't want to lose her. Niall went down the stairway, clinging to the railing. He was more exhausted than he ever remembered. *Poor Mary Margaret, how terrible this is for her.* He went to the study and took down the crystal decanter. He was not an enthusiastic drinker, but he did like a nightcap after a long day. The whiskey smelled strong and sweet as he removed the stopper. He poured an inch of the brown liquid into a glass, hesitated, and then poured another inch. *If there ever was an occasion for drink, this is it,* he thought.

The scream from upstairs echoed throughout the house. The sound tore from her throat, burning and searing as the child tore free from her body. Niall swallowed the drink in one long gulp. He waited, glass in hand, for the next scream to come. There was nothing but silence. *Was the child born? Is Mary Margaret all right? I have to know.*

He took the stairs two at a time and ran to her door and raised his fist to knock. A loud, lusty cry of protest came through the door from infant lungs. His son had been born!

Niall lowered his fist. "Thank you, God," he said softly. He leaned against the wall in relief, the strength gone from him. He heard the sound of the baby's cry again. Niall raised both hands in the air and let out a long high-pitched sound of exaltation. The beauty of the clear tone hung in the air.

The doctor's voice came through the door. "Quickly, help me! She's hemorrhaging!" Niall listened to the sudden new activity inside the room. The baby wailed, but no one hushed him. Niall opened the door and went in. The doctor and the midwife worked frantically over the bed. Niall saw the drained white face of his wife against the pillow, still wet from her ordeal. Her eyelids were still.

He went to the cot where the child screamed. He had kicked off the swaddling covers. Indeed, it was a son. *Why, he looks just like Donal,* Niall thought. He reached out and lifted him from the cot. A flood of joy swept over him. He lifted the tiny fingers tentatively and they curled around his own and held tight. The crying stopped. Niall hugged the tiny infant to him, letting the rush of love flow through him. On the bed behind him, the life's blood drained from his wife's body. She made no sound as her breathing stopped.

"She's gone," the doctor said. Niall turned at the words, but their meaning did not register. He looked at Mary Margaret in bewilderment. Instinctively, he held the baby closer to his chest. "I could not stop the bleeding. She's gone," the doctor repeated.

Niall went to her side and knelt by the bed, the baby still in his arms. The doctor and the midwife left the room. "Ah, Mary Margaret, it's sorry I am that you're leaving me. I did love ye, in me own poor way." Unconsciously, he had slipped into the old Irish way of speaking. "I hope ye'll be happy where yer goin'."

The baby stirred in his arms. Niall looked down at him, already so loved. "Thank you, Mary Margaret, for our son. Shall we call him Charles for your father? Charles Hammond DeCourcey. May he make us proud." He leaned over and kissed his wife's cold forehead, then got up from his knees and put the motherless child back in the cot.

None of the servants seemed to know what to do with the tiny infant, except to stand and admire him. The doctor said he would send a wet nurse for him, but Niall was uneasy about having a stranger feed and care for his son. He sent one of the servants for Kate. *She will know what to do*, he thought and waited impatiently for his sister to arrive.

Niall sat back and sipped his drink. The house was quiet and empty. He had not known such a void would suddenly open up when Mary Margaret died. They had taken her body away two hours ago, and it was as though the place had been stripped of its contents. Every sound echoed from the walls. He felt like he was sitting in a completely empty room.

Niall had finished his third drink by the time Kate arrived. The sound of the bell reverberated in the empty house. Niall rushed to the door as the butler opened it for her. He opened his arms, and Kate rushed into them. "Help me, Kate," he cried. "I don't know where to turn." Kate smiled reassuringly and led him back to the study. "How will I care for such a tiny helpless thing without her, Kate?"

"There are lots of people to help, Niall. We'll do just grand, you'll see." She waited until Niall was more relaxed, then asked, "Would you show your son to me, Niall?"

"Oh yes. Come with me." He led the way up the stairs. Mary Margaret's door had been closed, and the room across the hall they had decorated as a nursery threw a soft light across the carpet. He heard the servants' voices and led Kate into the bright room.

"My sister is here," he said. "You may all go back to bed. We'll stay with him until the wet nurse arrives." He went at once to the cradle which had been elaborately trimmed with lace and ribbons. He picked up his son and placed him in Kate's arms.

"Oh, Niall. He's beautiful!" Kate felt the soft, warm body in her arms. Inside her, the pain she had been carrying turned warm and began to glow. In six months' time, she would have her own baby. For the first time, the reality of it seemed not only possible but also acceptable. She hugged the sweet-smelling infant to her and allowed the tears to flow. "He's wonderful, Niall," she said through her tears. "He's just wonderful."

After Charles Hammond DeCourcey had been properly admired and returned to his bed, the two had a real talk for the first time in their lives. "I don't feel right having strangers feeding and caring for him," Niall said. "What am I going to do?"

"We have to have a wet nurse, Niall, and I'm afraid I don't qualify for that." She smiled as she remembered that in a few months, she would have ample qualifications. "Would you feel better if you had an Irish woman? You know, like the foster mothers back home? We could find a couple, maybe, who could live right here and become part of the family. The husband could help with the gardens or something. Would that be more acceptable?"

"I knew you'd think of something, Kate. That sounds good, but where will we ever find someone like that? Fostering isn't practiced around here, as far as I know."

"But the Irish know all about it, Niall, and I know just the couple. We have an Irish lass as a maid. Her brother and sister-in-law just had a baby a few months ago. She's still nursing. We just have to convince them to come here. I really don't think it will be a problem. They are overcrowded where they are and can certainly use the money."

"Send for them, Kate. Have her here before the one the doctor is sending gets here. I'd rather have an Irish woman nursing my son."

Kate was glad to have the infant, Charles, to keep her busy during the next weeks. It had all worked out as she had planned. Cluny's brother James and his wife, Fiona, had settled into Niall's household with their own three-month-old daughter, Cara. James had been happy to get his family out of the tenement in South Boston, and he was becoming an excellent groundskeeper. Charles thrived on Fiona's milk, and Niall was delighted with the whole arrangement. He and Kate laughed at Fiona's typical Irish baby talk to the two infants.

Kate found she was making an adjustment of her own. The more time she spent in the now-lively house with the two infants, the more she accepted the mother's role that had been thrust upon her. Often, she looked at Charles and found herself longing for her own baby to be in her arms. She ceased to fight the idea. It was no longer repugnant to her. Her nightmares lessened as the weeks went by.

Kate's greatest fear was that she would be an outcast among her friends and family. She remembered how the villagers at home turned against Maire, and dreamed at night of walking down the dusty street of Kinsale. She saw her old friends and neighbors turn their backs as she approached. She would awake trembling; and in the morning, she would rush to Niall's and hold Charles in her arms until her fear subsided.

As the time for Edward's arrival from London drew closer, her fears plagued her nightly. How could she face him, knowing she carried another man's child? Each day she retreated, spending more and more time at Niall's home. Often Jocelyn accompanied her, and Niall began to take up his old ways. The two of them would go out for an evening, and Kate suspected they spent most of that time at Niall's in-town flat. Kate was no longer shocked, for she knew neither of them would ever change. She simply could not understand such flippant behavior.

Kate knew too, by something Niall let slip, that he was seeing Maire. Declan had told her of the scene in Lowell, so proof that Niall was actually seeing Maire was not a surprise but she was still disappointed in them both.

Why could she not accept their behavior as normal? Perhaps if she could, it would be less difficult to carry off her own situation. Maybe then she would not be so concerned about what Edward would think when he arrived to find her five months pregnant. The fact that she had been raped did not lessen her feelings of guilt. Somehow, she blamed herself for what had happened to her.

Edward's ship arrived early in February. Kate begged off going to the wharf to meet him, saying Charles had the sniffles, and she was worried about him. "You know how disappointed he will be, Kate," Jocelyn said. "You don't think he came all this way to see me, do you?"

"I know, Jocelyn, but I can't see him in so public a place. I'm not sure how I will react."

"All right, luv. I'll make your excuses, but he's not going to forgive either of us, I know."

When Kate left Niall's house that evening, the chaise was waiting in front of the house as usual. She was glad to see it there, for she was unusually tired. Charles had indeed developed a serious cold, and no one but Kate had been able to comfort him. At last, he was sleeping and she was free to go home. She greeted the driver and gave a tired sigh as she climbed into the chaise.

Edward sat in the corner, his hat on his lap, his blond hair shining in the early-evening light. "Oh, Edward," Kate cried. "You're here." She could not keep the sound of welcome from her voice. She was so happy to see him again.

He held out his arms and moved toward her, folding them around her. "Kate. My darling, darling Kate. You don't know how I've been looking forward to this moment."

She cried softly as she nestled in his arms. *How can I tell him? I cannot bear to send him away, but how can I accept his love with this thing between us?*

"Kate," Edward whispered. "I love you with all that I am. Will you be my wife? I don't want to be separated from you ever again."

Kate stiffened in his arms. She held her breath. How she had longed to hear him say those words. And now it was too late. She tried to pull herself away from him, to escape from his arms.

"Don't move, luv," he said. "I have something more to say, and I want to say it while I'm holding you like this." Kate allowed herself to relax against him. She would enjoy the feel of him for another few minutes. She closed her eyes.

"Kate. My dear, sweet Kate. I know about the baby coming and about the priest. Jocelyn told me." Kate stiffened again in his arms, but he tightened his hold. "Don't move away from me, Kate. I don't want you ever to move away from me."

Kate held her breath. She wanted to die. Edward turned her face toward him and looked into her eyes. "I want more than ever to marry you, Kate. I want your child to be our child. I love you, Kate. Say you love me too. Nothing else matters. Nothing can come between us." He gently moved her head back so he could place his lips on hers. Kate felt the longing in his kiss, and she felt her own love rise to meet his. She could not refuse his love. She allowed herself to accept. Her tears ran freely down her cheeks and mingled with their kisses. "I do love you, Edward," she said as he brushed the salty tears away. "I want more than anything to be your wife." He kissed her again.

Edward was full of plans. He convinced her they should go west and buy land. "I've always wanted to own land," he said. "This is the opportunity I've been waiting for. As the youngest son, I'll never own the family property in England. The family inheritance will go to my brother, and he already has sons of his own."

"You mean leave Boston?" Kate asked.

"Why not, Kate? This is a big country, and there's lots of land out there just waiting to be settled. What's .n Boston to keep us here?"

"Well. There are my brothers . . . ," Kate began.

"Who are all wrapped up in their own plans, as they should be," he interrupted.

"There's Jocelyn," Kate replied, smiling at her friend.

"I think Jocelyn has some plans of her own, Kate, and you don't want to be a companion forever, no matter how wonderful my dear cousin is." He blew a kiss to Jocelyn.

"He's right, Kate, as much as I'd love having you here," Jocelyn said.

"There would be no Catholic Church in the west," Kate said hesitantly.

"Oh, Kate," Edward wailed. "Will you stop thinking the Church is going to take care of you? What has Catholicism ever done for the Irish? It was the pope who gave Ireland to the English in the first place! And ever since, the Catholic Church has been giving away Irish rights for the privilege of caring for their souls, and there have been many times when they even gave that away."

"But the Church gave us our faith. That's more than the English ever did."

"And can you still not have your faith, Kate, without a church to go to every Sunday? Is your faith not stronger than that?" Edward paced the floor. He stopped in front of her. "I'm not trying to blame everything on the Church. I know what the English have done to your country and your people, but they did it, for the most part, with the Church's blessing."

Kate looked into the deep blue eyes. "Why are we arguing about this, Edward?" she asked.

"I simply don't want you to use the Church as a reason for not coming with me to start a new life. You have your faith, Kate. No one can take that away from you. It's people like you who will strengthen the Church in this country. It's the people who count. The Church should serve them, not the other way around."

Kate remembered her talk with Declan. He would be going on the expedition to start a new church and build a town around it. The bishop said Benedicta would be the first of many such towns. They will fulfill the bishop's dreams, Declan said. *Well, maybe there was more than one way to build a church*, Kate thought. She had dreams of her own. Maybe she could build one that would bring more comfort than the old one had.

"Let's do it, Edward," she said. "The life may not be ideal in the West, but with land and faith, how can we lose?" Edward pulled her from her chair and into his arms.

"And what will you do, Jocelyn?" Kate asked when he released her. "I know your father wants to return to London soon. Will you go with him?"

Jocelyn smiled a secret little smile. "No, I'm not going back with Father. I'll stay here in Boston." She hesitated and then continued. "Niall and I have been talking. We think after a suitable time has passed that we will be married. Charles needs a mother, and Niall and I are good for each other. We think we can make a good marriage."

Kate rushed to her and threw her arms around her. "That's wonderful, Jocelyn! Now you truly will be my sister!" She kissed her friend on her cheek.

"I have one more favor to ask, Kate, if I may interrupt this hugging and kissing," Edward said. "Why don't we get married right away? We could be in St. Louis in a few weeks' time, and you could have the baby there. We could continue west when the baby is old enough to travel."

Kate breathed a sigh of relief. "Oh yes, Edward, let's do that. Let's get married just as soon as possible."

"I'll take care of everything, Kate," Jocelyn said. "All you have to do is invite your guests."

"Just my brothers, I think," Kate said. "I'll see Declan this weekend, and we'll go to see Donal. I wish Liam could be here too."

She thought of her brothers and the problems that had sprung up between them. She feared they would never be a whole family again. But she would have her own family soon. Perhaps that was the way it was meant to be. She reached out and took Edward's hand.

CHAPTER 35

PREPARATION FOR THE bishop's expedition to his selected site for an Irish farming colony and seminary took much longer than anticipated. Declan could not believe how much there was to do. Day and night, he worked with Father Murphy and Tim Ryan to interest the Irish immigrants of Boston in a move to the proposed farmlands of Maine.

The first expedition would be an exploratory one during which land would be surveyed and laid out. A tract of 11,358 acres of mostly woodland was located approximately seventy miles north of Bangor in the western half of what was known as No. 2 Township in southern Aroostook County. Bishop Fenwick had mortgaged his soul for the price of $13,597.50. The full price was due in six years, and the diocese could hardly afford the burden, but the bishop was anxious to begin.

Declan talked to families all over the Boston area about the rich lands and the healthy climate. Potatoes would be a natural crop, and the Irish already knew about raising potatoes. The purchase price for this prime land was $1.25 an acre, but even this price was beyond the reach of most of the tenement dwellers. Like himself, they had come to America with nothing in their pockets. They were lucky to get enough food for their families to eat. As much as they wanted to get out of the overcrowded city and own some land, for most, the dream would not be possible.

At last, a party was made up of eight families who agreed to purchase the land if they found it suitable. Accompanying them would be Father Murphy, his two top students (who would be his overseers of the project), and a cluster of young men from the Bishop's Basement who would help clear the land and operate the farm that would support the Church. They planned to leave in the early spring of 1832.

Declan wanted Chris to head the group of young men who would be going from the Bishop's Basement. Chris was an excellent judge of land and crops and was a natural leader among the laborers. He had been overseeing the farms near the Charlestown Convent since the beginning.

"Come with us, Chris," Declan urged. "This is the opportunity you've dreamed about. We'll be given our own plots of land. Where else could we get a chance to own our own farm?"

Chris shook his head. "If I leave the Boston area, the chances of finding Peggy are gone. She'd have no way of finding me, Declan, no clue to follow if she should get a chance to try." He met Declan's eyes. "I can't leave without my sister, without knowing that she is all right." Chris put his sunburned face in his hands. "It haunts me day and night." He looked up at his friend with desperate eyes. "What could have happened to her, Declan?"

"I don't know, Chris," Declan replied sadly. "It's been three years since the two nuns came for Peggy."

"Why won't they let me in the convent to ask? Even if I couldn't see her . . . if I could jest get some answers . . ."

Declan watched his friend with concern. He knew what he was going through. He knew the feeling of helplessness of being separated from his own family. "I asked Father Murphy to try, but he could find out nothing. Maybe it's time to give up, Chris."

"I can't give up, Declan. I can't. She's my sister. I brought her here. I must find her." He walked away with his hands thrust deep in his pockets, his strawlike hair falling over his hanging head.

Declan talked to Father Murphy again about trying to find out if Peggy was still at the Charlestown Convent. "It's been so long, Father. I don't suppose there's much hope of finding her, but if she's still at the convent . . . I thought maybe there would be some channel we could follow . . . the bishop, maybe . . ."

"I don't think we can ask the bishop to do anything, but let me try again," Father Murphy said thoughtfully.

Time passed quickly, and there were still hundreds of details to be worked out for the Benedicta expedition. The departure date was pushed ahead to early August. If they did not leave then, they would have to wait until spring or they would be trapped in the heavy snows of the harsh northern winter.

On the first day of August, Father Murphy called Declan into his office. "The bishop has asked me to go to the convent in Charlestown to hear confessions and say mass on Sunday. The priest who serves the convent has taken ill, and I'm to replace him. Would you like to assist me?"

Declan's face lit up. "Thank you, Father. I don't know what we'll be able to find out about Peggy, but at least we can try."

"I wouldn't mention it to Chris," Father Murphy said. "All this may lead to nothing. We won't be allowed to speak to them, of course, in the confessional, and I'm afraid I couldn't ask them."

"If you only knew her voice, you would be able to recognize her," Declan suggested.

"I'm afraid that wouldn't help. We'll have to hope she recognizes you. I wish I could have asked Chris to go, but I can't predict what he might do, and we can't have a scene."

"I know, Father. I'll be careful of what I do."

The wall surrounding the Ursuline Convent was somber and high. Declan had a sense of foreboding as he and Father Murphy approached the main gate. Heavy iron bars could be seen holding them locked from the inside. Little could be seen from the gate except for a cluster of dark weathered wooden buildings. There was not a soul in sight. Declan wondered if the occupants ever saw the light of day.

The convent was a seminary, established in 1820, which attracted Protestant as well as Catholic girls from six to eighteen years of age. They were educated by the Ursuline Sisters and operated a farm on the premises which supported the community.

There had been much controversy in recent weeks about the "nunnery," and once again stories spread about evildoings of Papist-controlled extremists. The strongly Protestant town was suspicious about what went on behind the secretive high walls and locked doors. They became convinced that the black-robed nuns were holding girls against their will. The sisters, behind their closed doors, knew nothing of what was happening in the community. They went about their business and kept to their privacy as was their custom.

Father Murphy pulled the heavy bell chain at the gate. A white-faced nun of indeterminate age shuffled her way from the main house to the gate. After asking for their names and their purpose, she acknowledged that they were expected and admitted them to the grounds, carefully replacing the heavy bar across the grillwork gate.

They were led without further conversation to a chapel behind the main building. In addition to the central convent building, there was what appeared to be a lodge, a farmhouse, a barn and stables, and a vine-covered summerhouse, all of ancient origin and built of wood.

The chapel, however, was exquisite. The high-pitched ceiling was of hand-hewn beams, and they gleamed richly in the candlelight. Its walls were lined with intricately carved statues of saints, all at least five feet high. The scenes of the Stations of the Cross were of a similar design in bas-relief. Pews were arranged in rows of two with matching kneelers of the same heavy, hand-hewn wood. At one side, a wrought iron grill shielded another row of pews, obviously meant for privacy, perhaps for the Mother Superior and other dignitaries, Declan thought.

The altar was breathtaking with gold filigree and inlaid tiles gleaming from the light of several large gold candleholders. The red light of the sacrament lamp beckoned one toward the golden altar rail. Declan was overawed at the atmosphere and sunk to his knees on the polished stone floor. He felt the presence of God here.

The coiffed nun motioned toward the single confessional booth in the shadow at the far corner of the hushed room. Father Murphy nodded. She bowed her head, genuflected before the altar, and left.

Father Murphy indicated Declan was to see that everything was in order for the serving of mass the next morning while he heard the confessions of the community of nuns and their students. Declan watched as the priest knelt in front of the altar and prayed. Rising, the priest placed his stole over his arm and went into the confessional booth, drawing the curtain over the entrance behind him.

Declan heard a shuffling noise and looked up to see a line of girls filing into the pews. Each wore a black long-skirted garment with a loose white top edged in lace. Their hair was pulled back under white kerchiefs tied at the back of the neck. Two black-habited nuns, their faces nearly hidden by their white-edged wimples, escorted them. On cue, they all knelt, and one of the sisters indicated the first in line was to enter the confessional. Two more nuns stood on guard at the entrance.

Declan walked across the front of the chapel, genuflecting before the tabernacle. He knew if these girls were anything like any other girl he had ever known, they would be watching him from beneath their lowered lids. He deliberately allowed his full face to be in view. If Peggy were among them, perhaps she would recognize him. The rest would be up to her. There was no way he could approach them.

Declan pulled a bench to a spot where he could observe the lines of faces as they awaited their turns. There were forty-six girls in all. The younger ones could be ruled out. Peggy was fifteen when he rescued her from the ship's fire. That was nearly three years ago. She would be almost eighteen now. Would he recognize her? The pixielike face and the close-cropped black hair were clear in his mind. The impish smile and the large black eyes as she had thanked him for her life and kissed his cheek had remained in his mind since he had last seen her. He had not forgotten. If he saw her he would know her, however much the three years had changed her. He remembered every detail.

Declan wondered how much he had changed in that time. Would Peggy recognize the young, blond, gangling boy in the face of a nineteen-year-old man? He had decided against growing a beard, and now he was glad. His square chin and high-cheeked bones would not be so different. He wanted to believe she would know him.

The girls slid over in the pew as yet another went into the confessional. As each came out of the enclosed box, she walked down the aisle and knelt briefly before the altar before taking a seat on the opposite side of the chapel.

Declan watched the five or six girls whom he judged to be Peggy's age. He could not get a good look at their faces. One by one, they went into the confessional box; and one by one, they came out and knelt before the altar.

That was it, he thought. He could pretend he had to check something on the altar when he spotted one of the older girls coming down the aisle.

He would not be able to see their faces too well, but they would be able to see his.

The first three of the older girls were obviously not the right build to be Peggy. They were too big-boned and moved too heavily. The next one caught his eye. Declan waited until she was halfway down the aisle, then he opened the door wide and stepped out. He would have to cross right in front of her to approach the altar.

Declan heard her gasp before he had turned full face. He raised his eyes and met hers. His heart skipped a beat. *Peggy! She looked the same as before, except now the face was that of a young woman.* Declan tried not to change his expression, but his eyes acknowledged he knew her. She bit her lower lip to keep from crying out, and then dropped her eyes, continuing to the altar rail. She knelt and bowed her head.

Declan crossed to the altar and rearranged the draped altar cloth, smoothing it with the palm of his hand. He genuflected slowly, knowing her eyes were on him. His heart beat faster and faster. *What can I do? How can I find out if she is all right, if she is happy staying here?* He rose and crossed back to the door of the sacristy. Turning, he watched as Peggy crossed herself, rose, and walked to the back of the chapel. He had the same feeling as when he had walked into the beautiful chapel, a recognition that he had stumbled onto something of great value.

Declan sat down on the bench and tried to think. Where Peggy sat was out of his range. He tried to quiet his excitement at finding her. *At least I now know she is still at the convent*, he thought. *Chris will be happy to know that. But what else can I do?*

There was no other opportunity for Declan to do anything. The girls were led out of the chapel the moment the last one came out of the confessional. Declan waited impatiently while twenty or so sisters made their confessions.

Father Murphy stepped wearily from the draped box where he had spent the last several hours. Sweat poured down his face, and the back of his cassock was soaked where he had sat for so long in the airless space. The same nun immediately escorted them to the gate. She reminded them that they would be expected at five o'clock the next morning for mass and ushered them through the gate, sliding the heavy bar in place.

It was not yet daylight the next morning when Declan and Father Murphy approached the iron gate of the convent. This time the sister was waiting on the other side with a small lantern, and they were promptly admitted. Once more they were led to the chapel and to the sacristy next to the altar. Declan had told Father Murphy he had seen Peggy and she had recognized him, and they tried to think of some way to speak to her but could not. "If she does not find a way to communicate with you, then I will approach the bishop about her," Father Murphy promised. "At least, we are now certain she is here."

Declan helped the priest into his vestments with nervous hands. He could hear the girls and the nuns filing into the pews. *There must be a way,* he kept telling himself. *I can not bear the thought of leaving her here behind the high walls and the barred gate.*

The mass was an impressive ceremony in such a setting. Declan wished he could concentrate, but his eyes and his thoughts kept moving back to Peggy. Carefully, he moved the Book of Gospels to its proper place on the altar and listened to Father Murphy's rich voice.

The time for communion came, and the shining faces of the girls lined up at the altar rail. Declan held the golden platen in place under each chin in turn as Father Murphy placed the sacred wafer on the extended tongue.

Peggy's face was suddenly before him. Her eyes met his briefly as she raised her head and opened her mouth. Declan felt something being tucked into his hand just as Father Murphy placed the wafer on her tongue. His eyes flew in panic to Father's face and then to Peggy's. Neither registered that anything had happened. Declan closed his fingers around the small scrap of paper. She had found a way to get a message through.

Declan thought the final prayers would never end, but at last, Father raised his hand in benediction, and Declan escorted him from the altar. Quickly, he placed the book on the sideboard in the sacristy and helped Father disrobe as he recited the required prayers.

Declan unrolled the wrinkled paper and read the note. He smiled at Father Murphy and read aloud. *Tell Chris to be at the rear wall at midnight on August 11. Throw a rope over where you can see the tallest tree. I'll be waiting. Peggy.*

CHAPTER 36

THE DATE FOR the departure of the expedition to Benedicta had finally been set; and this time, preparations were proceeding according to schedule. The eight families were packed and ready to leave. At the Bishop's Basement, there was a flurry of last-minute activity as most of the young men and boys who had lived there for the past several years prepared for the long journey. They would be leaving at sunrise the morning of August 12.

As the hot early August days passed, excitement rose. Declan paid a visit to Niall to say his good-byes to his brother and the rapidly growing Charles, who was now crawling around. Niall and Jocelyn were planning to marry in October, and Declan decided they were a good match. Jocelyn adored the baby, and she and Niall understood each other. It just might work, Declan concluded.

Declan told them of the letter he had received from Kate. Her baby daughter, Colleen, was thriving. She and Edward had decided to stay in St. Louis until the following spring when they would head west. Kate also wrote that she had seen Liam. He was working as a land agent in St. Louis and had taken Edward on as an assistant. Liam seemed happy, Kate said, and was seeing a very nice young lady who had a small daughter. Kate thought the relationship might be serious, though Liam had not mentioned marriage.

Declan also visited Donal, who was still working on the Boston-to-Lowell Railway. *He has moderated his drinking somewhat*, Declan thought, *and seems more content with his life.* He had moved in with the pretty barmaid called Kitty, and Donal admitted he no longer thought of Maire as often. Declan knew, without being told, it was when Donal was thinking of Maire and what had happened to their marriage, that his drinking began again.

As Declan walked through the city after he left Donal, he was startled at the ugly signs posted at nearly every corner. "Papists, Go Back to Rome!" said one. "The Pope is Antichrist," said another, which sported a crude drawing of the pope with a devil's tail. "Idol Worshippers Not Wanted Here!" said still another.

The anti-Catholic feeling had been growing steadily in the city for years and now approached an explosive stage. The northeastern area of the country had retained its English character from its early days, and the great influx of the Irish did not set well with them. Nearly ten thousand Irish had selected the Boston area during the last decade. Since these immigrants were willing to work for lower wages, they displaced many of the local workers. Some Protestant ministers even preached from the pulpit against these papist newcomers and urged their congregation not to hire Catholic workers.

Recently, Samuel F. B. Morse worsened the matter by publishing a political pamphlet condemning the expansion of the Catholic Church in America as a plot to gain control of the new government. "Our religion, the Protestant religion, and liberty are identical," he said. "And liberty keeps no terms with despotism."

At the same time, there was published a booklet supposed to have been authored by a young girl who had been held prisoner in a convent and had escaped. The book was widely publicized, although many prominent men in the city denounced it as fiction. It added to the existing high feeling against the Catholics.

Many secret anti-Catholic societies had sprung up. One particularly active group had recently joined with others, and it had become a large violent movement. It was called the Know Nothing Party, since its members, when questioned, would admit to knowing nothing about it. The General Assembly of Congregational Churches called on the people to save the United States from "Popery," and Baptist groups distributed anti-Catholic literature among the Irish population.

Declan was particularly disturbed by one poster. It was signed by a group called the Truckmen, and claimed they would demolish the "nunnery" in Charlestown on August 11. Declan stared at it in panic.

That was the night he and Chris were to help Peggy leave the convent. How would they ever get her away if there was a mass gathering of anti-Catholics near the convent that night?

Declan and Chris discussed what to do. There was no way to get a message to Peggy. They would have to be at the spot she mentioned on August 11. There might never be another chance.

It was almost midnight on the appointed night when Declan and Chris approached the convent. Angry crowds were already swarming near the front gate. The two boys kept their distance from the drunken rioters, hanging on the outskirts of the crowd just close enough to overhear their plans.

"Burn it to the ground!" the rioters shouted. "They worship the devil! Get rid of them!" shouted a female voice. The crowd increased by the minute. There was much drinking and shouting, and the sounds became loud and ugly.

The Mother Superior came to the gate escorted by two black-clad nuns. She tried to quiet the crowd and get them to return to their homes but to no avail. The sight of their black habits angered the crowd even more. They shouted her down, and the sisters retreated hastily.

While all this was going on in the front of the convent, Declan thought perhaps they could get Peggy over the wall and out of the grounds without being discovered. With Chris, he circled to a side gate in time to see through the narrow opening that the sisters were leading students out of the main building. The line of girls was led to the vine-covered summerhouse near the rear wall.

As they watched, one of their numbers broke away and dashed to the shadows behind the barn. "Peggy!" Chris whispered. She made a run for the clump of trees near the wall.

"Come on, Chris, let's get over to that tall tree," Declan whispered. They hurried around the wall. As they ran, they heard the sound of the main gate crashing and saw the first of the flames spring up from behind the wooden fence. "Hurry!" shouted Declan, grabbing Chris's arm as they skirted the seven-foot wooden fence.

Chris threw a rope to the top of the wall, catching the tool at the end on the rail. He tested its hold with a solid jerk of the rope. Quickly, he shimmied to the top. "My god, they've broken through the wall," came his voice from above. "Holy Mary, Mother of God! They're storming the main building!" he shouted.

"Can ye see Peggy?" Declan called up to him. "Hurry, Chris, throw the rope down for me." Chris dropped the rope and pulled Declan to the top of the fence.

"Jesus, Mary, and Joseph bless us!" Declan exclaimed as he got his first look at the rioters swarming over the grounds, breaking down doors and looting the buildings.

Declan saw three drunks stagger into the small chapel and drag out the carved statues. They threw them onto a bonfire that had been started in front of the main building. Declan remembered the beauty of the hand-worked figures and felt a pang of loss. He saw the unforgettable, gold grillwork of the altar in his mind. *Will it all be destroyed? How can this be happening,* he wondered. *How can God allow it?*

"Chris! Declan! Over here!" Peggy's voice came from below. "Help me up the fence!"

The two boys were quickly brought back to their purpose and lowered the rope. Peggy tied it securely around her waist, and they pulled gently as she climbed to the top of the fence. She threw her arms around both boys, nearly knocking them from their perch. They hurriedly lowered her to the ground on the other side of the fence. Declan drew the rope back up and tied it to Chris's waist, lowering him to a spot beside his sister.

After retrieving the rope one last time, Declan fastened it securely to the heavy rail and looked again at the convent. Every building was now ablaze. The rioters danced and shouted. The roof of the convent collapsed with a roar, and flames leaped into the sky. He saw the sisters leading their charges out the far back gate and across the street. Declan quickly lowered himself to the ground. "Leave the rope," he said. "Let's get out of here."

Peggy had taken off her white kerchief and the white cape of her uniform. Declan placed his jacket over her shoulders to cover the blackness of her long dress. "With the jacket, you'll look less like you came from the convent," he insisted.

Slipping it on, she asked, "Can we leave now? I've spent enough time cooped up behind walls. I thought you'd never come for me, Chris. But they wouldn't have let me go if you had. The only person who could have gotten me out would have to be a parent or a legal guardian, and I had neither."

"I tried, Pegeen. I really did," Chris said, putting his arm about her.

They ran down the street, the sound of the rioters following them. As they approached the bridge, Chris stumbled and fell. Declan tried to help him to his feet, but Chris could not stand. His ankle was broken.

"Get her to the Bishop's Basement," he told Declan. "If that mob discovers she is from the convent, who knows what they'll do."

Declan looked back at the rioters. As he watched, the overexcited mob drew closer, and he saw in his mind a frightening scene. They reached down and picked up Chris, holding him above their heads. "Kill him! Kill him!" they shouted.

Declan could see Chris still on the ground, rubbing his ankle. "Ye've got to get up, Chris!" he shouted. "They'll kill ye!"

Chris tried to rise but could not. "Get Peggy out of here, Declan, or they'll get her too!" he pleaded.

The angry crowd was not more than five hundred yards from them. Declan looked from Chris to Peggy. Chris was right. He had to get Peggy away. He reached down and made the sign of the cross on Chris's forehead. Grabbing Peggy's hand, he pulled her away from her brother. They ran across the bridge and hid in the park on the other side of the river.

The Mother Superior had warned the rioters that the Irish workers of the city would retaliate if the convent were harmed. The drunken crowd was now searching for these revenging Irishmen.

They had seen Chris fall to the ground and Declan and Peggy run across the bridge. Thinking they had uncovered a spy, they dragged Chris to the bridge. Three men raised him over their heads while others chanted, "Kill him! Kill him!" They carried the struggling Chris to the railing and threw him into the dark water. From across the Charles River, Declan and Peggy watched as his body flew from the parapet and hit an abutment of concrete.

Peggy cried out as her brother's body struck the water and sank below the surface. Declan put his arms around her and held her shaking body.

She shed her tears as he stroked her short cropped hair and her trembling shoulders. "I'll take care of you, my Pegeen," he crooned. "I'll always take care of you."

At last the rioters broke up, and Declan led Peggy through the city and across the causeway to South Boston. It was four o'clock in the morning when they arrived at the Bishop's Basement. Declan stared in amazement at the wagons lined up in a long row in front of the storefront chapel. He had completely forgotten the expedition was to leave at sunrise. Last-minute supplies were being loaded onto the wagons, and dozens of people were already crowding the street to see the expedition off.

Declan took Peggy to Father Murphy and explained what had happened. Father Murphy bowed his head and crossed himself as he heard of Chris's murder. "God rest his soul," he said. He looked at the young woman standing next to Declan, who had his arm about her shoulders. "And what will you do now, Peggy, now that your brother is gone?"

Peggy's eyes flew to Declan. He looked at the tiny pixie face. He did not ever want to be parted from it again. "Come with us to Benedicta," he said.

Her eyes lit up with the old sparkling light. "May I, Father?" she asked. Father Murphy looked at Declan with questioning eyes.

"I'll take care of her, Father. I'd like very much for her to come with us," Declan said.

"Let's go then," Father Murphy said. He turned to the waiting train of wagons. "Time to move out!" he shouted.

The members of the expedition climbed onto their wagons. Declan lifted Peggy to the seat and sat down beside her. Father Murphy raised his hand and made the sign of the cross. "May the Lord always look with favor on this family," he prayed. "As they are separated, so shall they be reunited in another world." He extended his hand to Declan. "Take this bit of the earth, and those you love will be always with you, though your journeys be far from this place." He dropped the fistful of earth in Declan's hand.

Declan stared at this beloved priest in amazement, remembering the night he had buried his mother on the rain-soaked hillside. A dark-haired priest had stepped out of nowhere and placed a clump of wet Irish soil in his hand and spoke the same benediction.

Declan extended his hand to Father Murphy. Their eyes locked in recognition. Declan slowly placed the handful of American soil into his pouch with the other. He mixed them carefully together and put the pouch back into his pocket.

Declan put his arm around the girl beside him and picked up the reins. "Benedicta," he said. He liked the sound. He slapped the horses with the reins, and they moved forward.

THE END